Tell No Lies

Fool's Honor

Praise for Fool's Honor

"*Fool's Honor* is a magical anthology like no other I've read, full of whimsical worlds and enthralling characters that tug on your heartstrings. I'd highly recommend it for fans of *Six of Crows* or *Caraval*."

-Bethany Meyer, Author of *Robbing Centaurs and Other Bad Ideas*

"You'll find masterful storytelling, magic, and brilliance living between the covers of this book — this anthology is filled with adventure, humor, trickery, and beautiful prose and poetry. I enjoyed each of the stories inside this beautiful book. This collection is sure to bring out the trickster in you."

-Devin Joubert, Author of *Freelance Fiancé At Mistletoe Inn*

"*Fool's Honor*, compiled by Anne J. Hill and Lara E. Madden introduces readers to an array of tricksters, from familiar faces like Peter Pan to thrilling new ones, like the ghost stuck aboard a spaceship. These dreamers and schemers will be sure to steal your heart - and possibly your wallet - as you follow them through their twisted tales. Standout stories include *Hoax of Hades* by Anna Augustine, *Fae Blood* by Hannah Carter, and *Won't Be In Today* by Lara E. Madden. It's hard to pick a favorite, as each story adds something unique and exciting to this collection. Perfect for those who love Loki and enjoy engaging twists and turns, *Fool's Honor* will be sure to keep you enchanted until the very end."

-Anna Ford, Author in *The Depths We Go To*

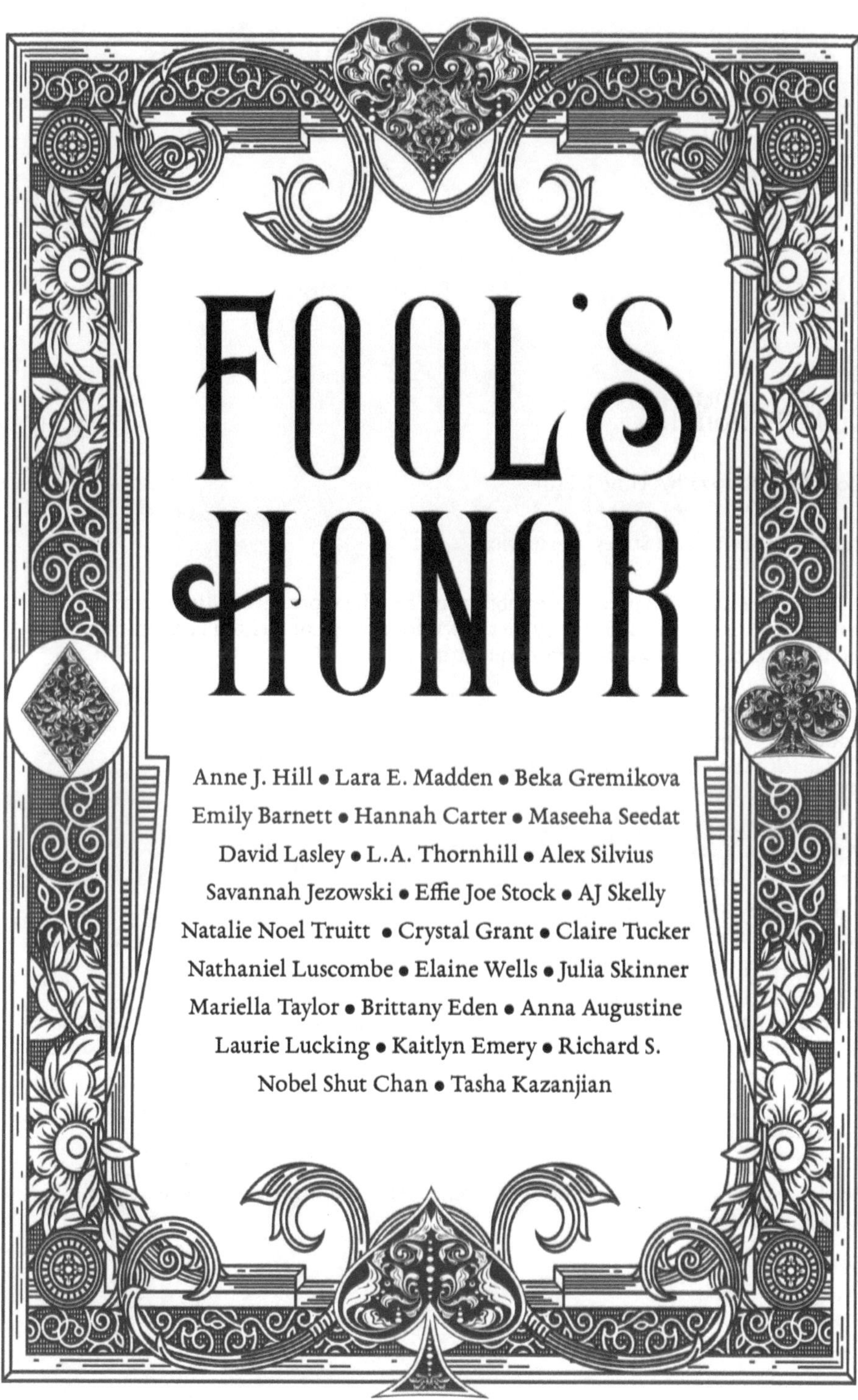

FOOL'S HONOR

Anne J. Hill • Lara E. Madden • Beka Gremikova
Emily Barnett • Hannah Carter • Maseeha Seedat
David Lasley • L.A. Thornhill • Alex Silvius
Savannah Jezowski • Effie Joe Stock • AJ Skelly
Natalie Noel Truitt • Crystal Grant • Claire Tucker
Nathaniel Luscombe • Elaine Wells • Julia Skinner
Mariella Taylor • Brittany Eden • Anna Augustine
Laurie Lucking • Kaitlyn Emery • Richard S.
Nobel Shut Chan • Tasha Kazanjian

FOOL'S HONOR

Paperback ISBN: 978-1-956499-03-2
Ebook ISBN: 978-1-956499-10-0
Hardback ISBN: 978-1-956499-04-9

Originally published in April 2022
Published by Twenty Hills Publishing

Cover Art by Fantastical Ink
Interior formatting by Dragonpen Designs
Publisher logo by Nathaniel Luscombe

Edited by Anne J. Hill with help from Andrew Winch, Crystal Grant, Hannah Carter, Anna Augustine, Maseeha Seedat, Beka Gremikova, Emily Barnett, Brittany Eden, and others.

Poems chosen by Elaine Wells

Book created by Anne J. Hill, head of Twenty Hills Publishing, with the help of Lara E. Madden

To Anne J. Hill's granddad,
Richard S., who was born on April Fool's Day
To Erin, her brother, who tricked his way out of being born the same day
To her loving father, the King of Dad Jokes

To Lara E. Madden's
family and their merry band of misfits

TABLE OF CONTENTS

LIES OF THE LEGENDS

Part Two: Jests of the Jokers

Part Three: Twists of the Trade

Part Four: Ruse of the Rogues

INTRODUCTION

TRICKSTERS HAVE ALWAYS been a favorite archetype in the long history of storytelling. From ancient myths to modern movies, these vagabonds, outlaws, and rogues have stolen our hearts and excited our imaginations. The wit and double-crossing, genius planning, and deep, dark secrecy of the trickster's antics both delight us and make our heads spin. In celebration of April Fool's Day, we decided to compile stories and poems that revolve around these untrustworthy individuals. *Fool's Honor* is a book filled with stories spotlighting tricksters who use their cleverness for good or evil.

In this collection, the actions of our wonderfully shifty characters have real-life consequences and determine whether they are the hero or villain of the story. Many of the stories in this anthology hit that concept on the nose, while others are here for your pure enjoyment. From villains to heroes, to the morally gray, our characters are defined both by their intentions and by the outcomes of their deception.

We hope you enjoy this book and that you get tricked, fooled, and blindsided along the way!

-Anne J. Hill and Lara E. Madden

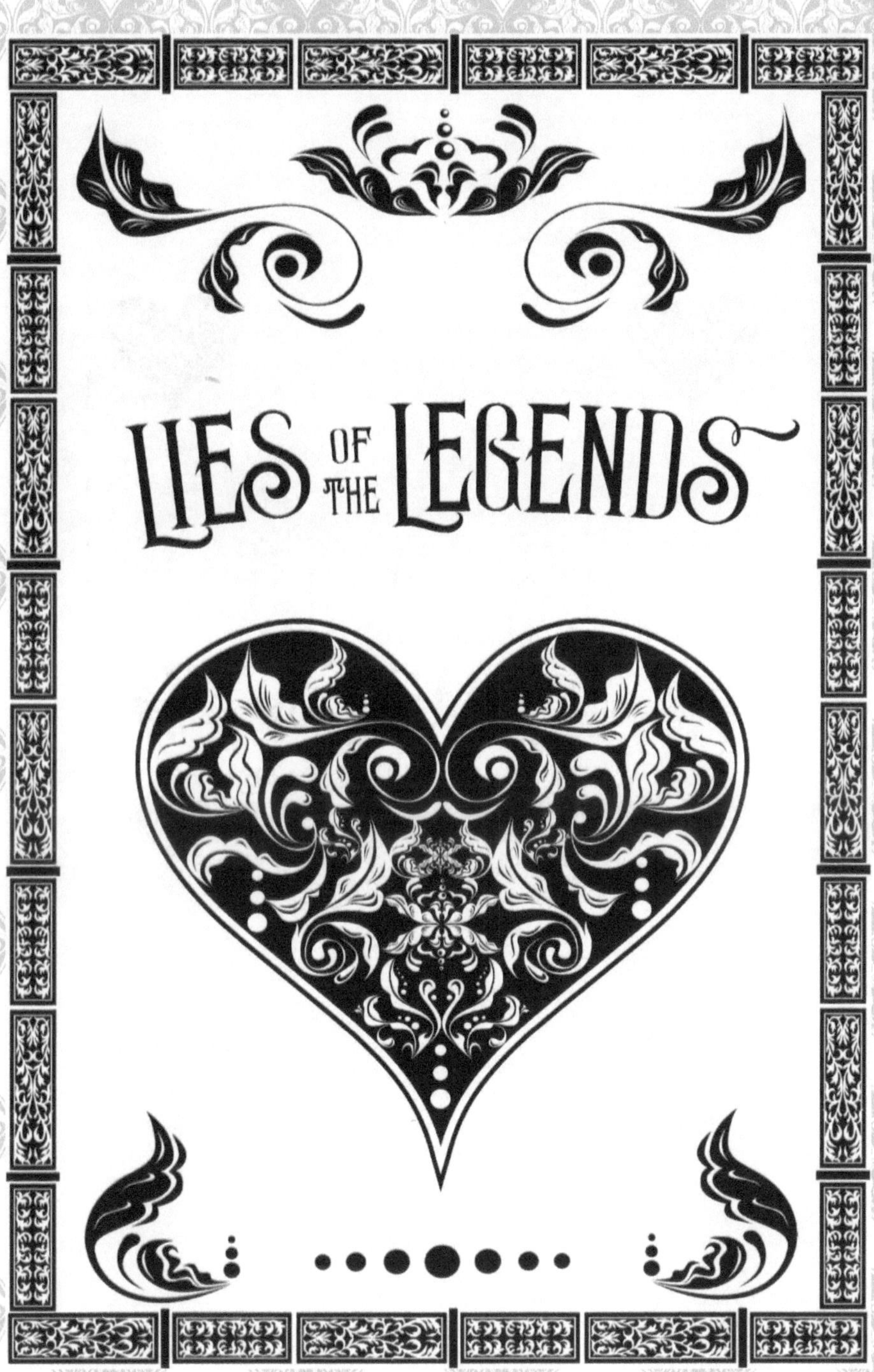
LIES OF THE LEGENDS

Telling the truth is overrated. Make

PROMISES

you never intend to keep.

DO YOU FIND the work of a trickster to be dull? Do you lose focus when trickery gets too complicated? Do you get down on yourself when it seems like your efforts are ineffective? Well, don't worry because you're not alone. This guide is just the thing you need to trick your way through life!

This first section is a transcribed interview featuring the world's most famous tricksters, and their tips are bound to inspire and motivate you. Just be sure to take everything you read here with a grain of salt. After all, they *are* tricksters, and even their most valuable advice is sure to be laced with a little bit of mischief. Happy Tricking!

1. "Tell no lies. Keeping track of lies will catch up with you, so always tell the truth. Or at least until a small lie gets you out of a sticky or potentially illegal situation. If it's for the better good, then, yes, in that case, lie away. Just be sure your lies resemble the truth as much as possible so you can remember them. But, like I said, generally speaking, tell no lies." -Robin Hood

2. "Telling the truth is overrated. Make promises you never intend to keep. But be careful not to use that too much on one person. People are, unfortunately, occasionally smart and will eventually catch on." -Rumpelstiltskin

3. "Speaking of smart . . . Always pair up with a sidekick who makes you look smart, even if they're more powerful than you. Then you can use them to surprise your enemies, but you'll get the attention." -Peter Pan

4. "If you want to surprise someone—disappear. Always disappear when you're done talking. Don't waste your time walking away. If you have magic, then use it for heaven's sake. If not, duck behind a wall or whatever is near. It doesn't matter. Just make yourself mysterious, powerful, and elusive." -Phantom of the Opera

5. "Forget everything that so-called ghost said. Why *disappear* when you can *appear* out of thin air? It's especially fun if your subject believes you're behind them. You might need magic to do this, but I'm sure you can figure something out if you don't. Trust me. It comes in handy." -Loki

6. "Repeat the same thing someone else said but in your own words with slight changes, because you're not creative enough to spin your own tale." -Rumplestiltskin

7. "Interject your opinions when no one asked and—" -Loki

8. "Settle down, you two. My advice is to make yourself look like the hero of the story. Then people will sing your praises for centuries to come until they look closer and realize you're a maggot. But by then, it won't matter because they'll be so loyal to the stories you've spun that they'll set you up as a hero even as you kidnap and murder other children." -Peter Pan

9. "Make your target think you're someone you're not. Sing like an angel if that helps. And then once you gain their trust, lure them into your dungeon. Make sure you lock them up, because no one blindly loves a villain, no matter what that little British boy tells you." -Phantom of the Opera

10. "Make bets, dearest, but only if you're certain you can win. And what's really fun is making them even when you're not certain. See where the cards land, as it were. Yes, that's the most exhilarating kind of trickery. I bet Loki will murder Pan." -Rumpelstiltskin

11. "Say you're sorry when you mess up, but make sure they know it was really their fault. Remember, you're better than everyone else. Never back down." -Peter Pan

12. "That's a good way to get yourself killed, kid. Instead, play dead. Every good trickster, at some point, must play dead. This is likely because we get ourselves into uncomfortable situations where everyone *wants* us dead. So instead of being killed, pull off a fake death stunt and start over somewhere else. Classic." -Loki

13. "Fake deaths can work, but even better—ignore reality no matter what. If ya think too hard about what's real, you'll realize death is a thing, and you can't actually do whatever ya want. And then you'll look weak and lose all your friends, if you have any." -Peter Pan

14. "Get friends, build a team of trustworthy misfits, wait for snobby rich people to come across your path, and then rob them of everything they're worth. Keep them alive if you can, though, because you may need them around longer for questioning or scare tactics. I find it quite effective to tie them to a tree and let them stand there contemplating their life choices." -Robin Hood

15. "If you're keeping them alive, then always wear a disguise, even if it only covers half of your face, so you never have to worry about some fool identifying you." -Phantom of the Opera

16. "Disguises can be removed by anyone with half a brain. Shapeshift. Turn your whole body into someone else. But if you're *normal* and bound by human physics, then I guess disguises can work. But you better be darn good at playing any part at the drop of a hat." - Loki

17. "And *always* pretend you know everything. People love smartness. But ya gotta act like you're humble at the same time. They'll never see through it." -Peter Pan

18. "Who invited this child here? Trickery takes years of practice. Snotty little babies can't give advice, especially if they never grow up. Listen to me instead, the literal *god* of mischief." -Loki

19. "Speak for yourself, Loki. You might be a god, but I can turn straw into gold." -Rumpelstiltskin

20. "This is going nowhere. I've kept quiet because I assumed you all could manage on your own. But clearly, you need a king to keep order. Be quiet and let the reader watch us in action. I'll go first." -Odysseus

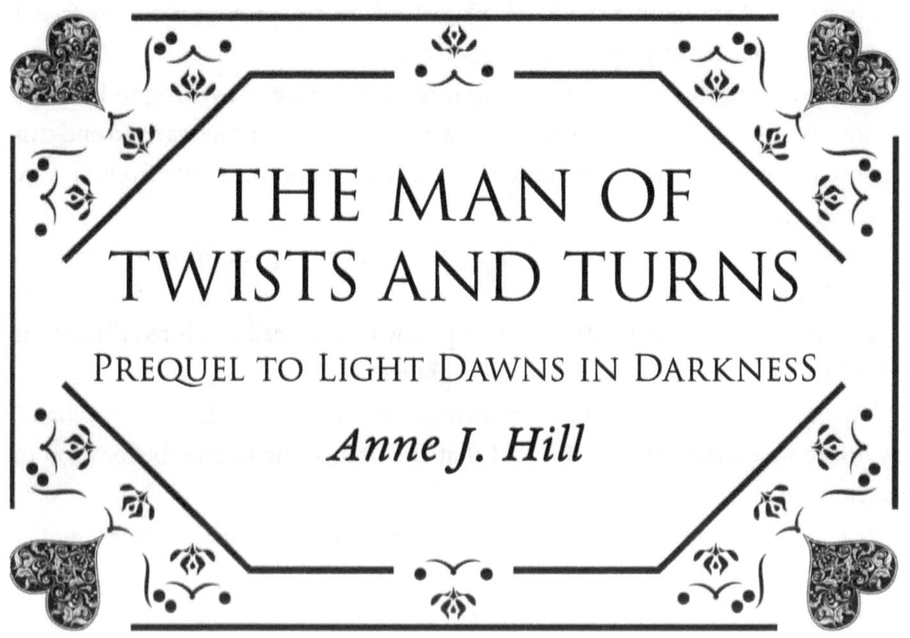

THE MAN OF TWISTS AND TURNS

Prequel to Light Dawns in Darkness

Anne J. Hill

THE WAR HAS been raging on for far too long. Most people want to throw the Emperor and his blood-born powers off his pearly white throne. I can't say I blame 'em, either. He snatched the scepter right out of his aunt's hand and took over our small corner of the world in one heartbeat. Having powers is already frowned upon, but taking orders from a blood-born is unthinkable to most. That, paired with his bold assassination, split the land between Emperor Loyals and the Revolter Majority. I'd be pretty miffed if some lowly crewmember of mine pushed me overboard and snagged *my* wheel, so I can understand the fury.

Then again, I'd *never* allow that to happen in the first place . . . .

I run my fingers over the edge of the *Wither* and brush blood from my brow. She's still a beauty but needs a good cleaning. We've been at sea for countless weeks and just finished a shootout with the *Novaturient,* another pirate ship, but their loyalties lie with the Emperor and his blood-born allies. They got away but not before I put a musket ball through the arm of their captain—some noble who turned to piracy—and left their sails in shambles.

Disheveled from the brawl, the *Wither* plows straight for the Siren's Eye. The Revolters seem to think there's something in the forsaken circle of rocks that will help them win this war. It's funny, actually. The people who think blood-borns are of the devil are willing to hunt down myths and legends to win a war. One is as foolish as the other, if you ask me. But I take orders in this war; I don't give opinions.

I press my chest against the *Wither*'s taffrail, misty water coating my face. I breathe in the sea air, tasting death on my tongue.

I can stomach this one last seafaring mission if I must. Anything to keep my wife and children safe from a world brewing with fire—to win the war and end this madness. After this last trek, I'm headed ashore to fight on the home front and see my family again.

"Captain?" A man puts his hand on my shoulder, jolting me from my thoughts.

"Yes?" I turn to him.

The gruff helmsman holds out a compass with the needle pointed directly at the rocks ahead. "Are you sure this is the right way, sir?"

"Aye, the tales hold true. You know them. *In the eye of the rocks, the siren sings.*" I try not to mock the old tales. It's said that the siren alone knows the location of an ageless creature, and the Revolters need that information.

The helmsman nods slowly. "You really b'lieve them old tales? Not even *all* the ancients did."

I shrug. "Don't matter what I believe."

"But you're the Pirate King. Surely—"

I snatch the compass from his hand. "That means nothin' now. Get your head out of the waves! Everyone must bow to someone, and I take orders just like you. This is war. We picked our side, and after it's over, we can go back to being our own masters, but for now, *you* do as *I* say. Steer the bloody ship toward those rocks!"

He shrinks like a beat dog and mutters, "Aye, Captain," before he bows an inch and heads to the helm.

I look back to the sea and study the rock circle. We're nearly on top of it. "Tie me to the mast," I yell, pressing my back to the pillar. My faithful crew quickly wraps jagged rope around my hands, feet, and torso, securing me. I inhale sharply. "Block your ears with candle wax! I don't need you dimwitted fools steering my ship into the siren's traps. I alone will hear her words." I'll be shocked if there's a siren at all, but the crew obeys nonetheless, just as I do. Wide-eyed loyalty to the bitter end. My first mate stands near me in case he needs to intervene.

Rocks claw the sides of the bow as we enter the Siren's Eye, and I cringe, thinking of the damage done.

"*Sodi*," a voice sings over me, and my muscles go tense.

My crew focuses on the ship, diverting their eyes from any temptations.

"I'm here, siren," I respond to the air.

Laughter erupts around me, coming from every direction. "I see that, Sodi. Finally, you've come. I've been waiting for you." I feel fingers run down my arm, and I glance over. Standing beside me is my beautiful wife. I haven't seen her in two years, and everything in me yearns for her.

My chest presses against the rope. "Pela?" The words croak out from my throat. Of all the things I expected, this is not one of them.

She moves closer so she's standing in front of me, a warm smile dancing on her face. Her blonde hair floats past her waist in the light breeze. "I missed you, honey. You're finally home." Her eyes glisten with tears, and all I want is to wrap her in my arms. There's been a mistake. This is my *wife*.

"I missed you too," I whisper. My head feels light, and my muscles relax. All the tension that's built inside of me during this war slips away at her touch.

My eyes glide down to her lips as her fingers trace my jaw. "Kiss me, and we can be together again," she whispers, matching my tone.

She leans forward so our foreheads are touching, and I breathe her in. Tears prick at my eyes. It's been far too long since I've beheld her. Her lips graze mine, begging me to show her my love. And I want to.

God above, I want to.

The death of men comes from a welcomed siren's kiss.

The ancient words play in my head, but everything in me wants to push them away, break my binds, and embrace my wife. Pela isn't a siren.

"Captain!" A boot slams down on my foot, and I yelp—my first mate shocking me into reality.

I blink several times. Pela isn't a siren . . . and she's also at home. This isn't home. The face in front of me is *not* my wife.

I jerk my head back from her, and she shrieks as Pela's features melt into ghostly horror.

"You would deny me? Your own wife?" Her fingers dig into my arms.

I tighten my jaw and close my eyes. "You're not my wife. You're a siren. Your kisses are poison." Her fingers dig deeper, and I stifle a scream. I flash my eyes back open and rally every ounce of resolve I have left. "Let go of me, siren."

My wife's eyes drop, tears drifting down her cheeks, and she steps away. "I'm sorry, Sodi. I just thought you loved me."

My chest tightens. *She's not my wife. She's not my wife,* I repeat over and over in my head, fighting back the fog that has overtaken me. "I love my *wife*. You are no man's wife!"

Her head yanks up toward me, and fangs shoot out as she hisses, her breath stale. "Tell me why you came, Pirate King."

Now we're getting somewhere. I am well versed in facing off with a foe. "You have something we need."

A smirk plays on her face. "Don't you mean I have something *they* need?"

I frown at her. "They. We. Same thing."

"You can't fool me, *Captain*." She circles around the mast. "I see the heart of men. I know you're a spy. An Emperor Loyal."

I glance at the others, afraid they might hear even though they have their ears blocked. This was the other reason I wanted them to hear nothing. "Fine. What is it to you where my loyalties lie? You have to give me what I desire. Isn't that how the saying goes? *Those who outwit the siren receive their heart's desire?*"

Her eyebrow raises. "I've tried to stay out of men's wars, but this one is different. This one is personal." She places her finger under my chin and lifts my head. "You've proven yourself strong of mind, and if I must take a side on this war, I choose the Emperor's. Not the empire, but her ruler. Long live blood-borns. So I will give you what you seek, but you must promise me it will find the hands of the Emperor."

I smile, the game won. "Thank you. I promise."

Something akin to sympathy spreads on her face. "Don't look so relieved yet, Pirate King. I require a sacrifice in exchange for the secrets I possess. As it's said, *All hope must come with a price.*"

I swallow. "Name your price."

She bends and whispers into my ear.

I feel my face pale as the life drains from me, along with my hope of growing old with my wife.

"So, what will it be, Captain?"

I've come here for one thing alone. To find hope for the empire. Hope that this siren can lead us to. The Revolters want me to find the location of an ancient immortal beast. They want to convince him to join them before he sides with the Emperor in his pursuits to rejoin the empire.

But I'm here to find him first and deliver the location to the Emperor myself. Nothing will stand between me and keeping my family safe.

Today is the day I put aside being a pirate and fight for something that actually matters—my final test.

I nod slowly. "You have a deal, siren. Now tell me. Where is the Ageless One?"

"Wise choice, Captain." She presses her lips to my ear once again and gives me detailed directions to the creature's island. "Now, be on your way home, and your doom will follow." The siren holds my cheeks in her hands, and I allow her to press her lips against mine. "Long live Sodi, the Pirate King."

My fate is sealed.

The chill of her kiss runs down to my toes, pulling the life from my veins. I've been marked with coming death, a sentence I can't outrun.

"Captain, no!" My first mate rushes over and yanks the siren off of me. She laughs and jumps back into the ocean, slithering through the waves.

One by one, the crew starts to take the wax from their ears.

"Onward!" I order from the mast as they untie me. "Let's get home."

"What did she say, Captain?" My first mate follows me as I stumble toward the captain's quarters.

"I need to write it down before I forget." I sit at my desk and furiously transcribe two copies. "In case the one gets lost," I explain. I hand my first mate the one with a false location, and I stuff the true letter into my satchel. I'd been collecting information over the last few weeks on the Revolter's plans and any information I could gather. But this is the key item—the location of the beast that never dies.

He reads over the letter and looks at me. "You don't look so good, Captain."

I run my hand through my greasy hair. "I think I need to lay down."

"You rest. I'll get us home." He leaves me alone in my quarters.

I pull myself into bed, nauseous. I'd allowed the siren to kiss me, to mark me with my coming end. *The death of men comes from a welcomed siren's kiss . . . .*

I don't remember the rest of our journey home, drifting in and out of consciousness.

"Captain." A hand jerks my shoulder. "We've hit shore."

I rub my face and stand on shaky legs. "My wife. I need to see my wife."

"Of course, sir. But then you need to report to the Revolter base."

I wave him away. "I know, I know. You have the letter too. I'm going to see my wife and children. You take the letter, and I'll meet up after."

He nods. "Yes, Captain."

I stumble off the ship and onto solid ground. My wife and I had chosen a house near the shore when we wed. Every winter, I'd come in from the sea and spend the freezing months with my family. That is, until the war started.

I make the distance home on foot, not stopping to find a faster transport. I have one thing on my mind—to hold my wife and children one last time.

I see the thatched roof in the distance, a welcoming cloud of smoke streaming from the chimney I built with my own hands. As I near, the glow of candlelight calls to me through the windows. When I reach the weather-worn front gate, I hear screams from inside, and the door flings open.

"Sodi!" Pela runs out and throws her arms around me. I hold her tight, her body pressed against my ragged breathing. She is real.

I cup the back of her head in my hand and stoop to kiss her. It sends heat through my body. I soak her in, knowing this might be the last kiss we ever share. "I love you," I whisper against her lips. My fingers trail down her back, and I pick her up.

"I love you, too. I missed you so much." She buries her face into my neck and takes a deep breath.

I carry her inside our home. "Are the children asleep?"

She kisses my neck. "Cali is."

I squeeze her and set her down. "Go get them for me. I want to see them." She rushes off, and I lower myself onto a chair, raking my fingers through my hair.

"Papa!" Cali runs out from her bedroom and throws herself on me. I hug her tight and set her down when Vivace approaches. He slinks over to me, his arms crossed. He has white stubble growing on his chin, and it makes my stomach churn with remorse.

"Vivace, my boy . . . you've grown up so much."

He nods, watching me with distant eyes. "I'm not a boy anymore."

He's right. He turned eighteen this last year. And I missed it. Just as I will miss every future birthday.

Vivace is like the Emperor—born with the generational powers passed to some. It is for him that I fight for blood-borns to live safely.

"I'm sorry, son." I hold my hand out to him.

My adopted child does not take my peace-offering. "You should have been here."

I stand to my full height despite the burning protest of every muscle in my body. "Vivace . . . You know why I have to fight."

"No, I don't! You've always hated what I am!" he snaps, and I blink.

"What?" When I first found out he was *special*, I admit I reacted poorly, but I've spent years trying to make up for that. My family does not know I'm a spy for the Loyals. They *cannot* know. My work and Vivace's shape-shifting powers must be kept a secret at all costs.

His eyes drop down to my satchel then back to me. "Going somewhere?"

"I have to report, yes." And then who knows if I will be back.

He nods and turns, heading outside. It chills me that I can't explain the truth to him before I'm gone, but it's safer for him to hate me as I fade away.

I sigh and pick Cali up, hugging her close. "I love you, honey."

She kisses my cheek. "I love you too, Papa."

"The sooner you report, the sooner you can return to us," Pela says.

My heart sinks, and I nod. "Right." I set Cali down and hug them both before heading outside. I don't bother saddling our horse, not wanting her to get lost when I don't come home.

I look around for Vivace to say goodbye, but I can't find him, and I know my time is running out. I can sense it. If I can make it to the duke's manor, from there, the letters will reach the Emperor. I trudge along as the setting sun casts blood-red rays across the sky. By the time I reach Brimwood Manor at the top of the hill, I can barely see the dark path before me.

I rap tired knuckles on the door, and the duke's ward pulls it open. "Oh. Can I help you?" She looks me over. I must be a sight to see with blood from the sea battle staining my clothes.

"Is the duke home?"

She nods and calls into the manor, "Mr. Claude?"

I smile when the Captain of the *Novaturient* steps into view. He looks just as exhausted as I feel, his left arm with a fresh bandage from where I shot him just days before.

His arms cross over his chest, and he leans against the doorframe. "Fancy seeing you here, Sodi. I haven't seen you in a while." His eyes twinkle with his lopsided grin.

I chuckle. "You'd be dead if I hadn't called my men off. Sorry for the damage. Had to keep my cover. You know how it is. Speaking of, I have letters with the Ageless One's location and the Revolters' plans that need to get to the Emperor." I tap the satchel at my side. "The unity of the empire could depend on it."

He nods and holds his hand out. "I'll take care of that from here. You head home."

I pull the satchel from around my neck and go to hand it to him when claws slam into my back, dragging me to the ground.

"Get back inside!" I hear the duke yelling at the ward who must have stepped out.

My vision blurs. Blood pools on my back. The duke yanks the satchel from my hands and feet scurry inside the mansion.

A wolf growls in my ear. My kiss-sealed fate has come.

But fate is not my master.

I twist around, grabbing the wolf's leg and throwing him off of me. He hits the wall with a whimper. Pushing myself up, I blink several times, trying to clear my sight.

The duke steps forward and slams the front door shut behind him, protecting his ward inside. He raises a flintlock pistol and aims it at the wolf. "Back, beast!"

The white wolf picks himself up and rolls his neck, baring his teeth. The duke cocks the gun, and I catch the wolf's eye.

I know this shape-shifter.

"Claude, no, don't shoot!" I grab his wrist and try to wrestle the gun from his hand. But the wolf has his fangs in my leg, and I scream.

A gunshot rings into the night. And the duke falls to the ground. I drop the gun and see red bloom across the duke's stomach. I land beside him, the wolf tugging me down. My head smacks against something hard and everything is muffled. My ears ring.

The front door creaks open, and the ward stands there, trembling. The wolf lunges for her, but I grab onto his neck and pin him. The duke grips the wolf's fur and curses him for going after her, then tosses the satchel to his ward. With his fading breath, he mumbles something to her, and she's off running to the stables. The wolf snaps at me, but I don't let go until I hear horse hooves clipping away, until my eyes grow heavy and my arms give out. The letters will reach the Emperor. I have succeeded.

Blood seeps from my body, and I cough, ragged. I try to mutter, to tell the wolf that he's wrong—that he should let the ward and the letters go. That they're bound for the Emperor and will help bring him a future world of peace. That I'm not a Revolter like he thinks.

But none of those words come out.

The wolf pulls out of my limp grasp and nudges my head with his nose. A quiet whimper escapes him, and he howls. I feel his fur in my fingers, and before I fade from this life, a single whisper slips from my mouth.

"I still love you, son."

ROBIN _ LXLY

Lara E. Madden

THE CELL WAS deep underground, buried beneath a mansion, its only entrance carefully hidden. The bare concrete chamber contained a hanging light bulb and a single chair where a bruised man slouched, his hands bound behind him and his ankles zip-tied to the wooden legs. His face was swollen, and his split lip oozed blood onto his green hooded shirt. He sat cooly, eyeing the hired thug before him with disdain and a half-cocked grin.

Many levels above them, a party was going on in the mansion. A charity event, attended by diamond-clad millionaires wearing watches worth more than most cars, getting drunk on $800 bottles of champagne. Of course, no one heard the battered man from the hidden cellar. How could they? The only way out was a hidden staircase behind a secret door in a little-used hallway.

He wondered how long it would be before his real adversary would slip through that secret door and down the steps to face him. He forced his breathing into a long, even rhythm. Counteracting the adrenaline and bringing his heart rate back down was a top priority. He would need to be collected for this meeting.

The henchman was still catching his breath and rewrapping his bruised knuckles when the chamber door opened. A man's silhouette appeared in the dark opening. The captive's long-awaited executioner, dressed for the occasion in a clean-cut tuxedo. The shadowy assassin waited a long moment, clearly enjoying the building tension. Finally, he called out to the interrogator.

"You can let our friend alone now, Maxim. I'd like a moment to speak with him."

The brute looked his prisoner over one more time, drove a heavy fist into his gut, and gave a self-satisfied grunt before stalking out of the chamber. The prisoner doubled over as much as his bound arms would allow, gasping for breath as his assassin stepped calmly into the room. He chuckled in painful bouts.

"Your henchman there hits like a cannonball; I'll give him that. Might not have much going on upstairs, but he can sure land a punch. I guess that's not difficult when I'm tied to a chair, though."

The tuxedoed man clasped his hands behind his back and narrowed his eyes. "You aren't what I'd pictured, Robin Loxley."

He'd used Robin's hacking handle. Robin_Lxly. His real name had been scrubbed from records years ago. People who knew him called him Robin. Those who didn't called him The Hood.

Robin was built like a fighter, held himself like a soldier, and had the dark, weathered skin of an outdoorsman. Not exactly the stereotypical profile of a hacker.

He sat taller and smirked. "Were you imagining some pasty kid who spends his days hiding behind a screen in his mother's basement? You gotta give a little more credit to someone who's managed to evade *you* for five years." He cocked his head. "Wait, I've seen you before. I competed against you in a shooting competition."

"That was *you*?"

"I won if I remember correctly." Robin leaned back in the chair and challenged his gaze.

The man began to circle the chair like a vulture eyeing its prey. "You've stolen a lot of money from my clients over these years."

"Oh, come on, *Guy*. That can't be your real name, can it?" Robin smirked. "You and I both know that you've been well compensated for hunting me down. If anything, I've extended your contracts. You're welcome."

He stopped pacing directly in front of Robin and crossed his arms.

"And anyway," Robin said, "stolen is a strong wo—"

"You siphoned tens of millions of dollars from corporate *and* personal accounts!"

Robin leaned farther back in the chair, passing it off as a cocky gesture while giving his bound hands room to fiddle with his sleeves. He felt for the thin razor blade that he'd sewn into his cuff.

"I would say that I helped them to give to the less fortunate," Robin said. "Like . . . involuntary philanthropy."

He maneuvered the blade into position, cut it through the fabric, and dropped it into his hand in a practiced motion just as Guy began to move around the room again. Robin slipped the razor to the back of his hand before the assassin could pass behind him and see it.

"And it's not as if the money was come-by honestly to begin with." He chuckled, trying to keep Guy distracted from what his hands were doing as he worked the razor blade underneath the zip ties on his wrists. He fumbled the blade but caught it again without even a flinch.

"With the tax evasion alone, I have enough blackmail on each of those corporations to keep the IRS on their trail for years. Seriously, you should look at their books sometime. The *real* books, not the *official* ones."

"How my clients make their money is entirely irrelevant to me," Guy said.

"As long as some of it ends up in *your* pocket, you mean?"

Guy said nothing. He stared at Robin, daring him to continue. Robin never dropped his gaze, even when his razor blade slipped and nicked his palm.

"How much were you paid to hunt me down anyway? I'm curious; how much am I worth to them?"

Guy's eyes narrowed, but he didn't answer.

"It's blood money. It was blood money before they paid you for my head on a pike." Robin had to keep Guy distracted for just a little longer . . ." Take Nottingham Inc., for example. The corporation that's putting on this charade of a charity event upstairs. You want to know how they keep their costs so low and profits so high? Their products are made almost entirely by slave labor. They outsource whatever they can to sweatshops overseas. And the local work is given to undocumented immigrants who get paid next to nothing but are afraid to quit because they could be reported. Nottingham's built an empire on the backs of desperate people who can't speak out against them, and they skirt around taxes so it all ends up back in their own wallets. And you're okay with that? With their coins jingling in your pocket?"

As Robin's undaunted gaze turned dark, the assassin shrugged and glanced away. "It's how the world works," he said in a thin, clipped tone. The muscles in his face twitched with tension, revealing the rage that was bubbling closer to the surface.

"There need to be people in the world who see injustice and do something about it," Robin said quietly. "I found one of those opportunities. I feel no remorse for taking it."

Guy's tight composure snapped. "Ha! You really are ridiculous, do you know that?" He snatched the gun from his belt and shoved it forward so quickly that Robin nearly lost the razor again. "So much sentiment from a grown man! You would think that by now the world would have bled your delusional hero-complex dry."

A silent moment of tension passed between them before Guy leaned closer and tapped the steel barrel against Robin's right temple.

"I'm disappointed, Robin," Guy said, so close that Robin could smell his spearmint breath. He took out a silencer and spun it onto the front of the pistol. "I was looking forward to finally meeting you. I thought I had a more formidable foe, but you are nothing. Just a silly little man blinded by your naive idealism." He hissed the words like a viper spitting venom.

"We'll see," Robin replied dryly, unflinching. Behind his back, the tiny blade finally cut through the zip ties, but he kept his freed hands tight together so Guy wouldn't notice.

"*Hmph.*" Guy grinned and took an arms-length step away. He chambered a round in the pistol, pressed it to Robin's chest, stroked and tapped the trigger. For a moment, the only sounds heard were shaky breathing, the tap-tap-tap of Guy's trigger finger, and Robin's heartbeat pounding in his head.

Guy looked half-remorseful. "I'm almost going to miss hunting you down Robin," he whispered. "But I think I prefer you dead."

On the other side of the door, gunfire rang out, followed by surprised shouts and thuds as bodies hit the floor.

In the half-second in which Guy turned his head, Robin knocked his arm aside and tackled him. The gun clattered across the room and the two men crashed to the ground. Robin landed hard with his feet still tied to the upended chair.

The door flew open to reveal three men in green hoods followed by a dozen or so men in suits. In an instant, the small room was full of fists, knives, batons, and bullets that ricocheted off the concrete walls. The largest hooded man had a .44 Magnum in each hand and shot with nearly perfect precision, though his sheer size and speed made his body a weapon itself.

"You all took your merry time, didn't you, John?" Robin shouted over the fray. He pinned Guy to the ground. His opponent roared and heaved himself to his side, turning Robin and the chair over with him.

"A thank you would suffice!" Little John replied. The pistol in his shooting hand clicked empty, and he switched to the other.

"All I'm saying is—" Robin had to pause to steel himself against a rain of punches coming down hard on his body. He waited, watching Guy, studying his rhythm. Right between a punch, in the middle of his breath, Robin managed to catch Guy's arm and drive an uppercut hard into his jaw. He felt bone break and used the brief moment of shock to pull Guy back down to the ground. "All I'm saying is you could have been here two minutes sooner."

"I'm going to pretend you didn't say that," Will Scarlet shouted from across the room as he wiped blood from a knife handle. He slid it across the floor to Robin and tackled an assailant to the ground in the same motion.

Guy glanced at his gun in the far corner and dragged himself toward it, but Robin latched onto his leg. When Guy broke loose and scrambled forward again, Allen Odell sidestepped an attacker and kicked the gun out of Guy's reach. In that brief moment of distraction, Robin snatched the knife from the floor and cut the ties on his ankles, finally freeing himself. He turned, grabbed the chair, slammed it down across the assassin's legs, and managed to stand again as Guy struggled to his feet.

Robin's men fought wildly until only three suits remained. Nottingham's last guards looked up in shock at the bloody hooded men and took off running without another breath of hesitation. The hoods had regained the room, but Robin and Guy were still fighting blow for blow. Robin felt a blade shoved into his left side. Adrenaline blocked the initial rush of pain, and in his shock, he pulled the knife from his abdomen and threw it across the room.

He staggered backward and glanced at the bone sticking out of Guy's ankle, though the steady flow of blood from the compound fracture didn't seem to slow him down. The two opponents locked together once more, hardly able to hold themselves up. Guy threw his weight on top of Robin, his hands crushing into his windpipe. Blood dribbled from his sadistic grin down onto Robin's face, and once again, Guy's face gleamed with triumph. But then Robin chuckled. Guy glanced up to see four guns trained on him, including his own.

"I'm a real good shot," Little John said. He held Guy's silenced pistol in his shooting hand and one of his own in the other. Guy rolled off of Robin and scrambled backward, his hands in the air, furious but submissive.

Allen and Will holstered their weapons and went to help Robin stand. Little John didn't take his guns off of Guy.

"Is everyone else okay? Is Marian safe?" Robin whispered.

Allen nodded. "She and Much are back at the van now. Our mastermind hacking genius did it again—everything went as planned. Marian was able to gain access to Nottingham's home office and she used his computer to break into his personal records. The funds have transferred successfully, and the press release should be going out as we speak."

Robin hung his head in relief. "Good job, men." He clapped his hands on Allen and Will's shoulders.

He turned to Guy. "You can inform Nottingham that he has just made a *very* generous donation to the charity he is hosting this fundraiser for. We've let all the local news stations know about it. After all, when you give *several million dollars* to help educate children in need, you've got to let the world know what a generous person you are. Oh, and his corporation may have made an anonymous donation to our organization as well."

"Mr. Nottingham is quite passionate about community development," Will added.

Guy shook with rage, but he didn't dare move.

"What are we doing with him?" Little John asked Robin.

"Leave him. We have more fun with him alive." Robin winked at Guy.

"You should kill me while you have the chance." Guy's voice dripped with grim fury. "I've seen your face. I've seen all your faces. You can't hide behind your internet handle anymore."

"We've seen your face too," Robin reminded him. "And it's only a matter of time before we know your *real* name."

Little John jammed the chamber door while two of the men put their arms under Robin's shoulders to help him up the stairs. His bravado left him as soon as they were out of their enemy's sight. Even with his hand pressed to his side, his wound bled freely.

"Sorry, boys," Little John said as he ran up the stairs behind them. "We're going to have to move a little faster than this." The big man unceremoniously tossed Robin over his shoulder and took off up the stairs. Robin yelped and grit his teeth. Each step sent shocks of pain through his ribs as they ran out into the empty hall, leaving a bloody trail the whole way. Will skimmed the blueprints to navigate toward a private back exit, but before they had gotten far, a new group of guards echoed around them from all directions. The hooded men barreled out through the exit with enemy shouts and footfalls not far behind. At the curb, their van was already running with the side door open, and they hurled themselves in as it screeched away.

"Toss me the med kit," Allen said once he had caught his breath. Marian reached for it as Much tore down the driveway and through a series of random streets until no other cars could follow them.

"Is he all right?" Marian dropped to Robin's side and glanced at the wound Will had his hand clamped against. Allen threw Will a fresh roll of gauze to replace the bunched-up shirt he was using to slow the bleeding.

"I'll be fine," Robin said through gritted teeth. He smiled at Marian's worry. "I'm just glad you're safe." He cleared his throat. "I mean that *all* of you are safe."

"Uh-huh, sure that's what you meant," teased Much from the driver's seat.

Marian didn't respond to the comment, but said, "I had time to transfer the funds and get into the safe in his home office. We have pictures of Nottingham's personal records . . . and cash. A lot of cash. We'll have plenty to finance tomorrow's community rounds."

"You're brilliant." Robin smiled, forgetting his pain for a brief moment.

Allen pulled on a pair of sterile gloves from the med kit and opened a suture packet. "Okay good news, we should have plenty of thread for that wound; bad news is we're out of lidocaine. So . . . this is gonna hurt."

Will gestured to Little John. "Why don't you get behind him and hold him still? Marian, you . . . distract him somehow. Just hold his hand and smile and do that flippy thing with your hair. He likes that."

"Will!" Robin shot him a look and Marian chuckled, her cheeks turning red.

"What?" Will shrugged. "It's not like it's a secret."

John wrapped his arms around Robin, and Allen poured alcohol on the wound. Robin writhed and screamed profanities, and Marian grabbed his hand on an impulse.

"Just look at me," she said calmly. Her voice was steadying. "Keep your eyes on me."

After a long moment, the pain in his side subdued a bit, and Robin took a breath, losing himself to the way Marian's eyes were locked on his. This beautiful, intelligent, spitfire woman, looking at him like that. He couldn't stop himself from smiling.

"AHHHHHHH!!" Robin squeezed Marian's hand harder than he meant to as the needle pushed deep into the wound. Little John held him tighter to keep him from throwing a fist in Allen or Will's direction.

Allen tied off the first stitch and chuckled. "Sorry to ruin your little moment, you two."

Robin winced and glanced at Marian. She met his gaze with kind eyes and squeezed his hand as Allen prepared the next stitch.

"This is going to be a long night," Will sighed.

The following evening, a familiar vigilante appeared on the city streets: a man with a green hood pulled down low over his eyes. No one knew his name. They simply called him The Hood, and very few knew that The Hood was not one man but many. That night, envelopes slipped under single mothers' front doors with enough cash inside to cover rent for the month. A large van-load of food and supplies arrived at a desperate local food bank just in time to feed the neighborhood. Homeless men and women were set up in motels for the week. Tuition fees and medical bills were mysteriously covered by an anonymous donor. Baskets of groceries appeared on doorsteps.

As Robin's men went on their missions throughout the city, he nursed his wounds and sat with an old friend of his, a priest named Tuck. He and the priest looked over a compiled list of individual needs in the community, and one by one, they had the pleasure of seeing those needs checked off. A surgery paid for. A box of diapers and formula delivered to a family with a new baby. A textbook for a student whose funds had run out. Tonight, all courtesy of Mr. Richard Nottingham.

WEEDING

Beka Gremikova

HUNGRY, DEAR?” THE old woman leans over the white picket fence, a basket of apples tucked under her arm, her wrinkled face open and friendly. “You look exhausted.” She clicks her tongue, her gaze on my pink-tinged pale skin. “You shouldn’t be out in this weather; you’ll get sunburnt.”

I snatch an enormous dandelion poking out between the cracks of the front walk. The elves hate weeds almost as much as they hate the Asperian queen for shutting down their mines. I give a vicious yank, and the plant gives, unearthing stem and roots. I wish it were this easy to weed out the Asperian queen. “I don’t mind a little sunshine.” I keep my voice level, even though my insides feel all sloshy like canned fruit. Trying to hide my shaking fingers, I add the weed to the growing pile at my side, sit back on my heels, and crack my knuckles.

I can’t show this woman my fear.

The old woman winces at the noise as if I’m back in the Asperian court, too loud and obnoxious than is proper for a princess.

“You’ll mind it if you burn your skin off,” she says, shaking her head. She nods toward the cluster of forest behind her, where I glimpse other cottages peppered between the trees. Close enough for false comfort, but too far to be much help if things go badly. “None of your neighbors are out today, I see.”

I swallow. My neighbors, as well as the seven elves who took me in, are all miners stuck searching for other work. I grit my teeth. Which *she* should know as the Asperian queen in disguise. "They have other matters to attend to," I say coolly.

She pushes the gate open and beckons me to the shade of the oak tree that grows in front of the cottage. "You should attend to other matters, too," she says, in the tone of voice grandmothers use on unruly grandchildren. "You need to eat."

My gaze falls on her basket of apples, shiny and tempting. *Too* tempting. My stomach tightens, and heat flares through me. I *won't* be tricked again.

Instead, it's *my* turn for trickery. My pocketknife suddenly feels heavy in the back pocket of my trousers. I've carried it around for months, waiting for this moment. I stand, stretching and yawning. "You're right. An apple shouldn't hurt."

Her eyelids wrinkle as she smiles, and she pats the grass next to her.

My body stiffens at the idea of getting so close again, of putting myself in harm's way. . . . But I force myself to sit beside her and take the apple she holds out to me. Its crimson skin glistens.

Sweat slicks my back. My mind wants to whirl out of control, panic nibbling at my consciousness. But I need to focus. "Shall we split it?" I ask, my voice coming out slightly higher pitched than I wished. I tuck a strand of hair out of my eyes. *Keep going.* "It's Asperian tradition to share meals with strangers." I tilt my head to the side, studying her reaction. "You're not Asperian, are you?"

She blinks innocently at me. "Telmakian."

Hmph. I don't believe that for a moment. She *sounds* Telmakian—she rolls her r's the same way Stef and the other elves do, but accents, with the right skills, are something that can be faked. I've learned that the hard way. If the elves hadn't come home in time, I'd be dead twice over.

If my stepmother thinks I'll fall for her disguises yet again, she's in for a surprise of her own.

Taking out my pocket knife, I cut the fruit in half, then wipe the blade on my trousers. I hope she doesn't notice the subtle brown smear left behind as I offer her the apple slice. I'm fairly certain this apple is poisoned—but if so, probably not with a substance that would hurt her with her witch blood. And if it's not, if it's just another of her mind tricks, I'm making *sure* it's the last one she ever plays on me.

She holds it, smiling, staring at me.

"What?" I ask.

Her small, beady eyes seem to gleam. "It's Telmakian tradition for the host to eat first."

My ears buzz. My mind screams, *Danger!*

But if I'm going to win this war, I can't show my hand. I nibble at my piece, careful not to eat from the side my penknife touched. Careful not to take a large enough bite to die. My body tenses, anticipating the familiar stinging burn of poison that I've felt so many times before—first, from a comb, then from laces my stepmother offered me for my best dress.

But there's no such burn.

Oh, *no.*

"Wait!" I shout, but the old woman's already taken a big bite of her apple piece—the slice I'd poisoned.

Her eyes widen. She slumps to the ground, her fingers clutching at her throat. My pocketknife slips from my fingers, lost in the grass I still need to trim. I lunge toward her, but the poison I used, potent enough to kill the hardiest witch, has done its job quickly.

The old woman stares up, unseeing, into the bright, hazy sky.

I stagger back from the corpse, clutching my own throat. My body suddenly feels too heavy, and the world around me starts to float.

This can't be happening. This can't be—

A snigger echoes from the white picket fence. I glance over, blinking blearily, and go cold at who I see.

A different old woman leans over the rails, her dark, beady eyes gleaming. "Hello, stepdaughter dear," she says, stepping through the gate. She passes the other old woman with a disdainful sniff. "I *thought* you might be onto me."

I scramble to my feet, backing away from her, only to run into the crackling bark of the oak tree. My stepmother advances, and this time I catch the flash of a dagger in her hand.

There's no huntsman to save me, no elves close enough to drive her away. And my poisoned blade is gone, lost somewhere in the tangle of grass and weeds.

I tried to play the trickster's game, and I've lost.

This time I can't run away.

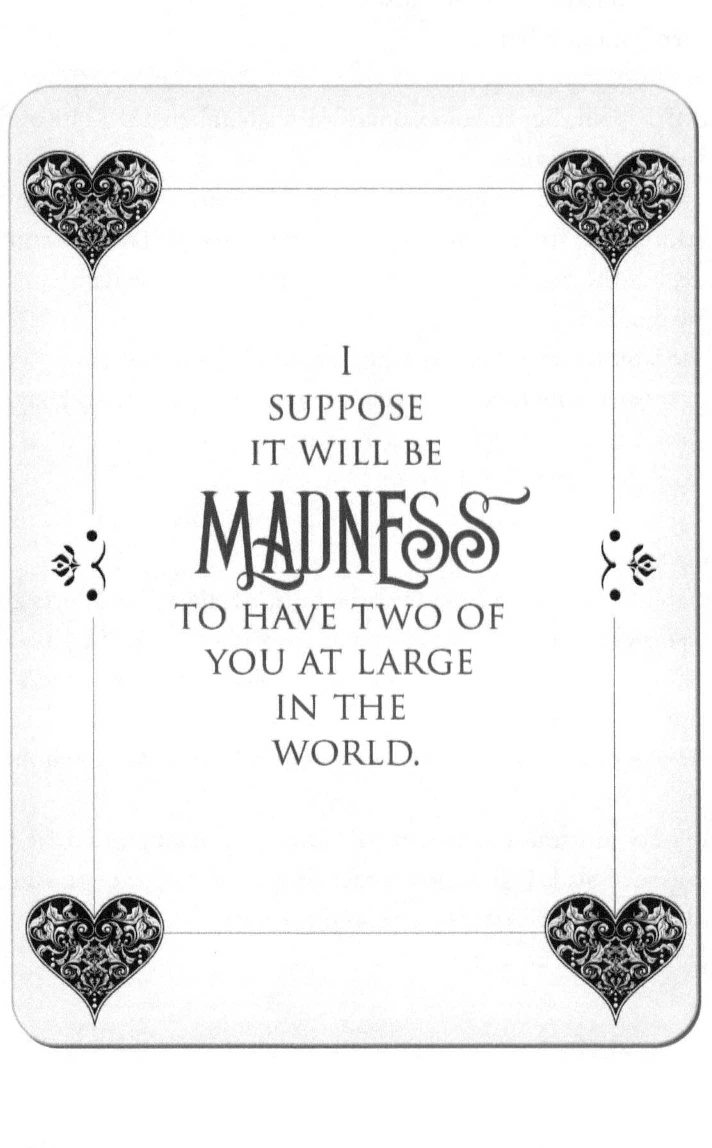
I
SUPPOSE
IT WILL BE
MADNESS
TO HAVE TWO OF
YOU AT LARGE
IN THE
WORLD.

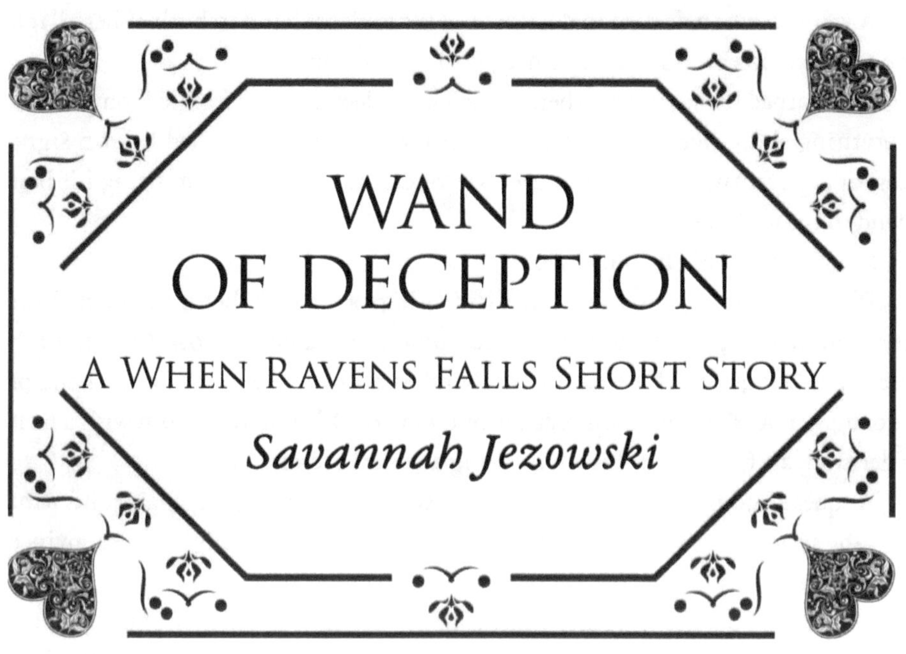

WAND OF DECEPTION

A When Ravens Falls Short Story

Savannah Jezowski

Things of destruction
seldom rest unguarded;
never sleeps the great wave-worm,
the wingless guardian eternal.

Those who will seek
the wand of great power
will find themselves shattered on sea-bone,
torn asunder by the maker of shards.

But he who returns
intact, empty-handed,
is blessed by the wing-steed to find
more fields of glory before Valhalla.

WAVES AS DARK as midnight peaked in frothy starlight, smashed against the rock outcropping where a young man stood. Lightning split the sky moments before a crash of thunder rattled the very stone beneath Loki's feet. Salty spray plastered his unruly dark hair to his face and neck. His heart beat as frantically as the waves pounding against the rocks.

A young woman dressed in doeskin and fur took his hand in both of hers. "You don't have to do this." She spoke softly, for his ears alone.

Loki turned his attention to her, admiring her deep eyes and freckled complexion. Everything about her was as familiar to him as his own skin. He'd known Signe most of his life, and he could not even say when she had gone from being his best friend to his soul mate.

She was the one. The only one.

If only everyone could see that. His teeth ground together as he shifted his attention to Thor, who waited in silence, content to watch him risk life and limb on a ridiculous quest. All because Thor found him *unworthy* to ask for the hand of his daughter. At that very moment, the burly son of Odin surveyed him with a hint of derision, as if he found this whole thing a useless exercise.

A squeaky cough down by his boot preceded a gentle tugging against his pant leg. "She's right," said the small red squirrel. "This isn't the only way to convince Thor of your fine qualities."

"What fine qualities, Tosk?" Loki's jaw tightened even further until it ached. "You heard what he said. He despises me. I'm a foolish boy. Selfish and untrustworthy."

"He didn't use those worse exactly." Tosk fiddled with his ear tufts but glanced away when Loki shot him a dark look. "Well, perhaps his meaning was rather . . . ahem . . . what I mean to say is—"

"Don't go. Don't do it. If you think I will let him stand between us, then you don't know me." Signe's grip on his hand tightened, and she leaned a little closer, earning a warning cough from her father. She growled under her breath but eased back an inch. When he coughed again, she shifted a step further away and let his hand slip from her fingers.

His hand felt empty without her touch, bereft like a ship lost on a stormy sea. "No," he said, words as cold as the pain in his heart. "I won't let him come between us either, and this is the only way. I need to bring him the wand."

"No, you don't!" Anger darkened her beautifully freckled cheeks. "By the shards, I am asking you not to go, Loki."

"I have to, Sig."

Lightning reflected in her eyes. "Fine. Go if you must, but I won't be here when you come back. I won't stand here and watch you kill yourself." With that bitter threat, she spun on her heel and strode away from him without a backward glance. She passed by Thor, but when he reached for her, she ducked out of reach and stalked from them both.

"I, erm, think she means it." Tosk scrabbled up his leg to perch on his shoulder, tiny claws digging into the furs warming his shoulders. "Perhaps we might reconsider? I mean, it's not like we have the greatest track record. None can fault our courage and honor, but perhaps our foresight has often been a little. . . ." Tosk trailed into silence as if too embarrassed to speak the truth. They had been friends for years and had entertained themselves with many adventures.

Recalling said adventures, Loki grimaced. No, he supposed he could not argue that their past exploits had been less than successful. Every time Tosk and Loki went on some fool's errand, they seemed to find themselves at death's gate. Quite literally, in some instances.

For the briefest moment, his resolve quavered. Perhaps Signe and Tosk were right. There must be another way to earn Thor's respect than to risk his life to recover some ancient relic. But when he shifted his gaze to where Thor stood glowering at him, beefy arms crossed over his chest, the doubt evaporated beneath a surge of determination.

He would show Thor—would show them all. Loki, the orphan, was worthy of the daughter of a king.

And then he would make it up to Signe later.

Without another word, he strode to the lip of the rock and leaped into the air. His boots landed in soft sand. Tosk squeaked and clawed at Loki's furs to maintain his balance. The entrance to the dragon's cave gaped before them like an open mouth with jagged rocks for teeth and salty spray instead of saliva. The storm growled with renewed angst as if displeased with their presence in this place.

Loki leaped against the rock teeth, back and forth, before landing in a graceful crouch just within the cave. As he strode into the darkness, the rumble of the storm and sea faded behind them. He pulled flint and torch from the pack slung against his back, and soon a warm glow pierced the gloom of the cave. Loki surveyed the path ahead of them that angled down into the ground as if it meant to tunnel beneath the ocean. The walls were streaked with dark stains that he refused to consider the origin of.

"I don't like this," Tosk whispered, flicking his tail. Loki brushed it away from his ear and plunged ahead despite the squirrel's misgivings.

"You don't have to come with me."

"Yes, I do." Tosk sniffed as if he'd been insulted. "Friends don't let friends venture into death realms alone."

The squirrel's words rang with a note of warning. A beautiful Valkyrie once warned Tosk about letting his friends get into trouble. But Loki brushed the reminder away. He didn't have time to be distracted right now. He needed to get in, get the wand, and get out.

Three simple steps. There would be no death realms today.

But they encountered their first hiccup when they rounded a sharp bend in the tunnel. The path before them disappeared into darkness.

It wasn't a normal darkness, but a *living* sort of darkness that writhed and hissed a warning to stay away. Loki lifted his torch to investigate closer, but the firelight could not pierce the dark shadows that lay between them and their prize.

"It's a distraction, an attempt to scare us off," he speculated. Tosk merely squeaked dubiously and nestled against the curve of his neck. His tiny frame shuddered.

Very well. Loki would have enough courage for the both of them. He slid one foot into the shadows and then another. All light from the torch evaporated as he eased them fully into the shifting darkness. He could feel it clinging to his skin like icy fingers. It even tried to claw its way into his eyes, so he squeezed them shut and continued to shuffle his way forward as Tosk shivered and wailed in distress. They continued in this horrible fashion for nearly ten minutes before the icy fingers slid away from his skin. He opened his eyes, relieved to see that his torch once again illuminated the underwater cave.

His skin began to warm too quickly, and then a fierce itch swept across his body. The itch grew to painful pinpricks over every inch of him. Tosk squeaked and danced back and forth on Loki's shoulder.

"Ow, ow, ow! It's stinging me!"

Loki scratched at his arm and plunged forward, the pain growing more intense with every step. Another distraction, he told himself with gritted teeth. He burst out of the tunnel and into a sloping cavern as the stabbing pains abruptly ceased.

Tosk wheezed and sagged in relief. "I don't wish to complain—a hero of my caliber never complains, naturally—but I'd rather not go through *that* again."

"That makes two of us." Loki met the squirrel's gaze and offered a commiserating smile.

The underwater cavern glowed with teal and blue luminescent lights embedded in the walls. Loki paused to investigate one of the lights, only to realize it *moved.* Scrabbled was more like it, on tiny glowing legs.

Beetles. The lights were giant, luminescent beetles the size of his foot.

"Don't let them eat me!" Tosk screamed and dove straight down the back of Loki's shirt. His claws shredded the skin over Loki's spine as the squirrel wormed his way to perceived safety. He hissed against the pain but forced himself not to yell at Tosk. He couldn't blame him for being nervous. The massive bugs were quite unnerving, even to him.

He scrambled away from the walls to put distance between them and the beetles just in case they were poisonous or inclined to feast on flesh.

The cavern seemed to grow larger the deeper he journeyed into it until the glowing beetles were tiny pinpricks on all sides of them. Stones skittered as he jostled them with his boots.

Then something grated ahead of them. Loki froze. Tosk emerged from his hiding place, nose quivering. Whatever moved in the darkness made a soft *shushing* sound.

"Well, well, well," a guttural voice filled the dimness of the cavern. "Either you're lost or dimwitted."

Loki spun around, trying to find the source of their unseen companion. "I am neither. I know exactly where I am, and I am no one's fool."

"Nor am I." Tosk's voice cracked halfway through his bold declaration.

The unseen force chortled. Loki lifted his arm higher in an attempt to see better. Something drifted through the darkness. No, he realized with a horrified chill, *slithered*. Coils of it seemed to be slithering closer to them. Closing in on them from all sides. Loki swung his torch and spun in a circle as he realized their escape had been cut off while the sea serpent glided around them. A triangular head loomed out of the shadows and into the torchlight. Gills and small fins fluttered along the serpent's neck.

The Jormungandr eyed him with a glowing emerald gaze. "What brings you to the sea realm, human?"

Loki swallowed the fear choking the back of his throat. "I've—I've come for the Wand of Destruction, serpent."

The serpent hissed between its teeth. "Is that what they're calling it these days? It used to go by another name."

Loki said nothing. He didn't care what the thing was called. He simply needed to have it.

"Who told you about the wand? It's supposed to be a secret." The serpent swayed back and forth as it pierced Loki with its unblinking eyes.

Loki considered briefly before answering. He supposed there was no harm in being honest. "Thor sent me."

The serpent reared backward a few feet. "Thor sent you? That's . . . interesting."

"Why?"

The serpent began to circle them, drawing in closer, inch by inch, foot by foot, until only a few yards remained around them.

"Why does it matter who sent me?" Loki demanded as he reached to pull a dagger from his belt.

"Because," the serpent hissed. "Thor is the one who tasked me with hiding the wand."

What? "Don't lie to me," Loki said, but the seed of uncertainty had been planted.

Something smelled off to him, and he didn't mean the pungent, fishy smell of the cavern or its inhabitant.

"I would not lie to you, human." The serpent lowered its head so that mere feet separated them. "I can give you the wand, but you won't want it."

"Do not presume to know my mind, snake."

The serpent laughed, parting its mouth to reveal teeth coated with pond scum. "I know your mind only too well. *Loki.*"

The chill in his bones turned to ice.

"And who is that with you?" the serpent continued. "Ah yes, the Tale Spinner. I wondered when he would find his way to me. He's visited all the other ancients in our world. It was only a matter of time before he darkened my door with his muddy little paws."

"Now see here—" Tosk began, but he choked off mid-sentence when the serpent's tongue licked out between his teeth.

Loki said nothing, and to his credit, neither did Tosk.

"You are determined then." The serpent sounded odd. Resigned somehow. "The wand is yours. But it will come with a cost, human. A terrible, terrible cost."

"Where is—" But he never had to finish the question. For one moment, his hand was empty, and the next, it held a wooden staff nearly two feet in length. The wand was made of thin branches wound together to form one single stick. The wood appeared blackened, perhaps charred, and gave off a foul odor.

He had the irrational urge to toss the wand away and put as much distance between himself and it as he could manage, as quickly as he could manage it. But his resolve remained unchanged.

For Signe. He could do this for Signe.

"Yes," the serpent hissed between his teeth. "*For Signe.*"

Loki waited for the deception to reveal itself. Of course, there would be a catch, some hidden terms in the exchange the serpent had deliberately withheld from him. Only a fool would think otherwise, and he was no fool. He would embrace whatever fate came for him with eyes wide open.

The serpent began to laugh, a terrible laugh that could move the caves that concealed him and churn up the seas that had spawned him. The cavern trembled, from within and without it seemed, and the ground bucked beneath his feet so that Loki had to stagger to stay upright. Shadows swirled, growing darker by the moment until even the light from his torch disappeared once again. The serpent's laugh reverberated around him. In his own head, his own thoughts. He could not stand the agony of the presence inside him a moment longer; the pain would surely rip him in two.

He collapsed to his knees, the wand between his palm and the damp cave floor, the torch held mere inches from a puddle of seawater that would have surely snuffed it out. When he raised his head, gasping for breath, he stared into a mirror.

Except, there was no mirror. The man that stood before him was flesh and blood—real, breathing, not a paltry reflection of himself.

And yet it *was* himself. Somehow, he stared at a duplicate of his own form, his own dark hair with the cowlicks nothing could tame. The scar on the back of his hand from a blunder in the forges. The glittering green eyes. The sly smile curving the mouth.

"What madness is this?" he rasped.

His other self smiled, cold and repulsive. "Oh, madness indeed. I suppose it will be madness to have two of you at large in the world." Even the voice that fell from that familiar mouth sounded exactly like his own.

Bile rose in the back of his throat. "I—I don't understand."

The other Loki crossed his arms and frowned at him, seeming disappointed. "Surely, you will have figured it out by now. No? I suppose I must spell it out for you then. I am the cost. The terrible cost of possessing that wand."

"A duplicate of me is a *cost?*" Loki shook his head and scrambled to his feet. He hated to admit he could not figure out what seemed to be happening here. Whatever the deception, it had taken him. He'd fallen prey to it.

The boy who swore never to be tricked again had fallen prey to a trick.

"Not a duplicate. A shard, Loki. A shard of your soul."

"Oh, crumb," Tosk squeaked.

Silence consumed the cavern as Loki processed what this meant, what it would cost him. Did he feel any different? Not really, except . . . he felt a little emptier somehow. As if something *might* be missing. Something he had not even realized he possessed.

"I am the darkest part of you." The shard of his soul offered a thin, cold smile. "You can never escape me. Everywhere you go, I will be by your side. What you love, I will hate. What you build, I will tear down. What you hold most dear, I will rip away from you. All you have will become mine in the end."

"You're lying," Loki rasped.

"Am I?" the shard asked. "You can feel it in your bones that I speak the truth. You, of all people, will know whether I am lying. So, which is it: am I a liar or the revealer of truths?"

With every fiber of his being, Loki wanted to believe the shard spun a web of deceit around him, but he found he could not embrace that belief. It felt hollow and empty, like what remained of himself. He had been torn in two pieces.

But what did that mean for him and Signe? Didn't it stand to reason that if the darkest part of himself had been removed, then she would like him the better for it? Perhaps, with this shadowy part of him removed, and if he could figure out a way to be rid of it, he could love her more truly, more purely—

"Now, who is the liar?" The shard's voice had become deadly soft. Loki felt as if he were walking along the rim of a sharp blade and had finally come to the tip, where he would turn around and save himself or fall to his doom. But he couldn't do either, could he?

If he went back, he would lose Signe. Without the wand to present to Thor, he had nothing to offer. But if he stayed this course, and if the shard was to be trusted, it would be the end of all he held dear.

He would lose her either way.

And Thor had known this would happen. If Thor had hidden the wand in the first place, then he knew the true power it possessed. He knew the true cost he was asking Loki to sacrifice.

"And now you begin to understand."

Yes. It sickened him to the core, but he understood. Thor had sent him on a fool's errand. He knew that whatever choice Loki made, he would lose Signe. Why had he not listened to her? He should never have come here. They could have stolen away together, found a place in the world to call their own.

But now, there would be no place for them in the world.

"This isn't fair," Tosk piped up in Loki's defense, a quiver in his voice.

"No," the shard said softly. "It isn't. But few things are, Tale Spinner. They simply are what they must be."

Tears pricked at Loki's eyes. Defeat pressed down on his shoulders, on his heart. Yet again, he felt as if he were breaking, but not in half. Rather to pieces. Hundreds of shards.

"So, if I give back the wand, then I will be free of you forever, and Signe will be safe?"

The green eyes grew more somber. "No. I will always be with you. *I am you.* But, in the end, that is what makes you who you are. You cannot be rid of me without ceasing to be. You must embrace who you were, who you could have been. Only then will you discover who you will be."

Loki didn't want to discover who he would be, not really, not if it meant he would be without Signe. He wanted her with him so badly the thought of losing her felt like a knife to the gut. But he could not put her in harm's way. And if being with him would hurt her, then he had to let her go.

It would break him, but he had no other choice. Thor had played his hand far, far too cleverly.

At last, he held the wand out.

The shard stared at him, eyes glittering in the darkness of the sea cave. "You are certain?"

"I am," Loki managed, eyes burning from the tears he refused to shed. "Take it back. I don't want it anymore."

The shard hesitated a moment longer, a slow smile spreading across his face. "It goes by another name, you know. Depending on how you translate the ancient words. Some say it means the Wand of Destruction. The destruction of the soul. But it can also mean the Wand of Deception and all the lies men tell themselves to hide who they truly are. There are precious few who have understood the true nature of the wand, and themselves, as you now do."

And just like that, the wand disappeared. One moment he clutched the horrid thing in his hands, and the next, he held empty air. And when he looked up, the shard was gone, the serpent had returned, its huge body coiled around him, and he felt a little more whole. His heart ached, but he knew he had done the right thing. It would break him, but he would not change his mind.

The serpent dipped his head, then, and in a slithering rush of scales and fins, disappeared back into his grotto. Loki made the return trip on legs that felt too heavy. He dreaded coming out on the other side of this and telling Signe he had failed.

He needn't have worried, though. When he emerged from the cavern, Signe kept her word and made herself scarce. He saw no sign of her as he returned to the place where he'd left Thor. Loki stopped in front of him. "You knew I would fail." He breathed the words because he feared if he spoke any louder, he might lose control and scream what he truly felt inside.

"Yes, I expected you would . . . ." Thor uncrossed his arms and took a step closer. The sea breeze riffled his long blond hair. "But you surprised me and didn't."

Loki paused, mouth opened to say the things he intended to say. It took him a moment to process what Thor might mean. "I gave the wand back. I didn't bring it with me."

"You were never meant to."

"But you told me—" Loki burst out before he managed to bite back the angry words. "You sent me to retrieve the wand."

"I did." Thor reached out and settled a heavy hand on Loki's shoulder. "You had to make peace with yourself, and until you did, I could not trust you with my daughter's heart."

Loki lifted his eyes, anger mingling with confusion and then the faintest ray of hope. He couldn't bring himself to ask what Thor meant.

The blond giant made him wait, a tick tugging at his cheek before a slow smile stretched his full mouth into a grin. "You'll have to win her over again. I fear she's rather furious with both of us. She has her father's stubborn streak." Thor said this as if it were something to be proud of. "But if you love her as much as you claim, and if she cares for *you* as much as *she* claims, then I expect you two will sort it out."

Loki tried to stop himself, but he whooped and broke into a run, Tosk screeching in alarm on his shoulder. Behind him, Thor snorted, but Loki didn't care what he thought. Not anymore.

He found Signe at the longboat. She stood on the deck, back to him, hair billowing in the wind as she stared out over the churning sea. He swung himself over the railing and hurried toward her, stomach stirring as violently as the waves against the hull of their boat. Tosk scrambled down and found himself a perch on the railing.

She said nothing as he stopped beside her, face pinched, eyes and nose red from crying. Loki hated that he'd upset her, but he'd been sure he was doing the right thing. He'd been so sure about a lot of things. Now, he was a little less sure, but one thing remained fixed in his mind. He wanted Signe to be with him for any future adventures he and Tosk might find themselves in. He didn't want to do it without her. "I should have listened to you," he said. "It was all a trick. Your father didn't even want me to bring him the wand, not really. He was just trying to make a point before he gave his blessing."

She sniffed and turned her face away slightly.

"I'm sorry, Sig." He hesitated and then reached to brush the side of her hand with his finger.

She did not pull away, but neither did she fall into his arms either. Instead, Signe wiped her cheeks with the back of her hand and angled slightly toward him, hurt still etched on her features. "He changed his mind then?"

Loki didn't know if he should look happy that Thor had given his blessing or unhappy because she still looked so sad. He'd known her long enough to know her moods were unpredictable, and no matter how hard he tried, he usually did the wrong thing. "He did," he said rather cautiously. "If you still want me."

"Oh, Loki." Signe's face crumpled a little, the tautness in her shoulders relaxing. "I've always wanted you. Even when you were that scrappy little fellow getting me into trouble. Why do you think I hung around all this time, waiting for you to grow a brain between those ears of yours?"

The ears in question grew suddenly warm as Loki blushed. "I admit I am a brainless oaf," he said contritely. "Your father was right. I am *not* worthy of you. But I swear on my honor that every day for the rest of my life, I shall endeavor to become so."

At this, a lovely smile tugged the girl's mouth, chasing away the shadows in her eyes. "I already think you're worthy, Loki."

Tosk made a contented sound from behind them as he shamelessly watched the spectacle unfold.

Loki realized then that Signe had never wanted him to prove himself to her. In fact, all the trouble he had gotten himself into was because *he* felt he had something to prove. Whatever flaws he may have, he loved her with all his heart and wanted to do right by her. It didn't matter that he was an orphan with no lineage, or that his only feats of valor had come while getting himself out of the scrapes his own folly had gotten him into. He might be flawed, might have made many mistakes in his life, but those flaws and follies had turned him into the person he was today.

He would endeavor to be the best version of himself for her, but he liked himself as he was. He didn't need to pretend to be anything more.

"Do you think your father will bludgeon me with his hammer if I were to kiss you, Sig?"

Her eyes sparkled, grin widening. "Are you willing to risk it?"

Tosk's sigh of contentment turned into violent coughing. "Oh, bother," he muttered. "I'll just make myself scarce then."

Signe giggled as the squirrel dove over the side of the boat and scampered back up the shore as if chased by wolves. Thunder rumbled in the distance, and the sky released a sudden torrent of icy rain as Loki kissed his lady.

THE OLD
CHOCOLATE

TREES CREAKED
IN A

CINNAMON
WIND.

THE TREAT TRICKSTER

Emily Barnett

The old chocolate trees creaked
in a cinnamon wind.
Twisting paths like candy canes,
drawing us further in.

A forest with its secrets
so sweet that they could rot
the teeth from our young heads.
And corrupt souls, if but caught.

A dark wood where a witch
spun a house of sugar-greed,
with gummies and orange toffee,
bitter sins in coated seeds.

Her mouth curled like rye pretzels,
eyes glinting with apple red.
My brother ate from her kitchen,
and staled like week-old bread.

But me, I did not cave
like an under-done cake.
I shoved her in the oven
And turned it high to bake.

The magic, I realized,
was in the candies she grew.
In the sickly sweet forest
slick as green apple goo.

The treat-trickster was tricked
by the treats that she had used
on apple-cheeked children
much too easily amused.

We left there, hand-in-hand
close by each other's side,
with the scent of flesh pie
trailing high to the sky.

But we never made it back
the night of her great defeat.
We found another strange path
to plant our curious feet.

Years have gone by now.
A new house has been built.
I stare from sugar windows
heavy with caloric guilt.

The witch had been prisoner,
chocolate trees, her cell.
The trickster, it would seem,
is the forest where we dwell.

With ripe saccharine secrets
not a stomach could handle.
Live a brother and a witch,
named Hansel and Gretel.

TRIALS
ALWAYS COME IN
THREES
DON'T THEY?

A TWIST OF GREEN AND GOLD

Laurie Lucking

Y*OU'VE GONE TOO far this time, Father.*

Tears blurred my view of the surrounding haystacks, impossibly tall and thick. *Don't cry, Abigail. You'll never fix your machine if you can't see properly.*

But what was the point? I elbowed the crank, eliciting a half-hearted *thunk*. Father had curried the king's favor at the expense of his fellow tradesmen ever since Mother's death.

Why would he treat his daughter any differently?

With a grunt, I reclaimed my screwdriver. Leaning against the side panel, I inserted a screw. Each twist brought my mistake circling back through my mind. Had I thought Father would be proud of my newest invention? Finally *see* me?

Instead, he saw status, wealth, power. And turned straight to the king, as always.

I'd turned five measly strands of hay into gold. *Five*! Yet he'd boasted I could transform an entire room. As an added challenge, His Royal Highness thought it'd be sporting to make me accomplish the task in one night.

Or die in the morning.

My shudder made my tool slip. I gritted my teeth and gave the screwdriver one last rotation.

Even when functioning properly, the contraption was slow and unwieldy. I'd passed thirty pieces of hay through, now a pile of golden sticks. A tiny fraction of the heaps of straw filling every corner of the room, yet enough to cause the machine to malfunction.

But I didn't have time to feel sorry for myself.

•••♥•••

I blinked, the grinding of gears irritating my pounding head. Tugging on the chain of my watch, I squinted at its black, ornamented hands and flinched. Only minutes from midnight. While my machine had resumed functioning hours before, I'd only transformed several hundred strands of straw, with—a glance around the room coiled knots in my stomach—thousands to go.

Grasping another handful, I inserted a piece of hay into the machine. Steam hissed as pistons bobbed up and down. Perhaps the Green Raiders would launch an attack, or the king would be required to investigate another sighting of his presumed-dead son, Prince Hieronymus. He might even appreciate my progress and give me more time.

King Auren, who'd give a peasant one day to pay his taxes before ordering an execution? I choked back a laugh. Appreciation and mercy were hardly his strong points.

"Your good humor is admirable."

I gasped and toppled from my stool.

A young man, probably a bit older than my seventeen years, offered his hand to help me up. "My apologies. I didn't mean to frighten you."

I stumbled backward, my chest tightening at the telltale emerald stripe edging his gray pants and jacket.

"You—you're a Green Raider. Where did you come from?" Had he crept through a doorway behind the tapestry? From within the wardrobe, perhaps?

"Be assured, I mean you no harm. Our only quarrel is with the king." He extended his fingers as though quieting a frightened kitten. "You may call me Rone. And this castle is crawling with secret passageways, but the less you know of them, the better."

"I see." Forcing my shaking legs to straighten, I resumed my seat on the stool. "I'm Abigail, but I'm quite busy, so—"

"Indeed. What is this fascinating contraption?" He rounded the table, taking in my machine from every angle.

With a huff, I fed it another cut of straw and rotated the handle. "Please, don't touch it. I can't afford any further delays."

"Is it—?" A stick of gold jangled into the collection bin. He picked it up, eyes wide. "It can't be turning the straw to gold."

I propped my free hand on my hip. "Actually, it is. By adding heat and the right combination of chemicals, it alters the hay's elemental properties until . . ." I threaded yet another line of straw into the opening. "I don't have time to explain."

"Surely, you aren't required to . . ." His gaze swept across the mounds of straw. "How long do you have?"

"Sunrise." I sniffled and lowered my eyes.

"Hmm, that won't do." A handkerchief appeared near my right cheek. Did this man make *any* sound when he moved? Assuming he wasn't just a figment of my frazzled imagination.

"Do you have enough chemicals?"

"What?" I pressed the faded cloth to my nose.

"Enough chemicals to transform the straw."

"Oh, yes. Each reaction consumes very little."

He lifted the top off the middle section, just beyond the glass tubes emitting steam, and peered inside.

"Careful!"

"Steam doesn't bother me." Removing his hat, he wiped perspiration from his brow. "The crank slows it down?"

Warmth invaded my face, likely turning my cheeks a blotchy red. "I have to turn the crank slowly, or it jams. The heating and cooling process takes time."

"So if we add more coal, we can achieve a larger flame. And perhaps another pool of water here"—he indicated an empty space near the collection bin—"would aid the cooling."

"I suppose."

His grin made a frantic moth take flight in my stomach. Despite his association with the volatile Green Raiders, Rone wasn't unappealing. Tousled curls hovered above his ears, and his bright eyes matched the stripe on his jacket. "I'll be right back." After several nimble steps, he added, "Don't try to follow."

"I couldn't if I wanted to." I gestured to the crank before wrapping my sore fingers around its handle.

"Good point." He glided into the wardrobe and disappeared from sight.

I returned to my work with a slight smile. I'd been right about the wardrobe.

•••♥•••

I glanced at my pocket watch. 5:30. *No*! Rone's ideas for the heating and cooling mechanisms had more than doubled the machine's efficiency, and we were so close. But the first rays of dawn must already . . .

Rone rotated his shoulders. "Anything we've missed?"

I scanned the room. Where once stood piles of straw, now rose tidy pyramids of golden bars. "N-no. There's nothing left."

"Excellent. Then I'd better—"

"Wait!" I clutched his arm. "I owe you my life. Surely, I can do something in return."

"Much as I hate to fuel King Auren's greed, it was my pleasure to help." He tucked a wayward strand of hair behind my ear. "Your life is well worth saving."

A warmth I'd presumed was gone forever wound through my veins. This stranger placed more value on my life than my own father.

"But I'd like to reward you somehow." I fumbled for anything that might be of use to this kind, quirky man. "My necklace? Or my ring?"

He gently disengaged my hand. "All I ask is that you maintain my secrecy."

"Thank you." The words seemed so hopelessly insufficient.

"Farewell, Abigail." His eyes held a perplexing intensity, as though our triumph had increased rather than diminished his concern. "We may yet meet again." Pressing a palm to each of my temples, he kissed my forehead.

Before I snapped my jaw shut, he'd disappeared into the wardrobe.

Father took a seat beside me on the wide, second-story veranda of the palace, his fingers thrumming the table's polished surface. "What, precisely, did King Auren say to you this morning?"

I swallowed a sigh. Father had been so full of life before Mother died. Eager to sail off on adventures, eager to return home to his wife and daughter.

Now he seemed convinced only the notice of the king himself could fill the void she'd left behind.

I fought to keep the resentment out of my tone. "He commended my fine work with the straw, instructed a guard to transport my machine home, and invited us to join him for afternoon tea." More like demanded.

A footman cleared his throat. "His Royal Highness, King Auren of Durbach."

I rose, nearly stumbling as my layered skirt caught my chair leg.

The king strode forward, his black cane clicking against the tiled floor. His tailcoat brushed the backs of his knees, and a top hat added nearly six inches to his average frame. But fashion couldn't conceal his graying hair or the power-hungry glint in his eyes.

"I hope I haven't kept you waiting."

"Not at all, Your Highness." Father swept into his deepest bow, and I lowered into a half-hearted curtsy.

King Auren claimed the third chair at the table, and Father and I resumed ours. Servants poured tea into delicate porcelain cups. I studied the gold filigree as Father and King Auren exchanged pleasantries.

"Miss Polek."

I lowered my cup, sloshing steaming tea onto my hand. "Yes, Your Highness?" I darted a glance at him before mopping up the mess with my lacy napkin.

"I must say, I'm impressed by the capabilities of your little contraption. Our technology hasn't progressed as quickly as I'd hoped, not since the loss of my dear Hieronymus."

My dear Hieronymus. From what I'd heard, the king's relationship with his son had been rocky for years before the prince's mysterious death.

I replaced my napkin. "Thank you, Your Highness."

"It makes me wonder what you might achieve if truly challenged. What new heights Durbach might reach with your help. We can't allow those Green Raiders to outpace us, after all."

I weighed my possible responses. Last night had been more than enough of a challenge, and I had no aspirations of royal service.

Besides, were the Green Raiders so bad?

"You flatter me, sir. The machine was merely a stroke of luck."

Father clucked his tongue. "Nonsense, Abigail. You have great potential, and I know you wouldn't hesitate to serve your king in any manner possible." He straightened. "I'm confident Abigail could achieve the task you set for her two times over."

I clenched my teeth. In any other circumstance, the compliment would've soothed like balm on a wound. But there was no way I could—

"Interesting." The king took an exaggeratedly slow sip of tea. "Let's put it to the test."

My pulse raced faster than a locomotive. "Your Highness, please. I finished the straw last night with only moments to spare, and—"

He silenced me with a dismissive wave. "Your father wouldn't make such a statement if he didn't have the utmost belief in you. We shall provide materials to enhance your machine, as needed." He motioned over a guard. "Miss Abigail Polek this night shall turn a room of straw to gold—a room twice as large as before. If she fails to perform her task by sunrise, she and her father shall be put to death."

Such prim formality. As though he were announcing a ball, not a death sentence.

Father barked a laugh. "Your Highness. Surely, you don't—"

"Surely, I do. If your faith in your daughter is so great, then you've nothing to fear. If not, well . . ." He replaced his cup in the precise center of his saucer. "One mustn't lie to his king."

"Of course, Your Highness." Father's defeated expression forged a new crack in my heart. As though he just now—finally—saw the king for who he was.

King Auren readjusted his hat and rose. "I must take my leave. Miss Polek, my servants will prepare your room for the night. In the meantime, stay and enjoy further refreshments. Mr. Polek, you may come and go as you please."

"Thank you, Your Highness." Father's bow held none of its usual confidence.

I dipped into a curtsy, not daring to speak.

King Auren strode out, the *clack-clack* of his cane accentuating his progress.

Father kept his head lowered. "He would kill you? Kill—me?" His trembling hands nearly upset the dainty table. "Abigail, I . . . When he mentioned a penalty of death the other day, you must believe I never thought he'd go through with it. Never dreamt . . ." His haunted eyes sought mine. He blinked through the tears gathering in his lashes and released a tremulous breath. "I—I'm beginning to see my error now."

The slightest thread of hope twined through my building panic and nausea. Would he finally cut his ties with the king? Be a father to me once more? But anger snipped it short before the dream could take hold. How much of a loving parent could he be when it had taken a threat against *him*, not me, to spawn his disappointment in the king?

I met his pleading gaze. There was so much I could say. Accusations, questions, failures. But we had mere hours together before I'd likely sentence us both to death.

Biting back a bitter retort, I placed a hand on his arm. "It's good to have you back, Father."

•••♥•••

So much straw.

A horse could've survived in this room for months. The table on which the servants had placed my machine rose like an island in the sea of haystacks. Across the room, another table hosted the promised tools and components.

My crazed laugh disrupted the machine's whirring. When was I supposed to build something new?

Rone's enhancements had allowed me to transform two piles of straw already. But the increased speed couldn't compensate for the room's larger capacity. I glanced about the chamber for the hundredth time. No wardrobe in sight—I was on my own.

•••♥•••

A low moan broke through my hazy thoughts. Jumping from my stool, I surveyed the machine. What could've caused such a sound?

A squeak followed, accompanied by a rustle of hay. To my left, a mound of straw toppled over. *What—*? A square of flooring angled upward, revealing a gray bowler hat.

"Rone!" I stumbled across the room and helped him climb out.

"I told you we'd meet again." He wedged a shoe beneath the heavy wooden plank. "Do you think they heaped straw over that trapdoor on purpose?"

"I—really couldn't say."

He rose and took in my shimmering dress and styled hair. "You look . . ." He swallowed. "Stunning."

Warmth crept into my cheeks. "Thank you. I never had the opportunity to change into something more practical before . . ."

"Oh, Abigail." He surveyed the room, the mischief fading from his eyes. "What have they done?"

"The faster heating and cooling is certainly helping, but—"

"It could never be enough." He kicked the nearest haystack.

"How did you know to come?"

His soft gaze landed back on me. "I suspected one demonstration wouldn't be sufficient for the king. Even this may not be enough. Abigail . . ." He took my hands, his palms callused but gentle. "If you want to go through with this, I'll do everything I can to assist. But if you'd rather escape, you'd be safe among the Green Raiders."

My breath snagged in my throat. If the rest of the Green Raiders were anything like Rone . . . But this time, Father's life was on the line. "I wish I could, but King Auren included my father in his death sentence."

Rone released my hands. "I see. Then let's get to work." He faced the table of extra supplies. "Continue with your machine, and I'll try making something similar."

I nodded. "Thank you, Rone. Truly. I—"

"It's my pleasure."

•••♥•••

I worked in rhythm with Rone's humming as he hammered, screwed, and chiseled, biting back the urge to scold him whenever he scrutinized a component of my machine.

His melody paused. "Would you take a look? The hay isn't moving through quite right."

I made my way to his table, pushing aside stray pieces of straw.

"My design is almost identical to yours, except with a foot pedal instead of a crank."

"Clever." I examined where he'd secured cut-up pipes instead of glass tubes. "You're not letting enough steam through here." I pointed to the small holes leading into each vertical pipe. "It's probably overheating."

He leaned close. "I bet you're right." With a recklessness that made me wince, he popped off the pipes.

I returned to my post, stooping to gather more straw. "I'm impressed you put that together so fast. Do you make your own inventions?"

"More than I can count." He fastened a larger bit to the drill. "Only about half of them work. I've attempted everything from a mechanical arm extender to a motion-activated squirrel trap." He wielded the drill against the small metal plate he'd removed from his machine. "Much better."

"I wish I could see your squirrel trap in action."

"You could give me tips for making it quieter. The racket scares the squirrel away before it's fully caught." He turned back to his discarded pipes. "What about you? You're clearly an experienced inventor."

"I started when my mother got sick." Grit coated my throat. "I made her a stand to hold her book when her hands became too weak, then a music box that played her favorite song."

"I'll bet she loved that."

"She did, but I came to hate it. The sound was so tinny. I never had a chance to fix it before she . . ."

"I'm sorry."

"I think the worst part was losing Father, too, in a way. He's never been the same."

Rone's breath hissed through his clenched jaw. "It's astonishing how losing a loved one can make a man turn his back on those memories and shared values. To put a stranglehold on everything else in a desperate attempt to seize some measure of control."

"You speak from experience."

"My mother died, too. And my father . . . couldn't be more lost." His posture sagged. "I'm sure your mother is proud of you."

"And yours, as well. You're a regular knight in shining armor, helping a damsel in distress."

He shook his head. "I hardly know what Mother would think." His knee bobbed as he pumped the pedal below his table. A *plink* followed. "It worked!"

He ran forward, lifted me from my stool, and spun me in a circle. "We'll keep you alive yet, Abigail."

•••❤•••

I forced a bite of potatoes into my mouth. The king appraised me with cold, beady eyes.

Tea was bad enough. Now he'd insisted on dinner.

"That's an interesting clock." I motioned to a timepiece featuring a set of intertwining gears.

"Indeed. Made by my late son."

I glanced at Father, who stared into his lobster bisque. With his rosy image of the king shattered, he seemed more disoriented than ever.

"You must miss him very much."

"His absence leaves a gap, certainly. Not only in my affections, but in the line to the throne." King Auren turned to face me. "Miss Polek, since the passing of my late wife, few ladies have made a favorable impression on me. But your skill and courage have me quite intrigued. I'd like to challenge them to one last test. You know the consequences should you fail, of course. For both of you." He inclined his head toward Father. "But this time, I have an offer in return."

Not again. My head swam with weariness, my hands protesting the thought of giving that crank even one more rotation.

"First to your father. Mr. Polek, my finest ship sits in the harbor. If your daughter succeeds tonight, you shall set sail on the morrow as its captain."

My chest ached at Father's anguished expression. His wildest dream could come true at such a cost.

"I thank you, Your Highness."

I squeezed his arm. "Congratulations, Father. They will be fortunate to have you." Perhaps on the sea, he could, at last, regain some portion of his former self.

"As for you, Miss Polek." The king's smile was too broad to be comforting. "If this greater success proves you worthy, *I shall make you my queen*."

•••❤•••

If I ever see a blade of straw again, I'll light it on fire.

My frantic rhythm kept further reflections at bay. Insert hay on right, turn crank. Thread straw on left, push pedal. Using my machine on one side and Rone's on the other, I produced a steady stream of metallic plinks. Not enough, but I shoved that worry to the back of my mind. The same place I pushed every thought about the king's proclamation at dinner.

Occasional breaks in the heavy clouds sent thin shafts of moonlight through the window. Based on the view, they'd marched me to the highest tower in the castle for this final challenge.

Out of reach of any secret passageways, no doubt.

Rain pounded, followed by a rumble. The noise grew louder, almost as though . . . I turned.

Rone perched on the windowsill, dripping water. "Trials always come in threes, don't they?" He removed his hat and shook out his hair.

"How did you get up there?"

"Vines aren't the only things that can climb trellises." A shiver belied his easy smile.

"You're soaked." I dashed to my discarded jacket. "A blanket would be better, but at least this is dry. Here." I wrapped the thin fabric around his shoulders.

"Thank you."

My laugh came out as a sob. "Don't thank me. It's my fault you've gone to all this trouble."

"None of this is your fault, Abigail." His green eyes searched mine.

"But why do you keep coming back? You don't even know me."

"I know you now, and I . . ." He traced a finger along my chin before letting his hand drop. "Well, I can't stand to see the king misusing people's inventions."

"But it's no use. I've used both our machines for hours, and . . ." I gestured helplessly at the heaping piles of straw. "I'm not sure I even want to succeed anymore."

I shall make you my queen. I shuddered.

"What?" Rone grasped my arms. "I know you're exhausted, but you can't give up. You have to fight back! And I came prepared today." He shrugged a rucksack from his back and dug through it, removing tools, scraps of metal, and glass tubing.

My eyes widened. "Won't King Auren notice the additional components?"

He glanced up, a lock of hair falling across his forehead. "The king won't notice anything but the gold."

"If you say so." I plopped back onto my stool. "I do appreciate this, Rone. More than I can express."

"Anything for more time with you." With a wink, he dove back into his bag.

Rone's new machine made a strange grinding sound but transformed handfuls of straw at a time. If only our progress brought more comfort. But with Father leaving and King Auren threatening to make me his bride . . .

I brushed a stray tear from my cheek.

Rone pursed his lips. "Did I tell you about the heating element that singed my eyebrows?"

"No, I think I would've remembered that one."

He regaled me with stories of failed inventions, Green Raider skirmishes, and adventures living in the forest. My heart lifted and pinched at the same time.

If only this night didn't have to end.

"What do you think King Auren will do with all this gold?" Rone gathered more straw into his arms.

I rubbed my aching forehead. "I suppose I'll find out soon enough."

"He may not let you within miles of the stuff once he's claimed it."

"I—" I bit my lip. He'd find out anyway when I became queen.

When I was on the receiving end of a Green Raider attack.

Pressing my eyes closed, I angled my head away. "The king plans to marry me if I succeed tonight."

"Marry you?" Rone's machine stuttered, leaving the room in eerie silence. "I suppose I can hardly blame him, but . . . congratulations."

"We did it!" I went to hug Rone but paused. His manner had assumed an air of cold formality ever since I'd revealed the king's unwelcome declaration.

"How can I possibly repay you?"

He cupped the back of his neck. "As I've said, I want nothing aside from your secrecy. It was my pleasure to spend this time with you."

My heart performed a little pirouette. "But there must be something. Once I'm queen, I can grant you any wish, no matter how grand."

"You can't go through with it." His lips curled into a sneer. "You'd marry the man who enslaved you to impossible undertakings under threat of death? Who—?" A vein throbbed in his throat.

"I don't want to marry him!" Indignation clawed my stomach. "But I doubt he'll give me a choice."

"There's always a choice." His eyes burned with a desperate plea. "Well, my future queen, I do have a request. I require . . . your first-born son."

"My what?"

He backed toward the window. "You said you'd grant any wish."

"But I never meant . . ."

"Your first-born son, should you follow through with this marriage. Don't forget I know the layout of this palace better than anyone and have the entire Green Raider force on my side."

Fear and anger coursed through me in nauseating waves. "You wouldn't."

He placed a hand on the windowsill. "I'd best depart before your *fiancé* catches me."

"Rone, please!" Suppressed sobs clung to my throat. "How can I change your mind?"

Rain dampened his sleeve as he raised the window. "Find out who I am." His sad, determined gaze collided with mine. "Goodbye, Abigail."

With that, he disappeared into the gray tones of early dawn.

I leaned out the window, watching him leap from the trellis and dash across the palace yard into the forest cover.

A feeble hope lit my chest. In all this mud, even Rone couldn't help but leave a trail I could follow.

•••♥•••

I willed the cloud obscuring the half-moon to move faster. *There*! I crept along the forest floor to the next footprint, my eyes roving the ground for another.

King Auren had paraded me about all afternoon, insisting I join him for tea, a garden stroll, and dinner with his simpering friends.

Bile soured my throat at the memory.

Guards had been posted outside my chamber after I'd asked to retire early. Fortunately, I could just reach the trellis below my window, and this room was only two stories from the ground instead of the six Rone had scaled.

Rone. I somehow already missed his company. Perhaps if I could find him . . . *No*. The gentleman I'd thought he was would've never demanded something so malicious.

Even so . . .

I glanced back toward the dark, eerie palace. Maybe I'd disappear into the forest and never return. Father was safe—I'd watched his ship depart from the harbor that morning—and even scraping by for survival was preferable to my impending marriage.

My corset and boots pinched as I edged forward. The clothes of my former life had disappeared as quickly as my freedom, replaced by trunks filled with bustled gowns and ruffled blouses.

A pinprick of light materialized ahead. I rubbed my eyes. The beacon remained steady, widening as I approached. It took every ounce of self-control not to break into a run.

The light emanated from the window of a small cottage with a steep, thatched roof. An *open* window.

I crouched, cursing every rustling leaf beneath my feet. Strange humming noises invaded the quiet night, punctuated by a man's muttering. Not daring to breathe, I peered through the window.

Rone sat within, draped across a rickety chair.

"Abigail despises me now." He buried his head in his hands. "Hieronymus, what have you done?"

Hieronymus. The pieces fell into place with jarring clarity—his animosity toward the king, knowledge of the palace's secret passageways, and exceptional understanding of mechanics.

"Prince Hieronymus." I clamped a hand over my mouth a moment too late.

He jerked upright, drawing closer as he scanned the dark night. My knees buckled when his bewildered gaze connected with mine. "Abigail. You found me."

Part of me screamed to run, but my feet remained rooted in place. "I'm sorry. I—"

"You have nothing to apologize for." His face crumpled. "Please, come in."

He stepped to the door and held it open. Inside, contraptions buzzed around us. Many were intricate clocks, but one produced an artificial fire, and another looked like it could chop vegetables.

He pulled out a chair and motioned for me to sit. "I'm afraid I have little to offer by way of hospitality." He ran a hand through his hair.

"I don't mind." I adjusted my skirt and sat, avoiding his gaze. "After last night, I had to find you. And now that I've discovered your name—"

"I never would've taken your child." He collapsed into his own chair. "It was a cold, heartless threat, and I'm so sorry."

My anger deflated in a relieved sigh. "Why would you say such a thing?"

"For so long, I've been disgusted by the way my father casts aside the needs of all but the wealthiest in our kingdom. My ideas for change met with nothing but resistance. When I wouldn't obey his every decree, he sent me away from the palace and faked my death."

"How awful."

"We're dealing with an awful man." Rising, he paced across the small room. "I'm not just one of the Green Raiders. I'm their leader. We hope that as heir to the throne, the people might one day accept me as their king. If I were replaced by a new heir raised in my father's image . . ." He shuddered. "But even that couldn't justify stealing a child."

I clutched the edge of the makeshift table to still my fidgeting hands.

"I was desperate to prevent you from marrying my father. I hoped the threat of losing your son might scare you away from the engagement." He stopped before me and dropped to his knees. "I'm sure you consider me a monster now, but please, Abigail. Don't marry that man."

"I have no desire to marry the king, but your father doesn't seem likely to release me."

"I'm afraid not." Rone—Prince Hieronymus—sat back on his heels, his expression a comical mix of terror and hope. "What if you didn't return to the palace?" With a graceful hop to his feet, he was pacing again. "What if you stayed with us instead? Being a Green Raider isn't easy, with few supplies and small, isolated lodgings spread throughout the forest. But you could stay with Emelie, at least for now, and we'd greatly appreciate your knack with machinery." He bent and captured my fingers. "Perhaps you and I might even . . . That is, I've so enjoyed my time with you, and you could still be queen one day if—" His cheeks reddened.

A fresh start. The opportunity to take a stand against King Auren's tyranny alongside the man I was growing to love, almost from the moment he'd startled me off my stool.

"I'd be honored to join the Green Raiders." The joy lighting his face set my insides quivering. "But we really must cover our footprints if we don't want your father's men to follow us here."

He chuckled. "Clever girl. We'll take care of it on our way to see Emelie." His gaze landed on my lips. "But I think it can wait a moment."

I tilted my head. "For what?"

"Oh, I—" He coughed and stepped away.

I followed. "I enjoyed my time with you too, Rone. Very much."

His grin warmed the room more than the artificial fireplace. "You don't know how happy I am to hear that." Circling his arms around me, he covered my laugh with a kiss.

SNAKE GIRL

Julia Skinner

ONCE, IN A forgotten room in a castle, there was a girl who spoke to snakes," Medusa whispered the old bedtime story her mother had once told her. She sat in the corner of the ballroom, near the servants' entrance, watching as couples gracefully twirled across the pale tile, in step with the thrumming orchestra. "The girl had been born a beloved princess, but by some terrible spell, her name had been erased—stolen away from every memory and heart."

To her left servants bustled around the long refreshment table, fetching food and drinks for various guests. Medusa shifted in her chair, keeping a firm hold on the tiny snake in her fist. Her hands were hidden by the traditional viridian shawl she always had to wear during events like this one. She held the snake's head gently between her thumb and forefinger, the rest of its thin body curled around her wrist. *Lapis Dente*, her mother had called it in her studies, *Fang of Ston*e. Even though it was small enough to fit in the palm of a hand, its venom could paralyze and kill a grown man within seconds.

"The snakes, however . . ." she murmured to no one as she idly scanned the ballroom. "They saw what others could not. They made her abandoned room a home and promised she'd never be alone. All they required was one *little* thing."

Medusa paused as the crier at the front of the room announced the arrival of the king. Her skin crawled like a hundred tiny snakes, twisting and burning. And then *he* appeared, dressed in his finest green suit. Green in memory of her mother. Green because today was the queen's birthday, and even though she'd been *gone* for eleven years, he refused to let anyone forget her. Flanked by his five personal guards, the king stode down the center of the room toward his looming throne.

After today, that throne would be *hers*.

"The snakes," she hissed to herself, "required her to become one of *them*. To trade her soul, to take their skin, to be as they are."

The king settled onto his throne, then immediately scanned the room, no doubt searching for his *monster of a daughter*. Medusa refused to flinch as his horrible, accusing eyes latched onto hers. With it came the nauseating guilt. The type that coiled around her stomach, squeezing and *squeezing* until she felt like clawing herself apart just to make it stop.

Liar. The familiar words were tiny reflections in his dark eyes. It was your fault. You are a murderer, murderer, murderer.

A shudder ran through her body, and she forced herself to look down at her veiled hands. *Soon*, she promised, *soon I will be free of this pain*.

She just had to become what he thought she was—a monster.

When she was little, her father used to be her hero. He'd take her on walks while her mother was busy working in her personal laboratory. And every night he'd sit down on the chair next to her bed, plant his elbows on his knees, and patiently answer her endless questions.

A sharp, bitter fang pierced her heart. That all ended the day her mother died, the day Medusa lied.

She squeezed her eyes closed, continuing the story. "'But I am human,' the girl said to the snakes. 'I cannot change.'"

"'All you must do,' replied the snakes, 'is say who you wish to become, and so you will be.'"

She glanced up at the ballroom's balcony. The oval tables neatly lining the space there were packed with aristocrats. Their whispers rustled in her ears, itching and incessant. *Probably gossiping about me*. They didn't know what she had done, but she was sure they could feel her father's paranoia toward her. And over the years, they had slowly grown to mirror it.

That was why she never spoke to anyone. That was why, year after year, she spent every party and event hiding away in her living quarters or on the sidelines.

But that was *fine.* Medusa tilted her chin up. She didn't need to dance. She didn't need to talk. She didn't need anyone to pay attention to her. Not yet, at least.

"The girl," Medusa hissed, "crouched down beside the snakes who had become her only friends, and she looked them in their beady, cold eyes." The cool, smooth scales of the snake she held in her fist sent a strange sense of strength through her, as if with it she could conquer the world. "*'I,'* the princess proclaimed, all alone in that forgotten room, *'am a snake.'* And from that very moment, a snake she became."

Medusa fell silent. The story was a dark blanket that softened the jagged shards of guilt tearing her up from the inside out.

"*The point*," her mother had said in her stern, clipped voice as she tucked Medusa in to sleep all those long nights ago, *"is that you become what you tell yourself you are."*

I am stone, Medusa thought.

An inconspicuous door—the servant's entrance—a few feet down, cracked open. Her new personal guard slipped in, looking slightly panicked. The moment he spotted her, relief washed over his young features. His polished boots clicked on the pale tile as he hurried over.

"Your Highness, I've been looking for you everywhere!"

She nodded, idly rubbing her thumb against the scales of the snake in her hand under the shawl.

The guard glanced toward the balcony. "Why are you all the way over here?"

It's as far away as I can get from everyone, she thought. *Off to the side. Not as brightly lit as the rest of the room. No one pays attention to this part of the ballroom.* "Waiting for you."

"You were supposed to do that in your room." His tone bordered on stern. "The King *specifically* assigned me to escort you wherever you need to go."

That was because her father didn't trust her. He thought that if he stationed a personal guard to constantly follow her around, she wouldn't be able to get into any trouble. She forced away the smirk that wanted to sneak onto her face. Despite all her father's efforts, she still managed to slip away from her guards.

"Are you going to go dance?" the guard asked.

"No."

He shifted his feet. "Will you at least allow us to move your chair closer to the King?"

"No." Medusa risked a glance at her father. He was no longer watching, but that didn't stop her from feeling sick at the sight of him. As long as he was around, she would never be free of the guilt that plagued her. And the longer he was here, the more it *spread* to others in the kingdom.

She pointedly shifted her attention to the food table. The white, embroidered tablecloth stretched all the way to the floor. "Did you see that?" she asked, scrunching her brow as if she were studying something.

"What?" He followed her gaze.

"Something moved under there!" Before he could answer, Medusa jumped to her feet, darting over. Servants skittered out of her way, confused. Her green dress brushed against the ground as she crouched to peek under the table, positioning herself in such a way that anyone watching couldn't see her slip one hand from beneath her gray shawl.

Beneath sat a small wooden chest, where she had hidden it earlier when the servants were setting everything up. A soft, almost imperceivable *hissing* came from inside it. *Hello, my beauties.* She quickly flipped the lid of the chest open, and tipped it onto its side. Lapis Dente snakes slithered out, shooting away from the table at an impressive speed.

She allowed herself the smallest of grins, then shoved herself backward with a panicked scream. The orchestra stuttered to an abrupt stop. The guests on the balcony turned, straining to catch sight of what had happened. Nearby dancers scattered as the tiny, gray streaks shot across the floor.

"Princess! What—" Her guard's mouth dropped.

"They just started pouring out everywhere!" Medusa said, pitching her voice higher.

He grabbed her arm, pulling her farther away from the poisonous snakes. The servants rushed over, trying to help the guests. Some of them would probably be bitten. But that was a price she had to pay. Her guard rushed her toward the throne, where her father sat, worriedly watching the ensuing chaos. His guards had formed a line in front of him, standing like a wall, their swords drawn.

"Stay here," her guard ordered, then spun to help.

She glanced toward her father, and a faint tremble ran through her. She was finally going to kill him. And there would be no one left who knew what she'd done. She'd be *free.*

Suddenly, she was an eight-year-old child again, standing over a glass terrarium in her mother's laboratory. She'd opened the top to try to get a better look at whatever snake was inside, but hadn't been able to see it amongst the dull gravel and sticks scattering the bottom.

"Medusa Gorgia Kaitel!" her mother yelled the moment she caught sight of her. "What are you doing? You're not allowed in here!"

Medusa rolled her eyes at her mother, then looked back down at the terrarium. What was in there? Most of the other terrariums lined in neat rows were filled with greenery or water, and contained bright green, or yellow, or red snakes.

"Medusa," her mother snapped, stalking over. "Get out before you mess something up!"

"I won't mess anything up." Medusa said. "I—"

"What is that?" her mother gaped at the ground. Medusa glanced down. Jagged glass was scattered beside the stool she was standing on, along with tiny black pebbles only slightly bigger than grains of sand.

"A cup." Medusa said. She'd accidentally knocked it over when climbing up to look at the cage.

"That—that had my Chine seeds in it!" Her mother's face flushed red. "They're my only way of growing that plant!" She dragged a manicured hand through her hair. "This is why you are not allowed in here; you always mess something up."

The words repeated themselves over and over in her head. They made her feel squirmy, and horrible—like she was stuck in a glass cage. She scowled. "I didn't mess up anything!"

"Oh really?" her mother grabbed her arm, pulling her down from the stool. "So you didn't knock the cup over?"

Yes, she thought. "No."

Her mother glared down at her. "Why haven't you learned yet that you can't lie to me."

Movement at the top of the terrarium caught Medusa's attention. A small, gray snake slithered out the top, body moving gracefully over the glass. It flicked an equally gray tongue out at her, then toward her mother, who stood right next to the cage.

I hope it bites her. Medusa thought, hot anger coiling in her gut. I hope—

As if it somehow heard her, the little snake flicked its head back, then lunged forward, striking her mother's arm. Her mother jerked, releasing her. Horrified, Medusa watched her mother stumble to her knees. Gray tendrils crept from the bite, up her arm, then her neck, across her face. Her eyes started to look like stone. But she didn't move. She knelt there, frozen, dying.

Someone shouted something behind her, and before she knew what was happening, her father was there.

"What happened?" her father yelled.

If she told him, he'd know she'd opened the lid. That she'd caused this.

"I . . . don't know," she whispered. "I found her like this." The lie wrapped itself around her neck like a chain.

"Medusa," he grabbed her shoulders, looked her in the eye. "Please, this is not the time for your games. Please tell me the truth. What did this?"

I did.

"I don't know!" Tears burned in Medusa's eyes, but they didn't fall.

Something changed in her father's eyes at that moment. They darkened, and a single, silent accusation filled their depths. Her father turned away, falling to his knees beside her mother. Medusa stood there, still as stone, as he ordered his men to bring all of the antidotes they had. Listened as he begged his wife not to die, to just hold on.

And she said nothing.

Medusa blinked away the memory, squeezing the snake hidden in her fist a little too tightly. She stiffened as her father turned toward her, eyes narrowed. *So untrusting.* It was as if he could see straight into her charred soul, as if he could see the holes and the poison churning deep inside.

"Medusa," he said, voice hard, "what did you *do?*"

It's your fault she died.

Your fault, your fault, your fault.

For a moment, Medusa felt her heart tremble, and a small part of her wanted to run from the room and go back on all her plans. But if she was ever going to be free of the guilt that tormented her, he *had* to die too. Then there would be no one left to remind her of her past.

I am stone, she told herself fiercely, clinging to the anger deep inside.

Stone didn't bleed with loneliness. It didn't bother to hear the whispers of all the things people said about her. It didn't care that she was responsible for her mother's death—or her father's for that matter.

"Nothing," she said, summoning a fake smile.

His jaw clenched, and he leaned closer. "We both know this has your trickery written all over it. I just didn't think you'd do it here, *today*."

"You never believe me." Medusa sniffed, looking away.

Her father fell silent. When she snuck a glance at him, she saw that he'd squeezed his eyes closed. Probably trying to not lose his temper. She took a deep breath, stilling her trembling hands. At her mother's funeral, standing alone by the casket, Medusa had turned her smile into fangs.

Her skin into impenetrable scales.

Her heart into a cold rock.

And today, she thought, *I will turn myself into a Queen.*

Slowly, Medusa removed her fisted hand from the shawl. Brushing it against the arm of the throne, she released the snake in one smooth motion.

This time she knew exactly what it would do.

The tiny, stone-gray snake flicked its tongue out, testing the air for prey. It inched closer to her father.

He took a deep breath, and opened his eyes. "Look, Medusa, I ignored your little pranks when you were younger, but this has gone too far. I cannot allow you to continue—"

The snake flicked its head back, then lunged forward. He jerked with a gasp as it struck the flesh of his arm. "Medusa, how—" his voice cut out as gray tendrils surfaced from the bite, spreading up his arm, rendering him paralyzed. Medusa crouched down to meet his eyes and saw the same shocked betrayal that had been there the day she'd lied.

"You should have believed me," she hissed.

Gray crept up his neck and face. The white of his eyes began to shift to stone. Standing, Medusa stumbled back a few steps. "Guards! Something—something's wrong with my father!" She twisted her expression into one of horror as the guards turned from watching the chaos across the ballroom. The subtle strands of gray were fanning out across her father's skin, becoming more apparent to the distant eye with every heartbeat. She covered her mouth with her hand, stepping farther away as the guards rushed forward, calling for someone to get the healer.

No one will ever suspect a thing.

Something dark and cold coiled in the pit of her stomach. Not guilt, not horror, not even relief. Just . . . stone. Hard, unfeeling stone hollowing her from the inside out. "Once," she muttered under her breath, "in a forgotten room in a castle, there was a girl who spoke to snakes . . . ."

THE CHILDREN
LOVED HIM.
THEY
ALWAYS
DID.

THE LEGEND OF VAN SKELM

Maseeha Seedat

SLIM SCANNED THE market square from the shadows for any bad signs. The vendors were already awake, unfortunately, raising their shutters and rolling out wagons piled high with colorful trinkets and souvenirs. They grumbled as they worked, fussing over the autumn harvest and the rainy seasons ahead.

Nothing out of the ordinary.

Slim turned his sharp gaze to the flat top of Table Mountain. It smothered the valleys of Cape Town in shade, a halo of mist revealing its bald head. He watched the smoke rise from the Dutch settlers' village beneath it, inhaling the sweet fragrance that drifted into the market. His stomach growled, almost as loud as the children as they raced through the market stalls, screaming at the top of their lungs about this bracelet and that toy. Easy for them when they didn't have to worry about their next meal or a place for the night. A pang of jealousy bubbled within him, and he shoved it down immediately.

The children are good, he reminded himself. They were the key to success. He turned his head west to the ocean, the roar of its waves somehow audible over the bustle of the market. Slim could hear the fishermen hollering across the water as they set sail for the day.

His gaze shifted to the clouds overhead. He still had time. He'd have to be fast, but he could still make it.

The sun peeked over the mountaintop, setting the rock aflame, painting the clouds red and gold. Daylight trickled down the mountain, the warmth welcoming the first wave of customers. Slim swallowed hard, pulling his hood over his head. It was busier than usual. That meant the vendors would be even angrier at him.

"Relax," he whispered. The kids loved him. They always did.

Slim kicked a wooden crate out from beneath an abandoned stall and into the center of the market square, dragging an enormous patchwork sack behind him. He positioned it right under the giant ash tree, sweeping the leaves of auburn and carbine off his dirt stage. He leaped on top of the box and faced the mountain before he cupped his hands over his mouth. It was showtime.

"Ho there!" A few heads turned. The merchants groaned, glaring at him. But they didn't kick him out. Maybe they actually enjoyed his performance. "Step right up, ladies and gentlemen. Come join me on this glorious day and let me tell you something magnificent, something that will change your life forever."

Some tourists started to gather around him.

"Heed my words. I know a secret that's been lost for generations, and now I have the honor to share it with you few lucky people."

The children squirmed to the front of the growing crowd. Slim grinned.

"And why should we listen to you?" spat one of the spectators.

Slim snapped his neck around. The voice belonged to a short, tubby gentleman with a big head and an even bigger top hat balanced on his curly blonde hair—bright blue with a black feather tucked into a black ribbon. Slim scowled but quickly smiled, swallowing his annoyance.

"I beg your pardon, sir. Is there a problem?"

"Yes. You. Why should we listen to someone like you?"

Slim lowered his head, staring at his hands. They weren't like the spectators' hands. Theirs were smooth and soft and clean. His were callused and cracked, his nails bitten down to the nub. Most importantly, his weren't the same color as theirs.

Come on. This wasn't the first time someone had pointed that out. *Get back up.*

He smirked, winking at the gentleman. "Because this story has always lived in my family, passed down from one generation to the next. My parents are dead, sir, and I got no siblings. I'm the only one left to tell it."

Top Hat grunted in dismissal, turning his back on Slim. *Why did he have to do that?* Now Slim had to get his crowd back. Great.

"Ladies, gentlemen, children." He bowed toward them. "My name is Slim, and I'm the last descendant of Van Skelm."

"Who'th that?" chirped one of the children, lisping violently.

Slim quickly hid his groan. Questions! Children *always* had questions. But children were important. He needed them to believe him.

He faked a laugh as if he hadn't been asked that question a million times before.

"Who's Van Skelm? *Who* is Van Skelm? Van Skelm is only the greatest person to ever live. You wanna know why?"

The children nodded eagerly. *Finally*, he had their full attention.

Slim sat on the crate, reaching into the sack behind him, pulling out a bottle of paraffin and a box of matches. He took a quick swig from the bottle and blew onto a lit match, spraying fire into the sky. The children gasped in awe as the adults backed off in fear. Slim did it once more, then wiped his lips on his sleeve.

"Close your eyes," he instructed. Only the children obeyed. "Now picture this. Long ago, long before your grandparents arrived on these shores, Van Skelm roamed the earth. He walked where you walked. He breathed the same air as you. He set fire to the sea as he robbed every ship he met, a pirate who never stopped searching for treasure."

Slim reared his head, imitating the cry of a seagull as he grabbed another bottle from his bag, splattering the crowd in seawater. As usual, some people didn't appreciate his showmanship and left, dabbing their faces with lace-embroidered hankies.

Oh well.

"One day, Van Skelm decided to retire." Slim pointed over his shoulder in the vague direction of the harbor. "He anchored his ship way over there and built a nice little house right under this tree. For a century, he was satisfied. He spent a third of it digging into the base of the mountain." A dull *thunk* rang through the market. "A third of it filling his cave with gold." *Thunk*. "And a third of it refilling his hole."

Thunk. The children shuddered as Slim slammed a metal cup against the crate, echoing the age-old scrapes of Van Skelm's shovel.

"But after he had finished the job, Van Skelm got bored. Horribly bored. He tried everything he could to escape it. He outlived his wife. His children all grew up and moved out. Every job he got was meaningless. Nothing would satisfy his craving to be free again, to fall asleep in one place and wake up somewhere completely different, to feel the ocean's breath on his face. But Van Skelm had sold his boat the minute he landed. So, as you do, he went down to the docks looking for a ship to work on. But no one wanted him on their crew."

"Why?" asked Top Hat. Slim furrowed his brow. Didn't he know it was rude to interrupt someone else's story?

"Because of this." Slim rolled up his sleeve, revealing every inch of his umber forearm. He glared at Top Hat and set his lips in a firm line, refusing to be silent. This scared off even more spectators, but Slim didn't care. He was from the Xhosa tribe, and he was proud of that.

But he wasn't stupid. There was no way he would say it out loud. They would kill him. He pulled his sleeve back down.

"No one wanted someone with a reputation as bad as Van Skelm. They all turned him away. He tried to buy a new ship, but no one believed that his treasures and riches actually belonged to him. Van Skelm was trapped."

Slim paused, dragging out the silence. He scanned the crowd again; they were still hooked. Even Top Hat looked mildly interested.

"Eventually, Van Skelm came up with a plan—a beautiful, twisted, genius plan to get a ship and sail it to the ends of the world and back. The first step was simple."

Slim leaned toward the girl with the lisp. Her brother pulled her back warily. Slim looked up at him, flashing his innocent brown eyes. He winked and reached behind the girl's ear, pulling out a small copper coin. His hand curled into a fist, and when he opened it, the coin was gone, encouraging cheers and applause from the children.

From his sack, Slim revealed a pile of kindling and two thick slabs of wood, and started a fire a few feet in front of his crate.

"Van Skelm vanished. No one, *no one*, went looking for him. The villagers didn't care. In their opinion, it was good riddance." Slim laughed to himself. "They were such fools."

Thick plumes of smoke rose from Slim's fire, the wind carrying the scentless fumes toward Table Mountain.

"A few weeks after Van Skelm's disappearance, one of the sailors noticed a white plume of smoke creeping over the mountain. By noon, it was gone. But it returned the second day, the third, and the fourth, each time larger than before. The fifth time, the smoke lasted a week, smothering the mountain like a tablecloth."

He looked up at the sky, watching the clouds waft through the air. It was time.

"Then came the second step." Slim held a metal sheet and stood. He waved it over his head, bending it back and forth, echoing a howling gust of wind through the market square. Slim lowered his head and deepened his voice—*one last step.*

"The mountain's roar filled the village, creeping in through the cracked walls, consuming the villagers' minds as they trembled, eyes wide in terror." Slim leaped off the crate, weaving his way through the crowds. "They never left their homes. They never slept. Soon, they ran out of food. At the end of the day, there was only one choice left."

Slim pulled a whistle out of his pocket and blew it, loud and shrill, scaring the market into silence.

"The settlers fled, leaving everything they owned, everything they loved. The village descended into ruin. No one dared to enter Camps Bay, fearing the pirate's spirit haunted it. The ghost town was left to rot."

"But what happened to Van Thkelm?" asked Lisp, big blue eyes staring up at him expectantly.

Why'd she have to destroy the tension?

"Don't worry. I'm getting there." Slim took a deep breath and kneeled in front of the children. "Van Skelm reappeared weeks later, happier than he had been for centuries. His plan had worked beautifully. You wanna know how?"

Lisp nodded. Slim tiptoed his fingers up her shoulder, pausing on her head of brown hair. "Van Skelm had climbed up Table Mountain." He blew into her face, growling in his throat. "And there he built an enormous fire that smoked over the whole summit while he bellowed into a speaking trumpet bigger than your head." She giggled. His fingers tiptoed down the other shoulder. "Then he came down as the sole survivor of a haunted village. He hauled all his treasure onto the biggest ship he could find and sailed into the sunset."

Slim looked at the other children, drawing them closer. "But that's not the end of our story, oh no. You see, Van Skelm is still mad about the way the villagers treated him. So every year, when the first leaves of autumn fall, he comes back to scare off little boys and girls like you."

Slim rose to his feet, arching his back, gazing at the mountain deep in thought. The children waited for him to do something, slowly losing interest as the seconds passed. Then, Slim's eyes widened. His hands started to tremble. He screamed, raw and hollow, his voice cracking as his fear infected the crowd. He raised a trembling arm, pointing at the mountain. The crowd turned to face it. The rolling clouds smothered the top, dripping over the edge, tumbling to the surface. The mountain's voice followed, the howling wind whipping through Slim's jacket, pricking the hairs on his arms.

He smiled to himself. It was showtime.

"It's Van Skelm!" he yelled, yanking the children to their feet. "Quick, get out of here." He pushed them away. "Run! All of you. Before he comes down to take us all."

The children, gullible as always, ran off in a panicked craze, skidding between the market stalls as their parents chased after them. Slim grinned. Everything had gone to plan.

His joy was short-lived. The market vendors marched through the terrified crowd with one target in mind: Slim. Turned out, scaring away customers wasn't the best for business. And if they couldn't get their money, Slim knew they'd at least beat out some of their stress.

Time to go.

Slim grabbed a log from his smoldering fire, lobbing it at the vendors. They ducked out of the way as it collided with a nearby stall, setting the fabric canopy aflame. Slim quickly pocketed any coins the tourists had dropped.

He hauled the sack over his shoulder and bolted back the way he had come. The men dashed after him, yelling insults at the top of their lungs. It was a good thing Slim didn't understand Afrikaans. He grabbed a loaf of bread from the baker's stand, barely escaping a rolling pin flying at his head, and flew past the last stall of the market, disappearing into the bushes and out of sight.

He held his breath, the pounding feet almost as loud as his heartbeat. The villagers soon gave up, returning to their mundane lives. Typical. Slim emerged from his hiding place and whistled as he walked, welcoming the shade on his back, the fresh roll still soft in his mouth. It had been a good day.

Two hands suddenly appeared on his shoulders. Slim whirled around, flicking a knife out of his pocket. His eyes landed on his attacker. It was Top Hat. This close up, Slim noticed the frayed edges of the hat. Top Hat's suit was even a little big for him and stitched pretty poorly as if it were some busted-up hand-me-down. He grinned at Slim's defensive stance.

"Stop being so scared," he laughed, slapping Slim on the back.

Slim tucked the knife away. "Only if you stop being such a pain."

"What did I do?"

Slim glared at him, mimicking his squeaky voice. "*Why should we listen to you? You don't belong here!*" He shoved Top Hat. "You almost cost me today's show."

"So? I was just selling myself as the skeptic."

"No. You were just making my life a thousand times harder. You try going up there in front of everyone. You're white! They'll listen to you."

Top Hat faltered back, staring at the ground. "Only my old man is," he mumbled, his voice trembling.

Slim extinguished his rage, patting him fondly on the shoulder. "Eish, Top, I'm sorry. You know I didn't mean that. We good?"

"Yeah, we good," Top Hat muttered.

"Come on, show me what you got. You know you want to."

Top Hat grinned, a chilling shimmer in his eyes. He yanked the hat off his head, pulling the wide brim outward, opening a hidden compartment inside. Slim peered into it, holding his breath in anticipation.

The hat was chock-full with treasure. Copper coins, silver coins, even a few rare gold ones. Some exquisite pocket watches that would fetch a beautiful price in Nyanga. A woman's emerald earrings, an engraved belt bucket, a gold heart-shaped locket, and a silver tooth.

"It's beautiful," Slim whispered. He looked Top Hat in the eye. "Seems like we gave you the right nickname after all."

Top Hat nudged him playfully. "Couldn't have done it without your storytelling."

"Van Skelm always scores big this time of year. Be grateful that the seasons work like clockwork. Who knows how long it will last."

Arms over each other's shoulders, Slim and Top Hat started the long walk back to their little cave in the mountain. As they reached the outskirts of the settlers' village, a little kid ran up to them. Top Hat tightened his grip on his hat.

Slim narrowed his eyes. Big blue eyes, brown hair. It was Lisp.

"Thlim?" she asked.

"Yeah?"

"I need your help. When I ran away from your show, I lotht my necklath. You didn't thee it, did you?"

Slim shuffled nervously on his feet. "What did it look like?" Top Hat prodded him hard in the ribs.

"It wath a gold heart with a painting of my grandma in it."

"Sorry, kid," Top Hat said. "We didn't find nothing."

"Oh."

Lisp trudged back down the path, her head hanging low. Slim turned to Tophat, nodding in Lisp's direction.

"What?" Top Hat hissed.

Slim narrowed his glare. "You know what. Give me the thing."

"No."

"Why not?"

"Because. I stole it fair and square."

"Yeah?" Slim crossed his arms. "What you gonna do with it?"

"I . . . I'mma wear it around my neck." Top Hat lifted it over his throat to make his point.

Slim slapped him over the head. "Give it back or so help me—"

"Fine!" Top Hat pouted.

"Thank you." Slim turned to the girl. "Hey, kid!"

Lisp raced back to them. Slim nudged Top Hat.

"Here," he muttered, revealing the necklace. "Is this it?"

The girl's face lit up. She clutched the pendant in her fist, flipping open the locket. Inside was a little portrait of her and an old lady smiling.

"Thank you!" she squealed, hugging Top Hat. He stared down at her, then at Slim, his arms pinned to his side and his face turning red as Slim tried to hide his laughter.

Lisp ran back home, skipping with the locket swinging around her neck.

"Why do we always have to be the good guys?" Top Hat whined.

"Because, did you see the look on her face? Did you hear the way she spoke to us?"

"Yeah. I'm not sure you did. Did the baker actually hit you this time?"

"No, Top. She treated us like people, like actual people. Lisp doesn't know the first thing about color. Her parents still have to teach her. And who knows, maybe she'll realize it's wrong. Maybe she'll help change the future for you and me."

Slim grinned at the utopia in his head. Top Hat flicked him.

"Get your head out of the clouds, Van Skelm," he joked.

"Oy! Don't talk about my ancestor like that."

Top Hat held his hands up in defense. "Fine. Come on, we still got a long way to go."

They continued their walk, planning out which other markets they would perform in. It would be dark before they made it back home.

Retelling of The Legend of Van Hunks, a South African Myth

KNAVE OF LOVE

Anne J. Hill

You said we're meant for life
I knew this was terminal
I should have seen it coming
'Cause you've always been criminal

We had this crazy love, you'd say
The arguing is what made it real
You just wished you could hold me
'Cause you didn't know what to feel

It's twisted the way you'd look at me
Like you're a joker, and I'm your queen
Just a puppet to fall in love with you
And use 'til the end of the scene

You're a clown with a gun, ready for crime
You'd kill anyone who looks at your doll face
But Mister Perfect is free to walk the line
With no care that it destroys me at the base

I've given myself the name of baka
For being so loyal to a jester
But I'll wear my scars with pride
To remind myself I'm my own master

I'm so done with this game
You can put away your ace of knaves
I'm finally free to live as me
While you go and make other slaves

THE CIRCUS OF MACHINES

Effie Joe Stock

I SEARCHED FOR MY muse in the crowd, adjusting the goggles on my face. *Vivian,* that beautiful creature of light. I had spent so many years crafting a persona from her likes and dislikes. Maybe tonight the façade would finally be perfect enough to trick her into loving the creature I had become.

But first came my circus—the magic I, the Ringmaster, had made for her. To awe her. To draw her in.

I crouched, perched on the metal grid overhanging the stage, taking in the bustling crowds, the warm smell of peanuts and popped corn, the screeching of metal against metal, the sound of turning cogs, the hum of anticipation—it was thrilling. But though my show was minutes from beginning, nothing could tear me from searching for the woman more beautiful than any doll I'd ever fashioned.

Box five was empty. The box I always reserved for her. A stab of vexation stirred me; she must be speaking with another guest. Perhaps another man . . . I took several breaths to calm the storm within me. No matter if she was. My annoyance faded to confidence. After tonight, she would never have need to desire another.

I cocked my head, humming through the gold-beaked mask over my nose and mouth, and peered through my multi-lensed goggles. Small knobs on the side of the lenses allowed me to see the distance with clarity, but I couldn't find her in the crowd either. I would have to wait.

I swung down a level of the metal rungs and pattered across a plank, my boots making more noise than I would ever allow if we were performing. Up here, in the gridiron, I was a god. I crouched and studied her empty box, waiting for her to emerge. From this angle, I could better see box five. She had to be alone tonight, or else it would befoul my plans. I would've liked to accompany her this evening, as I often did, but I needed to appear in my circus sometimes.

She finally stepped into her box, adjusting her lovely, ruffled blue skirts—my favorites. She brushed aside the ringlets around her face, the rest having been swept into a braided knot at the base of her neck. The design reminded me of the machines that had made my life magical. Her eyes were blue like the moon shining through the thick haze that hung over our overbuilt, industrial city. I once thought that haze was a curse, a testimony to the horrors that machines had brought us, but now I knew differently. Science was but another form of magic, and machines were the creatures that brought it to life.

A smirk lifted my lips. *Sweet, clueless Vivian.* Did she know that only a half-hour before, I had been the young man with the braided hair, tall striped hat, and ridiculously bright clothes with a red mask who checked her ticket and directed her through the maze of spectators? It was almost impossible for me to restrain the cackle of vibrant laughter that bubbled up in my throat.

A gong boomed, and the crowd quieted. My heart pounded in anticipation, the same thrum that hummed like a purring engine through the room.

They were ready. I was ready.

Let the show begin.

The butterflies raged in my stomach as I jumped to my feet and climbed through the bars—like a creature of the night.

The second gong sounded as I swung down the last rung and slipped. Barely was I able to catch hold of a rung to halt my descent. And there I hung, dangling over the whole arena as if trapped, as if I had accidentally fallen, and not planned this as my introduction.

The crowd gasped, then fell silent. I tried not to smile, tried not to think of how these people were so easily fooled.

Machines, magic, and mystery.

I let go of the rung.

Screams echoed through the arena as my body twisted.

The whirring of machines filled the air.

In a shower of sparks, wings spread out beside me and caught a draft.

My foot brushed the sandy floor before I shot upwards in a spray of gold sparks and wind.

The crowd went wild.

My performers dove off their platforms, their silver wings spreading and carrying them into the tall vaulted arena—the grandest circus arena of the Metal World.

I made it myself.

I made it for *her*.

My eyes darted to her dazzling blue eyes. She was standing and clapping. Her lips were parted in a smile. No matter how the silver wings around me darted and danced, falling and then shooting to the beautiful tapestry of clouds and stars above, her eyes never left me. I felt them on me like the hot metal against my back.

Everything went according to plan. How could it not? It was *my* circus—a whirlwind of chaos and trickery. My long dark hair fell traitorously into my eyes as I weaved through the machines, pretending to assemble entire creatures with my nimble fingers and quick tool work. To the audience, I was a genius, though it was all a hoax. No one could create an elephant in a few minutes.

Of course, if it weren't for my role as Ringmaster, the crowds would never identify me. They recognized my talents, not my face. It was magic I brought them, not my voice or my clothes.

Every show was different. Every machine and face, new, even my own. Last time, I had short blonde hair; the time before, I had dark skin. Once, I even had four life-like arms.

From the biggest machine to the smallest card trick, everything I had created was for Vivian—my first unwitting audience. It had been her face which lit up in wonder at the shapeshifting machine I made to dance to a violin; my first creation had drawn her smile.

That was back before I truly understood the power of illusion, of how you could trick the spectators not only into believing in magic but also anything else you wanted . . . even love.

If only she knew . . .

The night flew by in a blur. The show drawing to an end—a shower of gold sparks landed on the sand with me, my wings creaking at my sides.

"Ladies and Gentlemen! It is time for my finale! One of you shall scale the skies with me and my wings. Who is brave enough to scale the ether? Daring enough to soar the heavens?" Hands flew up, everyone desperate to prove their dauntlessness, to be close to the illusive Ringmaster.

But I only had eyes for one.

Vivian raised her hand, and I smirked. I knew her audacious spirit wouldn't let her deny this opportunity. "You!" I pointed, and our eyes locked. "In box five, lady in the blue skirts."

Elation lit up her face as she stood still in shock before running down the steps and through the crowd, hundreds of strangers' hands reaching out to touch her–the girl special enough to be chosen.

I couldn't look away from her as she drew closer and closer. *So close.* I was only minutes away from seeing if I had become the man she wanted. We had met a thousand times before, but I had never been perfect. She wanted something real, something she could touch and rely on. She didn't understand I was the most real thing she could have in this world.

She was standing in front of me now, appearing almost fake against the illusion of the arena.

I bowed low, a chuckle escaping my lips, sounding mystical through the mask and voice changer. "I'm surprised a lady like yourself would dare to scale the heights of the sky."

Her face lit up in indignation, the fiery spirit I admired so much in her. Reminded me of an engine who loathed to stop its roaring movement.

She planted her hands on her steel bone corset around her waist. It was old with tattered edges, fringed with rusted buckles, and decorative cogs. "And why not?" she snapped.

Rusted cogs, her voice was more beautiful than any music box I had fashioned. Was there a way I could trap her voice into something forever? Perhaps I could put it in a doll. Would she like that?

"You are so delicate . . ." I lightly brushed my fingers through her hair, watching as she shivered against my touch. "So fragile. The wind might blow you away."

She shook herself and narrowed her eyes. "Not as much as you think."

I could hardly drag my eyes from her lips. Roughly, I pulled her to me, one hand on her waist, the other cupping the back of her neck.

Surprise lit up her face. She could change faces as well as me . . . almost.

"Then you must prove it, *mon cheri.*" I brushed the beak of my mask against her ear, hearing her gasp lightly before I twirled her around, sparks entwining around us and making us like gods to the audience. Another illusion, of course, but in that moment, even I thought I could believe it too.

Somewhere, the announcer declared this the grand resolution. I could nearly feel the raging envy hanging in the air. Every woman wanted to be *her,* in the arms of the illusive Machine Master who could be anyone or anything you could dream of.

The wings spread behind me, and with quick fingers, I pulled her back to my chest and strapped the protective leather around her, binding her body to mine; then weightless, we rose into the expanse above the sand.

It was enough excitement for the cheering audience to see a mere citizen fly with the Ringmaster, but tonight, for Vivian, I had so much more planned.

The panels of the ceiling slid back on massive tracks with a shuttering groan, exposing the open night to us.

The crowd gasped with Vivian when they realized what I was doing.

"What's going on?" She struggled against me, against the straps holding her in.

"I'm taking you for a flight." I was grateful her back was to me so she couldn't see the smirk that decorated my lips.

"But only in the arena!"

"Oh really? I don't remember specifying."

"Let me go!"

I pressed my mask to her ear, and she stilled. "Do you really want me to do that?"

Her wide gaze shifted to the sand far below her, and then to the open night sky above us.

"Trust me . . ." My gloved fingers slid across her chin, down her throat, and she shuddered with a light gasp and quick nod.

The wings pushed against the drafts, carrying us quickly out of the dome, away from the frenzied crowd who thought a girl was kidnapped and the announcers who convinced them otherwise.

Her heart raced against me. Her breath caught in her throat as she looked down at our city.

My heart, usually a well-trained machine, betrayed me by mimicking hers.

"Where do you want to go?" I spared a quick glance down to her wide eyes. It seemed she couldn't take enough of the view in.

We were gliding now, the straps from the machine tight around her body, holding her steady against me.

"To the beach."

I wanted to tell her I already knew she wanted to go there, that we were already on our way, but I only nodded solemnly as if it were a great surprise. "A lovely choice."

She tried to look back at me. Her blue eyes shone in the night, but the little ringlets around her face kept flying into her gaze. What I wouldn't give to brush them out of her way. But I couldn't. Not as the Ringmaster. Not yet.

Then we were flying over the lake, big enough that our city called it the ocean. After all, few ever left the great Metal City. Most of us would die before seeing the true sea, before seeing anything other than this lonely stretch of sand on water. Of course, they could see the ocean if they came to my performances, to my circus. I could make the ocean itself. I could make the waves spray on their faces, and they would be able to taste the salt and hear the gulls.

I could make all their dreams come true.

Just as I had with *her.*

Our feet touched the sand, and, in moments, I released her from the straps that held her to me.

She lingered a moment longer before slipping away. I could feel the wonder from her. It was the same emotion I always felt when others were in my presence.

Not respect. Not fear. Not familiarity.

Pure wonder.

And I never tired of it.

I saw the yearning she held in her eyes for the magic that lifted me from the ground as I danced from foot to foot.

"You have a great deal of audacity, Ringmaster." The harsh tone of her scolding was not lost on me as she brushed the hair from her face and trained her narrow gaze on me. "My father will have your head for kidnapping."

I tried not to chuckle, tried not to diminish her suppressed annoyance and the way her eyes flashed with spark. I spread my hands before me, as if offering my innocence. "Taking a willing passenger on a midnight flight is hardly a kidnapping. And I haven't refused to take you home."

She raised her chin in a challenge, crossing her arms. "Then do so at once."

I let my shoulders sag slightly, my feet dragging the ground, just enough to trigger some guilt. "*Mon ange*. Shall we really end this night on such a sour note? I have not harmed you, and I do not intend to do so. Do you not trust me?"

Her eyes narrowed, and she shifted her stance, turning slightly to face me as I hovered on the wings. "Most certainly I do not, but if I am to stay, I must be permitted answers."

I licked my lips, my heart racing in anticipation. Such spirit, she had. "Very well, what is it you desire to know?"

"How do you do it?"

I landed in front of her, my hand extended. She took it after a long moment of hesitation. "Magic, *mon cheri*."

She laughed and shook her head, some of her hair falling from the braided knot and spilling over her shoulders. "Please, *monsieur*. I know it's not magic." She was lowering her defenses, I realized with triumph.

I clutched my heart as if wounded. "You don't believe me? You don't believe that this—" I extended my hand and twirled it a few times, swirls of gold shooting up to the sky like campfire sparks, "—is magic?"

The gold reflected in her eyes, and I knew in that moment, despite what she said, that she believed, truly believed it was.

"It's all a trick," she whispered, but she couldn't tear her eyes from the sparks, from the heavy wonder in the air that begged her to believe differently.

"Isn't everything just a trick?"

Her eyes turned back on me, and she said the last thing I ever thought she would.

"Love isn't."

If I had been a machine, I'm sure her words would have been a wrench stuck in one of my gears. *Love isn't.*

"Oh, but it is. Everything is."

Did she know even this lake was metal?

Not the water, of course, but everything it rested on. The basin was a metal tub, like a sink in one's kitchen. Even under the sand, we stood on a metal sheet.

"Everything in this city is a trick, a lie, an illusion." I didn't realize I'd said it out loud until she crossed her arms, a strange look on her face.

"Does that make people only a trick?"

I didn't miss a beat and merely shrugged. "Of course. They're always lying, saying one thing and meaning another, making promises and breaking them. The only true reality is the one we make for ourselves. Nothing else is real."

For a long moment, neither of us said anything, simply staring at each other as if waiting to see who would break the silence first.

She was taller than me in her heels, I noticed. Did she like that? I knew of ways to make my legs longer if she didn't . . .

Finally, she turned from me, her gaze wandering over the strange lake that stretched on for miles, held in by never-ending metal.

"This is my favorite spot."

"I know."

She turned to me, darkness shrouding her face. Her voice didn't hold the wonder it had a few minutes before. Something like suspicion had replaced it. "How did you know?"

Because you've told me so many times. Because you've brought me here before. I bit my tongue and drawled confidently instead, "I just guessed."

She tilted her head as if she didn't quite believe me. "Some sort of magic again?"

"A magician never reveals his secrets."

"Even to those he loves?"

This time I didn't stop the laughter that bubbled up. Thankfully the voice changer made it sound humorous. "Especially to those he loves."

"Why?"

"Because love is magic, and magic is only beautiful with mystery."

"So that is why you and your shows are so beautiful." A strange little smile lifted her lips. "The mystery."

I hummed in agreement. "Of course. It would be no good if you knew all the tricks."

"Then how do you have any fun? Knowing all the tricks, I mean."

I shook my head and chuckled. What a silly question. "Because, *mon cheri*, I *am* the mystery. I am everything I want to be and anything I can dream of being."

Her little mouth furrowed in ponder. "Then why do you do it?"

My eyebrows rose with surprise before my lips curled in a pleased smirk. No one before her had ever cared to ask. "I want everyone who ever lost sight of beauty to find it again. I want to show people that once upon a time, before all the machines, the steam, the clocks and cogs and gears, before all the blue haze, there was a world of majesty and magic. That a world of color and smells and tastes, of creatures you couldn't even imagine had existed. That even if you lived a hundred years, you would never tire of your reality . . ." I gazed hesitantly at her, unsure of where these words were coming from. Perhaps they came from that boy who had started this dream all those countless years ago the moment he saw the awe in a young girl's eyes. "I do it because I want people to be awed."

Suddenly, she was standing close to me. Much too close. I could smell her perfume—strong, intoxicating. It was a new scent; why had she changed it?

"I want to be awed." Her breath was warm on my face, warm in contrast to the cold winter air, calling me back to reality, or perhaps back to my imagination.

"And you haven't been already?" I raised an eyebrow at her, wishing I were taller than her right now so I could look down into her eyes. My fingers fiddled with the small nobs at my hips, and I felt the whirring in my legs. In a second, I was looking down at her, suddenly inches taller.

The surprise on her face was delectable. Oh, to kiss her in that moment to see what this surprise and awe tasted like. But to do that, I would have to take my mask off.

Unthinkable.

"H-how, wh—" she stuttered over her words, completely unable to fathom what she had just seen.

"Magic, *mon amour*. I thought I told you?"

"Impossible . . ." she whispered breathlessly, but her eyes told me she believed. She was fooled, just like everyone else.

"Or perhaps you want a different kind of magic? Perhaps you want me to read your mind? I'm sure I could know you better than any devoted lover."

Her eyes widened, and she took a step back. "You can't."

"Oh, but I can, Vivian."

She took in a sharp breath at her name, taking a few steps back when I took a few forward.

Feet sinking in the sand, I stepped around her, circling her. The façade of the Ringmaster was gone. I was the creature of the night now, teetering on loving this creature of light and fighting her. She was so tempting, so close to making me bare my secrets before her, but she was also so sweet to fool, so willing to believe anything I served her, and I never wanted that to change. She was my little fool, and I was her trickster. And if she could accept who–what–I was, then she would learn I could be so much more.

Taking a deep breath, I closed my eyes and hummed a light, airy tune. In a moment of her distraction, I switched the knob on my neck, changing my voice from the soft, higher pitch to a low, hypnotic tone.

"You like lower voices in men."

She gasped at the change and whirled to face me. Realization dawned in her eyes, but denial quickly clouded them.

"You like them to be more muscular." I dug my nails into my palms, three times with my right-hand ring finger, four with the left. The metal in my limbs shifted and changed, bulking. The change was painful, but it never showed on my face. This was magic now, not science, and while magic was frightening, it could never appear painful.

Her lace gloved hands tightened around her little top hat decorated in gears and clocks—a hat I had made her behind the face of an infatuated hat maker.

"You wear the blue dress—" I nodded to her skirts under her brown corset "—to your favorite occasions and red to ones where there will be eligible young men." Her dark painted lips dropped open, but I didn't pause for a moment.

"You've changed your perfume. You used to wear Joice's Autumn, but I believe . . ." I drew close to her and gently breathed in her scent, just by her shoulder. She stiffened, though she didn't move away. "This is a more flowery mixture, perhaps because the winter makes you long for warmer, greener days?" I didn't wait for her to answer.

Now, I was standing in front of her, our eyes locked, though I knew she wouldn't be able to see them well through the goggles. I, however, could see every fleck of brown in her bright eyes. I knew every freckle on her face, every little scar from when she used to play with machines as a child, even though she tried to conceal the marks under makeup. Like how she tried to hide from her father that she decorated her walls with cuckoo clocks and her hats and corsets with gears and old miniatures of someone else's grandmother.

"How do you know? How do you know all this about me?" The shock on her face was more like horror.

"Magic," I whispered in her ear.

She moved before I could stop her, and in one swift movement, my illusion was shattered.

Suddenly, my features were bare to the world, to her, to anyone who wanted to see; my mask was held tightly between her fingers.

For a moment, I could do nothing but stare into her eyes with my own, without the goggles or mask between us.

Dismay and the weight of failure slowly leaked onto my face, but I knew she wouldn't be able to see the emotions hidden behind the metal.

Her eyes widened as her eyes roamed over my face.

"You—you're . . ."

I waited for the words "hideous," "disfigured," "mutated," "broken." But they never came.

Her hand reached out slowly, hesitantly as if she were afraid I would flee. But how could I? I felt nothing more than dread as I waited to see how this would end. Only numbness in knowing that my muse might turn from me and leave, just as everyone else had before I became the greatest Circus Master in the Metal City, before I had made a million new faces for myself, before I had become something, *someone*, people actually wanted.

Her skin met mine, and I leaned into her touch, feeling her fingers trace over the half of my face that was metal, the half that didn't have a scar running over the little flesh that remained.

"You're—"

"An illusion," I finished for her.

She didn't have anything to say. I could see a war raging in her mind. If her mind were cogs, they would be spinning out of control.

"This . . . this is how you do it?"

I stepped back from her. "Yes. This is how I make magic." I held out my hands, and sparks tumbled from my fingertips. Not magic, just sparks from the mechanics that made up my body, or at least the parts I had improved upon myself, the parts the doctor hadn't been able to save from the gas explosion in the factory I was raised in.

Tears collected in her eyes, but I couldn't make out the emotion that drove them. "But, how do you know?"

"How do I know all those things about you?"

She nodded slowly.

A lazy grin spread across my face. "Because I am anything I want to be. An illusion, a reality, a lover . . . or a hundred lovers."

She studied my eyes, the only things that never changed; their dark green always remained the same.

Realization finally dawned on her face.

"You—"

I didn't let her finish and instead pressed my lips against hers. They were so soft, so sweet, so delicious . . . . So this is what her surprise tasted like. I knew then, and I wondered if she did too, that in the space where her flesh touched my metal, where our lips moved against each other, my hands on her waist, her hands pushing on my chest, *that* was reality.

She pushed against me, whimpered against the coaxing of my lips; I could taste the salt of her tears, but for a moment longer, I held her tighter, stealing the warmth I desired. *You are mine. My muse. You belong to me!*

I pulled away only for a moment, only long enough to whisper, "I am metal in a metal world. Everything else is a trick, remember? I am the only real thing you've ever seen, and so is my circus. I am everything you ever loved and everything you will ever love. You will never escape from me, your creature in the night."

Then, ignoring her breathless curses, I kissed her unyielding lips once more—a promise.

"I best be getting back, *mon ange.*" My lips wandered from her lips to her neck as I brushed my fingers through her hair.

She flinched from their cold.

Grasping her chin, I forced her eyes to meet mine. I searched them for love, for anything warm she might hold for this frozen, metal monster.

"Don't you realize?" My breath came heavy, my words desperate. "I can be anything, *anyone* you want me to be. You only need to say the word, and I will conform to your desires."

Her teeth worried her bottom lip, tears sparkled in her eyes. When her gaze met mine, I saw only rejection. "I would rather be alone."

Her words stabbed like a cold knife. I stepped back, narrowing my eyes down at her. "They'll be missing me at my circus." I let my golden wings unfurl from my back, never moving my eyes from hers, which burned through pained tears. "I will see you from behind another face." The wings hummed to life and lifted me from the sand. And I pondered, as I rose, what she would think now. Would she forever wonder if any man she met now or in the future would be real?

Bitterness and resentment ate at the cogs in my heart. If she couldn't accept my love, or metal body, then I would secretly consume her mind with my magic instead. Eventually, she would abandon her defenses, and she would be *mine.*

LOST NAMES

Hannah Carter

ONCE UPON A time, someone asked the question: what's in a name?

And I know the answer.

Everything.

And nothing.

For you see, in the past, I have gone by many names. Each name was nothing more than a mask I wore to suit whatever purpose I had.

To inspire fear, I used the name Baba Yaga, among others. Fear has always been such a good motivator for humans. At every bump in the night, they were willing to give me whatever I wanted to appease me.

Sometimes, though, I needed to use finesse. Outwit them. Charm them, even. Because when humans feel they have risen above such a primitive, base emotion as fear—well, someone needs to remind them that there is *much* more to fear than just fear itself. Someone more intelligent than them. Someone more powerful than them.

And so, I used the name of the Pied Piper to get what I wanted. I could trick them and disappear into the annals of their history, a name with no face. A threat that becomes a legend.

And still, I was the winner.

But the citizens of London grew complacent. They believed that all the old threats and fears their ancestors harbored had disappeared with the turn of the twentieth century.

It was my job to remind them that they were arrogant fools.

But I had one setback since my last name had been stolen from me: the lack of a human host. In my true form, I was nothing more than the dark shadow of a wolf, a herald of winter, of cold and hunger, but unable to impact the world as I could as Baba Yaga or the Pied Piper. Without a name, without a body, mothers and fathers could soothe their children after nightmares, tell them that I could not hurt them.

A snowflake escaped from my lips and froze a weed that dared to poke its green head out of the dark London streets. Yes, let the children believe the sweet lies that I was nothing more than the monster under the bed—it made it much easier to possess them and use them as my human hosts.

I slipped through the winding London streets in darkness. All sorts of emotions drifted on the night air to guide me. Oh, so many tantalizing ones. Wrath. Betrayal. Sorrow. Fear. They would certainly sustain me, but I grew tired of their taste, which felt dry on my tongue.

A sweeter smell ensorcelled me, much more poignant and flavorful than any of those. Yes, I could bend all the other emotions to my will, but it was too simple.

I smelled a prey much more satisfying.

Loneliness.

It drifted most potently from a two-story house.

I slithered up the ivy-covered stone wall to the open window. A young boy, barely out of his first decade, sat cross-legged on the floor. Tears stained his cheeks, and he sniffed as he trailed his hand below his nose. He clutched a pirate figurine with a missing hand.

The house was silent, save for sniffles and the loud *tick-tock* of a clock downstairs.

And then my voice.

"Home alone, child?" My voice was soft, soothing—no need to inspire fear or coerce this one. Lonely ones responded best to a listening ear.

The boy nodded. His eyes widened as he caught a glimpse of me on the floor. "Mmhmm." He shivered as a trail of frost formed behind me.

"Where are your parents?"

The boy stroked the wooden face of the sword-wielding swashbuckler. "I don't know. Out. Always are."

I murmured in sympathy. "Poor thing. If only you had some friends that might keep you company." I tasted vague impressions of his memories through his emotions. "But your schoolmates . . ."

The boy's face crumpled, though he didn't dissolve into hysterics. Neither did he have any words, but unbridled loneliness rolled off him in droves. So saccharine and potent—like chocolate that melted in my mouth.

"No schoolmates, either?" Emotions are so delicious, so mouth-watering, so *telling.*

"I'm better by myself," he finally said.

Delectable resignation. So young, and yet, so broken. Life had stolen this boy's light before he could even reach puberty.

I loved it.

"Are you?" The candlelight flickered as I spoke, and I grew and shrank in its glow. "Tell me, boy. If you could have anything, what would you want?"

The boy tucked his knees up to his chin. Hope flickered across his face before he squashed it—such a good little trinket. Already, my battle was half over. Someone who had learned that hope only leads to disappointment was ready to lap up all my machinations.

"Nothing," he whispered.

"Really? Nothing?" I circled him. His eyes followed my movements, but he didn't shudder. The lonely subconscious is open to any hint of fellowship, no matter how odd. "Not even a friend?"

"No." The boy shook his head. "No friends." But he tilted his head and stared down at the painted face of his plaything. "Maybe more toys. More pirates. Maybe a crocodile for them to fight!"

A flicker of excitement crossed his face.

"Toys are safe," I agreed. I could sound congenial when I desired. "They can't hurt you. They can't leave."

The boy considered my words. Digested them. Tilted his auburn head. "Yeah."

"But . . ." My promise lingered in front of him. "What if I told you I could find you friends that would never leave?"

His face darkened, and a wave of anger rolled off him, so potent—a three-course meal for me. I greedily slurped it up.

"Then you'd be a liar. Because anybody who says they'll never leave is lying." The poor boy gripped the trinket in his hand so tightly that I thought the head might pop off. "I know. Even Nanny Trudy grew up and got married and left me."

I circled him—a vulture surveying its prey—careful not to touch the pirate. I was unsure if the sword was made from metal or silver, and the latter made me wary. "But I can make you a deal. I can give you friends that will never leave you. Never grow up. Never abandon you. What do you say?"

The boy shook his head.

Ah, how pure it is to cling to innocent heartbreak instead of the promise of hope.

I heard the front door open.

"I'll come back," I assured him. "Don't worry. *I* will never abandon you."

And I kept my promise. Whatever names one might call me, one cannot deny that I was an honest creature when it suited my needs.

After all, did I or did I not get rid of those rats, just like the beggars of Hamelin asked me to?

Night after night, promise after promise, I filled that poor boy's lonely nights. I delivered toys and goodies, spun stories to elicit more emotions.

"You know," I began on one such night. "I know a place where no one *ever* grows up. We could go there."

"We could?" The boy shivered.

"We could. And we could bring as many people as you want." I rustled his figurines that were set up in line. "And have adventures. With mermaids, fairies, pirates—*friends*."

The boy swallowed. A tear slipped down his cheek until it froze from my breath.

Then he uttered the words I needed to hear: "All right. I want you to take me there and give me friends that will *never* leave."

I licked my fangs as if I could already taste the first meal I'd have once I merged my shadow with this boy's, took over his husk, and inhabited his mind through that dark connection.

"No matter the cost?" I whispered in the darkness.

"No matter the cost."

•••♥•••

I slunk through the alley, dressed in the boy's skin. His consciousness slumbered in the back of my mind. Perhaps he would wake and fight me. Sometimes hosts did, but he was so small. So innocent.

I smiled the boy's smile, though I wondered if anyone could see the wolfish shadows lurking on his face—the twisted satisfaction hidden behind his lips.

I turned onto a main street, the sun already painting the sky varying hues of pink, orange, and yellow above me. No one paid attention to a street urchin. Perhaps they did not think it odd that a young boy was in the park by himself. Perhaps onlookers thought I was just an older brother as I loomed over the prams of children when nannies weren't looking, out for one last walk before they were whisked off to the nursery.

I snatched the babes off instead.

That first night, I stole three new friends.

But what would the paper think? They would call me a child snatcher, and then everyone would be on guard. People would hunt for the culprit with the ferocity that they hunted Jack the Ripper, and if they traced it back to me, my new name and face would be ruined.

So I whispered stories into the ears of the distraught nannies.

I planted the seeds of a magical world inhabited by pixies and fairies and these strange children. I hummed lullabies and songs, infiltrated nurseries and dreams. The children were not *gone* or *taken*. They were merely *lost*.

More and more children wished to come to me. More and more children left their windows open and murmured my new name in bedtime prayers. Soon, all it took was one visit, and small ones would flock to me, even easier than when I'd twisted the tune of that minstrel and lured the babes of Hamelin out of the city.

Deep in the forest, we played.

By the shores of a lake, we played.

Hidden from all others, running wild in the trees, away from the world, we played.

Pirates and mermaids, fairies and crocodiles. Anything my host could dream up, I gave him using his imagination and a world of my own crafting. The joy of such innocents kept me entertained, and the little mishaps kept me sustained.

Like the one instance when one of the boys lost a hand.

I gobbled it down that night, my first taste of flesh in years.

Perhaps I got greedy after that.

But children's flesh—so supple, sweet, not yet tainted by adulthood—was my true sustenance, flavored by the emotions I yearned to feast upon.

My host was easy enough to manipulate.

Through my influence, he stayed younger than he ought. But I could only be a parasite to one person at a time, which meant that the lost ones I'd stolen did not have the same blessing.

They changed.

They morphed.

They *grew up*.

And to grow up meant to desert childhood, something my host could not allow.

Funny, no matter how many promises I fulfilled, he was never truly content. He merely became more desperate to keep his friends, to fill the loneliness inside of him, as permanent a feature on him as the green shirt he never outgrew. These friends became the dirty rags he shoved into the hole in his heart to stop its bleeding, but the thought of "how long until they inevitably fall out" always consumed him.

And I could use this to torment him even more.

"They're going to abandon you," I hissed one night as he tossed and turned in bed. "They will go away, just like everyone else did. Let me get you new ones. Leave these older ones to me."

For I had fed them a steady diet of things that I loved to taste, let their emotions run unchecked, like how one might soak a chicken in a desired sauce. My mouth drooled as I circled the boy's consciousness. "*I* will never leave you."

He allowed me control, as he often did.

And so we began to thin out the crowds. The eldest boys fell to me to do what I pleased with, and I stole my host's memories so that he would not remember their existence. No, to him, everything must be as it once was. There could be no growing up, no abandoning, no changing.

And for the others, the families left behind? Deceived by the stories I spread, they believed their missing children were actually in a better place, a place they longed to go, as well.

Such blissful ignorance all around.

So when did it all go wrong?

When that blasted girl entered the picture.

She was one of my most ardent admirers. The boy often perched outside her window and listened to her weave magnificent adventures. I lurked in the back of his consciousness, tasting her joy as she spoke my name, the idolization that whet my appetite. The boy, I could tell, had found another dirty rag to stuff his heart-hole with. He begged for me to whisk her away. I acquiesced.

After all, her sweet nature would make a rather delicious dessert in a short time.

So I slipped in, wearing the boy's skin.

I lingered over her bed until her eyes flew open. She gasped, her hands flying out, perhaps to throttle me, but she held back when she noticed who I was.

"You," she whispered.

I nodded. "Me."

"I knew you were real." She sat up, and I moved back so that we did not collide. She bathed me with exuberance and joy, her childish excitement at my very presence a salve for my soul. I resisted the urge to inhale deeply. During my time as Baba Yaga, I had learned that, for some reason, humans do not like to be sniffed like they are going to be dinner.

"Of course I'm real." I perched on the end of her bed, legs crossed in a carefree manner. After all, I had never been thwarted when I went by this name. What did I have to fear? "I love listening to you tell stories. Especially when they're about me."

The girl smiled. "I know all of the stories."

"Tell me one! Right now." Call me a prideful creature, but I never tired of hearing winsome fantasies which starred myself and my new name.

The girl adjusted her long sleeves, which were ill-suited for the summer warmth, but perhaps she had delicate female sensibilities. "All right. Can I be in this one, too?"

"I don't see why not."

The very prospect filled her with enough exhilaration that I could last a week off her pure jubilation alone.

"Once upon a time," she began, her voice breathless. "There was a little boy who refused to grow up."

I puffed out my adolescent chest.

"Every night, he listened at the window of a house he'd visited before, though . . ." She tilted her head. "I wonder if he remembered."

"I never forget," I assured her.

And it was true. *I* never forgot, even if my host did.

The girl smiled, and I felt the boy's consciousness prick in the back of my mind.

"Let me take control! I want to hear the story."

I'm snatching her tonight, boy. I must remain in control.

He turned sullen. *"You always let me have control when we're here."*

Leave me be. I'll make sure she stays your friend. Forever.

I shoved him away, tried to lull him back to sleep.

He seemed confused, but I redirected my attention to the girl. I'd already missed several parts of the story, which soured my disposition.

" . . . the boy crawled through the window one day to whisk the girl off on untold adventures. 'Where are we off to?' the girl questioned." She paused. Leaned in. I did the same until I could catch a hint of the lavender on her breath. The grandfather clock in the parlor chimed the first bell of midnight. "'*Neverland*.'"

I grinned wolfishly.

She continued. "A place with more magic and Lost Boys than you can ever imagine." The girl reached out and grasped my hand, and a thrill coursed through my veins, courtesy of the boy lurking in the back of my mind.

I caught a snippet of his barely-coherent thoughts, *"I like the way she talks about me. She thinks I can be better than I am. She tells me so in her stories."*

I almost snorted, but I didn't want to answer any pesky questions from a nosy girl. *Such adult thoughts from a boy who won't grow up.*

I'd missed another bit of the story, but it seemed the girl was only describing Neverland in great detail. It wasn't until she brought the tale back to me that I paid attention again.

"But what the boy didn't know was that the girl knew the truth."

I straightened. "The truth?"

"From a young age, the girl was obsessed with Neverland. She would tell her brothers the stories that she heard, and they believed, too."

Her brothers? Ah, yes. I combed through my memories until I vaguely remembered some boys that used to flock around her. But, really—they had been minor, unimportant players, and I often rested when my host was here. I scarcely remembered how many existed. Two? Seven? I couldn't say. After all, *they* hadn't woven stories of my greatness.

"And one day, one of the children got taken to Neverland."

I blinked. No—I hadn't. I hadn't taken anyone from this house, had I?

Unless.

Unless my host had.

Any mortal might have blanched, but I kept my bravado. There was nothing too accusatory in what she had said.

Except I noticed her grip on my hand was tighter, and her emotions subtly shifted to a bitter taste.

"Nicholas, the oldest boy, was whisked off to Neverland, while the girl, only ten at the time, hid under the bedsheets, unnoticed. But she heard everything and wanted to go, too." Her voice turned savage as she shifted her weight to her knees to take the higher ground. "She followed. There was no pixie dust, no flying. No second star to the right—those were nothing but fanciful myths to make children more compliant. But in truth, Nicholas, the sister, and the boy from Neverland merely climbed out the window and walked away."

I stood up and stretched to my host's full height. My influence had stunted his aging, so while I should have towered over the girl, I did not. We met eye to eye, hand still locked, all semblances of friendliness gone.

"The boy led Nicholas to a forest, not knowing the little imp of a sister crept behind. And there she saw *it* happen."

She advanced on me, and I attempted to wrest myself away as I growled, "Enough games. I'm done with this."

"*You* may be. But *I* am not."

A sudden influx of pain made me aware of my wrist. I howled and dropped to my knees. A band slid from her arm onto mine, her name engraved in the silver. She shoved me to my knees, a fireplace at my back, the burning metal on my wrist.

Sweat beaded down my face and back.

"Are you scared?" I hissed. I was cold, I was hunger, I was death—this little one should have quivered in her nightgown at my very presence.

But the fire in her eyes rivaled anything in the hearth behind me.

"Not anymore." She squeezed my hand until I wondered if it might break. "I've trained and searched for you for two years. I'm ready."

With my free hand, I tried to push the bracelet back on her. But the very touch of it made me jerk away, uttering words unfit for a nursery.

The story continued. "The girl saw the boy she idolized from the nursery tales shudder. She saw his shadow grow, stretch, and possess its host, like a grotesque puppeteer.

"'What did you do?' the shadow asked with the mouth of the boy—but gone was the youthful, innocent voice with the hint of loneliness. The voice that craved friendship and connection.

"There was no answer that the girl could hear, but she watched as Nicholas backed away. Perhaps he would have fled, and the siblings could have escaped back to the nursery and pretended that it was all just a terrible nightmare and that Neverland still existed in their dreams."

I hissed. I could recall the next part of the story. It had seemed so trivial at the time, a mere hiccup in my master plan.

The girl's eyes sparked and reflected the firelight as she continued. "'How old are you?' the shadow snarled.

"'Fourteen,' Nicholas replied.

"The shadow cursed. 'Too old. You're past your prime.'

"'My prime?' Nicholas asked."

Despite the pain in my arm and the heat on my back, I grinned. A droplet of sweat threaded past my upturned lips as I said, "Would it unnerve you to know the truth? That once a child passes the threshold into adolescence, they never quite have the same flavor as their youth? Or that I can still taste the flesh of everyone I consume?"

The girl flinched.

"Perhaps," she admitted. "Although, it's quite funny—once you witness someone cannibalize your brother, nothing else ever really seems quite as fearsome."

I sniffed the air. No. I didn't smell fear. Just pure, unabashed hatred mixed with vengeful, bitter glee to make it sweet.

She smiled. "But you do get a single-minded purpose."

And the girl grabbed a fireplace poker and whacked my head.

I cried out, but more so from the fact that it, too, burned my flesh. Silver. How had she convinced her parents to make everything in this blasted room silver?

She reared back, aiming the sharp end of her weapon towards my stomach. I attempted once more to shake off the bracelet as I rolled out of the way. It burned me several more times but finally clattered to the ground. I kicked it out of the way, baring my teeth at her.

"I wonder, does the sister taste like the brother?"

The girl arranged herself into a perfect fencing form; her makeshift blade pointed right at my heart. "Why don't you come take a bite?"

I lunged at her. She shoved me into the fireplace with the blunt end. My back hit the trim, and I heard the fizz of my host's hair as it burned. The acrid smell filled my nostrils, and I jerked away.

The girl fell forward, placing her knee on my stomach while a free hand went to my neck. I snapped at her a few times, but she had positioned me so that there was no way I could turn this pathetic human neck and bite her.

"You'll have to leave him," she hissed. "You'll have to leave his body if you want to escape the pain. I know you can. I've read all about your kind—the *real* you."

She pressed the poker against my chest and shoved my hair closer to the fire.

A bit of frost escaped my host's lips as I wriggled inside him. The girl shoved the silver closer to my skin.

"You think you want to face me in my true form?" I choked out.

"I would love to. Leave the human husk behind. Don't lurk in his shadow. *Let him go*."

I glared at her. If I stayed in his consciousness and she killed him, I would die, too. If I became his shadow, she'd sever my connection in an instant with her blasted silver. But if I left him completely, I could never re-enter, and my time in this body was over—every hour I'd spent cultivating my name, the stories, Neverland.

Wasted.

"Never," I snarled.

She drew back and bludgeoned my chest with the blunt length of the poker.

"You're letting me get hurt!" my host screamed.

We're merely biding our time.

"Until what?"

She thrashed me once more, closer to the neck. Blood spurted as the curved point of her weapon sliced my skin. My temper flared, and I yelled, both out loud and to my host, "Until we kill her!"

"*No!*" My host sounded like a tantruming child, and his consciousness attacked mine. It felt like he was pummeling me, throwing himself down on the metaphorical floor of our shared mind and throttling my spirit. "*I won't let you hurt her!*"

As if it's ever bothered you to hurt people before.

The girl squeezed until my vision began to darken. Stupid humans—why did they rely so much on blasted oxygen? Why was I as fragile as my host?

"I've never hurt anyone! I play with my friends—that's all. It's all pretend."

His voice sounded a bit hysterical. I wondered how he remembered it all. He couldn't conjure the actual memories, but did he know something was missing? Did he suspect? I'd toyed with his mind so much, erased so many people; I wasn't exactly sure what he thought of anything.

"Even the nightmares. They're all pretend. It's all in my imaginations."

I chuckled. I could taste the blood in the back of my throat. I could hardly see anything.

"Get out of my head! I don't want you here anymore! In her stories, she said that I didn't have to be bad because you made me do the things. She said that I could be good and get rid of you."

I could no longer address him out loud, but I could still direct my thoughts at him, though they grew less coherent as the girl choked me. *You'll be lonely again if you kick me out. You'll change. You'll grow up, that horrid thing.*

"Better to grow up and become the adult I should be than stay the child I always have been."

He gave me one more good shove, right as my consciousness was about to fade.

Fine!

If he was so in love with this maniac girl, let her kill him, not me.

An icy wind filled the room as I slithered out of the boy's consciousness and became his shadow instead, a dark wolf against the floor.

I fixed my red eyes on the girl and bared my teeth at her, which I assumed looked truly frightening in the glow of the blasted fireplace.

Frost inched its way up the open nursery window, and snow fell with every ragged breath I took.

"You wanted my true form, girl?"

She released her grip on my unconscious host, who looked pale and pathetic slumped on the ground.

"You'll yearn for the creatures of your nightmares by the time I'm done with you."

"Not likely. This is *my* tale now, and you die in it." The girl smirked. "Wendy Darling—wendigo slayer, rescuer of Peter Pan. It has a nice ring to it, doesn't it?"

Wendy advanced on me, poker at the ready. She swung at the floor and hit my abdomen. I roared, and the snow escalated to a blizzard. My teeth could not penetrate her without fully possessing my host. I could only hope to cause her frostbite or send her into hypothermia before she destroyed me.

"They say that some people have altered fairy tales to make them not quite as scary for young children. That there is always a hidden dark side. Won't it be funny in the future if I say I sewed your shadow back on instead of the truth? That I *murdered* the beast and freed Peter Pan of its influence."

She drove her poker against the wood where I lurked and severed my legs in one fell swoop. I howled as my connection snapped. I felt no pain now that I'd left my feeble host behind, but I'd destroy her for her impudence. No one could steal a name from me and live to tell the tale.

At least I could move freely now. I darted across the walls and out the crack in the door, but Wendy pursued. Silver trinkets lined the doors and hallways. How had her family not noticed her stockpiling these weapons?

I howled as I brushed against a silver statue of armor which had been pushed up against a door. I could hear a babe whimper inside, and another boy shushed him. I had found her brothers at last, but I couldn't possess them as my new hosts, either, now with their guard in the way.

"Every night I lock them in," Wendy said. I whirled around but found her behind me. "You can't slip under the crack without burning yourself, wendigo."

"Does your family think you're insane?" I growled. "Do they threaten to lock you away in an institution?"

"They'd sooner put up with my peculiarities than lose another child." Wendy's fingers curled around her bludgeon. "After all, my father slept outside in the doghouse for a week straight after Nicholas' death, in some desperate attempt to prevent anyone from kidnapping one of us. My family may be peculiar, but we're loyal."

I swore and tried to slip past Wendy. She swiped at me and tore a large hole in my body.

I heard a man's snore down the opposite end of the hall, but a similar suit of armor blocked my path. Silver bells littered the stairs and banisters, cutting off any escape.

It was just Wendy and me.

The closer she got to my heart, the lower the temperature dropped as I unleashed more of my wintery powers. Frost crawled up her arms, ruining any flavor they might have once possessed.

She flexed her arms to keep her elbows limber, taunting me through blue lips.

I blustered and blew; she burned and bruised. Suddenly her unseasonably warm clothes didn't seem quite so ridiculous. Her determination, hot like cider, pained my heart.

I panted, my body riddled with stab wounds, my shadowy form small, my fight all but gone.

And then Wendy Darling, wendigo slayer, drew back and speared me right through the heart.

•••♥•••

It took me years to fix myself. That's one thing about wendigos: unless you kill us inside of a host's body, we can only be defeated, never slayed.

Our shadows always reform, our wounds always heal. And as I watched the young family traipse through Kensington Gardens, I knew.

One day I would come for them again.

The auburn-haired woman bent down to the young redheaded girl, who wielded a stick. The taller man held a chubby boy in his arms, perhaps too scared to put him in the pram.

Perhaps he still remembered that part of the myth.

The small girl gazed upon the statue of Peter Pan. "Mummy, it *does* look like Daddy!"

Wendy cast her husband a smile over her shoulder. "Do you think so, love?"

Peter turned red. "I don't know. I don't really think I look anything like that."

His voice was much deeper than the host I'd once inhabited. Did I feel some kind of emotion?

Yes.

Bitterness. Rage. *Hatred.*

"Now, let me tell you a story." Wendy picked up a stick. "About Neverland. And shadows, wendigos, and darkness. It's our job to defend the world from these nightmares, my dear. So that all nurseries are filled with sweet dreams and stories."

Wendy picked up a stick and began to gently swat at her daughter's. "Once upon a time, there was a boy named Peter Pan . . . ."

I turned away. The Darlings were preparing for a rematch with me, so it was only fair that I return the favor.

•••♥•••

So, I ask again—what's in a name?

The people who have seen what I am, what I truly am, call me a wendigo. They say the name in fear, lock the doors and bar the windows.

But I will claim a new name.

Start a new legend, and the children will come.

Just as the children of the forest once stumbled into the domain of Baba Yaga.

Just as the Pied Piper once led those beautiful, delicious children out of the town of Hamelin.

Just as they whispered sweet stories in the nurseries, innocent dreams and wishes to have a visit from Peter Pan.

One day I will return.

I will always come to claim my Lost Boys.

THE OTHER CINDERELLA

Beka Gremikova

THE CARRIAGE CAREENED around the bend in the road, the echo of the horses' hooves thundering in my ears. I reached out to steady myself, trying to soothe the frantic pounding of my human heart. Beyond the carriage window, the night fell like a shroud of soft black feathers. The sliver of moon did little to lighten the gloom.

A shout pierced the air, and the horses shrieked, the carriage lurching to a stop. I flung myself back to keep from falling forward, reaching into the flowing sleeve of my gown. But my fingers closed around empty air.

No wand sat snug in my sleeve, waiting to be called upon. I had no magic to protect myself.

Cursing, I fumbled with the door handle, my fingers trembling.

Before I could get it open, Jacques, the coachman, poked his face through the open window, all gaunt, narrow features and glittering eyes. "Fairy—I mean, mademoiselle?"

"What is it?" I snapped.

"You have a visitor."

My heart hammered, and I sank back against the cushioned seat as though I might escape that way. Had Mathilde changed her mind? Had she come to snatch my dreams away from me?

Jacques stepped aside, and another face appeared.

My fingers clenched into the silk folds of my gown.

The girl's cheeks were smeared with ash where she had forgotten to wash it off; her eyes were soft and dark as midnight. Tendrils of silver gold wafted around high cheekbones, illuminating thin rosy lips that suggested dimpled smiles. "Please, mademoiselle," she panted, breathless. She shoved her fist against her mouth and coughed. Her entire body—what I could see of her, at least—shivered with exertion. She gripped the edge of the door with filthy fingers, her nails caked with dirt. "You're going to the palace, aren't you?" she rasped. "Please, please let me join you! I must get there!"

The idea of her, my enemy, sharing my coach, was preposterous. I tried to utter the merry laugh I'd heard other noble ladies do. It came out strangled. "My dear, you have nothing to wear—"

She shook her head, the rag that covered her hair whipping off in a sudden burst of wind. "I know the Tales! I'm supposed to have a fairy godmother—"

"Those don't exist," I said sharply.

Her head snapped up, her eyes glittering. "They do," she whispered, so fiercely that my heart stammered that *she knew*. Somehow, she must have learned of my trickery.

But no. That was impossible. Jacques, as well as Mathilde and the other fairies, were the only ones who knew the truth.

"They do," she repeated. "But mine must have forgotten me."

I licked my dry lips. The carriage felt hot and stuffy. But I didn't dare lean out the window, didn't dare get too close in case she could tell I was no true noblewoman. "If you know the Tales so well," I said, whipping out my fan and desperately batting it back and forth in front of my face, "you should also know that the girl does not reach the ball without magic."

The girl pursed her lips, narrowing her gaze as it roved the round, golden pumpkin in which I sat. "Yours came," she said softly. "How come yours came, and mine didn't? *I'm* a Cinderella. Cinderellas always have fairy godmothers! Cinderellas always go to the ball."

I drew myself up, nostrils flaring. "Perhaps you don't know the Tales well enough," I said stiffly. "There can only be *one* Cinderella in each Tale."

And this Tale was *mine*.

Her eyelids flickered. "Please," she whispered. "Surely you can—you'll still help me?"

"I'm afraid I can't. I have nothing for you to wear." I squinted past her, searching for Jacques. He stood several feet behind her, hands clasped behind his back, his eyes darting from her to me. He met my gaze, raising an eyebrow.

I gritted my teeth. Mathilde had insisted that her human god-son could keep my secret, that I needed to have an ally on my mission to take Cinderella's place. But I couldn't shake the sensation that he judged my every move.

The girl realized I'd stopped paying attention to her. She reached to grab my arm through the open window. "Mademoiselle, you must—" Her fingers snagged the sleeve of my gown, and I imagined it ripping, imagined my dreams withering from one tiny tear. I couldn't appear at the prince's ball in a torn dress, and my wish to the fairies didn't cover extras.

"Begone!" I snarled.

She tripped back, hacking through another cough. "Please—I can't go back—my stepmother—stepsisters—"

My chest tightened. "Ready the horses," I called to Jacques.

This girl was no longer my duty, no longer my responsibility. I wasn't a fairy anymore.

After one last look at the girl, the coachman clambered to his place on the carriage seat. Averting my gaze from the girl's crumpling face, I settled myself on my seat, back straight, fan clenched in my fingers. Though it didn't have the same comforting presence as my wand once did, it helped to have something to remind me of who I was now—a mysterious noblewoman about to snag the prince's heart.

With a snap of the reins, we leaped forward.

I let out a breath. My wish to the fairies had held, even in the face of the other Cinderella's pleas. I couldn't resist turning to watch the thin, forlorn figure grow smaller and smaller as the darkness enveloped her. We rounded another corner, and she was gone.

I pressed my fingers against the plush walls of the carriage, trying to steady my whirling, gnawing thoughts. *Thief. Traitor. Liar. Witch.* "You don't owe her anything," I said aloud, not caring if Jacques heard. "There can only be one Cinderella in this story!"

And, by hook or by crook, that Cinderella had to be me.

•••♥•••

"You have one wish," they said to me, their eyes glassy. The fairies surrounded me, ethereal in their gossamer gowns and with their sleek, translucent wings. "We ask that you do not make it, sister. No mortal man is worth Death. Death of body or of soul."

They'd been begging me for months, ever since I'd come to my decision to leave their ranks and join the mortal world. But they were all full-blooded fairies;

I'd been born with human blood and mortal desires, from a mortal father and immortal fairy mother. They had no notion of my struggles, no understanding of my longing.

They wept. Mathilde, our eldest, clutched me in her arms even as the others ripped my wings from my back. The pain was not physical—but as the wings left my body, I felt my kinship with these women break.

They drew away from me, my wings and wand in their arms.

All that was left was their blessing—their final gift to a sister who had gone astray.

To a sister who they would be forced to watch grow old and die.

But it was worth it to be with Etienne. I straightened. "I wish to take Cinderella's place."

Mathilde's lips thinned. "You understand the consequences?"

I nodded.

"Such trickery is beneath us," another fairy hissed.

"You cannot deny me," I said. "It's my right to be granted any wish."

Mathilde shook her head. "You are both right." Reaching out, she touched my forehead. Her fingers, smooth and heated, pressed against my skin, but it was her gaze that seared me. I almost stepped back, almost called it off. "Your wish is granted, girl. May you not live to regret it."

•••♥•••

My fingers trembled as I fiddled with my awful powdered wig. We'd arrived at the palace, but I couldn't bring myself to descend from the carriage. Jacques hovered by the door.

He cleared his throat. "Is this all really worth it?" He spread out his arms, indicating my silver dress, the splendid coach. "This whole charade?"

"I thought you were supposed to be my ally. Did Mathilde actually send you to try to change my mind?"

He pressed his lips together. "Do you not feel guilty? That girl—*she's* the real Cinderella—"

"I can be Cinderella." I leaped to my feet. Providence, Fate, Fairytale—they no longer bound me. The other girl, me—there were no longer any laws that said I couldn't *be* her. "Etienne won't know the difference!" The princes never did—they simply loved whoever the Cinderella in their Tale happened to be.

And now, *I* was this Tale's Cinderella, so Etienne had to love *me*.

Jacques threw up his hands. "But *you'll* know, and I'll know!" He scuffed his boot across the cobblestones before glowering at me. "And Etienne doesn't deserve to be tricked!"

I gathered my skirts, relishing their coolness against my sweaty skin. "Open the door," I snapped.

After a tense moment, he did so, offering a jaunty, slightly-mocking bow as I stepped down. "You have no right to judge me," I hissed at him, sweeping up the stairs to the palace before he could answer.

My heart pounded in my ears as I hurried through the halls, certain that at any moment, Mathilde would sweep in and snatch everything away from me.

But she never appeared, and the ballroom opened up before me, a swathe of dazzling lights and swirling gowns. My own dress seemed to glow in response as I stepped into the room, the power of twelve fairies fuelling its magical radiance.

Just as I knew would happen, all eyes turned to me.

And then I saw him.

Etienne.

He stood not far from me, chatting to one of the nobles. Like the rest of the crowd, he turned to look at the mysterious stranger—and our eyes met.

My heart swelled. All my worries fled as he strode toward me, the crowd parting to let him through.

For years, I'd watched him as I went about my fairy business; watched as he sprinkled joy on all his subjects; watched as he wept from loneliness when he thought no one saw—watched without ever meeting him, without ever experiencing those smiles, that kindness, for myself.

As he drew nearer, I trembled. Surely some spell would fall and break this moment. Surely the clock would strike midnight, and my gown would turn to dust.

He stopped in front of me. My vision blurred.

"Bonjour," he said softly. "May I have this dance?"

•••♥•••

We were to wed in the spring, by the edge of the lily pond in the palace garden. The day bloomed bright and sunny—the perfect day for a Fairy Tale wedding. Guests milled about the garden, sighing over the beautiful roses and daffodils. Etienne had opened the palace gates to allow commoners to attend, and peasant children skittered along the paths, giggling.

Then the fairies arrived to offer their congratulations.

Mathilde and her fellows looked as beautiful as ever, but their faces were stony, their lips pressed together. The only times they smiled were as they cooed over the peasant children and chatted with their parents.

They never approached me, and I avoided them, forcing Etienne to make the formal niceties, begging that I had to retouch my hair and makeup. Etienne, in his usual sweet, gentle manner, relented and let me escape.

As I returned, I glimpsed Mathilde speaking urgently with Jacques. Etienne had insisted the man drive our honeymoon coach—apparently, they were close friends.

Jacques shook his head at Mathilde's pleading, and her shoulders sagged before she nodded. He kissed her cheek and walked away, disappearing behind a copse of ash trees.

Mathilde glanced up, caught me looking, and her face went stony once again.

I shivered and hurried to rejoin Etienne, who stood by the pond with the officiant. He took my hand, patted it, and nodded gravely.

"You're so serious," I murmured, squeezing his fingers. My eyes skimmed the crowd, but I caught no trace of ash-blonde hair and a soot-streaked face.

"It's a serious day," he said, but there was a strange note to his voice. Before I could question further, the ceremony began.

It felt like hours, standing there, gripping Etienne's fingers, waiting for the final word that would make me his forever, safe from threat of fairy interference. The sun vanished behind a coiling cloud, and the soft, sweet breeze of the morning faded. The air grew hot and stifling.

When the ceremony finally ended, and the rings were exchanged, we received guests in the garden's pavilion. High, trilling music whispered in the background.

A tall, proud woman was one of the first to approach. She touched my outstretched hand with cold, bony fingers. "I congratulate you on your happy day," she said in a high, nasal tone. "Prince Etienne is blessed to have such a beautiful wife." She smiled thinly at him. "May you live not to regret your choice."

I startled at her words.

Etienne kissed my knuckles, his lips soft and cold. Then he smiled at the woman—a long, knowing smile that looked odd on his usually open features. "I will try my best," he said.

She nodded stiffly and turned aside. Two girls trailed after her, glaring at me over their shoulders.

Then, crossing the garden, came the fairies. They walked slowly, whispering, their gazes trained on me, gnawing like gnats.

I blinked past a sudden wave of dizziness. The air pressed in on me, and I clutched Etienne's arm. "May we—leave early?"

Etienne followed my gaze. "You wish to avoid the fairies?"

There it was again—that note in his voice I couldn't fathom. There was a keenness, an alertness to him now that hadn't been there before.

I nodded. "They make me nervous," I whispered.

"Very well." He led me across the garden. We dipped through the gate into the cultivated wilds, where our carriage waited to carry us to our honeymoon. Flies buzzed around the horses' heads, and they stamped their hooves, snorting.

The coachman was nowhere to be seen.

"Where is he?" I snapped at Etienne. "Stuffing himself with pastries?"

"Don't you mind," Etienne said. "I'm sure he'll be along sooner than you think." He guided me to the carriage and handed me up—then, after a pause, gave a jaunty, half-mocking bow.

My heart nearly stopped. I gripped the handle of the carriage for support. "No," I whispered.

Etienne—no, the *coachman* with Etienne's body—glanced up at me and smiled. "Hullo, fairy," he murmured.

I swayed, holding onto that carriage door, praying I wouldn't faint. "What did you *do*?" I hissed. "Where's the real Etienne?"

"*I'm* Etienne." No note of the former Etienne remained in his steely voice now. "As much as you're the real Cinderella." He leaned against the carriage, arms crossed, a cruel smile twisting his lips. "You're not the only one who can wish upon a fairy to trade places with another. If there can only be one Cinderella in this Tale, there can only be one prince."

"But—but—" My mind whirled. "*Why*?"

He met my horrified gaze, his own unabashed. "Because Etienne deserves better than *you*, you deceitful witch."

Desperate, I reached into my pocket for my fan, fluttering it in front of my face. But still, the heat threatened to overwhelm me. "Mathilde betrayed me, then," I whispered, remembering her cold warning.

Etienne-who-wasn't-Etienne offered his hand. "Come. I'm tired of standing."

Reluctantly, I took his hand.

His gait stiff and his hold on my fingers disparagingly polite, he guided me to the front of the coach. Together, we clambered onto the bench. As soon as we were seated, he gathered the reins and shot me a scathing glance. "Mathilde wanted me to look after you; she wanted to see if I could appeal to your conscience and change your mind." His lips curled. "She overestimated you."

I swallowed, rubbing my hands over my arms. Over the last few months, Etienne had been nothing but sweet to me, forgiving every slip of my tongue, dismissing any doubts I felt. This man . . . this man would not let me forget my sins. "Where is the real Etienne now?"

He shrugged languidly, cracking his knuckles. "Far away from you, I expect. Mathilde will ensure he's safe and happy." His gaze narrowed. "As he deserves to be."

My nostrils flared. "And what about *you*? You don't deserve to be happy?"

He smiled thinly. "Let me just say that for Etienne, I'm willing to sacrifice a lot." He gave the reins a snap, and we rolled forward. I sat petrified, trapped by my own trickery. Unable to leave without causing scandal. Unable to point out the truth without being called a liar.

As we rattled down the road, we passed a young woman weeding a garden. Her ash-blonde hair glistened in the sunlight, and she gave a small, sad wave as the carriage went by. Jacques waved back—no, False Etienne waved—no . . . Oh, who *was* he now? Who was *I* anymore?

I didn't realize I'd stood as though to address her until the coachman clucked his tongue. "No take-backs," he murmured, pulling me back onto my seat. "There can only be one Cinderella, remember? And in *this* Tale now, my dear, that's *you*."

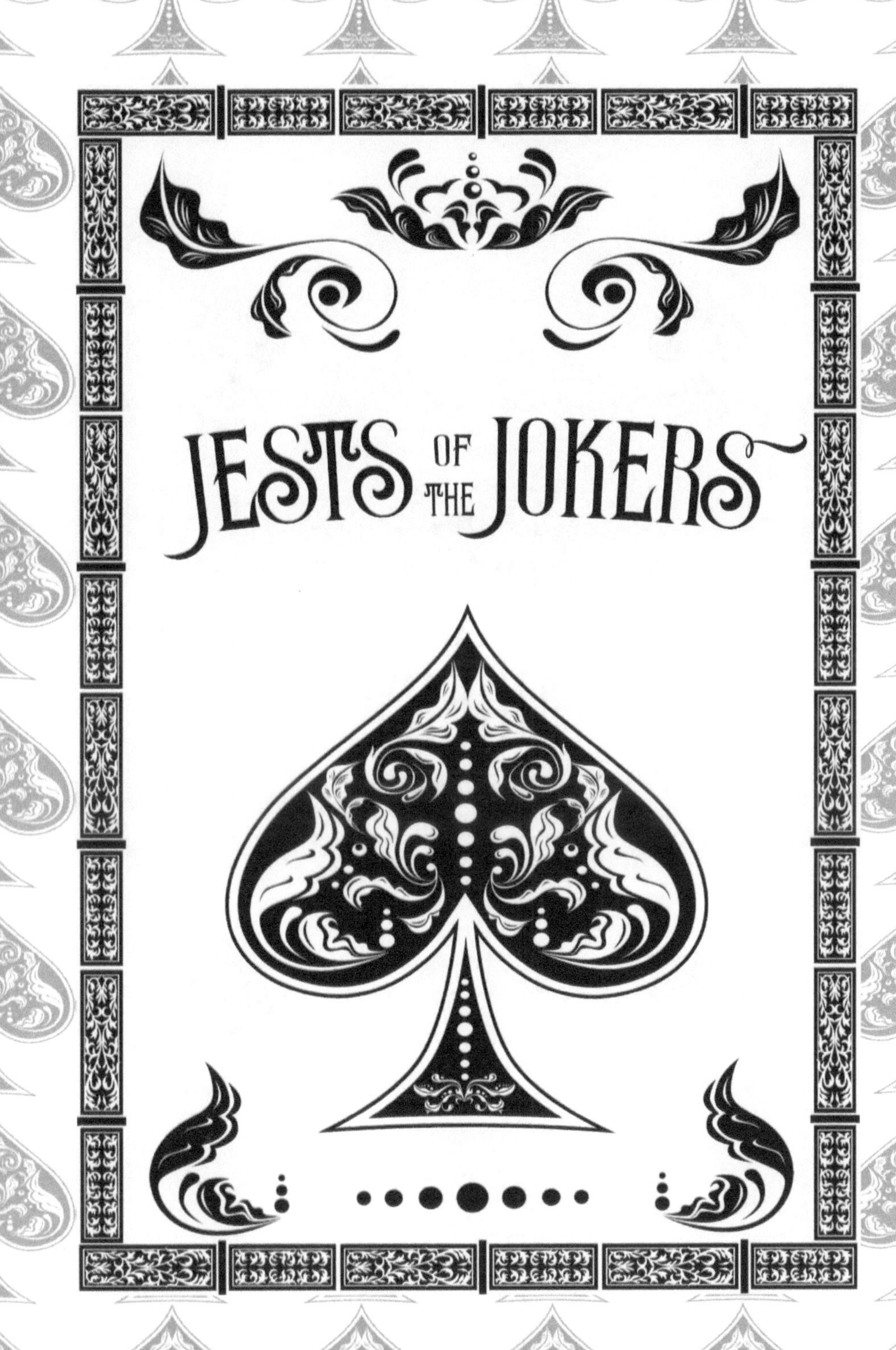
JESTS OF THE JOKERS

Don't
Underestimate
a
Rodent.
That's all.

FOOL'S GUIDE TO TRICKERY

PART TWO

Anne J. Hill

AS YOU WELL know, not all tricksters share the same disposition. Some are grave and serious, while others prefer more whimsical and comedic mischief. Thankfully, there's plenty of room for both in this world, and the following guidelines are for those of you who wish to have an occasional laugh or even transfer entirely from somber to silly in your trickster pursuits.

1. Master the art of wit. Figure it out yourself. Easy.

2. Don't try too hard. Seriously, don't. People can tell if you're forcing it, so don't force it! Instead of coming off cool, you'll look like a fumbling fool. And that is the opposite goal. Understand? Have I clearly explained myself? Short and sweet. Calm and collected! Got it!?

3. Wiggle your fingers. When you're plotting an evil plan, hold your hands together in front of your face and wiggle your fingers while you laugh maniacally. Be sure to practice this when no one is watching, or else everyone will think you're insane when you do it later, and no one will fall for a crazy person.

4. Surround yourself with exceptionally boring people, so you look hilarious by comparison. Or with people who will chuckle at anything you say to build the illusion that you're funny, even if you're not. And funny people are trustworthy people, right?

5. Don't kick puppies. No one trusts someone who would kick a puppy. Don't be that guy. You won't make friends. And without friends, who will you trick?

6. Don't care. People seem to find it humorous when you don't give a hoot about walking the line between good and evil. Jumping from one to the other puzzles the viewer and creates laughter, even if it's nervous laughter. So, whatever you do, don't care. Or do. Whatever. I don't care.

7. Don't underestimate a rodent. That's all.

8. Find a companion you can tease and have banter with. They could be your arch-nemesis, best friend, lover, or loyal sidekick. Unless you're too dim-witted to pull it off.... Nah, just teasin' ya.... See? You think I'm funnier already, right?

9. Never do or say what you actually mean. Living life like a riddle can confuse your opponents, making them easier targets than a one-eyed magician at a bake sale, and you'll have fun while doing so.

10. Practice your laugh. Whether you're out to save the world or burn it, you need a good laugh. But especially if you're a villain, because nothing is scarier than a cackling villain. *Mwahahahaha!* See? Terrifying, right?

11. And finally, above all: Never get caught! But you already knew that, didn't you? Too bad I'm right behind you! *Boo!*

WON'T BE IN TODAY

Lara E. Madden

Subject: Won't Be In Today
From: <Lara E. Madden>
Recipients: Hill, Anne <imtheboss@workmail.com>
CC: <HR@workmail.com>

Dear Ms. Boss Lady,

I AM WRITING THIS email to inform you that I won't be in the office today and to try to explain why. It's a bit of a long story. But I'm sure by the end of it you'll be more than understanding.

Okay. So.

It all started when the helicopter landed in my backyard . . . .

Crazy, right?

I realize that, at this point, you probably think that I'm lying to you. I mean, I would think that too if I were in your position. When has a helicopter ever just appeared in someone's yard?

Except it turned out to be aliens. They were flying a helicopter-shaped UFO because they thought their normal spacecraft would draw too much attention.

So anyway, the aliens—they were a kind of sky blue by the way, not green or grey like in the movies, and they were sort of formless, like a walking liquid-plasma being, not solid like us—they told me it was an emergency. They used radio signals or something to speak through the translation app on my phone because they couldn't speak English; only the sentences kept getting jumbled, so I'm not exactly sure *what* the emergency was supposed to be. I just knew they *really* wanted me to get in the helicopter.

And I did. But you can't blame me, really. I'm a deeply curious person, and the opportunity for an adventure happened to present itself. In my backyard. Via helicopter spaceship.

And this adventure seemed important. Life-alteringly vital. I thought they might need my help to save the world or something. So obviously, I went with them. You would have too if you were in my shoes.

It was a small helicopter, but being the only solid life form in the vehicle, it wasn't hard for me to fit in beside the four or five aliens. However, we rose in altitude much too quickly. They tried to apologize through Google Translate, saying that they'd forgotten from their Earth Lifeform Studies that humans are so sensitive to changes in air pressure. I was slightly peeved about being called "sensitive," but I decided to let it go.

Anyway, I had never been in a helicopter before, so I couldn't decide whether I should look out the window and marvel at how *far* away the *ground* was or look over my shoulder and marvel at how *close* the *aliens* were. I settled on doing a bit of both. You know, in case staring was rude in their culture. (Do you think aliens have culture?)

Well, apparently, they didn't really need me to save the world at all. And they didn't even need me for research exactly. They said they already have plenty of human research and weren't taking more applications for test subjects at the moment. "And besides," they managed to explain to me, I was "much too strange." They usually look for either extremely ordinary humans or extremely advanced ones to use as test subjects, and I was just . . . I think the word they used was "odd"?

But that was *definitely* the pot watching the kettle boil, or whatever, because these aliens turned out to be tourists—*tourists!*—and thought I would be an entertaining guide. When I heard this, I imagined that being a tour guide of Earth could be a pretty sweet deal if I got some free travel out of it myself. So I said, "Oh, good. Well, we have lots of interesting things to see on planet Earth! How about the seven wonders of the—"

They cut me off. They knew all about the Seven Wonders of the Ancient World. Been there, done that. What they REALLY wanted to see, more than anything, were America's best . . . cornfields.

Cornfields? Really?

But, hey, when space aliens demand that you entertain them with stories about the cornfields they want to visit, you don't ask questions. So that's what I did. All night and late into the morning, I told them about the cornfields we were passing over. (I know jack about corn, by the way. Or fields. But they must not have realized that because they seemed absolutely riveted the entire tour.)

Well, we were running out of fuel in the spacecraft-copter, and I was getting tired—because I have a *human* brain and it requires *sleep*—and they agreed to return to my backyard and drop me off. But first, the feistiest alien, who was apparently the youngest, convinced the others that they should graffiti one of the fields. It leaned out of the helicopter, jiggling as if it was laughing, and reached out a vapory blue appendage toward the field. It shot a sonic ray toward the ground that struck so hard that the helicopter was thrown back by the force. The alien collapsed in what looked like uncontrollable fits of silent laughter. The helicopter righted itself, and I looked down at the Earth to see farmers racing out of their houses toward a field that was now printed with a network of perfect circles.

Well, we landed in my backyard again, and I realized as I glanced at my watch that I was late for work. At that point, though, I was starting to rethink my career choice. I mean, it's not every day that someone tells you in broken electronic English that you *really should* consider becoming Planet Earth's Official Cornfield Tour Guide. They said goodbye (I think), and I watched them fly away as I reconsidered whether I wanted to go to work today at all.

And you know what? I don't. I don't want to go to work today. I'm tired. It's been a long night. I think I'm going to go back to bed. I might watch Netflix. I might research cornfields. I might think about taking the extraterrestrials up on their job offer.

But also, I sneezed today. So, you know, I probably shouldn't be in the office anyway.

(Mostly) Sincerely,

Lara E. Madden

THIS IS THE
SECRET
OF THE BUTTER
BANDITS.

THE GREAT BUTTER PIRATES

Elaine Wells

The great butter pirates of Braxton Bay,
A name that strikes fear in sailors to this day,
As the legend goes
They are ruthless men,
Thieves of the sea
That take only one thing:
Butter,
Just butter,
But pounds of the stuff,
Poor trade ships left empty,
Their stock rounded up,
That terrible butter gang
Leaves all other goods,
Gold and silver completely ignored,
While a confused ship captain shakes in his boots,
They take their loot and flee the scene,
Vanishing away in their bathtub boat.

You may ask, "Why?"
"What is all this butter for?"
And this question, my dear,
Has been asked for years,
But I'll tell you now,
Listen close, keep it down,
This is the secret of the butter bandits.

'Bout ten miles from the bay,
On the island of Skay,
A beast hides deep in the ominous cave,
Winged with claws
And scales like a snake,
A mean and horrible thing he is,
He demands only butter,
Near a barrel a day,
He gobbles it up,
And sleeps again.

As the story foretells,
The marauders never sell,
Even an ounce of the butter they take off the shelves,
And though they pillage and steal,
There is nothing to fear,
They only do it to keep the dragon away.

JUST A LISP OF A THING

Crystal Grant

NEVER PARTNER WITH a chipmunk.

My father's cryptic statement drifted back to me. I understood now. Not only were they hard to understand, but they were impossible to work with.

I pushed my sunglasses on top of my head and glared up into the trees after my furry accomplice. "Kethie, would you get down here?"

Her high-pitched chatter echoed in my mind. "*Juth a moment! I'm checking the p'wimeter.*"

"You mean perimeter?"

"*That'th what I thaid.*"

I squeezed my temples and sighed. This was my own fault. I'd spent the majority of my young adult life playing around, pulling pranks, and making people laugh. Or really annoyed at me. I was too busy not taking life seriously to be taken seriously myself. Until adulthood finally caught up to me, and I wasn't ready for it.

My family had long been animal whisperers, though most had the sense to partner with creatures of size or ferocity. Together they patrolled the streets and surrounding woods, guarding our busy, suburburn town from trespassers. By the time my turn came, no one believed I had what it took. And they were right. I couldn't get a single animal to even partner with me. I should've admitted it then and there and asked for help.

But instead, I let my pride get the better of me and dared my brothers to select my partner. Because, after all, I could work with anything. When they paired me with a chipmunk, it was too late to back down. The joke was on me this time. Now I was stuck guarding the eastern edge of town with a very excitable, very *tiny* sidekick.

The sound of tiny claws scratching across bark fell on my ears. "Are you done fooling around?"

Kethie darted down the tree and circled my feet, chirping loudly. *"It'th coming! We'th gonna catch it!"*

Even as her words registered in my mind, I shushed her. "Quit making so much noise, or you're going to end up its prey."

She spun to a stop and twitched her nose at me. "*Oh no. A panther will never catch a chipmunk. Never, no, no! We're their gweateth enemy*!"

"Sure." I could just see it. A massive black panther run out of town by a tiny rodent.

"*He'th coming thith way*!"

I jerked at the mental warning. "Why didn't you tell me that before?" I ducked behind a tree just as a branch snapped in the woods ahead. The sound of soft, heavy feet approached.

She squeaked and disappeared up the same tree I hid behind. *"You didn't athk."*

I gripped my automatic rifle, making sure it was set on stun. If at all possible, I'd talk the big cat down and convince him to leave. If he didn't comply, I'd take stronger measures.

"*He'th coming*!"

The brush parted, and a huge, black feline appeared, his eyes yellow and piercing.

I took a quick breath and stepped out, my rifle held loosely in my hands. "Stop right there, stranger."

The panther halted and cocked his head. *"What is the meaning of this?"*

"You're trespassing. Go back to your territory."

He sat primly on his haunches. "*How insulting that I should be greeted in such a fashion by one of your two-legged kind*."

I blinked at the haughty tone. Was this cat talking down to me? "Listen, I don't want any trouble. Just go back to your own domain."

One side of his lips lifted in a snarl, exposing bone-white fangs. He stood and paced back and forth in front of me. *"Who are you to order me around like a common house cat?"*

Yep. He was definitely talking down to me. My fingers tightened around my gun. "I'm the town guardsman. If you don't leave, I'll have no choice but to use force."

A rumble sounded deep in his chest. He was laughing at me. "*I've heard of the young whisperer who likes to play. The one who couldn't even get a partner.*"

Tension crawled down my back. Somehow I knew I was not going to talk this big guy down.

He turned and faced me, his muscles coiling. "*And don't think that stun gun is going to be enough to stop me.*"

My fingers itched to change the setting on my rifle, but if I moved, he would be on top of me in an instant.

Just then, acorns pelted the panther's head from above. *"Take that, you big puthy cat!"*

What was that idiot chipmunk doing?

The panther shook his head, growled, and shifted to pounce. I raised my gun, but before I could shoot, a little brown blur whizzed past me.

My heart jolted in my chest. "Kethie, no!" Visions of the panther's fangs piercing her little body flew through my mind. This was my fault!

But despite my cry, Kethie slid to a stop before the panther; her tiny paws stretched out in front of her. "*Thtand back, you fiend, or there will be dire conthequentheth!*"

If the moment had not been so grim, I would've rolled my eyes at the pitiful display of valor and the squeaky threat. "Kethie, get back before he swallows you whole!"

But the panther stared down at Kethie with wide eyes and backtracked, stumbling over his own feet. *"Oh, the horror!"*

Kethie took another step forward. *"You shall not path!"*

The cat shook his head, trembling. "*Do not come any closer. Please!*"

I stared, my gun forgotten. "What?"

"*Don't let it speak*!" The panther retreated another few hasty steps. "*I did not know there were any more of this species in the land. They speak with devilry*!"

"*That'th wight, we do*!"

"You're scared of a *chipmunk*?"

"*Don't act thurprithed.*"

"Ach!" The panther collapsed and covered his ears. *"The tongue of sorcery!"*

I gaped at him. "Are you talking about her lisp?"

Kethie cocked her head. *"What lithp?"*

The panther let out a shriek. "*All right, I'll go! Just keep that . . . thing back.*"

My brows shot up to my hairline. This big guy was terrified of Kethie's lisp? I scratched my head, but there was no point in missing the opportunity. "You promise to never return?"

"Yes, yes!" He pushed himself up, still gaping at Kethie. She watched him intently, her black nose twitching. He trotted a few steps, then cast an apprehensive glance over his shoulder.

"*Do not thop, or I, Kethie, shall give chathe.*"

"NOOO!" With that, the panther bolted.

I stood rooted to the spot. Never, in all my wildest expectations or craziest dreams, could I ever have imagined what I'd just witnessed.

Kethie twittered and ran in circles, tail up in the air. *"We did it!"*

I let out a weak chuckle. "I didn't do a darn thing." Nothing like a chipmunk to keep one humble. My legs felt as solid and stable as forest vines, and I wiped sweat from my brow with a shaking hand.

She blinked up at me with big, dark eyes. *"You faced him vewy bwavewy."*

"You mean bravely?"

"*That'th what I thaid.*"

I stared down at her, feeling smaller than her six inches. This panther had not taken me seriously, which could have gotten both me and Kethie killed. Other animals had refused to partner with me for the same reason. My own reputation had put us in danger. But for whatever reason, Kethie had not only accepted the request but put herself in harm's way to save my life. For a chipmunk, she wasn't so bad. Even with the lisp. "Well, Kethie. Let's go back and tell everyone about our grand adventure."

"*Yeth, yeth! Leth do that*!"

I turned to head back home when a realization stopped me in my tracks. "Wait a minute. Your name's not even Kethie, is it? It's Kessie!"

"*Of courthe. That'th what I thaid.*"

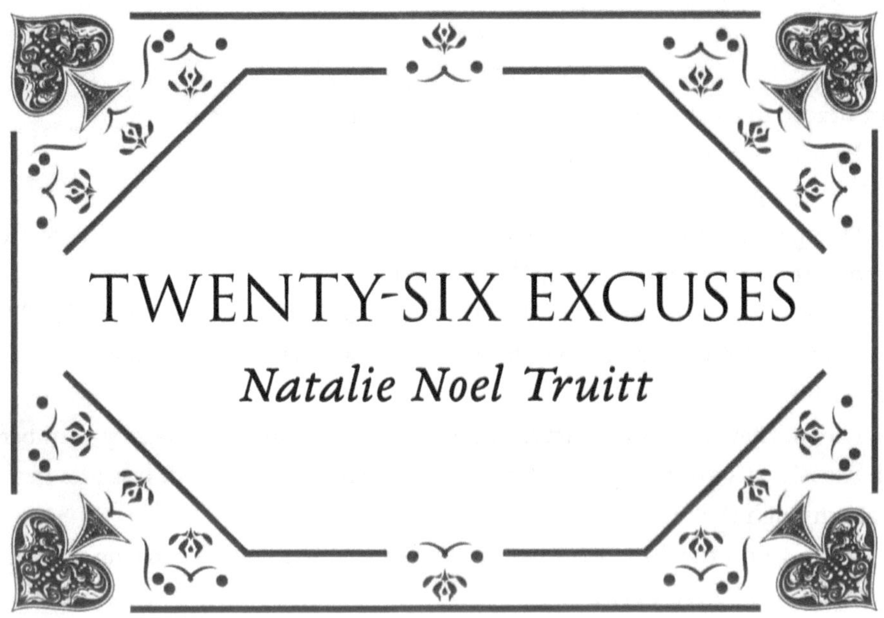

TWENTY-SIX EXCUSES

Natalie Noel Truitt

IT ALL BEGAN with a bet. Matt had recently been dumped, so his best friend, Dylan, conjured a little game to lift his spirits—who could get the most dates in one week. The loser had to do the winner's laundry for the next month, so, being a college student, Matt was determined to win. Everything had been going perfectly.

Until every single one of Matt's dates were scheduled for that Saturday.

And Matt had twenty-five dates.

"So, you never said I actually had to go *on* the dates to win. I just had to *get* the dates." Matt rolled a Magic 8 Excuse Ball in his hands. He and Dylan stood in the toy section of the dollar store that Friday evening.

Dylan rummaged through a bin and pulled out a plastic blue bat. "I guess that's right. What are you going to do? Cancel on twenty-five girls last minute? They're going to beat you up." He waved the baseball bat.

Chuckling, Matt glanced down at the Excuse Ball. "How about this? A new bet. If I use this Excuse Ball to cancel on all my dates, then you still do my laundry."

Dylan tucked the bat under his chin in thought. "Tempting offer. Let's make it even better. You can't skip a single excuse or you lose. And you have to call, not text."

Matt ran his thumb over the ball and nodded slowly. "Deal."

"These girls are going to send you to the hospital."

Matt headed to their dorm, Dylan following, baseball bat in hand.

"You know," Matt said, "you don't have to be here for this."

"I'm not going to miss out."

They got back to their dorm to find that it was already unlocked. "You've really got to start locking the door, man," Matt groaned.

"My bad." Dylan shrugged. "Wouldn't want to get all of our ramen stolen."

Matt entered the messy room, sat at his desk, and pulled out his phone. "Here goes nothing."

The first few excuses were actually pretty decent. Headache. A family member is in the ER. His great aunt died. Studying. Broken leg. Killer cold. Just like that, he was through the first six girls on his list.

Dylan sat on the floor, working on homework, occasionally looking up with an amused smirk on his face.

Next on his list was Annika, a beautiful girl he'd love to go out with on any other weekend. He debated just rescheduling.

She answered on the second ring. "Hey, Matt!"

"Hey, beautiful. How's it going?" he asked, leaning back in his desk chair.

"Pretty good. How are you?"

Matt smiled and leaned back further. The chair tipped and he grabbed the edge of his desk, steadying himself. His heart pounded in his chest. Dylan laughed from across the room, and Matt ignored him. "Uh, I'm good."

"That's good to hear," Annika said. "So, why are you calling? Any particular reason?"

"Well, actually, it's about our date tomorrow." Matt took a deep breath.

"Are you as excited as I am?"

"Well, actually." Matt cleared his throat. "I'm going to have to reschedule."

"Reschedule? How come?"

Matt gave the Excuse Ball a shake. He raised an eyebrow when he saw the results. "I'm actually too drunk to come." Realizing how lame that sounded, he added, "Uh . . . sorry."

He glanced at Dylan, whose face was red from laughing, and threw a pillow at him.

"You're . . . too drunk to come on our date *tomorrow*?" Annika's skepticism bled into her voice.

"Yeah," he said. "Rough week."

"You're a jerk."

"So . . . can you reschedule for next week?"

She hung up, leaving Matt to deal with a hysterically laughing Dylan.

"You *are* a jerk," Dylan teased, throwing the pillow back.

Matt lobbed it back at him. "Shut up."

He looked down at the ball. Why did it have to pick that exact moment to betray him? But he was committed to winning, especially with Dylan sitting there cracking up.

For excuse number eight, he had to tell the hottest girl on campus that he cut himself shaving and was now too ugly to leave his dorm. Next, it was that he had to bake cookies with his grandma. That one got him an *awwww*. The ball then said that he had a cat sitting on his lap, and he couldn't disturb it by getting up . . . for a whole day, apparently. Two more excuses and he was already through the first half.

Matt moved from the desk and hopped onto his bed, shoulders tense. The Beatles and Dylan's laughter played as background music. He looked at his stack of textbooks he had abandoned and thought about the test coming up on Monday. But he couldn't lose this bet. "I'm going to fail this test because of you."

"But think of how much extra time you'll have to study without needing to do your laundry." Dylan smirked.

Matt looked back at his phone, his determination growing. He wasn't going to let Dylan win this one.

He called the girl on the volleyball team, Heather.

The phone rang several times. He almost thought she wasn't going to answer, but then she did.

"Hello?" Heather said.

"Hey," he responded, now laying down on his bed, feet propped against the wall. "So, I'm going to have to cancel on Saturday."

"Oh, that's fine," she said. "Did something come up?"

"Yeah." He shook the ball, and his face immediately went red. This was a bit much, even for him . . . . He glanced at Dylan. But he made a deal. "I have to poop . . . a lot."

Dylan buried his face in the pillow to muffle the sound of his chuckles.

"Oh." Heather went quiet.

"Yeah."

"I didn't need to know that." She cleared her throat.

It was quiet for another long, drawn out moment.

Heather finally said, "Well . . . feel better, I guess."

"Yeah, thanks . . . ." Matt hung up.

"That one was bad," Dylan said as he tried to catch his breath.

Matt glared at him. "Yeah."

Dylan smirked then shook his head. "I'm going to run down to the cafeteria."

"I'll go with you," Matt said.

"I'll grab you something," Dylan offered. "You'd better keep on making calls if you're going to get through them all by midnight. I'll try to make it something that won't be too hard on your stomach so you can stay off the toilet."

He left, his laughter echoing down the hall.

As obnoxious as Dylan was, Matt knew that he was right—so he continued to make calls.

Pot brownies. He had to take his plant for a walk. His cat really missed him. And then he had to tell a girl that he was *literally* stuck to his chair and she almost called the fire department to rescue him.

Twenty minutes later, Dylan came back with two styrofoam containers from the cafeteria.

"So, what was your best excuse while I was gone?" Dylan asked, handing Matt his box and then plopping down on the floor. "Anything top your 'too many poops'?"

Matt looked at the food. Tacos. "I don't know about the best one, but this thing is kind of obsessed with cats."

"You give up yet?" Dylan asked, then took a bite.

"Hey, I've got to be committed to something."

"Maybe make it a girl next time instead of something you picked up at the dollar store," Dylan suggested.

"At least I can get a date," Matt said. "Twenty-five of them for one night, to be exact."

After he ate his tacos, he called Jessica Reynolds, a girl on the basketball team.

"Hello?"

"Hey, Jess."

"Hey," she said. "What's up?"

"So, funny story . . ." An excuse generated and he cleared his throat. "I'm grounded."

"Uh . . . don't you live on campus?" Jess asked.

"Yeah, about that. My parents are really strict." He paused and rubbed his temples, glancing at Dylan.

"Seriously?" she said slowly. "You can't just sneak out?"

There was no way she would fall for this.

"They track my phone and everything."

"They're seriously going to be suspicious if you get dinner two miles off of campus?" she asked, voice raising.

"Jessica, I know, it sucks. But they will. And they're probably tracking this phone call, so I probably should go. I'll talk to you later."

"Okay. Fine. Whatever."

Matt stared up at the ceiling and took some deep breaths.

After the next four excuses, he was convinced that the ball was out to get him. He had to tell someone there was a raccoon in his dorm, while Dylan pretended to fight it off. Then, he had to say he had a sneaking suspicion that the world was about to end. The next excuse—there was an earthquake—might have worked if they didn't both live on the same campus. And finally, he had to tell one of the girls that he was going to be up all night shampooing his cat.

Matt ran a hand through his hair and then pinched the bridge of his nose, trying to ward off a headache.

"What's up?" Dylan asked.

"Dude, I can't do it." Matt slinked off of his bed and crumbled onto the floor. "The excuses are getting out of control."

"Let's up the stakes then. We'll add in twenty bucks."

Matt paused, thinking about how many boxes of ramen that would buy him. He could get his money back for the stupid ball and then some, too.

Matt took a deep breath. "All right."

He looked over the list of the last five remaining phone calls. He was kind of impressed that he had a list in the first place. Second semester of sophomore year had made him so organized. His parents would be proud.

He dialed Victoria's number, and to his dismay, she answered on the second ring. She was a gymnast, and he did not want to call off a date with a *gymnast*.

"Hello?"

Imagining those legs almost made him turn back.

But no, he was committed to this bet and nothing else.

"Hey, Victoria, so, unfortunately, I'm going to have to cancel."

"Oh." She sighed. "How come?"

He gave the Magic 8 Excuse Ball a shake, and his eyes bulged. Oh, *heck* no. He was not saying this. There was no way.

Matt pressed mute and said to Dylan, "I need another roll."

"No way," Dylan said. "If you don't say it, the bet is off."

Matt groaned and looked at the ball.

"It can't be that bad." Dylan snatched the ball from him. "Oh, this is way worse than I expected."

"Matt?" Victoria said.

Matt glared at Dylan. "*Quiet.*"

Dylan managed to collect himself, looking like he would burst at any moment.

Matt took a deep breath and then unmuted, bringing it back up to his ear. "I'm on my period."

"You're on your *what*?"

Matt felt heat rush to his face. "Yeah, I'm on my period." He cleared his throat, trying to muster some confidence from who knows where. Because where was he going to be able to find even an ounce of confidence after a proclamation like *that*? He didn't need this spread around the school.

"I don't think I'm hearing you right, Matt. You're on your *what*?"

"You're seriously going to make me say it again?" Matt's voice cracked at the end. "I'm on my *period,* Vic."

And then he hung up.

Dylan said, "These are getting worse."

Matt shot him a glare.

His face flushed and his heart hammered in his chest. Was this what it felt like to die? But he had to press on, despite Dylan's incessant snickering.

He took a few minutes to recover, scrolling through apps on his phone, but he couldn't stop thinking about how this was going to end up all over campus.

"Giving up?" Dylan asked.

Matt shook his head and called a girl named Cassidy this time.

She answered.

"Hi." His voice came out in a rush. "I need to cancel our date."

"You do?" she asked. "This better be good if you're canceling last minute."

"It is." He gave the Magic 8 Excuse Ball a shake, and his stomach filled with dread as he saw its answer. "I have to walk my cat."

"You're a terrible person."

"I'm sorry," he said.

He was met with silence.

The thing was, Matt had started to *feel* like a terrible person. Ironic. He was pretty sure his reputation was ruined. He could just see girls sitting in their dorms or coffee shops talking about the jerk who canceled on them last minute with some weird excuse. What if he had to change schools?

Excuses for twenty-three and twenty-four had to do with cats. Why was this thing so obsessed with cats? *My cat fell asleep on my lap! My cat is making me dinner and will be disappointed if I don't join.*

But it was almost over now. One last call and he would be done. Done with these dumb calls and these stupid, cat-obsessed excuses. He was almost there.

He laid back in his bed and looked at the last phone number, and dialed.

"I'm going to have to cancel." He looked at the little blue screen on the ball. "I'm . . ." He took a deep breath. Was this really worth twenty bucks?

"You're . . . what?" she asked.

"Dead," he said with a tone of finality.

"You're . . . dead?"

"Yeah, and unfortunately ghosts can only use the phone for a couple of seconds so . . . got to go."

He hung up, feeling like the ball was going to drop at any minute. There was no way any of this could end well.

The next day, Matt tried to move on from his disastrous phone calls and forget they ever happened. He sat through his classes, looking forward to the rest of the weekend. Who thought Saturday classes were a good idea in the first place?

When he got out of class, he headed back to his dorm, but when he tried to unlock the door, it was already cracked open.

He didn't think much of it, assuming his roommate had left it open again. He stepped into his dorm and froze, face-to-face with all twenty-five women that he canceled on. *Oh no.*

Annika looked at him, arms crossed. "Still drunk?"

"Yeah, where's the cat?" another girl asked.

"I brought you some tampons," Victoria said, tossing them on his bed.

"And some Pepto Bismol," Heather seethed.

Jess glared at him. "What's your excuse this time?"

Matt slowly reached for his backpack, dug the Magic 8 Excuse Ball out and shook it. At this point, it couldn't get much worse. "My wife said I can't go out tonight."

I ONLY
WANTED
TO IMPRESS
THE GIRL.

HONOR OF A FOOL

AJ Skelly

I only wanted to impress the girl.
To make a grand gesture,
To give it a whirl.

Girls love flowers
And it was time for the dance
Here was my chance
Only a fool cowers

I picked them with care
All colors of the rainbow
One of each to be fair.

The day approached
And I lost my nerve.
Gutless, I shoved the flowers and took a swerve
I remained anonymous, silently reproached.

I watched from afar
As she opened her locker
Her mouth hung ajar.

Shock written all over her face
She coughed, she wheezed
She was not pleased.
My gesture, I wanted to erase

She screeched, still wheezing
Her nose started swelling,
Primed and ready for sneezing

Jumping into the fray
I grabbed the slightly used tissue
From my pocket to solve the issue
Shaking, I thrust it towards her. "Hey."

"My hero!" she declared.
And ferociously blew her nose
With the tissue I'd prepared.

Cringing as her snot mixed with mine
She lamented her mottled state.
"I'll never get a date!"
"Come to the dance with me, you're *fine*."

The words escaped without any warning
Her face brightened
Saving my morning

"Yes, I'll go with you.
Definitely not with the jerk
Who put flowers here to lurk.
I'm allergic to all but a few."

Speechless, I smiled like a fool
Blood freezing inside
Knowing I was an utter tool.

So here I am at the dance
With the girl of my dreams.
Her nose four times too big it seems
But finally, this is my chance.

My honor in tatters
I've still got the girl.
Is that all that matters?

She hates the one who left her the gift.
Her guy would never
Her good health sever.
It would cause such a rift.

She thinks I am so cool
That my honor cannot be questioned.
Pity, it's only the honor of a fool.

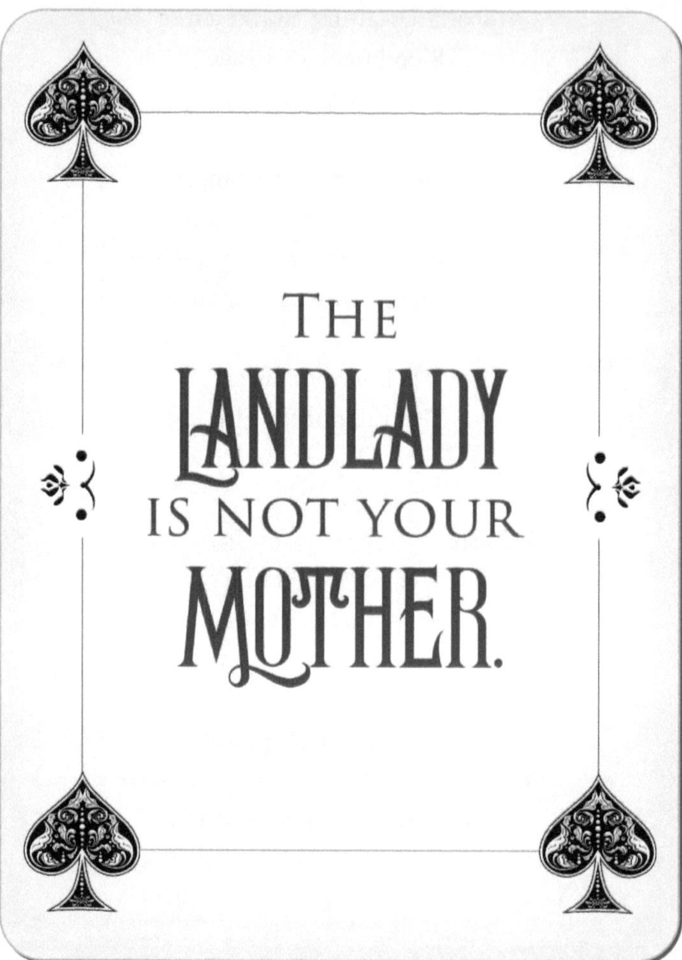
THE
LANDLADY
IS NOT YOUR
MOTHER.

LEASE AGREEMENT

Lara E. Madden and Anne J. Hill

THE RULES UNDERWRITTEN apply to a single-month rental of a room at 528 Fair Way, Nowhere, Florida 12345, forthwith referred to as "the property," and will be reviewed on a month-to-month basis. Violations of this lease may result in immediate eviction at the discretion of the Landlady.

1. Rent is due on the first of the month and includes utilities, renters insurance, fire insurance, and fees for the use of the basement gym (see #3 below). The Landlady understands that times are difficult but cannot extend the grace period for rent longer than 15 days. "Free Performance Tickets" will not be considered as rent replacement or as payment for debts owed.

2. Absolutely no large or exotic pets will be allowed to reside on the property. This includes but is not limited to horses, zebras, cobras, tigers, tarantulas, birds of prey, or primates of any kind. *Domestic breeds* of cats and small, well-trained dogs will be considered on a case-by-case basis.

3. For an extra monthly fee, the basement gym is available for use. The steel support beams and high ceilings are safe for up to an additional 5,000 lbs load-bearing capacity and may be used to install various apparatuses. However, all ropes, slings, hooks, hoops, crash mats, etc., must be cleared away by the final day of the lease. The Landlady is not your mother. If she has to clean up after you, she will keep both your equipment and your deposit.

4. The Landlady takes no personal or legal responsibility for any injuries sustained by renters or their visitors on the property. The Tenant agrees that no legal action will be taken against the Landlady for any accident resulting in injury that may occur on the property. This includes any degree of burns, knife injuries, paralysis, broken bones, fall injuries, death, or dismemberment.

5. If an accident does occur, blood or other stains on the floor, walls, or ceiling must be cleaned immediately. Irremovable stains, holes in the walls, or other damage created by the renter's equipment will result in loss of deposit as well as repair fees.

6. If any stunts lead to death, surviving Tenants are absolutely prohibited from disposing of the body on the property. The authorities must be notified, and the Landlady will not be held responsible for Tenants' failures. Any fines or fees must be paid by the responsible party, be it a surviving Tenant or the estate of the deceased.

7. There are strict quiet hours between 10 p.m. and 6 a.m. This is generous, so do not take advantage. If the neighbors call the authorities due to loud noises, explosions, blaring music, or roof jumping, the Tenant is responsible for any repercussions, not the Landlady.

8. Roof access is safe and permitted for sitting, walking, eating, or casually socializing. Sword fighting, weaponry, dance performances, parkour, and the use of fire or explosives are strictly prohibited on the roof. All Tenants and their guests must use the stairs to and from the roof to access this space. Any other entry or exit will result in loss of roof access privileges.

9. There will be *no* roof jumping, defined as jumping from one roof to the next. Tenants are only permitted on the property's roof and not on neighboring roofs. Neighbors *will* call the cops.

10. Tenants are permitted to use the backyard for fires, pyrotechnics, and/or explosives. However, flammable fuels must be kept locked safely in the storage container provided, and a hose and extinguisher must be available and accessible at all times. If any part of the property is burned down or damaged, the offending party will have arson privileges immediately and permanently revoked and pay for damages.

11. Crash mats, throwing knives, archery equipment, etc., may only be used outdoors. Large semi-permanent apparatuses which do not fit in the basement space may be set up in the back yard as long as this does not interfere with another Tenant's use of the space. Any disputes between Tenants will be settled with a competition, as judged by the Landlady.

12. Tenants are permitted to have guests and visitors, but any vagabonds, nomads, or self-proclaimed starving artists who stay longer than one week must be added to the lease and contribute rent payments.

13. The trash must be taken out every Tuesday before 8 am. This is the responsibility of the Tenants, as well as keeping common-use areas of the property clean and free of any potentially hazardous elements. Dishes must be cleaned and put away after use, and any laundry that's hung outside to dry must be hung on the line provided, *not on the highwire rig.*

14. The opinions and instructions of managers, trainers, and/or ringmasters do not and never will trump the rules of the Landlady while living on the property. DO NOT disobey the Landlady! This may be a house for circus performers, but it is not a circus.

The undersigned parties agree to all rules and regulations of the month-to-month rental of a single room at the Big Top Guest House, 528 Fair Way.

Landlady: *Anne J. Hill* Date: 4/1/22

Tenant(s): *Lara E. Madden* Date: 4/1/22

SOME SOULS ARE
TAINTED
BEFORE THEY

LAIR OF THE LEPRECHAUN

Emily Barnett

IT TOOK ROY Bivens forty-two days to find the end of the rainbow. He rode through the red ribbon forest, yelled at some yellow-bellied yaks, and scaled the indigo icebergs. Finally, Roy evaded a pack of violent violet velociraptors that everyone assumed to be extinct. Breathless, sore, and hungry, he found the end in a dank cave. But after all Roy had been through, he no longer feared the unknown.

Dragging himself inside, he found a crooked old woman with mold-green skin that barely reached the height of his waist. "So, ye found the Lair of the Leprechaun. I'm the Keeper of thee Gold." Her lips and words were cracked with age and disuse.

"Aye," he said, sniffing at the leprechaun. He had assumed their kind was jolly and ornery, not a heap of rags and bones. A shiver trailed his spine. "I'm here for my gold." He tipped up his chin arrogantly. He'd come on a promise that if he found the end of the bow, the leprechaun's hoard would become his.

The woman smiled. "Are ye certain thee desire's gold? It's been said to taint souls."

Roy snorted.

The leprechaun cocked her head, greasy black hair hanging limp. "But some souls are tainted before they arrive." She shifted, looking deeper into the cave. Roy followed her gaze to a towering pile of shining gold that had been hidden moments before. His breath caught. It was marvelous! He took a step forward, and the woman's hand slithered out to grasp his wrist.

"Make thee vow, Roy G. Bivens, before ye touch a single coin." Her touch was ice, but the gold gleamed warm.

He nodded, dragging out the page he'd stolen from the forbidden archives. His hand shook as he read the words that would give him all he desired. "I vow to always be the keeper of the coin."

Wind tore through the cave as pain tore through Roy. When he stopped screaming, he looked at his gnarled hands. They were mold green. And he had shrunk at least three feet.

"Did I forget to mention?" a beautiful woman said from the entrance of the cave. "You might be the gold's keeper, but the gold keeps you as well." She winked. "But thanks for setting me free."

The woman slipped away, leaving behind an old leprechaun sitting on his hoard of gold at the end of a rainbow.

MUSE

Anne J. Hill

"Oh, sweet muse, hear my cry
Grant me inspirations this day
This book desperately needs done
So, lead me on my way."

Though the writer knew not
That he was actually quite near
And the kind muse she spoke to
Had freckled skin and pointy ears

On her shoulder he sat
Muse, rather proud of himself
She was his author
And he was her elf

He patted her head
And whispered in her ear
All the wonderful ideas
She needed to hear

You see, Muse was picked
Just for her by his kind
One elf for one year
With a writer in mind

So proudly he sat
Watching her type away
And the joy in her eyes
Made his tiny heart sway

Little Muse grew content
His eyes drifting closed
And atop her shoulder there
He started to doze

When he finally awoke, he saw
She'd closed her writing docs
And on the couch now she lay
Watching the magical box

But worst of all were the trolls
Dancing on her head with delight
Muse curtly pulled his bow
And marched toward the sorry sight

He lifted arrow to string
"Who are you?" he begged
"Leave her alone, or
To the dogs you'll be fed."

"I am Net," said one troll
As he laughed and sneered
"And I am Flix,"
The other one jeered

Muse shook his head in fury
"She needs real rest!
Don't you see the way
You both are making her stressed?"

"The magical box is rest,"
Flix said in fiendish wile
"Might even give an idea,"
Net sang with mischief in his smile

Muse had enough of that
And rang his arrow true
A warning shot indeed
It zipped between the two

"Yes, it can be rest
But not the kind she needs
At the moment, at least
And not with your crazy deeds."

The Fairies of Rest
Through the window they flew
With wonder and grace
As if summoned on cue

"Ah, at last! Save our author,"
Muse pled on his knees
The fairies scooped up those trolls
Tossing them to the trees

The little elf sighed
As his author stood to leave
And out the door she went
On a walk in the breeze

The fairies fluttered after
Helping her truly rest
Giving her mind a break
From epic tales and quests

Content again, Muse sat
Perched upon her shoulder top
Preparing for his next task
Collecting inspiration and thought

The trolls would soon come back
But for then, they stayed away
Bothering another helpless author
Until their return the following day

And every morning, Muse scolded
And fought with them all
Until the author's mind was taken
And someone would withdraw

Sometimes Muse rose victorious
The words written with determination
Or the Fairies of Rest did their best
To refocus her attention

Sometimes though, the trolls prevailed
And then nothing got done
No real rest to be had
And all songs left unsung

But everyday, Muse stood fast
Against the trolls, Net and Flix
And magical boxes of different sizes
Nothing was too hard for him to fix

THE HOAX OF HADES

Anna Augustine

THE SOULS OF the damned moan in agony as I flop onto my throne, rubbing at my throbbing temples. One of my slaves stumbles forward with a tray of my favorite fruit. I glance at the pomegranate then flick my hand. It holds no interest to me.

"Will someone stop that infernal wailing?" I demand, slamming my fist against the armrest of my throne. "Gods! You'd think this is Hell or something."

"It—it is, Lord Hades," whispers the slave, eyes sunken into his narrow face.

"Right." I draw the word out and smile, my teeth gleaming in the blue glow all around the throne room. The vaulted ceiling carries the echo of my eternal slaves, those destined to endure unending torment. A few, like the slave at my side, have a lesser sentencing, but all men fall to me in the end. It is only a matter of time. Some worship my 'all-powerful' brothers in life—the gods of the sky and sea—but I truly am the one to fear. There is no escaping death.

"Lord Hades, I can try and get them to stop." The slave's voice quivers, his throat bobbing.

"No, it would be pointless." I grin again at the agony they suffer before the smile falls into a scowl once more. "How I wish Persephone were here. She at least makes Hell brighter."

My wife is off visiting her mother. Demeter is unbearable on the best of days, all sunshine and roses. While my wife has a bit of that light, she has her rage and temper too. But nothing in all Olympus nor Hell could persuade me to visit Demeter. I'd rather be stabbed in the eye a million times over.

A guard pokes his head through the door. "A messenger for you, Lord Hades."

I straighten on my throne, gesturing to the guard. "Show him in!"

The large ebony doors grate open, and in strides Hermes.

At the sight of him, I slouch back on my throne, resting my chin in my hand. "Good gods, what have you done now?"

Hermes heaves his eyes upwards. "Good to see you too, Uncle Hades."

He wears the archaic toga that many of my fellow gods wear. I prefer the suits and styles that currently fill Earth and make a show of unbuttoning my jacket so I can sink back further on my throne, steepling my fingers.

"You never bring me good news, Hermes. Spill it. What mess must I clean up this time?"

My nephew sighs. "Fine. Eros did something."

"Eros?" I raise a brow. "That bumbling idiot cut himself with his own arrow. How much trouble could he possibly get into?"

My nephew laughs nervously, clenching and unclenching the sash on his toga.

"Hermes . . ." I draw out his name, feeling my temper shorten with every second he doesn't share his news. "Tell me your message. This millennia, please."

"Well, I may have accidentally saved someone."

"You . . . what?" I launch to my feet. "Do you know what that can do to the balance of reality?"

"Yeah, yeah, I do. And that's why I thought it would be a good idea to kill them myself."

The headache comes back in full force, and I rub at my temples. "And?"

"I may have grabbed Eros' bow instead of Apollo's." He laughs again. "Kind of a funny mistake, huh?"

I glare, and he snaps his mouth closed.

"So, what's the problem?" I ask.

"Well, this man is now madly in love with this beautiful young lady who also loves him and I . . . I just can't bring myself to kill him."

"You meddling little—" I suck in a sharp breath and grab my scepter. "Then I'll have to do it."

"Uncle, it's not that simple!"

"Then tell me what the problem is, Hermes, or I swear on the sky and the sea I will—"

"Okay! Okay, yeesh. So after I used the wrong bow and made a giant mess of things, Aphrodite butted her nose in." His face twists with disgust. "She placed a protection over them. None of us can directly touch them, or we will be cursed forever!"

"I am the god of the underworld! If that man was marked for death, then none of you—not Eros, Aphrodite, nor you—should have *dared* to interfere." I step closer to my nephew, and he flinches.

"Sorry, Uncle."

"'*Sorry, Uncle*' doesn't fix this," I say. "Do your parents know about this?"

He gulps. "No. Mother would be enraged."

"Your father won't be happy either, because I'm going to see him."

"You can't!" Hermes whines.

"Oh, yes, I can, and I will. And I may just require your . . . methods later." I roll my eyes at the word. Tricks were more like it. "Come along, nephew of mine."

Hermes continues to whine as we make our way down the river and up the winding path to the top of Mount Olympus. He tries to make a deal with me, and when his persuasion falls, he tries to make a run for it. My grip on the back of his toga prevents this. Growing up with Zeus as a brother had its perks—I knew how to out-trick his trickster son.

We reach the temple in short order. Hermes has slipped into silence—thank the gods—and I drag him up the twelve marble steps and past the pearl columns into the throne room. Zeus sits on his throne, spinning his lightning bolts around his wrists. Hera watches him with her adoring doe-eyes. Why she is still attracted to my philandering brother is beyond me. It's not like us gods are the model of fidelity or anything, but you'd think with her jealousy, she'd go for someone who could stay out of other women's beds.

"This one yours?" I ask, shoving Hermes toward the twelve thrones. Besides the ones Hera and Zeus are perched on, only one other throne is occupied. Aphrodite is busy brushing her hair, humming under her breath, and she pays little attention to Hermes and me. The little vixen looks far too innocent to me.

"You know very well he is." Zeus glares at me. "What is the meaning of this, Hades?"

"Your little prat may have just ruined the reality of all mankind."

Zeus shrugs. "How does this affect me?"

I growl. Zeus cares little for mankind. All he worries about is food, lust, and war. Quite possibly in that order.

"Brother, he has denied me one of my own. If I do not kill the mortal—" I let the threat hang.

"Then what?" Zeus looks thoroughly puzzled.

I rub at my temples in frustration. "Did you forget everything Father Cronus taught us?"

"We've been gods for millennia, Hades. What do I care about a few ancient rules?" Zeus flicks his hand in dismissal. His eyes keep flicking to Aphrodite, but the goddess is too enthralled with her looking glass.

"We have to fix this!" I resist the urge to stomp my foot. I'm a god, not a toddler. Although, the ones sitting across from me tend to act like children most of the time.

Hermes scrambles to his feet, and his eyes flick between his father and me. "Father, you can fix it, right?"

"I am the god of the living, not the dead."

"He's not dead yet," I say through gritted teeth. "He was marked, but your little Soul of the Dead henchman went and screwed him up, so now he *can't* die. And you!" I jab a finger at Aphrodite, who presses a hand to her chest, eyes wide. "You went and put a spell on him. *A spell*. Knowing good and well that he's supposed to be *dead*!" I'm screaming now, not caring what the others may think of me.

"So?" Aphrodite shrugs one of her perfectly tanned shoulders. "He's madly, completely in love with the woman he's married to. He doesn't deserve to die."

I pound my fists against my temples now. "No, no, no, no, *no*! That's not how this god thing works! If he is supposed to be dead, then he needs to die. Only now I can't touch him."

Aphrodite shrugs and goes back to looking in the mirror.

"Sweet Chaos," I mutter, "this cannot get worse, can it?"

The door swooshes open, and Poseidon glides into the room, glaring at me as he slinks to his throne. "Demeter is here to see you, Zeus."

"Oh, gods, what does she want?" I groan, turning and striding to one of the many windows along the left side of the hall. All you can see is blue sky and clouds. It's boring. Hell is much more interesting, with the River of Souls, decaying bodies, and the blue fire that torments my subjects.

Hermes slips up to stand beside me, and I shoot him a withering glare. "I blame you for this, just so we're clear."

He grins and opens his mouth to reply, but the door banging against the wall interrupts him.

Demeter comes striding in. "What's happened to the human realm?"

"What?" My brother growls, throwing his hands up in exasperation. "Why is everyone so worried about that stupid realm all of a sudden?"

"Is someone else worried?" Demeter arches her slim brow, eyes glancing around the throne room. When they land on me, they lower. "Is this your fault, Hades?"

"Contrary to popular belief, not everything is my fault, Demeter." I clasp my hands behind my back to keep myself from strangling her. "No, this is Hermes' fault."

Poseidon snorts. "Honestly, Hermes, you cause more problems than there are fish in the sea."

"Trouble follows me around." Our nephew throws his hands up in the air. "I can't help it."

"No, you can." I wave my finger in his nose. "You just like wreaking havoc on everything and everyone."

Hermes huffs a breath, waving the light brown hair off his forehead. "Fine, maybe I could work on it. But Father's the one who made me the god of tricks and thieves. I can't help *that*."

Yes, such a stellar job to bestow on your child, brother.

With a sigh, I cross my arms and turn to my mother-in-law. "So, what's wrong with the humans?"

"Nothing with them, per se." She sniffs, as if addressing me is beneath her. "But the flowers are singing a song of death."

I turn to Poseidon and Zeus. "Does this not make you think that—just perhaps mind you—that I may be right? This man that Hermes messed with is destined to die. Keeping the human alive is affecting the balance of the universe."

"The dead are your business. Fix it." Hera sniffs. "Why should we meddle with your affairs?"

"*Because you already did!*" My hands need to smash something, so I turn and pound them against one of the pearl columns that line the throne room. It shakes the whole of Olympus, and my scream shakes the crystal chandler. "You're being foolish, Zeus. But that is nothing new. You've always been an arrogant, insufferable brute! But just remember this: it may be my problem now, but if I can't fix it, do recall that I came to you first."

I send a withering glare over them. Aphrodite looks far too smug as I stride out of the hall, dragging Hermes with me.

He's whining again. "Why do I have to come? Like Father said, you're the god of the dead."

"And you're the Bearer of Souls. Therefore, you have to be with me to bear this one. That, and the fact that you're the one who screwed this all up in the first place. If anyone touches the man, they go—" I wave my pointer finger by my temple. "—and you're already halfway there, so it won't be a problem for you to deal with this."

Hermes huffs and crosses his arms, pouting.

I ignore him. "Where's your flying horse?"

"We can't ride Pegasus into the human realm!" he protests. "If anyone sees him—"

I flourish the cape I have draped over my shoulders, silencing him. "Do you know what this is?"

"A cape."

"Oh, your father really didn't teach you anything." I clear my throat. "No, not just a cape."

I flick the hood up and watch Hermes' eyes double in size. He reaches out to touch me, but I step to the side. He laughs, eyes flicking everywhere but where I stand. Lowering the hood once more, Hermes laughs again. "Amazing! A cloak of invisibility!"

"Yes, and I can do this"—I flick the fabric, and it doubles in size—"And now it will cover Pegasus as well as us."

Hermes pumps his fist in the air. "Looks like it's time to fix what I screwed up!" Spinning on his heel as he takes off down the hall.

"Yeah," I say flatly. "Whoopie."

•••♠•••

"Are we almost there?"

I grit my teeth at Hermes' incessant complaining. He's thumping his head against my back, and I'm fairly certain I have a bruise.

"Will you shut up, or I'm throwing you off this animal."

Pegasus tosses his head and looks over his shoulder at me. If horses can raise their eyebrows, then he certainly is.

"What?" I ask, glaring at the beast. "I'm fairly certain no one would miss him."

He whinnies, as close to a laugh as he can make, and pumps his wings a few more times to gain momentum.

"We've been on Peg for hours!"

"If you don't shut up, Hermes, I swear I'll—"

My threat is cut short by Pegasus tucking his wings to his side and pointing towards the ground. Hermes screams, high and shrill. My ears ring as I clutch fistfuls of the flying horses' fur, relaxing my grip only after he throws out his wings and glides to a running stop in a small open clearing.

Hermes slips off Pegasus' back and throws his hands into the air. "Oh, thank the gods!" he cheers before kissing the dew-soaked grass.

I roll my eyes and throw the cloak of invisibility over Pegasus.

"How are we going to do this?" Hermes asks, bouncing on the balls of his feet.

I point between us. "*We* aren't doing anything. *You* are going to figure out how to kill this guy without getting us cursed or dooming humanity."

A curse for a god or goddess would be a dangerous thing. A crazed immortal could level all the three of the realms, killing all the other gods. It would be worse than the Titan war!

With an eye roll of epic proportions, my nephew snaps his fingers, turning his toga into the typical human-style jeans and a white t-shirt. There's nothing that can hide his looks, however. With high cheekbones, curly light brown hair, and a million-watt smile, Hermes is a looker. His list of girlfriends is lengthy. It is a trait he'd inherited from Zeus.

I smooth my hand over my short black hair, and straighten my black suit before adjusting the collar of my light gray dress shirt.

"Snazzy, Uncle." Hermes points his fingers at me like they're human weapons and clicks his tongue.

"'*Snazzy*'? Honestly, where do humans come up with these words?"

Hermes laughs. "You like the ingenuity of humans."

I scoff and motion for him to follow. Out of the cluster of trees, I can see down the hillside. A small-town lies below us. The houses all look the same. Same brick exterior, same gray shingled roofs, same green grass. It's a touch disconcerting.

I rub my temples. "Where are they?"

Hermes rattles off a string of numbers and directions I don't understand. I blink at him, and he groans. "Follow me. I'll lead you to their house."

I follow him down what he calls a *sidewalk* and then up to one of the houses. I stare at the pretty pink flowers. They remind me of Persephone. I reach down and brush one with my finger. The soft petals shrivel at my touch, curling inward before crumbling to dust. I curse, straighten and follow Hermes to the door. He presses a small button, and a bell chimes within.

"Yes?" A man with brown hair and eyes pokes his head out. Thick, speckle-framed glasses are perched on his nose, and he glances between Hermes and me with a divot in his forehead. "Can I help you?"

"You need to die," I say flatly.

"Uncle!" Hermes laughs and shakes his head. Turning to the man, he says, "He's a touch . . ." He whistles and spins a finger by his head.

The man's face morphs from shock to pity. "And you think I can help him, is that it?"

"Yes, that's exactly right." Hermes nods enthusiastically. Perhaps a might too enthusiastically. "*You* can help my uncle."

"Come in, both of you," the man says.

I follow behind Hermes, keeping my mouth shut and my eyes open. The foyer of the home is pristine. The oak floors gleam, the picture frames don't sport any dust, and not a fuzzy is to be seen on the red, circular carpet.

"Is your wife here?" Hermes asks.

"No, she's out shopping with my sister." The man smiles at me. "I'm Alfred Benawitz, by the way. And you are?"

"I'm—" Well, I can't very well say *Hades, Lord of the Dead* now can I? Although I am supposed to be insane. So I say just that.

Alfred's eyes go round. "Okay then." He draws out the first word like he isn't sure what to make of me. "Come into my office."

Hermes pads after him, and I swear once more. This is going to be harder than it first appeared.

The office is painted blue, with the same oak flooring. The carpet is a cream color, and on his walls are pictures with friends and family. Three windows are behind his desk, looking out at the hill Hermes and I had come down only a few hours before. Alfred directs me to a couch, and I perch on the edge, ruffling the sleeve of my jacket as I watch my target. Hermes is bouncing from picture to picture, being no help whatsoever.

"When did you start thinking you were Hades?" Alfred asks, picking up a pen and a notebook.

At the dawn of time. Instead, I say, "I *am* Hades."

"Denial never solves anything." Alfred smiles, and if it wasn't for Aphrodite's blasted curse, I would have leveled him right then and there.

Instead, I shrug. "I'm not in denial about anything. I am Hades."

"See, he needs help!" Hermes frowns, selling his part a bit too well.

"Well, let's try this." Alfred pats the couch. "Lie down."

I glance at my nephew, who shrugs with a mischievous curl to his lips. I don't like that, not even a little bit. Shaking my head, I stand. "I'm not doing this. I am Hades, Lord of the Dead, Keeper of the River of Souls! I do not *lie down* for anyone."

Hermes steps to my side, and I grab him by the nape of his neck. I hiss the words, "Kill him, or I'll kill you."

"It's not that simple!"

"Make it simple."

Alfred's cold fingers touch mine, and I yank my hand back, eyeing the man. His eyes are hard now, his jaw set. "You want to kill me?"

Oops. "No, I want him to kill the mouse I saw."

Alfred goes very, very pale. He leaps onto the couch, eyes flying around wildly. "M—mouse? Where?"

"Right there!" Hermes points and, using his gift of trickery, makes the shadow of a mouse dart from behind a filing cabinet.

Alfred screeches, clutching at his chest. His eyes go round, and he tips off the couch. As he tumbles to the floor, his head cracks the corner of the coffee table with sickening finality.

Hermes pokes him with his foot. "Alfred?"

The man doesn't stir. We wait for nearly an hour, hoping that Mrs. Benawitz doesn't make an appearance.

"I think he's dead," Hermes says as the shadows in the room begin to lengthen.

I kneel beside him, holding a hand over his mouth. No breath wafts across my cold skin. "You know what's odd?" I ask Hermes.

"What?"

"He was ice cold." I glare at my nephew. "He's not a human, is he?"

When he doesn't answer, I reel back and kick the limp figure in the stomach. He *oofs*, rolling onto his back as he shifts from Alfred Benawitz to none other than Aphrodite herself.

I swear. "What in all the Underworld is going on here?"

Aphrodite sits up, cradling her stomach as she glares at me. "I thought it was obvious."

"We got you!" Hermes laughs, dancing around the couch with a crazed giggle. Gods, he can be such a child sometimes.

I want to kick Aphrodite in the gut again as she sits up and waves a hand over her body, shifting into a sparkling blue toga. She fluffs her blonde hair and chuckles at me. "We did *get you*, as Hermes said."

"For the love of Olympus, *why*?" I ask with a threatening glare.

"You've become stodgy." Hermes shrugs. "You needed a good heart pumping, mind working puzzle to figure out."

"Plus, it was fun to torment you." Aphrodite smirks. "Demeter was all for it. Apparently, Persephone was saying you've grown . . . boring."

"Boring?" I ask, disbelief clearly in my tone.

"Stodgy," Hermes repeats.

Aphrodite waves her hand in a circle. "Borderline Zeus himself."

I bristle. "I'm more reliable than my brother will ever be."

"Boring." They say in unison.

"Oh shut up!" I snap, crossing my arms and turning my back on them. "So the human realm was never in danger?"

"Only of becoming stranger by the day." Hermes' voice pitches up an octave. "Do you know they now have devices where you can call someone and see their face? That's a miracle if I've ever seen one!"

"Hades, are you mad?" Aphrodite asks.

"You lied to me! Of course I'm mad." I scowl. "So this was all an elaborate prank?"

They nod in tantum, and I growl, raking a hand through my hair.

"And where is the real Alfred?" I ask.

"On vacation." Aphrodite huffs a breath. "We paid for him to win a trip to some tropical island with his wife. Don't worry, it was all above board. He's fine."

"Was he ever marked for death?" I glance at Hermes.

"Not that I saw." My nephew shrugs. "We didn't want to endanger the mortal realm, Uncle. I swear it!"

"Good," I say. "If either of you try something of this ilk again, I swear on the sky and the sea, you will regret it!"

Aphrodite and Hermes' eyes widen. I turn sharply on my heel, muttering under my breath as I stride out the door. I reach Pegasus, throwing off the cloak and straddling him. He snorts in irritation as I goad him into a run, trying to outpace my fury along with it. Spreading his wings, Pegasus launches into the air. Even without Hermes' head thumping into my back, I can't enjoy the ride. Something about this whole thing doesn't sit well with me. Not in the slightest.

The foreboding doesn't leave me as I reach Mount Olympus. Because of it, I don't bother speaking to Zeus and Poseidon, heading back down into my domain with the fire still pumping in my veins. I reach my throne and ease into it with a sigh.

Be it ever so dreary, there's no place like home. Just five seconds of silence, please.

A knock sounds on the large ebony doors.

"I didn't mean a literal five seconds!" I grumble before, I call out, "What in all the realms do you want?"

A slave steps in, arms shaking as he gestures behind him. "A new arrival, Lord Hades."

A man—one I know all too well—gazes around my throne room. "Where am I?"

"The Underworld." I pinch the bridge of my nose. "Oh gods, you shouldn't be here."

"My plane crashed on the way to Bora Bora." He pushes the bridge of his glasses up his nose. "Am I . . . dead?"

Rubbing my temples, I raise my gaze to meet the brown eyes that are wide with fear. "Yes. Yes, you are, Alfred Benawitz. Welcome to Hell."

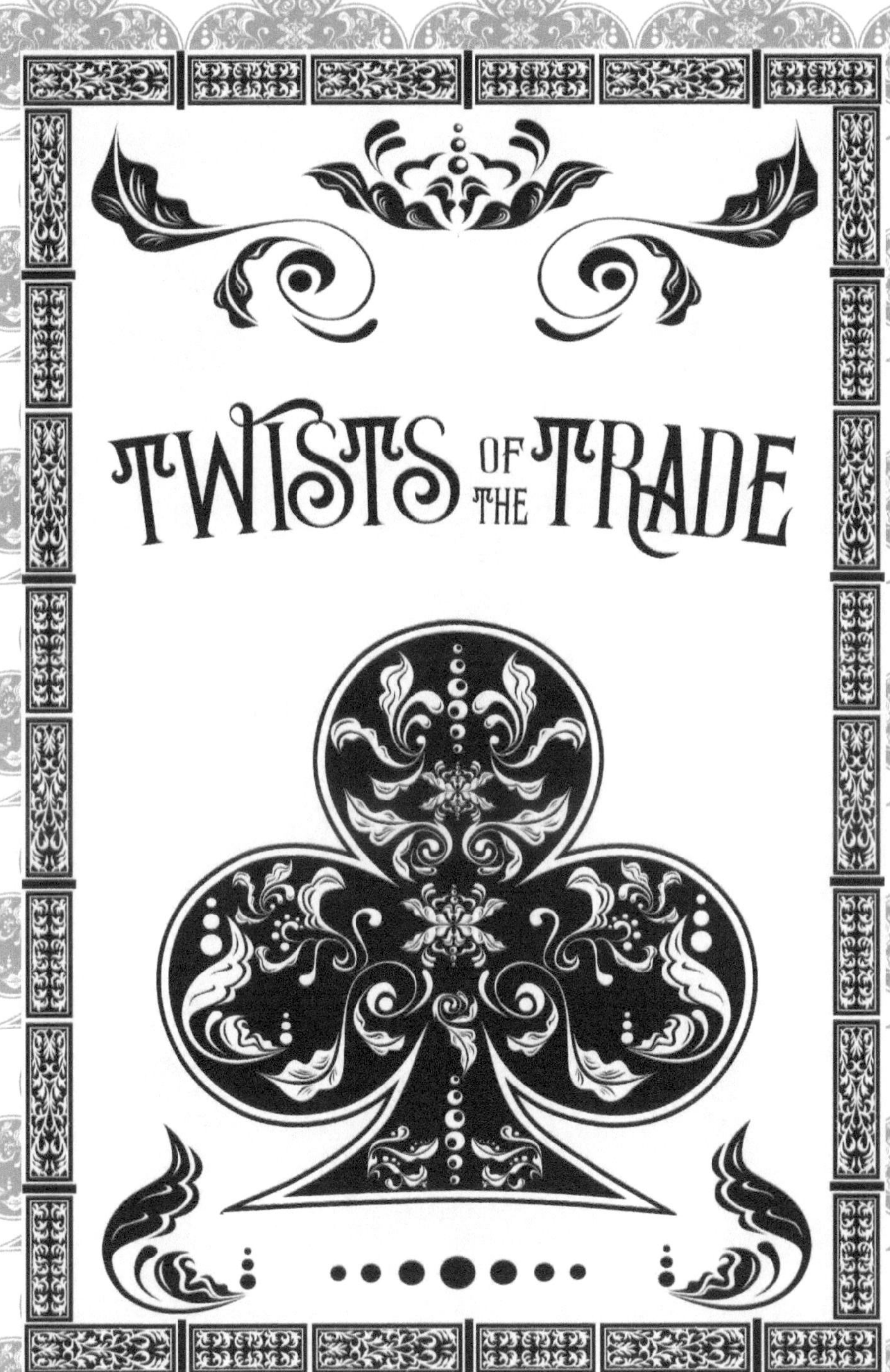

TWISTS OF THE TRADE

TAKE NOTHING

FOR GRANTED.

FOOL'S GUIDE TO TRICKERY

Part Three

Anne J. Hill

THE ART OF deception—of twisting something on its head—is a skill every trickster needs in their toolbelt. There are many different ways to go about doing this, and every situation is different.

Here are just a few good places to start.

1. Cultivate a persona of absolute integrity. This will allow you to get close to the people you need to and then flip everything on its head.

2. Knife.

3. Take nothing for granted. Even if someone or something seems irrelevant or out of place, notice it, lock it away in your brain for later. It has a purpose; most things do.

4. Stabby stabby.

5. If you're hoping to disguise yourself as a villain in order to save the day, then make sure you study the group of criminals you're trying to impersonate. Now, stand in your bathroom and pretend to be them in front of your mirror until you can't tell if it's you talking, or the criminal. Once you've mastered the villain act, you're ready to infiltrate and take them down from the inside out. They will never see it coming.

6. Blood.

7. Have a foolproof plan. Anticipate your opponent's every move so that you have your counteracts set in place. This will twist every single move they make to your advantage.

8. Murder.

9. Don't even tell your companions your plans because you might need to steal from them.

10. Death.

11. Always do the unexpected. Make your enemy think they know you and your goals, but then do the exact opposite. It works every time.

12. Make sure the person you tried to kill actually stays dead.

13. Oh, look. They're alive.

WITHIN A DREAM, WITHIN A DREAM

People Watchers Part II

Lara E. Madden

I START DOWN THE running path, relishing the feel of my sneakers pushing off against the dirt. I check my watch. I'm moving too fast. I have to slow down, or I'll miss my window. Jeffery is a creature of habit. He starts from the same point every day at 7 a.m. on the dot. I need to run close enough to him that I can observe him, but not so close that he'll notice me.

I know what he should be doing right now—stretching, bouncing from one foot to the other, warming up to begin his morning mile. I am rounding a corner of the trail at the exact time that he will be starting his run, about 150 meters ahead of me. The sun is just beginning to come up over the treetops. The air is still cool and fresh. I take in deep lungfuls of it and grin, anticipating the moment I'll see him, trying to decide if I'll talk to him today.

The trail forks, and I take the path to the left. Just ahead of me, Jeffery is—

Blank. Nothing.

Shoot! What is Jeffery doing? Suddenly the words just aren't coming, and I can't see the scene anymore. When I imagine it, all I see is the empty trail in my mind's eye, and no Jeffery. I attempt to force myself through the next sentence of this crazy writing exercise but can't finish it. After a full three minutes of staring at the blinking cursor on my Word document, I close my laptop lid and groan. I hate it when characters go rogue.

No! I am the author! I am the only person who gets to decide how this story goes.

I open the computer again, a bit too aggressively.

Jeffery is

I want to write that Jeffery is exactly where he should be, that he's wearing the expression he has when he's worried about something, that he's a blur of gray in his ridiculous tracksuit that he's convinced is stylish.

But I can't do it. The words refuse to be written. I decide to try something else.

Jeffery is nowhere to be seen. There is no sign of him at all. He has not broken his running routine in the three years and eight months that he has lived in this neighborhood, except on three separate occasions when he was sick with the flu and for one week after Jasmine broke up with him. But this morning, for no apparent reason, Jeffery is not where he should be.

And suddenly, the words start flowing.

I continue my run, but with no sign of him, not even the marks left in the dirt trail by the unique tread lines of his sneakers. When the trail takes me past his street, I veer off for a detour. His apartment is situated such that from the sidewalk, I can usually see into his living room. But on this day, unlike most other days, all of the blinds on the windows are closed, and the curtains are drawn behind them. I glance out across the apartment building's parking lot. His car is not in its usual spot.

Okay, then. I'm going to have to do this the interesting way.

His spare key is poorly hidden above the frame of his front door. I check to be sure no neighbors are watching before letting myself in. He doesn't speak with many of them, but he also has very few visitors, so my presence could seem suspicious. I quickly slip inside and glance around the almost spotless room, still unsure what I'm looking for exactly. Something to hint at the cause of this unusual change in routine.

My hands fly across the keys now as I picture the apartment in my mind and continue to write myself into it. This is the best way I've been able to come up with to get to know Jeffery before I write him into a novel. By making up these little scenes of ours. Following him. Being in his world.

I glance at the stack of dishes in the sink and wish for a moment that I could just write them away for him. I would only have to type a few words, and the chore would cease to exist. That might startle him, though. I take a few treats out of a jar on the table for the cats. The little gray ball of fluff and two rescue tabbies hear the sound and come out from hiding in the living room. The smallest cat, who usually stays under the couch, rubs her head against my ankle.

Nothing unusual. There's a notebook in the living room filled with thoughts and ideas for the book he is working on, but when I flip through it, I see he hasn't added much to it recently.

The living room is orderly except for a pile of mail tossed on the coffee table. Bills, a credit card offer, a coupon for some local grocery stores and a shooting range, a high school reunion invitation.

Hmmm, that would be interesting, seeing him at his 10th high school reunion. I know it would likely be out of character for him to attend, so the scene wouldn't make much sense to write . . . but I would learn so much about him if I could get him there. I wonder what he was like in high school. Probably quiet. Likely kept few friends. I doubt he dated much. Maybe he went out for sports but wasn't enough of a jock to fit in there. Definitely got good grades in math. Probably in English, too, although if he had started to write novels by then, he likely kept them secret.

I glance out through the blinds to the parking lot—still no Jeff. Okay, the coast is clear. I probably have some time to look around. I start up the stairs to his bedroom and a low, guttural sound gives me pause—a growl. The cats scamper back to their hiding places. I freeze on the step, confused for the few seconds it takes me to register that there is another animal in the apartment. The bedroom door nudges open, and a squashed, fanged face pokes around the corner to glare at me.

He has a dog! When did he get a dog?

I try to soothe the bulldog with some calm words as I back slowly down the stairs and ease my way toward the front door I came through. I am just about to turn my back on him when the growling turns to barking and snapping and he's scrambling down the stairs, so quickly that he is almost at my heels when I slam the door shut behind me. I hear the dog run into the other side of the door and then explode in a fit of scratching and barking. I lock up and put the key back above the frame where I found it.

He bought a guard dog. Interesting. I stop typing and sit back in my chair, spinning silently and chewing my lip. Why would Jeffery need a guard dog? He lives in a safe neighborhood. He doesn't have any enemies. He doesn't even really like dogs. I close my laptop, thinking I'll go for a walk and come back to the problem in half an hour. But the walk yields nothing, and when I try to write again, I feel blocked. Every time I attempt to write a new scene, the words just won't come.

Days pass in the real world, and I just can't get past a few sentences without staring at the blinking cursor. I try writing myself into the cafe that Jeffery hangs out at. I start a scene where I am driving past his office, but all I can think to write is, *His car is not in the parking lot at 5 p.m.,* so he must be leaving work early.

I finally decide to step away from my computer entirely and just start carrying a notebook around with me, trying to write a scene whenever I think of a new place he may be.

Is he . . . hiding from me?

It's game night. Surely he won't change this. I'm sitting in my car in the parking lot of Jeffery's apartment complex, waiting for his car to pull in. My eyes are trained on his huge living room windows. The blinds are still pulled, but behind them, there is darkness. He's not home. Game night is supposed to start in twenty minutes, and he's not home yet.

I'm getting *very* tired of this.

Fine. In the world of Jeffery's story, I'm going to wait outside his apartment until something changes. He has to come home at some point. Or, in other words, if I wait here long enough, I will have to get inspired to write some kind of action on his part eventually.

Let the waiting game commence.

I lean back in my driver's side seat and watch. A Pink Floyd song is playing on the radio. Time passes slowly, and I amuse myself with the ticking seconds on my watch. Thinking about the essence of time and space. Trying to see how many thoughts I can think between the tick-tick-ticks. Wondering whether time exists at all. Whether I exist at all, or Jeffery, or the world I've materialized only in my imagination. I consider this whole silly game I've made up while the stars begin to creep out from behind the cloud cover. This game of playing with people who are in my head, writing their stories, determining their lives. Writing myself into their lives to get closer to them, to make them more real. It is very strange. And all the while, I pass a few minutes in the real world, writing something that takes hours in the fictional world, while another scene that may follow a handful of minutes in the story world could take days to write in mine.

I glance at the green number on the dashboard clock. It's three minutes to midnight. I lazily look back toward his apartment. No lights on. I close my eyes . . . .

TAP TAP TAP

Isit straight up before I even realize that I'd fallen asleep. Something metal is rapping against the window.

I jump when I see Jeffery standing outside my car.

What?

He's holding a gun.

WHAT?!

The black metal object is tucked discreetly into the shadow of his overcoat. The barrel is pointed at me.

"Get out of the car," he says. As I fumble for the door handle and step out, I take mental note of his serious tone and the matching expression on his face. Terror and anger. Interesting. I can tell he's trying to steady his breathing, but the hand that holds the gun is visibly shaking. None of this is real for me. But it is for him.

"Jeffery," I say calmly, putting my hands up.

"Why do you know my name?"

"I can explain—"

Can I explain? What could I possibly say to legitimize the way I've been following him without causing an existential crisis?

"You're the woman from the cafe," he says. His voice is trembling, and the words begin to tumble. "From the running track, my job, my parent's freaking vacation home. Your face in my window at night. I see you everywhere; you think I don't notice, but I do. You're the one who's been stalking me!"

He reaches for his phone, keeps his eyes on me, tries to hold the gun steady, and dials 9-1-1. In his panicked state it seems like too much to handle.

"Don't call the police, Jeff." I reach out my hand a little too casually, meaning for the gesture to be comforting. He nearly drops the phone. I forgot that he thinks I'm mortal and a gun will scare me. A 9-1-1 call might complicate things though. He hits the call button.

"Look, Jeff, the operator isn't going to pick up."

He looks at me in horror while the phone rings. It ends in a busy signal. He tries again, desperately, and gets the same painful beeping tone. His eyes fill with dread and confusion. I sigh as he tries a third time.

Maybe I should just tell him the truth. If it goes badly, I can always hit delete and rewrite the scene.

"Okay," I say. "I'm going to tell you what's really going on. But I want you to put down the gun."

He chuckles, but the sound is strained as if he's either going to laugh or cry. "There is no way in hell I'm doing that," he says.

"It's not for my safety; it's for yours. What I'm about to tell you . . . well, you'll want to sit down. Maybe we can go inside; I'll make you some tea—"

"You're insane! Who are you?!"

"I'm . . . My name is Catalina."

"You're stalking me."

"I'm learning about you. I'm doing research. For a book."

"What?"

"A book about you . . ."

"Why would you want to write—"

"Jeff, give me the gun." I take a step closer to him. He is shaking so hard now that I'm afraid his finger will depress the trigger by mistake, and—

BOOM

A shot explodes from beneath his overcoat. I feel nothing. I watch the twist of absolute horror on Jeff's features as my body goes limp and blood pools across his boots.

Okay, let's fix this.

I regenerate a second later, standing behind him. Jeff stares in shock at the ground where my dead body had just been. He spins around when I say his name, about to pull the trigger again from the sheer force of the shock. I snatch the pistol away from him, release the magazine, and unload the chambered bullet in a smooth motion before tossing it back to him. A quick kick sends the full mag spinning underneath a parked car somewhere behind us.

If only I could be this smooth in real life . . .

"Jeff, you're a character in my novel. I'm your author. I'm following you for research. I don't know how to say this, but . . . you don't exist."

"I'm dreaming . . . ." His voice is so faint that he's almost whispering. His eyes are wild, glancing everywhere, trying to make sense of what he has just seen and what I've told him. "I must be dreaming . . . . This is just . . . a dream . . . ."

"Well, you aren't entirely wrong, I guess. But it's not your dream. You're only real in my imagination, so it's sort of mine."

Predictably, Jeffery faints.

This seems like a good time for a break.

I smirk with self-satisfaction and close my laptop. Time to celebrate. The wayward character has been found once again. There is a very good chance that I've ruined him forever, but this has been a very interesting experience. I suppose in my next writing session, I'll need to explain things to him further. But overall, he seems to have gotten the idea. I was surprised by the gun though. I didn't see him being the type to carry.

Everything clicks into place. The changes of routine, the guard dog, the coupons and receipts from the shooting range. He *was* hiding from me. Huh.

I decide to treat myself. I'm buying myself a drink in honor of my lost-and-found Jeffery. I'm still thinking about him when, five minutes down the road, I feel a strange thought, like a voice echoing through my mind.

Pull over the car, Catalina.

I ignore the thought. But a second later:

Pull over up ahead here.

"What? Why would I want to pull over?" I'm surprised by the fact that I'm speaking this thought aloud. It feels out of character for me. Forced. But not by me.

You're going to want to be parked for this.

I stop the car slowly as if testing the strange voice that seems to reverberate through my consciousness. It feels right. I don't know why I do it, but I find a parking space and change gears. I wait a second, curious. Then I turn the key to cut the engine.

"Hello, Catalina."

A woman appears in my passenger seat, and I scream. She waits calmly while I hyperventilate between shrieks, struggling to get my seatbelt off, to get out of the car, away from her.

She smiles. "My name is Lara E. Madden."

My head is spinning. I am about to cry. I dread what she might say next and what it might mean. I am in a dream. This is a dream. She takes out a notepad and writes the words, *Catalina feels suddenly calm.*

A false tranquility washes over me, and my mind clears with no explanation. I should be panicking. I should be panicking, but I'm not. Why am I not panicking?

The woman smiles kindly again, almost apologetically. "I'm your author."

No one's

EVER

been able to
teach *me* a

LESSON.

EPITHET

Tasha Kazanjian

London
November, 1851

A SOOTY FOG SEEPED down the sides of the houses and pooled between the cobblestones. Simon could scarcely see his own feet, and his boot stamped deep into an icy puddle. Frigid water instantly soaked through the torn soles and tattered leather. Muttering a curse, he dragged his foot out and shrugged deeper into his coat, his fingers tightening around the coins in his pocket. The street was crowded and, likely as not, full of pickpockets.

"Four years on Jacob's Island, and you're still scared of pickpockets?" Dec would say, then shake his head with a smirk. "You wouldn't last a day in St Giles."

Dec's family hadn't lasted much more than a day there, either, but of course, Simon didn't say anything about that, just took the insult. It didn't make sense to him how Dec could even joke about St Giles, but then, Dec could turn anything into a joke.

Simon clenched his fist even tighter and the coins bit into his palm. A week's wages—he hadn't even spent a farthing of it crossing the Thames, since another dockworker gave him a lift—and he meant to keep them this time. He was on Shad Thames now, nearly home. Instead of following the street, however, he turned towards the River Neckinger, which was not so much a river as a grease-smothered cesspit—the Thames taking a piss, Simon had thought the first time he saw it. Jacob's Island, the rookery around the Neckinger, boasted perhaps the worst smelling tenements in London, crammed to the gills with thieves and beggars—and magickers, who were the worst of both.

There was an apothecary down by the water, where Simon sometimes helped the old chemist mix his powders. Behind the shop was an alley so narrow Simon had to shuffle through it sideways, which meant it was nearly always empty. Months ago, he'd pried a brick out of the wall just at his eye level and hollowed it out. There was a small trove of coins in there now, but not nearly as much as Simon wanted. This week's wages would make it a pound.

He began walking faster, the fog slinking away from his footsteps, and nearly tripped over a bundle of rags. The bundle made a small noise, a tiny whimper. Simon, stumbling, peered down at it. A pair of eyes stared back up. The bundle was a young girl, wrapped in a tattered assortment of shawls and skirts. Her hair was probably blonde, but muck and grease left it sickly grey, as though she was an old woman. Her blue eyes seemed to take up her whole face—somehow the only *real* thing about her, Simon thought. The rest of her was fading away, like coal dissolving into ash, but her eyes were clear.

She reached out a hand to Simon without speaking. He caught his balance, his hand still tight around the coins, and hurried to the end of the street. He'd made it to the docks, a cramped spit of cobblestones separating the buildings from the river. A thrill of excitement rose in him as he reached the embankment, but then he stopped dead.

Dec was already there.

He hadn't caught sight of Simon yet—at least, Simon didn't think he had. The dock was crowded with people, with Dec in the middle as usual. Simon couldn't even see him, but Dec's voice carried.

"Come on, give it another go. Sure, your luck'll change this time."

There was a roar from the onlookers, some jeering, some goading. Dec said something else, and there was a loud retort and then a cheer. The game was beginning again. Probably écarté. That was Dec's favorite, at least when he wanted to make money.

Simon stepped back. He could get around to the alley another way. He was so close now, only a few buildings over, and even if he got a bit muddled in the maze of lanes and passages, he was sure to find it soon enough. Except that if Dec was on the docks, then Merlo was, too.

And Merlo would've already spotted him.

Simon glanced around the docks, though it wasn't much use. It was long past dusk, and while torches and lanterns studded the waterfront, in the fog they seemed to cast more shadow than light. That, of course, was a convenient excuse to ignore the truth: even in broad daylight, he would not see Merlo until Merlo wanted to be seen.

So Simon grit his teeth, forced himself to pull an empty hand from his pocket, and strode onto the docks. One or two people recognized him and called out a hello, and he waved back, caught between a spark of happiness at being safely part of this place and disgust that anyone in Jacob's Island would know his name.

"It'd be easier if you forgot," Dec had told him once. "Pride won't get you anywhere in a rookery."

Dec hadn't forgotten, Simon thought, but he didn't say anything.

The throng around the two card players was noisy and jostling, and Simon didn't try to elbow his way through it. He was tall enough to see over most of them. Dec and his opponent sat across from each other on either side of a crate, which was scattered with cards and lit by a few candle stubs. The man across from Dec dropped a bottle onto the cobblestones and threw down a card. There was a shout from the onlookers, and Dec let out a long groan.

"Told you your luck would change, didn't I?" he said, snatching the bottle himself and taking a swig. Then he held it up as though toasting the throng. "But don't change your bets just yet, boys," he added with a grin.

Simon could see the glint in his dark eyes and winced. He knew that expression. Dec meant to lose. Then his opponent, now considerably drunker than he had been at the start of the first game and crowing over his victory, would play again, and Dec would gut him like a fish.

Nearly everyone on the dock had to know it. If Dec's opponent had any wits at all, or if his wits weren't drowning in gin, he would've noticed how few onlookers were betting on him. But there was always some idiot newcomer on St. Saviours Dock, along with a few idiot newcomer friends, that Dec could trap.

Declán Ó Sí, he called himself. It had taken Simon far too long to realize the surname was a lark. An epithet, Simon thought when Merlo finally told him what *sí* meant—like a Homeric epithet, *cunning Odysseus, great-hearted Aeneas, bright-eyed Athena,* though he didn't quote the Aeneid to Merlo. Declán Ò Sí, fey-like Declán. Gifted by the *sí*, or maybe even fey-blooded.

Fey-fingered Dec, the best cardsharp in London.

Certainly the best two-fingered cardsharp in London. Then again, Simon wasn't sure how many cardsharps in London got along without three of the fingers on their right hands.

A mingled cacophony of groans and cheers went up from the onlookers, and Simon blinked. Dec was shaking his head and tipping the bottle back (though he wouldn't swallow more than a few drops) while the other man jumped up, laughing as he slapped the cards scattered across the crate.

"You thought you could rob me, *boyo*?" the man jeered as he seized a handful of coins out of Dec's proffered hand. His eyes fixed on the empty scar where three fingers had been. "Looks like I'm not the first one to teach you a lesson. I reckon an Irish whelp won't learn unless it hurts."

Laughter rang through the crowd. Simon tugged a lock of fair hair over his eyes, grimacing. The man was making it so *easy*.

Dec staggered to his feet, banging the bottle on the crate and leaning towards the man. "Maybe it hasn't hurt enough yet. One more round."

He might actually be a little angry, Simon observed, recognizing the flash in his black eyes, but he was still playing a part. With his chin jutted up and his fists curled, he seemed like a boy instead of a grown man—just a child, mad and easy to beat. Dec was slight—*fey-lissom Dec*, Simon thought—and his oversized coat made him look even slighter.

"All right, if you want another whipping," the man replied with a broad smile. "I can see through your *sí* tricks easy enough."

Simon let out a sigh, which was lost in the cheer of the crowd. The man was done for.

Something touched his sleeve, and his hand dove instantly into his pocket, grasping for the coins. They were still there, all of them, cool against his skin. Simon slowly extracted his hand and then flushed, realizing his mistake.

Merlo was perched on top of a barrel, several paces away, cradling a paper sack. As Simon watched, Merlo extracted an oyster from the sack and sucked out the meat. But those falcon eyes were on him the whole time, half hidden by overlong black curls. Simon would need to cut that wild tangle again soon. It was perhaps the only job Merlo trusted him to do better than Dec.

Merlo was another epithet. *Blackbird*. Or sometimes it was Merlin, another kind of bird, or a wizard. Blackbird, black magic. But Merlo's only magic was blackmail. There was no place Merlo couldn't get into, no wall thick enough, no lock strong enough. Merlo knew everything, and everyone knew it. Most people thought it was magic, bloody gypsy boy with his soul-reading magic, but Merlo wasn't a gypsy, or magic, or, for that matter, a boy.

"I suppose that would make you *Merla*," Simon had pointed out when he first learned. He'd been shocked; he hadn't meant to let the witticism slip. Merlo gave him a scathing glare and called him something in Italian that Simon understood well enough, even if he'd never heard the word before.

Merlo took another oyster from the sack and cocked her head. Simon broke away from the huddle around the card game and drifted over to her, his arms crossed defensively over his coat. She smirked very slightly—Merlo did not smirk with her mouth but with her eyebrows—and held out the oyster.

Almost against his will, Simon loved the salt-and-vinegar tang of the shellfish. He'd never eaten one when he was a child, not even when his father brought him along to the docks. He always kept a tight grip on Simon as they walked, only letting go of his shoulder once they reached the warehouse or the clerk's office. Simon barely even knew his own way to the shipyards, as most of the time, his face was pressed up against the stiff wool of his father's overcoat.

He could still smell it, the musk of damp wool and tobacco.

"What're the stakes?" Merlo asked, pulling Simon out of the memory.

Simon shrugged. "I didn't hear."

She snorted, clearly unimpressed with his lack of attention.

"Did you find anything today?" Simon asked.

"A little," Merlo replied. "Investments."

Investments. Merlo's word for secrets that she couldn't sell just yet. She, like Dec, could pass for much younger than she was and, therefore, could still join the fleet of boys who worked any odd job on the streets. She could haunt a railway station and tote luggage; she could buy scraps from cooks to sell as hogwash; she could run messages, sweep streets, or sell anything she happened to find. And what she usually happened to find, as she roamed all over London, hanging around shops and houses and stations, was information.

When Simon learned Merlo's secret, he'd asked, still in shock, *why*. Merlo glibly replied that she could sneak into more tight spaces wearing trousers than a pile of petticoats. While this was true enough, he realized almost immediately how foolish the question was. He knew for himself what it was to be a boy alone on the streets, no family, no home, no money. He didn't want to think what that would be like for a girl.

It had been Merlo who found him four years ago, just after he turned twelve. She had appeared in front of him, somewhere in the warren of alleys around Whitechapel, and said bluntly, "You walk like you have money."

"I haven't," Simon replied, almost too exhausted to be frightened. He hadn't eaten in two days, hadn't slept except in snatches.

Merlo smirked. It was not a comforting expression. "Even worse. Thieves around here, they don't take disappointment well." But then she turned around and said, "Like this, you see? No sticking your nose up. Follow me; I will show you."

And because he didn't have the strength to argue, Simon followed.

She knew, of course, about the merchant John Dromley and how he fell deep into debt financing his ships, only to lose everything. She'd heard about his sudden death, almost certainly caught the rumors that the man had killed himself—he *hadn't*, Simon snarled at her when she'd asked how his father died.

"The boy needs work," she'd told Dec simply. "So, you take him with you to the dockyards." It wasn't a request. Merlo only had to tilt her head and lift an eyebrow, and Dec agreed.

Simon's father always planned for him to work around ships, though as a clerk, not a laborer. Somehow Simon still hoped that he could work his way up, prove to *someone* that he wasn't like the rest of the dockworkers, just living from day to day and content to spend his life lugging cargo to and from the warehouses. He was meant for better than that.

"*Meant* is a funny word," Dec told him one night when he'd foolishly vented this complaint. "My father meant for me to spend my life working the land of some noble English arse."

"But you got off the better of that one," Simon argued.

"The English arse didn't," Dec said. "You're just sore because you think you deserve better."

Simon stared at him. *Don't I?* he wanted to snap, but instead, he retorted, "Didn't *you*?"

Dec rubbed his jaw. "Probably not. But I don't think we're the ones who decide what we deserve or what we're meant to be. You're here, aren't you? Then odds are you're *meant* to do something here."

Yes, Simon thought. *I* mean *to get out of here*.

In the meantime, he would save his money whenever he could.

Merlo was looking at him. He glanced up, slightly unsettled, and realized she was holding out the sack, offering him the last oyster. As he took it, she asked, "Did you find work today?"

"No," Simon lied. It was believable enough. The docks were crowded every morning with men desperate for a day's labor.

"Tomorrow, then." Merlo rubbed her vinegar-stained fingers on her trousers and then straightened up. "He is about to win."

Simon didn't see what was so exciting about that.

The onlookers leaned in even closer around the crate and the cards, their voices tense with anticipation. Simon started towards them, wary of what might happen next, but Merlo nudged him with her foot. "Wait. He does not need you."

"What if there's a fight?"

Merlo just shook her head, her eyes on the crowd.

A sudden howl went up from the onlookers, mingled shouts of triumph and disappointment, followed by a chorus of, "Cough up, that's tuppence you owe me," and, "All right, all right," and "He's a cheat, he is, the dirty *sí*, you won't get a farthing from me."

Dec's opponent was on his feet, his head lowered like a bull ready to charge.

"That's five shillings for me," Dec said lightly, as though the man wasn't glowering over him. He quickly gathered up the cards and tucked them into his pocket, then used his arm to scrape the little pile of coins across the crate and into his waiting left hand.

Grabbing Dec's shirt and yanking him to his feet, the man growled, "You used magic, you bloody Irish fey."

"I didn't use magic any more than you did," Dec replied, and he spread out his hands. With a flick of his arms, he shook his sleeves, showing that there weren't any cards stowed away. "And I didn't cheat."

There was a long, lung-squeezing moment. Then the man shoved Dec away and spat, "All magickers are cheats." Muttering a curse under his breath, he reached down for the bottle, which still had a few drops sloshing about in the bottom.

"Don't take it so hard," Dec said with a wicked grin. "No one's ever been able to teach me a lesson."

The man whirled around then, but before he could strike, Dec's left fist, still clamped around the coins, landed in his face.

Chaos broke out, men roaring and punching, coins flying, the crate overturned, and the candle stubs knocked into a puddle. Simon, suppressing a curse, rolled back his shoulders and made to join the fray. Before he could move, someone grabbed his sleeve and pulled him away. He turned, expecting to see Merlo, but it was Dec. He was laughing, though there was a bruise beginning to bloom on his cheek, and then he darted off towards the street.

No one had ever been able to best Dec, not even the English lord who caught him poaching. The lord considered the Irish a people still mired in the Dark Ages, and therefore only the old laws were strong enough to deal with them. So Dec lost three fingers, the punishment for thieves. But Dec never *quite* lost, not really. He always outsmarted his opponent, somehow.

And as he stumbled away from the lord's castle, bleeding and feverish with pain, he was grimly satisfied because it was his right hand that was maimed.

Dec, after all, was left-handed.

Really, it wasn't so surprising that Simon had barely been able to save a pound over the last year. Reluctantly, he cast one last look at the apothecary shop, but the brawl behind him was getting louder. He hurried off after Dec.

Merlo was already waiting for them, poised like a bird about to take flight. Instead of breaking into a run as soon as they caught up, though, she reached out and clasped Dec's hand, whispering something. He glanced down behind her, a flicker of pity crossing his face, and nodded.

The girl still sat there, curled up in her rags, her head leaned back against the brick wall. Merlo crouched down and dropped something that *clinked* into the girl's lap.

With a start, the girl looked up, her luminous eyes somehow growing even larger. Merlo had already shot off, and Simon, after a second's hesitation, followed.

They took the long way home, in and out of alleys, through tiny archways and into courtyards, paused to buy hot potatoes, and then finally reached their own building. There were no lights in the windows—even if there were any candles burning inside, Simon doubted the light could've penetrated the grime-coated glass—and the steep roof had a nasty habit of molting shingles, which pitched down onto the street below. The tenants learned to approach the door with caution, as Dec did now.

After making it inside unscathed, the three started up the narrow stairs to their own room. Yet Dec paused at the bottom of the last staircase instead of going up to the top floor. Simon watched, puzzled, as he went to one of the doors and knocked. A young woman cracked the door open, suspicion shadowing her thin face, but when she saw Dec, she relaxed.

Simon frowned, annoyance smoldering under his skin. At least, he thought sourly, they'd bought dinner *first* this time.

Dec spoke quietly to the woman for a few minutes, asking after her children and if she'd found a new job yet. The woman replied that she hadn't, rubbing her arms anxiously. "They're worried I'll try and use magic to grease the machinery," she explained. "As if I didn't know it would jam the ironworks. Or that I'll cast a glamour and get them in trouble with the Verity Board when I can't even *cast* a glamour."

"Something'll turn up, you'll see," Dec said with an encouraging smile. "There's a house on Tooley Street you might try tomorrow. Merlo heard they're looking for a kitchen maid."

The woman's face brightened. "Really?"

"Sure. I'll show you the way myself in the morning." Dec smiled and pressed the woman's hand. She blinked, beginning to shake her head, but he spoke before she could protest. "Go on. It's all right. Just a loan until you get a new position. You'll be paying my rent next month; see if you don't."

Shaking slightly, the woman nodded, pressing her hand over her mouth. She whispered her thanks through her fingers, and Dec brushed it aside.

As the three of them made their way up the last flight of stairs, the question that had been growing in Simon's mind throughout Dec's conversation with the woman finally solidified.

"Dec," he called uneasily.

Dec was already on the landing, but he leaned against the wall and looked down at Simon. "What?"

"How much did you give that woman?"

Absently, Dec whisked a card out of his pocket and began twirling it between the two fingers of his right hand. "All of it. Five shillings."

Simon's gut jerked into a knot. He turned to Merlo. "Then what did you give the girl in the street?"

"*I* gave her nothing," Merlo replied, quirking an eyebrow. "You did."

Stricken, Simon thrust his hand into his pocket. It was empty.

Of course it was empty.

"You—" Simon started, his teeth clenched. "I *needed* that."

Merlo spun around, taking a step towards him. "Stop squawking. What do you need, Simon? You had dinner, yes? Half of mine, as I remember. You earned money today and likely will tomorrow. You have a place to stay tonight. She had nothing."

"You can't keep stealing from me, like you steal from everyone else," Simon hissed.

Dec cocked his head. "I told you, Simon. You stay with us; you live like us. If you can't, then go. We aren't keeping you here."

Silence. Simon's breath came in hot, angry bursts as he glared at the two of them. They stared calmly back at him.

He remembered Merlo teaching him how to walk like he had no money. He remembered Dec doing card tricks for him that first night and buying him coffee and bread the next morning. And he remembered his amazement the following evening, when Dec used both their wages to buy a bedraggled little girl's entire basket of flowers, still full even after a day of her trudging through the city. He gave the posies away to every woman he met on the way home, saving just one for Merlo.

Simon wasn't sure why Dec and Merlo decided to keep him instead of sending him on his way with a handful of coins. He wasn't anything like them. He knew them now, understood them as well as he could, and he also understood that they were different from him, different from nearly everyone he'd ever met, both before his father died and after.

It was a kind of different Simon didn't want to be, was *afraid* to be.

"Simon," Dec said quietly. "*I* took your money, not Merlo, and all right, I admit it was stealing. I stole from that halfwit on the docks, too. You really think I wasn't cheating?" He twitched the card to his left hand and deftly flicked it into his sleeve, only to pull it out of the air again with his right thumb and forefinger. He tilted his head back, grinning. "But that's what we do, and you know it." His voice dropped. "Isn't that what we did with you?"

"Am I paying out a debt, then?" Simon snarled.

Dec glanced at Merlo, then back at him. "Of course not," he said, raising his eyebrows. "Have you ever seen me collect on a debt?"

Simon hadn't. The woman downstairs *wouldn't* be paying next month's rent, even if she did have the money, and they all knew it. Infuriating, really. Somehow he wanted to strangle Dec, and yet at the same time, he felt a sudden sting of guilt. Merlo must've seen him walk away from the little girl and her outstretched hand.

Falcon-eyed Merlo. Fey-fingered Dec. Simon was the only one who had no epithet, and suddenly he wondered what his would be. He'd always thought of Dec as the cunning, not the great-hearted, but perhaps he was both. Simon was fairly certain just then that he was neither.

"All right," he said, the words like a sigh.

Dec and Merlo both smiled, the most honest smiles he'd seen from them all day, and then their arms were around him. Merlo began to recount, with wild gestures that nearly slapped Simon in the face, a bit of gossip she'd heard earlier, while Dec cheerfully poked holes in the wild story just to irritate her.

One more night, Simon decided. Maybe tomorrow he'd try to stow his wages away again, and maybe this time he'd be successful, but more likely, he'd fail for the hundredth time.

Or maybe, he thought, he'd give it away himself, before Dec and Merlo had the chance.

FOOL'S APPRENTICE

Kaitlyn Emery

THE CARVED SCENES on the face of the casket looked alive, despite its intended purpose, and with it, I would bury my nightmare.

The shop smelled of fresh-shaved cedar, delicate curls collecting in small drifts upon the dirt floor as I poured my pain into finishing this task.

The shop door scraped open, startling me from my creative trance. A fair-haired cherub entered, her rosy cheeks forming into a bright smile. I recognized her as the duke's daughter before she spoke to me. "Good afternoon."

I quickly set aside my tools and bowed. "May I help you?"

"Oh," she cried, noticing the casket behind me. "It's beautiful!"

"Thank you, m'lady." I moved my foot to discreetly sweep wood shavings over a stain on the floor as she stepped forward and traced her fingertips over my carvings.

"Is this for my father's carpentry contest?"

"No, m'lady." What was she *doing* here?

The duke's daughter continued to run her fingers along the smooth surface, tracing the tangled vines attempting to choke out the delicate flowers carved into the wood. "Is it your master's work?"

"No, it is by my own hand." I had carpenter's blood in my veins and the calluses on my hands to prove it.

"Your master must be proud to have such a fine apprentice."

"Yes," I lied.

She glanced at me and frowned. "You're wondering why I am here. I have many virtues, according to my father, but patience is not one of them. I've been longing to see the masters' preparations for the contest, so I decided to go through the shops for a little peek." She seemed amused by this. "You should enter this casket in the contest!"

"Thank you, m'lady."

"If I were a boy and allowed to practice such a craft, I would have the finest craftsmen in the region teach me." Stretching out her hand, the girl reached for the clasps on the casket.

"Don't!"

Her green eyes glanced towards me, confused. "Why not?"

I cleared my throat. "M'lady, please, it's bad luck."

"Oh rubbish. I don't believe in such things, and neither should you." The duke's daughter flipped up the clasps and lifted the lid while I held my breath. "Sand? Why is it full of sand?"

"To keep the wood dry," I answered, perhaps too quickly. "If the wood gets damp before I oil it, the wood will swell and split apart the joints."

"Ah, I see. Trade secret." She winked. "I won't say a word."

"Thank you, m'lady." I dabbed the sweat trickling down my face as she replaced the lid.

Something else caught her attention. "What is that on your cheek? Has someone hit you?"

My fingers fluttered over the bruise on my face. "My master has a temper, occasionally."

"Well!" She puffed with outrage. "He ought not strike such a skilled apprentice. Shame on him for putting such an ugly mark on a fair-faced lad. Call him out so I might speak with him!"

I shuffled my feet. "He is away presently."

"When will he be back?"

"I can't say." I stared at the shavings on the floor, nervously smoothing them out with my shoe.

She scowled. "I must go before my father finds out I have left and sends a search party, but I will have him come by."

She hastened to the door, then paused. "I could have my father buy that coffin, perhaps? Grandmother is quite ill, and the physicians say she hasn't much time left. You could use the money to start your own shop."

"Oh, no, I couldn't! This is one I made special . . . for my master." I refastened the clasps and dusted the lid off with a horsehair brush.

Concern crossed her face. "Someone in his family died?"

"Yes, m'lady." I nodded. "But I can make a better one if it pleases you."

She beamed and nodded. "I shall see that my father comes to you." Sunlight shone around her silhouette, creating an angelic aura as she bounced out the door and down the street.

Once she was out of sight, I bolted the door. As the latch clicked into place, I breathed a sigh of relief and clutched my aching ribs.

Slowly, I sat down on a stool, my knees trembling. So close to ruin . . . I swore I'd felt Death's icy breath, his great scythe suspended over my neck, waiting for the moment the girl noticed more than the bruises under the dirt and grime on my face. Things like my freshly-shorn hair, delicate facial features, or my girlish figure I had bound in wraps.

That last night when my master came for me, I knew I would rather die than suffer at his hands again. His anger over my carpentry hadn't kept him from selling my work as his own. He pretended his wrath was righteous—defending society against a female craftsman—but I knew what angered him more was that his housemaid could produce finer work than his own.

Now I had crafted my last piece for the tyrant, just to spite him. I pondered my sudden good fortune. If the duke ordered a casket from me, I would earn enough acclaim and money to build a future for myself.

I set to oiling the casket, protecting the wood and bringing out its reddish hues. As I buffed the front panels, I thanked God for sending me the duke's daughter. I thanked Him that she hadn't noticed me brushing shavings over the blood-stained floor. But mostly, I thanked God that she hadn't smelled my master's rotting corpse through all that sand and cedar.

YOU'RE NOT
THE BEST
TRICK
IN THE SHOW.

RULE NUMBER TWO

L.A. Thornhill

"THAT'S PHUZZEY WITH a 'P-H.'" Benjamin Phuzzey cast one of his charming smiles at the audience. "P-H-U-Z-Z-E-Y. At your service."

He gave a sweeping motion in front of his table, adorned with such a simple gold fabric on the front with gold tassels on the end. It sat on a wooden platform with the banner "Benny Phuzzey Tricks Extraordinaire" in bold red letters. Among the long chain of displays in The Bramble Train Carnival, it would be easy to get lost among the mechanical wonders, the magicians, and the freaks. But Benny took no issue with his placement and how far removed he was from the noise and bustle.

The attendees would hear him. And they would be drawn to him.

It was inevitable.

"Now all eyes on me," Benny said as he picked up his juggling pins off the platform and began his act. First with three and then four. "Be sure to blink, or else your vision will get *fuzzy*."

Some of the audience groaned at the terrible pun on his name. A group of street urchins laughed heartily in the back of the audience. A few people condescended to smile at him.

This was good. It was all good. All eyes were on him.

"Sydney, if you please," Benny cued, picking up speed with the juggle.

Sydney, a rectangular automaton with a barrel organ built in his chest, tilted forward on his short legs—the closest thing he could do to bow. "Of course, Master Benjamin."

His right arm turned in full circles, winding up the music instrument within. The tune came out quietly at first and then built up to drown out the nearby melodies of the other carnies.

Benny didn't repress his smile. And why should he? Everything was going well.

As he bungled with his fourth pin, he stole a few glances at his audience, choosing the next stage of his act. There were a few potential targets. A young couple looking a little nervous, perhaps a first date. An older man with a slick tailcoat. And one broad man who looked a bit too eager to prove him wrong. Potential.

Benny attempted to pick up a fifth pin and dropped the rest. The audience erupted in laughter. He shrugged and kicked the pins off the platform.

If they had any idea how difficult it was to look this believably clumsy.

He whipped out a pack of cards from his coat pocket. This part of the act was embellishment, furthering the confidence in the audience.

He flicked the cards between his hands, and half the deck hit the platform—more laughter from the audience. Benny made a show of picking up the cards. This part wouldn't last long. He truly was inept with cards.

"Extraordinaire, my baited breath," someone hollered from the crowd.

Benny stood up quickly and foolishly. The tiny earplug in his ear slid out slightly.

Cursed Fathers! Don't overdo it!

He pretended to scratch the inside of his ear to push the plug deeper inside. As he did, he stole a glance at Sydney, whose bulging bulb eyes were directed at him. Sydney wasn't the most sentient automaton that ever came out of a factory, but he understood his purpose, and he was never to play while Benny was unplugged. Benny waved his index finger in a circular motion, signaling Sydney to keep playing.

Sydney's music wasn't strong, and that was deliberate. A hypnotized audience would draw unwanted attention. However, an influenced audience, one already eager to be pleased by the madness of the carnival, were much easier to camouflage and manipulate. If his music had been any more influential, then even the earplugs wouldn't protect Benny from swooning under its power. Just the slight interference of the plugs, along with his awareness of the tunes, allowed Benny to take advantage of Sydney's unique music.

Benny dropped a few stale jokes, testing the crowd. Everyone closest to the stage readily laughed, including the man who had been giving his skeptic glares the entire time.

Perfect. Now for the real show to begin.

"Ladies and gentlemen, flesh and mechanical, keep your eyes on me," Benny said, sitting at his table. He swept both hands over three shiny blue cups, glistening in the sunlight. "For this, I will need a volunteer."

Several hands raised immediately. Benny scanned the crowd and then selected a young man with a mechanical hand sticking out from his coat. He had mousy brown hair and had more freckles than an automaton had bolts. The mechanical stepped up on the platform and stood opposite Benny.

A mechanical was the perfect first mark for his show—people with metal appendages were thought to be lesser beings by most of the realms. Benny personally didn't care if mechanicals were lesser or not. He only cared about setting up the perfect trick.

"You seem a sharp lad for a mechanical," Benny said, smiling.

The young mechanical rolled his eyes. "Aye, well, what do you want me to do?"

Benny wiggled his fingers over each cup before lifting the middle one to reveal a small ball underneath. "Follow the ball."

"Right. Got it," the young mechanical replied.

Sydney's music picked up the beat, slightly altering for the game.

Benny cracked his knuckles over the cups and then worked his magic on them. The cups moved smoothly across the table's surface, flowing under his touch. He glanced up once to make sure the mechanical kept his eyes on the cups. To his credit, he appeared to be on track.

"Right!" Benny said, removing his hands. "Which cup has the ball?"

The mechanical looked up once and met Benny's eyes. "The left one."

Benny grabbed the cup and raised it over his head. "And he is correct."

The crowd applauded.

"Now that you've gotten your feet wet, let's make it interesting," Benny said, reaching into his coat pocket and dropping three silver coins on the table. "Are you a betting mechanical?"

The mechanical grinned and reached into his own coat. He dropped three of the same coins on the table next to Benny's. "Aye."

"Once, or do you need a two out of three?" Benny asked, laying his hands on the cups once more.

"Once," he replied, setting both his flesh and mechanical hands on the table. "I'm on my lunch. Let's do this."

Benny indicated the ball, still under the left cup. He then worked his skill over the cups, weaving them in and out of each other. Again, he lifted his hands and asked the mechanical to pick a cup.

Their eyes met.

"The middle one."

Benny sighed and lifted the cup. The ball sat perfectly in the center. "Congrats, lad."

The mechanical scooped up the coins in his metal hand and pocketed the coins. "Thanks."

"All part of the risk." Benny waved to the audience. "Who is next?"

More hands raised, this time with a little more eagerness.

Benny pointed at the big man who had been sneering at him through the whole show. As the man stepped on the platform, Benny gestured to Sydney.

The music picked up tempo.

"I'm still waiting on those extraordinary tricks of yours, *Phuzzey*," the big man said.

Benny grinned. You're already in one.

"Let's go straight to the betting," the man said, reaching into his pocket and removing six coins. "And we'll make it two out of three to give you a fair chance."

"If you insist." Benny matched the coins on the table. "Keep your eye on the ball."

Benny worked the cups over the table, making *whoop, whoop* sounds with every turn of the cup.

"You're slow at this," the big man said with a smirk.

"We'll see," Benny replied, stopping.

Benny decided to have a little fun with the man. Two out of three, after all. He lifted his hands off the cups, and the music slowed. The big man reached for the far right cup.

"Think hard now," Benny said. "You don't want to be outdone by that mechanical lad, do you?"

The man paused mid-grab, his hand lingering over the cup. He blinked, and Sydney continued to play. Benny looked down quick, stealing a look at the middle cup. The man reacted immediately and snatched up the middle cup to reveal . . . nothing.

A few in the crowd chuckled, others cheered the man to keep trying, but all applauded.

The big man's face burned at his first fault. But Benny ensured the man won the second time easily, not playing any mind games, and keeping the music steady.

Two out of three.

"I'm getting those coins of yours," the big man spat.

"I'm sure you will." Benny smiled.

Again, Benny spun the cups, and again the big man followed his every movement. This time the crowd watched with a hushed eagerness. The only sound was the scraping of the cups on the table and Sydney's music.

Benny raised his hands dramatically. Sydney's beat shifted ever so slightly. So few would notice, but Benny knew it well.

"Choose wisely," Benny said, unable to restrain a snicker.

"Baited carnie," the man said under his breath.

There were several ways to influence a person to choose a cup. A hand a little closer to one. Not-so-subtle eye drop on another. A tick in a finger. Things that the guesser would try to read in the dealer, but Benny was always in control.

In this case, he did a slight tick in his index finger toward the left, knowing full well the ball was in the right.

The music played on.

The man's confidence waned.

He chose the left.

Benny lifted his hat with one hand and the cup in the other. "Pleasure playing the game with you, good sir."

"There's some kind of trick!" the big man bellowed, grabbing the table and lifting it. Their coins flew all over the stage. "You got a hole in this thing or—"

"No hole. No trick." Benny scooped up the cups and started to juggle them. "I'm in a generous mood today, sir. For being such a good sport. You may take two of your coins back."

The audience laughed. The big man scoffed as he replaced the table and picked up the two he was permitted off the platform.

Benny's grin widened as the man left. The cups and ball trick was an old one, and everyone had their theories on how it was done. Disappearing ball. Stuck in the cup. Hole in the table.

And they never once looked at Sydney—the real trick.

Out of the corner of his eye, Benny caught sight of a skinny, dirty hand slide toward one of his coins on the edge of the platform. He did a quick jig toward the edge, still juggling, and stomped at the hand. The young urchin lass withdrew her hand, her face twitching.

The show went on for another hour. Him doing his act to a growing crowd, interested in seeing what they might gain off him, or lose.

Benny always played it carefully. He chose his marks, lost when he chose, won when he chose. He never bet for anything too valuable; it was far too dangerous. But he always walked away with enough coin to weigh down his coat pocket and a few items worth pawning for a few extra coin.

Though today he had nearly overdone it. He had coaxed the young couple on stage, winning a few coins from the gentleman and something quite unexpected from the lady. Benny had caught sight of an unusual necklace. A simple chain with a hideously unfashionable wooden frame. But he could swear there was a small piece of tustium metal in the frame—the rarest metal in all of the realms of Imperium. Even a small fragment such as that was worth more than the fancy pocket watch he had won off another.

Benny had to have it.

Something that hideous but adorned on a young woman must have been for sentimental reasons. There could be no other. So with a few quick signals to Sydney, a faster tempo was played from sound five in his bot's programming.

He wanted the young woman to trust him and his game.

She did, although the instant she lost, the spell of the song nearly broke in an instant. But Sydney, the intrepid automaton that he was, kept playing. And she left the platform, looking a bit shellshocked. Benny was certain the music would wear off by the evening. But by then, he would have made his coin off the necklace.

A few hours later, Benny took a break for lunch. His fingers were sore, and his eyes strained. He hunkered behind the curtain to his platform and nibbled on some dried fruit and a pasty as Sydney played a ditty for the audience. Just as he lifted his mug of grog to his lips, the ringmaster of the carnival, Gideon Bramble, approached.

"High afternoon, Benny," Bramble said, his bright red tailcoat glistening in the noonday sun.

"Conductor," Benny replied with a tip of his top hat. Even after six months on the carnival, Benny wasn't used to calling the ringleader conductor, even if the show was built around Bramble's beloved train.

"How're the people treating you?" Bramble inquired, pushing back his glossy black conductor's cap with goggles. It was Bramble's silly attempt to combine a conductor's hat with the class of a top hat. It looked more like a glop of grease with goggles on the man's head.

"Can't complain."

"But there was a complaint toward you," Bramble said, his voice lowered.

Benny set down his mug. "A complaint?"

"Aye, from a doctor that claims you swiped his lady friend's necklace."

Benny's brow furrowed. So soon? Usually the influence of Sydney's music didn't wear off for several more hours.

"I didn't swipe nothing, Gideon. I make the risks clear before I—"

Bramble held up his hand. "Ah, let's not pretend there's not a gimmick to your show. I might not have figured it out myself, but that doesn't mean I can't smell the rotten cheese in your pantry."

Benny returned his mug to his lips to conceal his smile.

"I pacified the doctor, but you need to choose your marks more carefully. And speaking of being careful." He crossed his arms. "What are my three rules?"

Benny sighed. Not this again.

"The rules," Bramble reiterated. "What are they?"

Benny sat up straighter. "Rule number one: never reveal your secrets. Rule number two: never underestimate an urchin. And rule number three: never betray you."

"Right, and yet, what did I see? You tried to stomp an urchin's hand."

"She tried to take my coin."

"Don't be a fool, Benny. Those urchins are clever. They survive on the streets by their genius and teamwork. You attack one, and they'll come at you like a swarm of bees protecting their queen."

Benny rolled his eyes. "You think too highly of a bunch of dirty children."

"Rule number two exists for a reason, Benny." He removed his pocket watch and looked at the time. "My show is about to start. Mind what I told you."

"You just keep that whiney doctor off my back about the necklace." Benny eyed the watch. "Is that new?"

"Aye, lost the last one."

"That's, what, your third watch this month?"

"By the realms, I hardly know anymore."

Benny smiled, enjoying Sydney's music a little more.

That reminds me. I never did pawn his last watch. Better do that tonight with today's earnings.

Swallowing his last bite of pasty, Benny stepped back on the platform to renew his performance. As before, he told jokes and juggled while Sydney played his songs.

Benny scanned the new crowd. An older lady with her grandchildren. A few couples. A handful of working class mechanicals. And, of course, the same group of urchins as before. Children were more attracted to Sydney's music than adults.

But there was one new urchin in the group that caught Benny's attention. He was a blond boy, surprisingly clean for an urchin. Some sentimental fool must have donated some clothes to him. He wore a cap and suspenders over a dark blue shirt.

But the urchin's eyes glared at Benny.

Benny continued juggling. Let him glare. It was only a matter of time before he too would fall under Sydney's hypnotic music. Even the girl he had nearly stomped on was watching him with some enthusiasm, clearly having forgotten the whole exchange.

As his performance went on, Benny was aware that the strange boy walked closer, his glare ever present. He kept drawing near, until he was at the foot of the platform.

Benny called for volunteers, pleased at the number of hands raised.

The urchin raised his hand as well.

Benny ignored him and selected the person directly behind—a middle-aged woman with her own automaton in tow. It was tempting to gamble for the bot, but such a win would surely turn some audience members away.

It was always best to allow the first targets to win, making it more comfortable for more to try.

And they did try. A young man trying to impress his new bride lost his wedding ring. A female mechanical won two coins. An older gentleman lost his cufflinks.

On and on it went. Some wins. Some losses.

The urchin still glared with his hand raised.

Benny continued to ignore him.

It unsettled Benny to his core that the boy didn't look at him favorably. The boy seemed unaffected by the music, jokes, or tricks. At one point, Benny wondered if the lad was deaf. To test this, Benny returned to juggling and asked the audience a few questions about their day, making funny comments about them.

Benny looked at the urchin. "Having fun today, boy?"

"Yes," the boy responded, face unchanged.

"Then perhaps you could smile a little. You look like you're lost."

"I'm only lost to how you're supposed to be entertaining."

The audience erupted in laughter, far more than they had at any of Benny's jokes. Benny grunted and moved on. The boy was certainly not deaf.

He returned to his cups and once again picked someone other than the lad. He had to get the boy out of his mind.

Rule number two.

Bah! Gideon Bramble is mad, and he doesn't have a hypnosis automaton. What have I to fear?

He stole a glance at the boy again as his next target stepped on the platform.

The urchin was gone.

Finally, the lad had gotten bored and moved on. Now he could focus on his work.

Benny was in the middle of scamming a gentleman out of his gold tie clip when a voice interrupted him. "Master Benjamin."

"Sydney!" Benny shouted, nearly losing the cups in his hands. "I told you to never—"

"Someone is inside my gears, Master Benjamin."

Benny spun around just in time to see the curtain behind Sydney move. Sydney rocked back and forth, his entire back plate hanging on a single screw. Benny dropped the cups and ran through the curtain. He looked for the culprit but saw no one.

He gritted his teeth. Urchins had a reputation for being slippery.

Rule number two.

Benny hurried to Sydney and examined his insides. One of Sydney's glass tubes was missing. It was a minor thing, but Sydney could lose power quickly if not replaced. Good thing Benny had spare tubes in his train car.

"Sorry for the delay, folks," Benny said as he twisted the screws back in place. He didn't have his screwdriver to make it secure, but it'd at least hold the plate upright until he returned. "My automaton partner needs some quick maintenance. I'll be right back."

Benny leaped off the stage and raced to his train car. He hoped that Sydney's music kept the audience appeased until he returned. He found a spare tube in a box under his cot and ran back to the platform. Sydney still played as Benny returned, but the sound dragged slightly. Benny couldn't put the tube inside the automaton fast enough for his liking.

Feeling he had no choice, he conceded defeat to the gentleman he had last played. The man walked away with six of Benny's coins.

Benny had never lost so much before.

I'm going to drop that baited runt into the Ethereal Depths for this.

Not ten minutes later, while fumbling with his cards, the urchin reappeared at the back of the crowd.

He was smiling.

Benny dropped his cards and pointed at the urchin. "Did you touch my bot, boy?"

The boy nodded.

"What do you want?" Benny bellowed, his face heating up.

He didn't know why the urchin irritated him so much. Perhaps it was because he refused to leave his stage. Or it was the glare.

Or the fact that Sydney seemed to have no influence over him.

"I want to play against you," the urchin replied, still smiling.

"If you play, will you go away?"

"Sure."

"Then get up here!"

Benny would have never talked to a child that way in front of an audience, even a street urchin, if not for Sydney's music.

The boy made his way to the platform, and Benny took his seat behind his table.

"How many tries, lad?" Benny asked as the boy stood before him.

The lad was barely tall enough to look down on the cups. And up close, the urchin was much younger than Benny thought. Six, maybe seven years old. His eyes were bright blue and sharp. His stringy blonde hair fell over his ears, even with the cap on. As the boy approached, he awkwardly adjusted his cap over his right ear.

The boy crossed his arms. "Name's Watts."

"I don't care, and that doesn't answer my question."

"I just want you to remember my name . . . for later." He looked over the cups. "How many tries to get that necklace?"

"What?"

"That tustium necklace you swiped from my friend Claire. How many tries?"

Benny sat up in his seat. All that stalking and annoyance was about an ugly necklace? "None. I won it fair and square."

"Right, fair and square." The boy rolled his eyes. He then reached into his pant pocket and dropped a pocket watch on the table. "I can barter for it. Will this be fair?"

Benny paled at the sight of the watch. It was Conductor Bramble's that he had forgotten to pawn. The boy had been in his train car!

"Thank you for showing me which car was yours," Watts said. "Me and my mates found a lot of fun stuff there. Thinking about telling the conductor about it."

Benny's hands trembled. Was he really being blackmailed by an urchin? "What makes you think he'll believe you?"

"We could find out together."

Benny paused. He didn't want to face the conductor, not when he had such odd respect for urchins. Worst case scenario, he would have Sydney playing nearby to help his case. But it wasn't a guarantee.

"All you want is the necklace?" Benny asked.

"Aye."

"And if you lose?"

"You get the watch, and I walk away."

Benny reached into his pocket and placed the necklace next to the pocket watch. "Walk away and say nothing to Conductor Bramble."

Watts nodded. "Done."

"The necklace that important to you?" Benny cracked his knuckles.

"Claire is."

Perhaps that's why the music hasn't persuaded him. But this close, he has to be influenced. Maybe I can use his feelings against him.

"She your sister or something?" Benny inquired.

Watts shook his head. "Employer."

Benny's face contorted. "And you're how old?"

"Don't know."

This is going nowhere. I just need to shuffle him out.

"Two out of three," Benny said, gripping the cups.

"Four out of six," Watts said. "I want you to know that I beat you."

"You even know how to count, urchin?"

Watts grinned. "Count and spell. Thanks to Claire."

A literate urchin. Just what the realms need.

Benny wiggled his fingers over the cups, signaling Sydney. The music picked up the tempo.

"I guess you need all the help you can get," Watts said.

What does he mean by that? He can't possibly know.

"You're all talk, lad," Benny replied. "I hope to the Master above that you can talk your friend Claire into feeling better without her necklace."

"I'm not worried."

Benny went to work on the cups. There would be no playing or manipulating wins and losses. He wanted to be rid of his child. Four wins, and he would be gone.

Rule number two.

The boy's eyes followed Benny's hands.

"Middle," Watts said as soon as Benny stopped.

"Wait until I remove my hands," Benny snapped.

"Still the middle."

Benny grunted and lifted the cup. The audience cheered the boy, giddy and oblivious to the battle between the two, thanks to Sydney.

"You're not very good at this," Watts said.

"You're not very good at being a good sportsman," Benny retorted.

Benny resumed his shuffling of the cups.

"I heard your jokes, saw you juggle . . ." Watts continued. "I'm *phuzzey* on why so many people like your show."

Benny growled and lifted his hands.

"Left cup."

Sneering at a second loss, Benny shuffled again.

Watts kept on prattling. "Biggest surprise of all was Claire. She'd never risk losing her necklace. It means the realms to her. And then you stomped at my mate Twitchy, and she still liked you. Middle cup again. I just couldn't make sense of it."

Benny shook his head. The boy only needed one more win. How did this happen?

Nothing worked. None of his usual twitches, gestures, or glances worked. The boy kept talking and wouldn't let Benny say a word to influence him.

This had to be the best shuffle of Benny's life.

His palms sweated over the cups.

"So if you're not the best trick in the show." Watts snickered. "Then it's Sydney."

Benny swallowed but kept shuffling.

"So that got me thinking. What's so special about a music bot?"

Benny stopped shuffling and lifted his hands.

Sydney played the best song of his metallic existence.

Watts looked up at the sky. "Then I got the idea. Maybe I'm the one that's special. Cause there is something about me—"

"Pick a cup!" Benny shouted.

"Fine, guess you won't learn my trick." Watts reached out and lifted the middle cup, revealing the ball. "You lose."

"Blast you, baited child!" Benny slammed his fists on the table. The audience recoiled at that one, despite Sydney.

"Now, who is a poor sport?" Watts reclaimed the necklace. "Keep the watch, Phuzzey. I'm sure Conductor Bramble would want it back."

Benny looked up and saw Gideon Bramble walking toward the platform, led by many urchins.

It was over. The real trick was over. But perhaps he could work his way out of a few broken bones with Sydney.

"By the way," Watts added, adjusting his cap correctly on his head, "I got my name because I've tinkered with electrics thanks to my pa being an engineer. Claire doesn't like me messing with machines; she thinks I'm too young, but I just can't help myself sometimes."

"Master . . . Benjamin . . ."

Benny turned around and saw smoke billow from Sydney's back.

"Something is not right."

"Sydney!"

The automaton made a coughing sound, his eyes flashed rapidly, and his organ came to a halt. He tottered on his feet and then fell on what would have been his posterior. "I need to rest, Master Benjamin."

"That's for Twitchy," Watts said.

Benny turned back to the boy. "You did this."

"Sometimes what's put in a bot is more important than what's taken out," Watts said, chuckling.

"How did you do it?"

"A coin in the gears."

"Not that, you filthy urchin. How did you ignore the music?"

Watts smiled again.

Conductor Bramble reached the stage, now accompanied by two of the locomotive's crew members.

"Benny," Bramble said as the crew members grabbed him by the arms. "I want a word with you."

"Conductor Bramble, I can explain!" Benny struggled against the men.

"What are my three rules, Benny?" the conductor shook his head. "I hear you've broken all three. The first two are bad enough . . ." his voice lowered, "but to betray me is unforgivable."

"Conductor . . ."

Bramble turned to the audience. "Ladies, gentlemen, and mechanicals. I apologize for the disruption of the show. If you've been offended by this man, see me at the end of the day. I'm sure we can work things out."

He turned to Watts and shook his hand. "Thank you, lad."

"Your watch is on the table, sir," Watts said.

"You want the bot?"

"Naw, I only wanted Claire's necklace back. And I got it."

Bramble cocked his head. "You sure?"

The boy nodded.

"How did you do it?" Benny screamed again.

"Oh, right." Watts removed his cap and lifted his hair off his right ear. A strange scar, almost like a burn, ran from his inner ear and into his hair. "Lost my hearing in this ear. That's why Claire doesn't like me working on machines. She worries."

The air left Benny's lungs. One ear. The urchin was deaf in one ear. It must have been enough interference with Sydney's music, like Benny's earplugs. Combined with the lad's determination to avenge his friend, he had unwittingly stumbled on the real trick.

Watts replaced his cap, eyes on Benny. "Claire thinks she takes care of me, but I take care of her. Always will, got it?"

Benny scowled. "Whatever."

The boy leaped off the platform and ran, calling out for his friend as he did.

"Clever lad," Bramble said. "He might just have a good future ahead of him. You, on the other hand . . ."

Benny struggled against his captors, but it was useless.

"Come back to my train. I'd love for us to have a conversation without Sydney."

Benny swallowed. *Rule number two.*

TO WIN

Nobel Shut Chan

My sister and I look alike,
Though I am much more full of spite;
She was more a tender girl,
Who wooed the boys with furtive eyes.
Never mind, she's long gone now
With all her pretty lies as well;
Now I lie in her love's arms
And now she lies in burning Hell.
"Mira," in his midnight voice,
He turns to kiss me on the lips;
"Mira, dear, your sister was
Never quite as good as this."
Never quite? She was a fool
Who couldn't kiss to save her life,
Only he would fall for her
And leave behind his faithful wife.
Never mind, he's long gone now

His skin turns darker by the day;
Nighttime stalks him while he sleeps
And every dawn chips bits away.
Of course he's fool enough to drink
The heady things I leave for him,
My sister too, that stupid thing,
Who downs a glass without a sip.
Little sisters always take
Things that are not meant for them;
Older sisters take them back,
Revenge is such a loving sin.

Mira, Mira, down the hall,
Who's the luckiest of them all?
Mira, dearest, in your heart
Did you really think he could tell us apart?

HEARTS OF FLESH

Nathaniel Luscombe

I USED A DAMP cloth to wipe the gears. Dried blood and oil coated the smooth surface, clogging the spaces where they were supposed to fit together.

Beside me, Lillian wrung her cloth into the bucket of pink, bloody water. "You need to keep your machine clean. If it's always dirty, you can't expect it to run properly," she huffed.

"I don't always have time to clean it," I protested. I knew how important it was, but the battles were growing more frequent. I hardly had enough time to sleep between them, much less give my weapon a bath.

"Well, they're going to lose if they send their fighters out in machines like this." She shook her head and smiled triumphantly. "Here's the problem. It's like I thought. The gear has a little crack, and now it's crooked. That's why your left leg is struggling to move smoothly."

I took the gear from her and inspected it. Even the smallest change threw the machine off its rhythm. "I really need to get guards." I looked at the ones hanging on the wall. They came in all shapes and sizes, designed to keep the gears protected during the wars. Along the legs of my machine, there were exposed sections—the Achilles' heel. A direct hit would be enough to knock me down. I spent more time on defense than offense, protecting myself in hopes that I would survive.

"Why don't you get guards?" Lillian asked. She was bent over her work table, searching for the right size gear. I watched her for a moment, noticing the way she bit her lip as she concentrated. Her eyes looked up and locked on mine, a light flush flooding her cheeks. "What?"

I looked away, mumbling, "Nothing."

I refused to fall in love with my best friend. But love, like gears, often fell in and out in unexpected ways. I'd never even expected to meet someone like Lillian. She'd moved here a few years ago with her dad, a traveler from another village. It was luck that brought us together. Or fate.

Lillian finally found one, took it out of the box and replaced it with the damaged gear. I knew she would stay up late one night, hovering over a fire as she worked on fixing the gear to sell to someone else.

I was proud of my machine. He'd gotten me through many wars, from the first time I was drafted until the battle that almost killed me yesterday. The cockpit was on the top, a small space with a seat and all the controls. It rested on four legs. Two of them were large, jutting forward to give it more mobility. The ones in the back were shorter. They gave me balance.

"You didn't answer my other question," Lillian reminded me. She oiled the gears, working the new one into its place. A thin line of sweat ran down her forehead. "Why won't you get guards? The fights are becoming too frequent. You have to protect yourself better."

"I can't afford it." I kicked a loose stone.

"The army pays well, doesn't it? I would give an arm and leg to make the amount you do."

"Yeah, but between supporting my mom and helping Mrs. Devers, I don't have enough to put toward the machine." I sighed. The world was so unfair. Only a month ago, I'd never worried about Mrs. Devers, the old woman downstairs. She had a son who was a decorated war hero. Until he died.

Now she relied on my money to get her enough food. I didn't mind doing it since my mom drilled into me the idea that everyone around us was family, but it was beginning to drain my resources. The military was losing money, and pay cuts were made.

Lillian wilted. "I would give them to you for free if I could, but money is tight for me too."

I hated that she felt guilty for not sacrificing her tools to help me. "There's nothing you can do about it. I've survived many battles. I'm sure I can survive a few more. I'm saving up."

Lillian didn't answer. She was too focused on making sure her modifications didn't mess up my machine. I walked around it and climbed up the front leg. The top rose, and I stepped inside. It wasn't big, but I had grown familiar with it,like a second body.

"What are you doing?" Lillian called up.

"Checking the needles. They've been irritating me lately." I bent over the chair and activated it. A lining of needles emerged from inside the material. They would run down my spine, allowing me to control the machine better than my hands could.

I saw the problem immediately. One of the needles near the top was bent. The tube inside was still intact, but it pierced more skin than the others, making it more painful while I was piloting. I groaned. "One of my needles is twisted."

Lillian popped up, her chin resting on the edge of the machine. "I have needles around here somewhere. I don't use them very much. You can take one free of charge."

"I don't—"

"I won't take no for an answer, Clarence. Take them, and later we'll figure out a way for you to get guards too. I would rather lose money than have you die." She jumped down, her feet echoing on the cement floor. I waited, listening to her rummage through the mess of supplies until she came back with a needle in hand.

"Here. I'll watch you put it in." Her dark eyes followed my every move as I removed the chair's cushion. The skeletal structure was ugly—thin metal spokes waiting to be covered. Lillian handed me a pair of pliers, and I carefully extracted the crooked needle.

"Am I good to just put this in?"

"As long as it connects with the others. Try it. They're pretty easy to replace." She grinned as I leaned forward. While I was pretty comfortable on the battlefield, Lillian was at home in the shop. She knew everything there was to know about the war machines.

I slid the needle into place. "Is this good?"

"Move, I'll check." She pulled herself into the cockpit and made sure it was connected. The air felt tight with her so close. She looked up at me and seemed to notice her face was inches from mine.

"Uh—" I stuttered, rubbing the back of my neck.

She just shook her head. "Keep yourself safe, Clarence. I want to see you back here in one piece."

"Yes, ma'am." I saluted her mockingly. "I wouldn't worry too much. I'm not fighting the borckensher."

"That's not funny." She frowned. The borckensher was a beast every soldier feared. The enemy used it during their battles, but its presence was not common. Lillian clambered out and watched as I sat down. The needles entered my spine, and reality shifted, switching between me and the machine. I stepped forward, leaving the shop and Lillian behind.

•••♣•••

The battle alarm blared early in the morning, jerking me awake. My heart started pounding, adrenaline pumping through my veins. I pushed my blanket off and slipped into the cold night air.

The alarms only sounded when a battle was getting too close to the village. They needed backup. Fast. I pulled on my boots and grabbed a shirt from the floor. In the room beside me, I heard my mom quietly sobbing. She hated listening to me preparing for war.

The house was dark and quiet. I opened the door that led outside and headed down the stairs along the side of the building.

The grass glimmered from the dew. Along the horizon, a gentle stream of light pierced the sky. I ran to my machine, which rested beside the house each night and climbed up the side. It opened, and I climbed in. The needles entered my spine, and I was jolted into the inner workings of the machine.

It was always a bit jarring at first. It didn't hurt, as my body had grown used to the jabbing needles, but a cold feeling always washed over me, like ice around my bones. It was only for a split second before I gained control over the machine, but sometimes I feared that I wouldn't leave that stage. I would just be paralyzed within my machine.

I moved out onto the path that led through the village. Coordinates flashed across the screen, filled with general statistics. It looked like two scouting parties had collided, and now there was a bigger force on the way. More machines joined me, and we ran toward the conflict.

It was just a border skirmish, no doubt. They were common and didn't usually mean many casualties.

I heard the sounds before I saw the fighting. War machines were not quiet. Each arm ended in a long blade, and they scraped against each other, screeching metal against metal. My machine wavered a little, still slightly off balance. I crested the hill and looked down at the battle below.

There was a clear line between our land and theirs. We called it the ridge, a thin crevice. Our side was green, running up the hills that held our villages. Across the ridge was the desert that housed our enemies. Dry and cragged.

There hadn't been any casualties. A pilot only died when their machine had been crushed, and there were no machines lying on the ground. I ran down the hill. A few others passed me—a wave of power coming to save our fellow fighters.

I became hyper-concentrated when fighting. The machine became my body, its metal my skin and gears my muscles. I fought with everything I had, sweat running down my body. The scouting party was backing up, pushed further away from our village.

An enemy machine lumbered toward me, swiping at my legs. I used the arms to guard myself and gave it a push. The other machine started falling backward, but its back legs caught it. It reared forward and smashed into my left leg. I stumbled back. Over its shoulder, I spotted a larger party approaching. They didn't join the scuffle. The scouts turned and began heading toward the new arrivals, following unheard orders. It was a retreat. Only one machine was down, and it was one of their scouts. I watched breathlessly as the enemy machines ran away.

Most of the fights ended up being short. The enemy just wanted to keep us occupied so that they would have more success taking over the other villages. It was all part of some complicated plan. The best we could do was fight back and try not to get overrun.

It was always them that retreated. We weren't the real target yet, but one day we would be.

"Head back to the village. Report any damages on your machines before the next shift," the voice of the commander rang through the cockpit. I turned my machine around. I could tell something was wrong. It walked crooked, struggling to lift its left leg.

I opened up the channel in the machine. "I'm limping. I'll get it fixed right away."

"Copy that, number seven."

The other machines were ahead of me. Their legs moved faster, smoothly carrying them across the ground. I focused on walking in a way that wouldn't destroy the machine more. If a gear were to slip out of place, the entire leg would buckle, and I wouldn't be able to move it.

The sun was fully in the sky by the time I reached Lillian's shop. She stood by the door, clearly expecting me. Her eyebrows furrowed, and she shook her head. I retracted the needles, putting the machine into manual mode. Coming out of fighting mode was always weird. I felt like I was slammed into my body, suddenly conscious of the fact that we were separate, I a being of flesh, and it a being of metal. The top of the cockpit opened.

"Hey, Lillian!" I yelled.

"Good morning, Clarence." She stood back and let the machine enter. The cool interior of the shop felt nice. My skin was still wet with sweat, shining almost as brightly as the oily metal on the machine. "You seem to be broken. Again."

I chuckled, bringing the machine to a sudden stop. I pulled myself up and climbed down the leg. "I think I *really* need a guard. What can I do to get one?"

She frowned. "I'll think of something. I know you need one."

I groaned inwardly. Her father worked day and night to make the guards for all the different sizes of war machines. He didn't have any legs, so he spent his days in the same place, working over candlelight to make them. I couldn't take them without paying. I also didn't have the money.

"I'm not asking you to give me one, but I know that I only have a couple battles left in this condition before my machine falls apart. I need to do *something*."

Lillian studied me for a moment. "I do have an idea. I know you're not going to like it. But you don't really have a choice."

"What's your idea?"

"You let me fight in one of your small scouting skirmishes, and I'll give you guards for half the price. I can cover the rest with some of the money I've saved up. I just want a few hours in a war machine." She smiled, leaning forward to gauge my reaction.

I sputtered. "This is ridiculous. Surely you're not serious."

Sparks ignited in her eyes. "And why shouldn't I be serious? I'm just as capable of running the machine as you are. In fact, I would probably be better at it. I know how these work."

"But . . ." I trailed off, unsure of how to continue.

"But what? I'm a girl?" She growled, menacing and dangerous. "I can't believe you, Clarence. I thought you were different. Turns out all pilots are the same, stuck up and unable to see beyond their own noses." She grabbed her tools and headed to the machine, huffing the entire time. I didn't dare go near her. I just cleared space on her desk and sat down.

War had always been a man's game. The women had their place, tending to the matters in the village, but it required a true man to take another's life.

In this fight for land, the victors would be the ones to flourish. If our village lost the land, the army would continue advancing toward the capital, burning down the country on their way. Our village, and the others like it, were the only things keeping our enemies on their side of the border.

The women were just as vital to this war but in different ways. Lillian kept many of the machines running, as did other women who ran shops in the villages. A woman had never been a pilot before. It was not something I'd even thought of.

"Why would someone *want* to be a pilot?" I asked her, curious to know but also desperate for the silence to be over.

Lillian muttered under her breath, yanking on gears and cursing. She finally dropped her cloth and spun around. "So you've decided that I'm 'man' enough to have my own aspirations?"

I shrugged, unsure of how to respond. "I just don't see why someone would want to be in a war machine. It's horrible work. It's kill or be killed." I shuddered.

Her eyes softened for a second, but they steeled over soon enough. "And you don't think I know that? I deal with machines that have been completely crushed, the insides filled with the pieces of the pilot. I listen to the radio chatter between you. I hear people scream in terror as they face death. I just want a chance to protect the village. I want to fight against the monsters that have killed my people."

"You listen to the radios?" I hardly ever talked on the radio. It was distracting. But I knew that some people relied on it to stay sane.

"Yes. I hooked one up to your channels. I want to be part of this, even if it's just for one fight."

"It's dangerous. I don't know how to even go about putting you into the war."

She lit up. "I made a plan yesterday. I know how we can do this."

As much as I hated the idea, the way she responded made me happy. I couldn't deny my feelings for Lillian. If this was the thing that would help fulfill her dreams, then I wanted to have a part in it. Besides, she could join a scouting party. They knew I was quiet, so she wouldn't even have to talk to them. The chances of being attacked were low, and if they were, the defense would come in quickly.

The more I thought about it, the more I realized it wasn't as dangerous as I first thought.

"What's your plan?" I asked, pushing myself off the table.

She laid it all out so well. She would go on a simple scouting mission. She didn't need to fight. Driving the machine was more than enough. While she was out, she would connect the machine to the shop's radio. That would allow her to talk to me if she needed help with something. I would hide in the shop while she was gone. My only task was to make sure no one knew that I was there. By the time she got to the end of her plan, I was as excited as she was. This was an easy way for me to get guards. All I had to do was sit in the shop for three hours while she rode the machine around the borders of the village.

And it was all happening tomorrow morning.

I knew it would be safe because there had never been a scout war two days in a row. The enemy attacked different villages, but they were strategic in the way they worked, moving from one to the next to weaken the entire border.

"Which guards do you want?" Lillian asked. She stepped back and let me look at them all. They were hung on the wall in sets of four; two larger ones for the front and two smaller ones for the back.

"I'll take those ones." I selected sleek, black guards. They didn't stick out too much, but they would do their job. Some people chose fancier guards, but I thought it made their machines stand out. I wanted to blend in with everyone else.

She took them down and handed them to me. We put them on together, hiding the gears.

"It's never looked better," I commented, stepping back. Immense pride filled my chest. I couldn't wait to ride this out. I turned to Lillian and let out a surprised grunt when she threw herself on me, wrapping her arms around my neck. "Thank you for letting me do this," she whispered.

I stood still for a moment before bringing my arms around her. "You're welcome. Just don't hurt the machine."

"Pretty sure I'm too weak for that." She smiled teasingly.

I couldn't stop myself from staring deep into her eyes. "Just be careful tomorrow. If you need any help, let me know."

She leaned in and left a small kiss on my cheek. "I will. It'll be fine. If anything happens, I know you'll help me."

I was too stunned from the kiss to even respond to her words. For a moment, I imagined her dying tomorrow. It would be my fault. I pushed the thought away, unable to even approach the subject. I'd gained her trust, so next, I would try to earn her heart.

Evening drew closer, the afternoon having slipped past during our planning. I had to get home before Mom worried too much about me. I left the machine there for the night. Lillian wanted to do some work on it before she took it out the next day.

•••♣•••

The cold morning air left my face feeling numb. I buried my hands in my jacket and hurried to the shop. The lights were on, and the door was unlocked. I stepped into the warm interior.

Lillian looked up from the desk. There were lines across her cheeks, a testament of the night she'd spent sleeping there. She ran a hand through her hair and smiled. "Good morning, Clarence."

"Good morning." I approached slowly, still half asleep. "How are you feeling?"

"Tired and excited."

"Not nervous?"

"Nope. Not one bit." She laughed, then yawned. "It was hard for me to sleep. I've waited my entire life for this."

"I'm glad this means so much to you. We could both get in a lot of trouble, so it has to be worth it." I grimaced. If we were caught, it could mean a cut in my pay or expulsion from the military.

Worse, Lillian might get hurt.

Lillian stood and hurried to the war machine. She went to climb, then turned and ran to me. She grabbed my hand and closed the distance between us with a kiss. Time seemed to pause. All I wanted was for this to never end. Our relationship, not the kiss. Though the kiss was short, it ignited something in my soul. Her eyes shone as she looked at me, and she smiled. "I would be nervous if I didn't know you were on the other end of the radio."

"I'll keep you safe." I blushed, stumbling over my words. "Just let me know if anything happens."

"Of course." She hurried back to the machine and pulled herself up into the cockpit. It closed over her, shutting her off from me. I sat down at the desk.

The radio crackled. "Can you hear me?"

"Loud and clear."

"Good." She moved the machine forward. It lumbered out of the shop and into the quiet street. I closed the door behind her. I had to make sure no one realized I was here.

The first shift started. I played with my thumbs, knocking them against each other as I listened to Lillian breathe. It was such a personal sound. I almost felt like I was invading her space. It was nice, being this trusted.

The first half-hour was quiet. The gentle thump of the machine's footfalls were a constant reminder of what we were doing.

Letting Lillian command my machine was not something I ever thought I would do, but there was no way I could say no when she asked. I just wanted her to be happy. Besides, what the soldiers didn't know wouldn't hurt them. As long as this scouting went as planned, things would be fine.

And when the bell rang, that's when I realized how poorly I'd judged the enemy. Lillian's breath hitched. "We're receiving news of a force moving along the edge of the village. We're getting sent to check it out."

"I doubt they'll attack you," I assured her. "Stick to the back of the scouters and don't get involved if you don't have to."

“Okay.” She took a deep breath. I placed my ear against the radio. Away from her voice and the footsteps, there was another sound, a quiet screech that seemed to shake the war machine.

Dread filled my stomach. “Turn on the radio for the other machines.”

She flipped it on, and voices poured into the cockpit. Through the ruckus, I heard one thing mentioned again and again—a borckensher. My breathing quickened, and my heart began to pound.

The reports were flooding in. Outside, the thump of machines echoed in the streets. A startled scream filled the sky. I felt powerless inside the shop, unable to move, unable to protect.

“What’s going on?” Lillian asked.

“There’s a borckensher.” I explained.

“I know that.” She snapped, tense. “What am I supposed to do?”

“Don’t get close. It won’t hesitate to rip you apart. They’re only used in bigger attacks—they attack anything that moves.” My voice shook. It was almost impossible to survive a direct attack from a borckensher. I’d never faced one, but I’d heard rumors of them tearing down entire villages.

As she grew nearer, I heard the horrific sounds of a battle. The borckensher’s savage screams and the tearing metal sent chills down my spine.

“How close are you?” I stood up, sweat running down my back.

“It’s tearing apart the middle street. There’s blood everywhere, and I can’t move back much farther.” Her panicked breathing filled the radio. “Clarence . . . at least five machines are down.”

“Can’t you turn and run?” I turned the radio up and ran for the window. Her shop was close to the center of the village. Even without the radio, I could hear the battle. “Come back and we’ll switch spots!” I yelled.

“I can try.” Her voice had turned to a resigned, flat tone. She was prepared to die. To sacrifice herself to save the village.

I ran back to the radio. “You have to run, Lillian. Get out of there. You’re not a trained soldier.”

The fear in her voice had turned to a resigned, flat tone. She was prepared to die. To sacrifice herself to save the village. I pulled the radio close. “You have to run, Lillian. Get out of there. You’re not a trained soldier.”

“But—” Her voice paused, and she seemed to halt for a moment “—I don’t think I can.”

I pulled away from the radio. “No . . . no, Lillian!”

“I want you to know something,” she said. “Just know that I love you, I always have. Thank you for believing in me.”

I picked up the radio, cradling it close to my chest. It was the last thing I had of her. "Lillian, you have to run. If you truly love me, then run!"

She sniffled on the other end. Her silence scared me. This wasn't a normal response. The borckensher screamed as it drew closer. She wasn't crying as hard as I thought someone would in that situation. Even I would be crying while facing a borckensher. Skills didn't matter when up against demons.

The claws dug into the side of the machine. Lillian screamed, fighting back. I heard the blades struggling to turn as Lillian tried to stab the beast. The crash shook the radio, the borckensher battling her to the ground. After that, there was just startling silence.

That was when the world ended. We were all dead. Everyone in this village. I wanted to go home and get my mom and Mrs. Devers out of there, but I also knew that she would hate me for letting Lillian go. I killed the only girl that I'd ever loved. My heart shattered.

I pushed myself up from the table. The borckensher was coming closer. Its shrieks pierced through the walls. I knew then that someone had to warn the villages around us. If this town was overrun, it would mean an end to this part of the border. We were about to be pushed back.

If I could get some backup, we had a chance to stop that from happening.

I staggered, the weight of everything pushing me down. I opened the back door and started for the hill that rose behind the village. Once at the top, I stared at the world before me. The villages were spread out, small wisps of smoke rising into the smoky sky. Black clumps of enemy machines marched in the distance, heading toward the border in the endless fight to steal our land.

The land between us was flat. Grass wavered in the wind, tall enough to hide in. If I could reach it before anyone noticed, I had a chance of getting to the nearest village.

Tears ran down my face as I started down the hill. The burning remains of Lillian's kiss lingered on my lips, reminding me of the promise I'd made to protect her. I could no longer keep that promise, but I could try to save others who still lived in the world that would never stop crumbling.

I ignored the tired, painful resonance that buzzed around my head. I'd never felt such a range of strong emotions before. My legs moved without command. This was surviving. Even though I wanted to die, there was a will pushing me to my limits.

I heard the town ripping apart at the seams. I imagined the borkensher tearing into my home, knocking down the walls and grabbing my mom's frail body in its bloody claws. I turned, hesitant, and looked for signs of the battle.

Smoke drifted over Lillian's shop. I saw flames reflecting through the glass as a small fire grew into a blaze. I forced myself to run in the opposite direction.

More enemies emerged along the horizon.

The savage growl of the borckensher sounded much too close. I turned and saw it barrelling down the hill. Behind it, the broken walls of the shop shattered, falling in a flurry of glimmering sparks. There was just open ground between us now. It was a good distance, but not enough. I tripped over my feet, tumbling into the tall grass. I knew I was going to die. My heart pounded loudly, blood rushing to my ears.

I wasn't ready to die.

The borckensher's head pushed through the grass. Its black nose emerged first, followed by the yellow eyes that narrowed when they caught sight of me. Sharp canines hung past its bottom jaw. Blood tinged saliva dripped off its fangs.

"Don't kill him yet." A voice spoke from beyond the grass. I jerked, almost sobbing. It was Lillian's voice. I heard her drop to the ground. She stepped into the small ring of flattened grass. Her body was not broken or mangled into the folds of twisted metal.

"How are you alive?" I gasped.

"Because the borckensher won't kill me." Her voice was like steel, holding no emotion, but her eyes were full of turmoil.

"What's going on?" I backed away from them. The borckensher growled.

"I'm just another tool in this war, Clarence. I was planted in this village to help bring it down."

I stopped and stared at her, bewildered. "You're a traitor?"

"No, since I've been on their side all along. I'm a *spy*. But even with my training, there's one thing they couldn't predict. My heart. I fell in love with you, Clarence, but this war can't keep both of us alive."

"Not even if I'm in love with you?" I almost regretted saying it out loud. She looked so torn, and I felt sorry for her. My shattered heart was breaking into more pieces. Even though she was the enemy. It had come down to a fight between Lillian and herself. I just hoped she would make the right choice.

The borckensher opened its mouth, revealing sharp teeth. I stumbled away as it approached. The smell of blood covered its body. Lillian grabbed onto its thick hair and pulled herself onto its back. She settled between its shoulders. "When you die . . ." her voice broke. She just stared at me.

The borckensher lunged. I rolled away, but I couldn't escape without leaving trails in the grass. There was no place for me to hide. I was only delaying the inevitable. I felt the warm breath of the beast on my neck. It came for me again, its fangs almost closing over my skin. Lillian screamed and the borckensher stopped.

"Don't hurt him!" She held up her hands, standing between me and the borckensher. It snapped at her, its eyes still focused on me. It had its own programming to follow. She flinched, but didn't move out of the way. They circled one another. Predator facing predator.

Lillian made the first move. She grabbed onto the borckensher's neck and whipped out a knife. It pulled away, but she drew drops of blood from its matted fur. It roared in pain and betrayal.

They tumbled through the grass, biting and stabbing at each other. I backed away. While I knew Lillian couldn't win, I also felt wrong leaving her there. There was blood slowly spreading through the grass. Lillian didn't let out any cries of pain, but her movements were slowing.

I stood back, fists clenched, unsure of what to do. My instinct was to save Lillian, but now that I knew she was the enemy, my training was setting in. Anyone who was an enemy had to die.

She spun to get out of the borckensher's way, and her eyes met mine for just a moment. I stepped forward, ready to save her, my heart beating faster than ever before. She misstepped and tripped. The borckensher closed its jaws around her midsection. She let out a scream, her blade burying itself in the beast's neck.

"Lillian!" I yelled, running forward. The borckensher dropped her, staggering back with its own wound. I grabbed her and held her in my arms. The ground shook as the borckensher tumbled and died. "Clarence," she whispered, her body arching with pain, "I'm so sorry."

I wiped a tear off her cheek, but it was replaced by my own. I leaned down and touched my forehead to hers. "Stay with me," I pleaded.

She gasped, her hand reaching up to touch my cheek. She couldn't speak. The bitemarks were too much, and she was slipping away. I felt myself losing her.

"Please! Lillian!" I couldn't lose her twice in one day.

She didn't move. Her body drooped, and she left me behind. There was just me, her body, and a cold wind that tore through the grass. This was how it all ended. The girl I loved died protecting me only minutes after almost killing me herself.

Life was too cruel.

I bowed over her body. The battle was still raging on, but I couldn't move. I held her until the village began to grow quiet. Without the borckensher, the fighters would have to hold their ground. If they fell back, there was some hope for us yet.

I looked up at the distant villages. I had to go. I laid her gently on the ground, leaving her as peacefully as I could, and forced myself to get up. The sorrow quickly turned to anger. I ran, fierce energy coursing through me. I was now fighting the urge to fight something, burning with the desire to *kill.* Before I did that, I had to warn the other villages. We had to regain our footing.

I was going to stop this war once and for all. I just had to see the enemy's tricks before they were sprung on us.

FAE BLOOD

Hannah Carter

"Do you know what color fae blood is?
Green, my son, naught but green—
So go now forth and slay their queen.
But beware, for she seeks her mate,
And only death can stop this fate.
For if she steals one of your kin,
She must die for you to win."

JAN FINISHED THE story and smiled at her little brother in the firelight.

"I don't like that story. It's too scary." Tommy curled up in his blanket, only his eyes and the tip of his nose visible from inside his cocoon.

Jan closed the picture book and left it behind on her chair before she padded closer to his bed. "But it used to be your favorite, Tommy. Why don't you like it now?"

Tommy glanced away. "Because. I just don't."

"Fair enough." She sat down on the edge of the bed, brushed a kiss against his baby-soft skin, and lingered there. "But it's okay, you know. No fae will ever hurt you. I promise. I'll keep you safe."

A few tears trickled out of Tommy's eyes as he shook his head. He pulled his makeshift hood closer around him and sniveled. "Why didn't the fae leave a changeling in Dad's place when they killed him?"

Jan furrowed her brow. "Well . . ." She reached for his dark hair so that she could stroke it.

"Why?!"

Jan started. "Shh! Don't wake Mom. I just got her to rest."

"Is she going to die, too?" Tommy's dark eyes flashed with a fire that turned Jan's stomach. "'Cause of the fae poison?"

Jan pursed her lips and reached to hug him—only to feel something hard beneath his blanket. She jerked back and pulled the covers away.

He clutched an iron dagger in his hands.

"Tommy!" She slapped her hands over her mouth as she twisted out of bed. The door remained fastened, and no whimpers sifted through the wall from the other bedroom. Jan dropped her voice down to a forced whisper. "What do you think you're doing? What if you rolled over on this in your sleep? You could have killed yourself!"

"I have to protect us from the fae, just like Dad used to!"

Jan took a deep breath and forced her shoulders to relax. "Love, Dad did not sleep with his knife in his bed. He'd impale himself if he did. *Please* put it down. You can protect us from the fae well enough if it's on the floor."

Visions of Tommy, eviscerated in his white phoenix pajamas, danced around in her head. They didn't recede until he held the dagger over the edge of the bed. He slowly lifted each finger, one by one, until it slid down the crack between his bed and the wall and clattered to the hardwood floor.

"There. But you don't have to protect us from the fae, you know. I told you. They can't hurt you." Jan settled beside him on the bed and ran her fingernails lightly up his pale arm.

He shivered but otherwise didn't move, although a few more tears slipped out of his eyes.

She kissed the salty droplets. "Why are you crying? If you cry, it makes me want to cry."

"Because." He sniffled and ran his arm underneath his nose. Since she'd just reprimanded him for almost accidentally murdering himself, she decided to let bad manners slide this once. "Do you think if we killed the Fae Queen, Dad would come back, and Mom would get better? Like in the story?"

Jan brushed another kiss against his freckled cheek. He still smelled like the lavender soap from bath time. Her heart pounded, pumping out fierce emotion with every thud. "Dad wasn't replaced by a changeling. It was his job to fight the fae, and they killed him. They poisoned Mom because she's a hunter, too. Defeating the Fae Queen wouldn't save them. They're not changelings like in the story."

Tommy turned on his side and slipped his hands underneath his pillow as he snuggled up next to Jan. She propped her head up with one arm and traced a pattern across his forehead and down his nose with her other hand.

His face crumpled a little bit. "Do you think . . . if I could kill the Fae Queen . . . it would save you?"

"Save *m*—"

Jan choked on the rest of her words.

Tommy yanked his hands out from underneath his pillow to reveal the twin blade to the one he'd dropped earlier. He plunged it into her abdomen once—wrenched it out—stabbed her again—

Jan couldn't even screech and had no time to raise her hands up to defend herself. She could only stare, eyes wide, mouth agape, fury frozen in the back of her throat. Green blood gushed from her stomach. She snapped her teeth at him, which turned pointier as her glamour faltered.

"Give me back my sister!" Tommy screamed. "Give Jan back!"

He drove the iron into her chest, so far in that it pinned her to the bed. She clawed at the weapon as the world began to fade just a little bit; Tommy's beautiful, enraged face blurred.

Jan cackled and choked on the emerald liquid bubbling up from her throat. "You know I'll just be back, love." Blood dribbled down her cheek. The pillows and sheets turned green. "You're mine . . . . You can't kill the Fae Queen so easily."

"I said, give me back my sister."

He shoved the weapon down to the hilt.

The front door burst open as the real Jan stumbled in, her face smeared with blood and grime. "Tommy?"

Tommy's smile seemed to glow in the fading light.

"So beautiful," the Fae Queen whispered.

"Jan! You came back!"

Do you know what color fae blood is?
Green, my son, naught but green—
So go now forth and slay their queen.

YOU'RE

PERFECTLY

SAFE.

DEEP DIVE

Beka Gremikova

Y*OU OKAY?* ELI'S voice tickled Iris's mind.

She rubbed the itchy spot behind her ear where the purple telepachip had been inserted. *Just nervous.* About the dive, about this new telepathic technology . . .

He chuckled. *Aren't you a pilot?*

She glanced out the plane window at the clear lilac-blue sky. Somewhere, thousands of feet below them, lay the earth. *Being a passenger is . . . different—less control.*

It's okay. He patted her shoulder. *You're perfectly safe.* He nodded to the plane's locker, where extra parachutes peeked out in hues of yellow, orange, and red. *Our parachutes are in excellent working order. Did you read our company guarantee on the website?*

Errrr . . . It was a very long-winded website.

He buckled himself to her harness. *The gist is we may be a new company, but DiveCo takes customer safety very seriously.* He tapped his own ear. *That's part of the reason why we're using the telepachip. If you start to panic during freefall, I can guide you through it.*

She exhaled. *Oh . . . okay.*

Don't worry; we're not trying to get your deepest, darkest secrets. He laughed, but Iris's throat closed.

She turned to Sandra, the work friend who'd dragged her here to begin with. *You go first.*

Sure thing! Sandra grinned, adjusted her light purple harness, and stepped up to the open plane door. *You'll be fine, girl. I've done this hundreds of times.* Then, before Iris could blink, Sandra jumped forward—and fell.

Iris peered out the door, her pulse racing. Then, a few heartbeats later, a puff of plum appeared as Sandra's parachute bloomed. Iris locked her legs and gripped the threshold of the doorway.

It'll be all right. Eli pushed her gently forward, closer to the edge. *It's only scary for a moment, and then your telepachip will activate the parachute.*

Wait, they're connected to the parachutes*, too? I thought they were just communication devices!*

Eli chuckled. *You should have read the website. We're using a multifunctional prototype. Pretty handy. We're aiming for a world where . . . incidents . . . will happen less.*

A newspaper headline popped into her head: *Tragic Skydiving Accident—Young Man Dies From Parachute Malfunction.*

Yeah, incidents like that, Eli said. *You ready?*

She swallowed. Thankfully the telepachip couldn't access her deepest memories. But she'd have to be careful to control her thoughts. She closed her eyes, breathed out once . . . twice.

Yes.

She pried her eyes open as they jumped.

They plummeted toward the earth. The wind beat against Iris's face, and she choked on a breath.

Spread out your arms. Eli demonstrated.

She obeyed, mimicking his outstretched limbs. Cloud wisps streamed away from her reaching fingers. The world below looked almost . . . shimmery, like a desert mirage.

She counted the seconds in her head. Just as she reached sixty, Eli, sounding breathless with anticipation, announced, *Deploying parachute . . . now!*

Iris waited for the break in the fall, for the dizzying floating sensation, for that puff of purple to appear above their heads.

Nothing happened.

Her pulse spiked.

It's going to be fine. We'll be okay. Eli's calm, reassuring tone did nothing to assuage her.

She was going to die. And unbidden, the thought popped out. *Just like Garrett.*

•••♣•••

"I'm so excited!" Tiana's voice echoed through the tiny plane to where Iris sat in the cockpit.

"It's just skydiving, Tia." Garrett sounded annoyed. Iris's fingers clenched around the control wheel.

"I've wanted to do this for a long time." Iris could picture Tia crossing her arms.

Garrett's voice lowered. "Well, why did she *have to be our pilot?"*

Iris kept her eyes focused on the soft lavender clouds that swirled in the blue sky. Chills swept along her skin.

"Listen, I know you don't like her, but she's my best friend, and she's taking us up for really cheap." Tia's voice wavered, then sharpened. "No, don't take the purple parachute! I want it. Iris told me to use her favorite color. For luck."

"Fine, I'll take the yellow one then." Garrett's stomping footsteps shook the small plane. Iris heard buckles snap and Tia doing breathing exercises.

The outer door opened with a thud, and air swelled through the plane. Then, sixty long seconds of freefall later, Tiana's scream rippled as Garrett plunged to his death.

•••♣•••

You were there? When someone—this Garrett—died? Eli's question snared her like a mousetrap.

Iris's stomach twisted. She didn't want to die without telling someone what happened. *Garrett . . . was awful. A cheater.*

He cheated on you? I'm so sorry. Eli's voice was soft, cajoling. As comforting as a handhold during the spinning terror of their continued freefall.

She latched onto that comfort, tears stinging her eyes even as the wind ripped them away from her. *No, he was my bestie's boyfriend. She didn't believe me when I tried to tell her.* She paused. *He started getting between us. It was just so easy to mess with the parachute . . . .*

The sky blurred into a blue-purple smudge. The earth closed in—so little time. Her thoughts tumbled into one clear, cold statement: *I killed him.*

A sudden, blinding flash. Then she hit a cloud—*hard.* She lay there, blinking as the sky faded into a lavender interrogation room. Her ears throbbed.

Eli's weight lifted from off her back. "Crap," he muttered. "Guess the reality-altering feature overloaded the chips."

Reality-altering? Fear skidded through her.

"Oh well. We got our confession." Sandra sat at a small table in a police uniform with her hands folded primly.

Iris struggled to breathe, her mind scrambling to what little she knew of law. "It—what I said wouldn't be admissible in court!"

Sandra adjusted her collar as Eli hauled Iris to her feet. "You gave up the information. We didn't force it out of you."

"You trapped me. *Tricked* me! I was hysterical."

Sandra's brows rose. "Really? Seems like a pretty clear confession to me. Not our fault you didn't realize it was a *virtual* skydive." She swiped at a speck on her uniform. "You really should've read the website."

SHIFTING SANDS

Mariella Taylor

NEVER BEFORE HAS the Nile River gone dry. Craters of cracking, drying mud pock its bed, and the people restlessly avoid it. But who can avoid the parch of arid heat forever? Deep cracks gouge the earth's surface, burying into unstable land, the drifting sand on the breeze not nearly enough to fill them. Without water, her people will die.

Hehet stands, hands folded before her, next to a balcony overlook. Once, this balcony held a crystalline view of the Nile, of the boats drifting up and down her length, of the children splashing near her shores while their mothers gathered reeds. Today, even the great crocodiles have hidden themselves. Without water, even the arms of the gods may die.

"Will you not help us?" Hehet murmurs to the blazing, flickering sunlight. Amidst the angry heat, even the sun appears a mirage. As if Ra is hiding from them. Hands fisting in her tunic, Hehet casts a frown to the east. It is out of her view now, the oasis, but she knows it lies there, can feel its magic even at this distance.

Turning her back to the view, Hehet leans a hip against the stone-carved railing, watching her husband argue with his advisors and officials. All of them have gathered around him in their flowing robes and finery, demanding their answers. What is to be done, they ask. What is to be done about that troublemaker, Set?

Hehet says nothing, simply watches the man she calls her husband, for his word is law, and she will not speak until he allows it. He is Pharaoh, esteemed and beloved by all of Egypt, great king and god over all. And yet, he is hers—her Asim, her morning sun, her all.

Asim's fingers tap a slow beat against the arm of his throne, his gaze cold and harsh as the desert nights while he oversees this shouting mob. At last, he raises his heka from its place in his lap and gestures with the shepherd's crook at one of his guards. "Carry a message to Set," he orders. "Tell him that his Pharaoh will see him."

With that, Asim stands from his throne, crossing the crook and flail across his chest to dismiss the crowd. As these men scurry from their master's presence, Asim's eyes find hers across the length of the room. Servants gather at her husband's command, relieving him of his godly regalia until he stands at the foot of his throne—merely a man. Then, he comes to her.

Hehet keeps her place at the balcony, studying the weary slump of his shoulders, the red of his kohl-rimmed eyes as Asim stands before her. "He will not come," she says.

Asim lifts a hand to brush the backs of his fingers over her cheek. Bending his head to rest his forehead against hers, he says, "Love, you should not say such things."

"You may call a dog," Hehet replies. "But that does not mean it will come."

Asim sighs, the rest of his body still. Finally, he straightens, resting both hands on her shoulders. "Maybe this time, my beloved will be wrong."

Hehet casts a doubtful look up into his dark eyes as Asim turns from her to face the empty riverbed. The creases at the corners of his eyes and mouth tighten, and he braces strong hands against the stone railing. His skull looks so fragile from this angle, scraped smooth and defenseless. If he did not bear the marks of war on his body, she would worry for him. Hehet rests her fingertips on the faint beating of his heart against his ribs.

"Let me go before him," she requests. "He will listen to me. I will petition Set. For you. For our people. Let me do this thing for you, Asim."

"No." The word is firm, quiet.

"If you worry for my safety—"

Asim shakes his head and straightens from the railing. His fingers brush across the sparkling carnelian gems of the pin at her shoulder, the slim line of them running down her side, holding closed the wrap-around dress.

"I must do this," Asim tells her at last. "It must be my doing."

"Why?"

"I cleaved this throne from my brother's grasp."

"The people have faith in you. They know their Pharaoh will protect them," she argues, her fingers fisting in the loose material at his neck. "You have already proven yourself worthy of this throne. A thousand times over."

Her husband smiles a weary, crooked grimace, and bends his head to brush his mouth against her knuckles. "But have I shown myself worthy of you?"

"Asim," she whispers. "Yes. Yes." She cups his jaw in her hand. "Always yes, my sun."

He smiles then, a true and tired thing. "Let me prove this," he says. "One more time. Let me remind my wife that I am worthy of being her choice."

Hehet wraps her arms around his neck and tucks a kiss there. "You will always be worthy," she whispers as his arms encircle her.

•••••••

The magic of the oasis never fails to draw her. She hates it in some moments, the way it lingers on the edge of her consciousness, and she wonders if it is purposeful on his part. Hehet's rooms may be vast, but they face the eastern desert, and every single one of them offers her the sight of that place in the distance. She thinks tonight of the Nile River, still dry, and the man who holds her people, her husband, captive in his palms. They will die without Set's help, and he knows this.

The tricks began small. Little words, little spells, little bits of desert magic meant to inconvenience Asim, meant to make him appear weak in his people's eyes. A reminder that though Set has left them, it was once his birthright to rule over Egypt's people. And now . . . now they are here. Her husband tired and broken, her people crushed beneath the feud of two powerful men, her own mind confused.

She feels him sometimes, from these windows. She feels Set's spirit in the sand, lingering close to her. The breeze carries him through the city, for the desert sands go wherever they wish. And for some reason, that place is here.

Hehet returns to her room many nights to find his offerings. Gentle, beautiful things. Pendants, gems, small scent bottles, delivered by the butterflies that flock to her balcony. Their brilliant wings–colored azure, lapis, and kohl with delicate lines of white and gold–bathed in the crackling firelight from her rooms as they rest their tired bodies on her thick curtains. Sometimes she is ashamed to say that she keeps the gifts—a reminder of the things that could have been between them. She does not love Set the way she loves her sun, but there is a place in her chest that cracks like the riverbed, and that place misses him.

Glancing back over her shoulder toward her husband's slumbering form, Hehet tucks her fingertip beneath the tiny black legs of one of the butterflies, gratified when it delicately steps aboard. "Tell him he must stop," she whispers to the insect.

"He must stop hurting my people." The insect does not reply, but it flutters its wings and takes off into the night sky.

Hehet studies the shadowed lines of the oasis in the flicker of the firelight coming over her shoulders. She imagines that she sees him–the same arms that once lifted to catch mighty falcons, raised to allow her butterfly to land.

"I must stop this," she says to the darkness.

"Who are you speaking to?" Asim mumbles from the bed. She glances back at him, his eyelids hefting open and shut as he drifts on that edge of consciousness, waiting for her reply.

"No one, my sun," she answers. "Go back to sleep."

He obeys because he trusts her, sinking back into that sweet, much-needed oblivion. The light flickers over his skin the same way it does over the butterfly's wings as she slips beneath the blankets beside him. Asim's body curls around hers, a protective shell, but Hehet does not sleep. She watches the other butterflies resting quietly on her curtains. She must go to him; she knows. She must go before Set to save her people.

For six nights, Hehet slips from her bed and goes to the temple to pray. The riverbed lies dry, and rather than dancing at the water side, children lie crying in their beds—weakening. So on that seventh night, when the moon is high, and all seven planets are visible in the sky, she goes, with a single guard and a handmaiden to guide her. She rides her camel deep into the dunes before dismounting and handing the reins to her handmaiden.

"Wait here," she tells them both when the guard tries to follow. "I will face no harm at the desert's hands."

She does not believe for a moment that he will remain, but she places distance between them as she walks further into the dunes, giving her the semblance of loneliness. What must it be like, she wonders, to be so alone here, to live in this vast, endless nothing?

Stopping beneath the bright of the moon, Hehet searches the rolling dunes. The oasis is yet far off, but she needn't venture farther. Taking a knife from her belt, Hehet slips it across her palm and turns her hand to let the dark droplets plop into the sand and disappear. Three of them. To honor the goddess, Isis, and her Knot of Life. Isis brings all things together—the past, the present, and the future; the unborn, the living, and the dead. And tonight, it is magic she will bring.

"Come to me," she whispers.

She doesn't see him come. She only knows that one moment she is alone, and then, she is not. The sand stirs beneath his feet. Set is the same, always the same. A thick mane of dark hair. Bright, expressive eyes. She remembers the color of them, so opposite Asim's, the same colors of those butterfly wings. His wrists no longer bear gold, but instead, leather gauntlets protect the skin there. She cannot see the color of his tunic, but she knows that it will compliment him.

Set towers, broader than his brother, if not as tall. Chiseled and coarse where his brother is refined. But there is something in his eyes when he sees her, something that breaks Hehet's heart, chipping at that place inside her that misses him in a very palpable way. It's charming, the uncertain, half-smile that rests upon his face.

"You have come to me," he says, his voice filled with warmth and awe. "Finally." There is so much weight, so much longing in that single word.

"Yes." Hehet slides her knife back into her belt and closes her fingers around her bleeding palm. And suddenly, her mind, her heart, is filled with so many questions. Is he safe? Is he well? Is he lonely? She swallows them back and asks the pertinent one. "Did you receive my message?"

"From the soldiers?" Distaste fills Set's voice, and he tips his head down to look at her, stepping closer, a mere handbreadth away from her. He is the heat of the desert itself. Sweat crawls down Hehet's spine as she lifts her head to meet those eyes. They had smiled at her once, as a child, from his angular face, mischievous as he whispered his tricks and games to her. They had all played together in their youth—Hehet, Asim, and Set—before he disappeared into the oasis in pursuit of . . . well, she does not know. She only knows that he had returned a very different, very broken soul—after seven years, for a single day, and he had broken all their hearts. So much so that Asim had cast him out into this desert alone.

"My butterfly," she answers.

Something softens in his face, and Set nods.

"My people are dying, Set," she tells him. "Can you not hear their cries in the wind?"

"I can."

"You hold their lives in your hand." Hehet clenches her jaw to keep her voice steady. "You are the answer to their prayers. Why have you not released the curse you laid upon the land?"

"It is nothing my brother does not deserve." A sneer ticks at Set's lips. "He is a king, a god. *Pharaoh*. Can he not prove himself?"

"Set," she fills the word with reprimand, and he falls silent. Hehet curls the fingers of her free hand around his arm beneath the gauntlet's grasp. He stills, listening, gaze fallen to her fingers, fixated on that point of contact before they venture slowly back to her. "Do this thing for me. Heal the land, Set, and I will ask my husband to pardon you and bring you home."

The words linger between them for a long while, Set's gaze falling to the ground. His shoulders lift on a noiseless sigh, then sink, and in that vulnerable moment, he looks so much like Asim. Finally, he raises his head and pulls back.

"I will do what you ask," Set agrees. "For you. But do not speak to Asim on my behalf."

"That is your request?"

"Come back to me," he says, refusing to meet her gaze. "One more night. Do this, and I will fill the great river. I will pour down water from the skies. Whatever you ask, Hehet, if you grant me this request." Set meets her gaze then, his body still, barely breathing.

"One more night," Hehet answers, squeezing his arm. Set's smile is breathtaking—brighter than the moon, the stars, the planets, brighter than Ra's sun. It lights up the night, and the desert sands swirl at his feet, a breath of excitement and hope.

He does not thank her, does not speak. Merely reaches for her wounded hand. When Hehet opens her palm for him, Set smooths his calloused thumb over the broken skin, and it closes beneath his touch. He closes her hand, dwarfing it in his own, then vanishes from her sight. That night, when she crawls into her bed, she can still feel the grains of sand and magic in her palm.

•••●♣●••

When Hehet appears at the dunes on that second night, Set is waiting for her. He sits on the sand, his feet digging deep into the dune, a flask resting by his side. The moonlight glints off his dark hair and softens his features. The start of a beard traces his jaw, a curious thing; she has never seen him with facial hair. She seats herself beside him, looking up into the sky in silence.

After a long while, Set lifts the flask and uncorks it, raising it to his mouth before extending it to her. Hehet takes the flask from his fingers and drinks. A smooth, honeyed red wine. She wonders where he's taken it from. Set's gaze is back on the sky, but he allows her to pull the cork from his fingers and plug the cask. Then, she watches him, the strained planes of his face easing into peace. How does he do this, she wonders. A free spirit such as him, a man who once thrived in the arms of other people, who laughed and played and loved and protected. But not here, not now. Now, he is none of those things.

"How can you not be lonely?" Hehet whispers into the darkness from her seat beside him, laying gentle fingers against his back. She feels the muscles tighten, bunch as he hunches against the weight of her question.

"It is a pain I have learned to bear," Set answers. He tucks a fist against his heart and looks over his shoulder at her. "And now, you are here."

"I cannot stay, Set," Hehet reminds him. "Asim is waiting for me."

At the mention of his brother, Set grimaces. "There are other wives," he says.

"But none like me," she answers.

Asim had many wives; that much was true. It was the way of a Pharaoh. Having wives, consorts, slaves to bring him glory by bearing his children. Something Hehet had never been able to do, but she pleased his heart and comforted his mind. She gave Asim peace in ways they never could. She could have gone into the desert with Set instead, this warrior prince with the cerulean eyes. She could have chosen him. Instead, she chose her people, her home, and Asim—and she does not regret it.

Hehet squeezes her fingers in Set's tunic then lowers her hand when he speaks. "There is no woman like you, Hehet. Not even among the heavens."

She does not answer.

"How did I never see it?" Set speaks quietly. "Your eyes hold all the colors of the desert. Every layer of brown and red and gold at the heart of us. How could I never—"

Hehet's hand snaps up, curling tight around his arm to stop it from touching her face. "Don't," she whispers. "Protect your heart, Set."

The man stares at her for the longest time, his blue eyes flickering. His outstretched fingers close into a fist, and his eyes shut along with them. Finally, he pulls his arm from her touch and stands to his feet, sand gusting from the folds of his clothing.

"Come back with me," Hehet begs, looking up at him. "I will beg mercy for you. Forgiveness. Come back to your family, Set."

"Do not come back to the desert a third time," Set answers. "Isis' magic lies deep in these sands. Already, her Knot grows tight around you. It wants you for its own, Hehet. The spirits—" He breaks off then, his downcast features etched in pain. "This is a magic you cannot understand."

"I understand that you are alone here, and you are hurting," she argues, standing.

Set looks at her then, fierceness in his gaze. "The sands will not give up their right."

"They hold no claim on me."

He grimaces, plucks up his flask, and replies, "Not yet."

•••♣•••

"Wake up, Hehet," her husband's excited voice whispers in her ear. "Open your eyes, wife."

"What is it, my sun?" she murmurs into his chest.

Joy cradles his sleepy voice the way his body cradles her. His hands cup her face, fingers buried in her hair, and he smiles something like relief.

"Listen," he says.

Hehet grins against his skin and kisses his chest. She knows. From the moment she laid at his side, she has listened to the sound of rain on the rooftops. Set has kept his promise; the Nile will run full again.

•••♣•••

Seven days pass. Her people return to their lives, their boats, their work, their play. The children splash in the Nile . . . and their joy hurts her heart. They all remain here, in the city, untouched now by those parching sands, thank Ra. And Set sits alone in the desert, planning yet more sins against his brother. But his butterflies come nightly–sometimes bringing gifts, sometimes merely resting. She thinks now that this is his way of being close to them. He knows she is there, he knows his brother is near, and maybe that gives him peace.

That seventh night, Asim does not come to her immediately, and so, she does the only thing she can think to bring the brothers together. She lifts a butterfly from the curtain and whispers to the breezes full of swirling sand, "Come to me."

Then, she turns her back to her balcony and waits. The fluttering cascade of butterflies around her announces his presence, and she turns to face him. It's different in the sunlight, looking up into Set's face. Here, in this place, he appears harsher, angrier, sharper, suspicious.

"I told you not to come to me a third time," he says.

"You told me not to return to the desert. You never said I could not call for you."

Something cracks in his eyes, the way the earth cracked when he recalled the waters. "A wise woman," he praises. Hehet smiles back. Banished, perhaps, but no less a prince, Set assumes a relaxed and lordly position before her, leaning against the balcony ledge. The sunlight catches on the sword at his side as he speaks. "Tell me, my queen. Why have you called for me?"

"My heart hurts for you," Hehet told him. "You are only half yourself without us."

Set frowns, lines gathering in his forehead. "Hehet, we spoke of this. I do not wish you to speak to Asim. You will not beg for me."

"Then speak to him yourself."

"If I wished to speak with him, I would answer his messengers."

"Does the hate run so deep?" Hehet snaps. Set's expression remains flat, unfathomable now. "Can there be no forgiveness between brothers? You belong here with your family, Set. Why must you fight him? Why must there be all these tricks and games?"

Set sighs and steps toward her, closing his eyes. "Hehet . . . the wounds between us. There are cracks in the earth that do not run so deep; you must understand this."

"Cracks may heal with time and rain," she answers. "He will be here soon, Set. Stay. Speak with him."

"I will not—"

The sharp closing of the bedroom door intervenes, snapping Hehet's concentration. Her hands rest on her hips, and the frown on her face is mirrored by the one on her husband's. Set opens his eyes slowly, but the expression that darkens his features is one of a jackal. He edges back toward the balcony with slow, steady steps. "Brother."

Asim's teeth grind audibly as he steps to her side. "Why are you here, Set?" Set lifts a shoulder in her direction.

Hehet lays a hand on her husband's arm, pulls him closer to her side. "My people will not be safe until the wounds between you are settled. I wish this. I wish Set home with his family and the two of you together. As it should be."

Asim's gaze never leaves his brother's face. "I have called for you myself. Why did you not come?"

Set scoffs, a sneer pulling across his face. "Am I a dog that you call, and I must come?"

"No." Asim slides his arm from her grasp and around her shoulders. "A dog would obey. A *slave* would obey."

"And I am neither to you, *brother*." Set's body bristles, and Asim tenses at the reminder.

"Don't," Hehet whispers, though to which of them she is not sure.

"You left the people," Asim replies evenly, his arm beginning to push Hehet behind him. He stretches to his full height to look down at his brother, cold and lordly, Pharaoh. "You left us. You made your choice."

"Is that what you've told yourself?" Set asks, his hand curling around the pommel of his sword, ready. "That *this* is what I chose?" He shakes his head, and Hehet does not know what to say. Who is to say where the root of these pains lies, for either brother?

"This is not helping," she pleads, pulling at her husband's arm.

"I told you, little Hehet," Set looks at her sadly. "Some wounds cannot be healed." His gaze flickers over Asim. "You failed to best me last time, brother. Be prepared." And then, in a gust of sand and wind, he is gone.

Asim clutches her to his side, a shaky breath escaping his lips. "Do you still say I am worthy?" he asks.

"Yes," Hehet replies, slipping her body against his.

"Then obey your husband and stay away from that man."

•••♣•••

She tries.

Dear Ra, she tries. But the sands are relentless. The vicious sandstorms ring their city, smashing homes and shops, relentless in their destruction. The sand fills every crevice, and Asim fumes. He cuts his hands, three drops in the air, and screams for his brother to come to him to end these foolish games. He begs—for her, for their people, for his pride. But Set refuses to show his face. The butterflies no longer come.

And so, when her husband falls into a restless sleep, Hehet presses a kiss to his shoulder. "I will fix this," she whispers to him. "All will be well." Asim does not stir as she slips from the room and out into the screaming wind. She does not know what will happen this time. Set told her not to come a third time, but she must. She must—to save all that she holds dear.

When she stumbles across the dunes alone, camel abandoned, sand in her eyes, praying it is the right direction, she can hear them. The anguished cries buried beneath the wind—Set's cries, sounds of grief and agony. She's not certain how many drops of blood splatter the sand when she cuts her hand. Only that one moment she's screaming Set's name, the sand sucking at her feet, pulling her down, down, down. And then, she opens her eyes to silence. She rests on her back, staring up into blazing sunlight, and the world lies still. Too still.

"I told you not to come here," Set's voice reaches from beyond her, broken, hoarse, tired. "The sands—they never forget."

Hehet turns slowly to her side, body aching, searching for him. Green grasses, reeds, and trees scatter the surroundings of the small oasis, and Set sits on a stone nearby, dark and ragged. "How did I come so far?" she asks him.

"The desert has collected its due," Set replies. He looks at her, red streaks amidst the blue in his eyes. "You gave your blood to the sands three times. Now, you belong to us."

"Us? Who is—" Hehet echoes, pushing herself to sit up. Her head spins, throbbing, and she presses her forehead into her undamaged palm. She pauses then, raising her head to look at him. "What will it take for you to cease the storms upon my city?"

"They have stopped," he answers.

Stopped? Oh, thank Ra. "Good. Good. You cannot remain alone here." She feels bleary as she stumbles toward him. The world shifts restlessly beneath her feet, and Hehet stumbles.

"I am alone no longer," Set's voice reaches inside her fog, and his hands on her arms steady her before he seats her on the stone beside him. The scent of him is grief. Hehet leans into his side, drawing in slow breaths until the spinning, aching feeling in her head subsides. Alone no longer, he said. Alone no—

Hehet's head snaps up, jolting the warrior at her side. "You must return me, Set," she warns. "Asim's wrath is something even you will regret."

He chuckles, low and weary, letting his arm slide from its place around her. "I am the desert, Hehet. I carry it in my veins. I am subject only to its will. Not even the great Pharaoh may command me. Who are you to demand I do anything?"

She swallows hard, the words tasting sour in her mouth when she answers. "Once, I was your beloved."

Set shudders. "Not once," he answers. And she knows. Perhaps she always knew that he loved her, that he had not given that up even after so many years.

"You must return me, Set," Hehet repeats quietly, laying a hand over his fist. "I cannot be yours."

"You already are," Set answers, tensing all over as he straightens. "You gave yourself three times to the sand. By Isis' Knot, you are now bound to us, to this desert." He opens his hand beneath the cover of hers and takes it firmly in his own.

"I will escape you," Hehet stands slowly.

There is something sad in his voice as he watches her. "You may try."

She's not certain how long it is that she struggles, fighting the magic and the sand to make her escape, to get home, to return to her people and her husband. But she knows that Set watches her, the sand tightening its hold on her with each flicker of feeling across his features. And at last, she collapses at the edge of the oasis, trembling and exhausted, gulping down water.

"A game," Set says, rising to his feet.

"What?"

"A game." He moves closer, stripping a length of cloth from the hem of his tunic. He dips it in the water and squeezes it out before crouching before her. Hehet watches suspiciously as the man reaches for her, flinches at the first touch of that cloth to her face. Then, she closes her eyes and lets him wash the burning sand from her skin. "Senet. You know it, yes?" Hehet nods. "Play with me. If you win, I will ask the desert to release you to your kingdom, and I will bother your lands no longer."

"And if I do not?" She opens her eyes.

"You will remain here. With me." Set pauses cleaning her hands to gently close the open wound on her palm before looking up at her. "Close to my heart."

"I will add terms," she says. "For each turn taken, you will tell me a truth of my choice."

He hesitates, then nods. "Done."

Set steps back from her, gathering a handful of sand from the earth. He throws it across the stone where they earlier sat and murmurs words she does not understand. In place of the sand appears a shimmering board covered in square markings. Hand-carved butterflies adorn its surface, waiting neatly at the head of the board. Hehet looks up at him slowly, and Set offers her a pair of dice. Part of her feels victory. It is not a long board. With enough luck, she will beat him, and she will gain truths along the way. Hehet studies the tired creases of his face as he sits across the board from her.

Taking a deep breath, Hehet casts a silent prayer to Ra and rolls the dice. They clatter to the board and clutter together. A seven. Lucky. She smiles up at Set, and this time, he smiles back.

Hehet gently moves her butterfly into place and waits for Set to take his turn. A three. Also lucky, Isis is with him. "My truth," she says. Set's fingers tense as he drops his butterfly into place. "Why did you leave your people?"

"I was young and foolish. Searching for a thing I could not have." The brusque answer is less than satisfying, but Hehet rolls again. "May I ask you for a truth?"

"Only one," she answers. "When I win." Set chuckles quietly as the dice change hands once more; Hehet's piece continues to lead down the board. She glances up at him, watches his gaze traversing the board before he rolls. He remains behind her, but her lead is slim. "What were you searching for?"

"Worth."

The single word holds more emotion than any Hehet can think. Again, they roll, keeping an even pace.

"Would you not have found that amidst your people, Set? A Pharaoh is god to his people."

Set's voice cracks. "A crown I could be born worthy of. That is not what I sought."

The dice clatter from her fingers. A two. Not so lucky. This turn, Set pulls ahead. Hehet grimaces, a trembling beginning in her arms. She will hold out, somehow. Somehow, she will win and return home to Asim and her people; Ra help her if she doesn't.

"What more could you be worthy of?"

"I had nothing to make me strong enough," he answers. "Nothing to set me apart from any other boy. I thought the magic would make me worthy. I did not understand what it would take in return."

Another roll, and Hehet's heart begins to sink. A desperate sensation clogs her chest as Set maintains his lead, growing closer to the end of the board. He hesitates in handing the dice back to her.

"What did it take?"

"Everything," he answers.

"What did the desert take from you, Set?" she asks gently when he refuses to look at her.

"That's a second question."

"Will you answer it?" she asks as she rolls. Set hunches over the board.

Two turns pass before, at last, he speaks, "I could not return. No matter how much I wished. One day every seven years I might step free of this desert without the spirits' interference." Set scrubs a hand over his face. "The desert calls me worthy, but I am not . . ."

"You used that day to visit me. When I called for you."

"Yes."

"The desert, its magic, its spirits, have done this—not you." Set does not answer. "You love your brother. And you love me."

"Very much."

"Does Asim know this?"

"He said I lied. Said that I was selfish, that I only wished to take you from him, that I did not care for my people or for him."

Hehet startles, clattering the dice across the board. Two. Her chest seizes anxiously as she watches his pieces advance farther ahead.

"Is there no way to break this curse?"

"Not without death," Set replies. "The sand always takes its dues. There must always be sacrifice."

He picks up the dice for his final roll. She will not win, Hehet knows it now. Set knows it, rolls the dice in his fingers, hesitating. Hehet slides her knife slowly from her belt. If it must be death . . . then so be it. Tears burn her eyes. It is not what she wished, but . . .

She's trembling when Set's butterfly crosses the finish marker.

"May I ask for a truth?" he asks, his voice thick with emotion, as if for once, perhaps, he did not wish to win.

"Yes."

A hand slides across the board and covers her own, the thumb brushing gently against her wrist. "Was I ever worthy of you?"

Hehet tightens her grip on her knife and presses her lips firmly together. Yanking her hand from his, she launches forward to swing a fist at his face. Set bolts, snatching her fist in both of his before it can strike him. But it does not save him from the knife she plunges into the side of his neck.

Set stares at her, shock creasing his features. "No," he chokes, stumbling down to one knee. Tears streaming down her face, Hehet pulls her knife free of his neck and watches him crumple to his knees at her feet. He shakes his head, or tries at least, hands clutching at his neck as blood seeps from the wound. The sands rush from his skin, his veins bulging blue and thick beneath his skin as the writhing spirits shriek to escape his collapsing body. Hehet gasps when they surge like burrowing insects into her instead. She can feel the strange magic like a swirling, rage-filled fire in her blood. Set's sounds grow strangled as he struggles, still trying to escape death. He tries to get up, so she stabs him a second time, as deep as she can, and twists. Part of his flesh comes away when she pulls the knife free.

"Be free, Set," she says, trembling as he collapses forward into her hands. "Be free."

As she lowers his body to the ground and herself to her knees beside him, a great weight bends her shoulders. His blood stains her hands, but she covers her face with them anyway and presses her lips tight together against the keening sounds rising in her throat. Set is dead. She will not walk among her people again, will not sleep beside her husband. Everything that had once meant something is gone, and she is filled with roiling seas of angry sand spirits. She belongs to this desert now—to Isis—in the same way that Set once did.

But she has one day every seven years, she reminds herself. One day to make things right.

When she straightens slowly and wipes the tears from her eyes, a cerealien butterfly perches on her thigh. Slowly, Hehet slides a finger beneath it. She will find a way to send a message to her husband. She must let Asim know what has happened, tell him the truth about his brother, let him know he must not come. She will come to him when it is time.

For now, she whispers to the insect as it beats its tender wings, "Be with him, so he is never without me."

And as the butterfly disappears into the sun-drenched distance, Hehet stands. She may not be able to leave this oasis, but she will not be Set. She will not allow these sand spirits to control her; she will find a way to best their games.

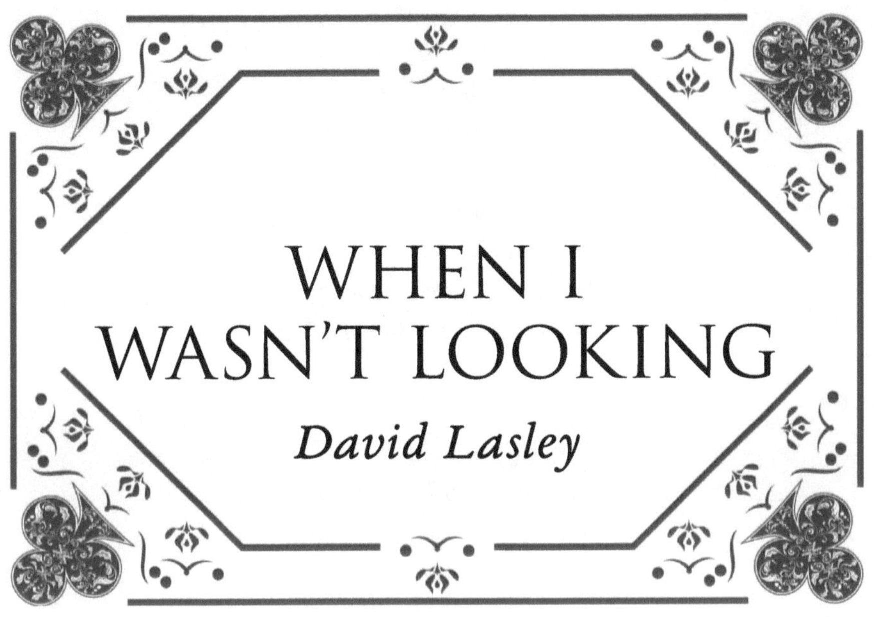

WHEN I WASN'T LOOKING

David Lasley

You snuck into my home when I wasn't looking
my fortress hidden
bolstered
through independence
Its watchword: self-reliance

You, my grinning prankster
middle child with that smile
I didn't know I needed
that deep belly laugh
the kind where we throw our heads back
eyes closed
not from hiding
but from holding
inside this mirth
abandoned to it
You duped me into this
You, my little golden haired girl

youngest child with those eyes
bewitching me again
that extra tale
you want to share
transfixing me
until we know it's ending
and it's the invitation
it's in the sharing
these unknown worlds
in which we go exploring
I always thought I'd do that alone
But I was taken in

You, my thoughtful artist
first born son with a song
so pure it makes me pause
long enough
to finally be still
a captivating
misdirection
you and your attention
not just to excellence
but also to beauty
and the curiosity
of how long it all could go
this crescendo
You pulled me into it

You, my closest friend, lovely bride
with that wide
open door you never close
to everything
pent up from my
perpetual hiding
an invitation to be heard
when I always thought
those words would hit
unwelcome ears

too great a risk
why would anyone want to listen to me?
if you didn't
You sure fooled me

You snuck into my home when I wasn't looking
Tricksters, all of you.

Now
I must be the
Jester
once more.

FOOL'S CROWN

Claire Tucker

CANDLELIGHT FLICKERS THROUGH the great hall of Chateau d'Angers, illuminating the silent men-at-arms eating their dinner. I'm sitting a few places left of France's under-age king, studying his every move.

He's rotating his glass, leaning back with his right foot tucked under the chair and his left stretched out beneath the table. Simple.

But the way young Charles rotates his glass after dinner is the one thing I haven't been able to master. In these two weeks, I've learned every expression, every gesture, every preference, and am ready to step into my role as him.

Only I haven't mastered this, the thing he does so casually after every meal while he stares unseeing at the spot between the ornate candlestick and silver serving dish with the remnants of roast chicken on it.

Charles has been rotating the glass, only half full of wine tonight, with a pattern for once. The thumb slides back along the stem and pushes. Fingers fan briefly as he adjusts them to be straight. A ring catches the light. Repeat. I'm surreptitiously imitating him with my own wine glass.

If he keeps this up, then I'm ready.

He shifts, presses the base of his glass, and pushes it around. I've gotten into a rhythm and the change in his pattern upsets mine. A little wine splashes from my glass and seeps into the wooden table.

"The men are quiet tonight," Charles says. I sit back and smile, the court jester once more.

The Count of Angers, seated to Charles's right, looks at the youth.

"Come, Triboulet, entertain us," Charles calls.

I rise, pushing the carefully formed thoughts of his habits and preferences from my mind as I slip into the role I've played for two weeks. Charles's two dozen men-at-arms look at me, doubtless wondering if the entertainment will be at the monarch's expense. While I have used my resemblance to the youth before, it would be unwise to call attention to it tonight.

"Majesty, your men are tired because their tasks have been too hard," I say. The Count of Angers snorts.

Well, at least one of them caught the joke.

"Consider how straining it is for a man accustomed to work and training to be required to do absolutely *nothing* at all."

I move around the king's table and into the middle of the hall. Several of the men smile. Some watch me through narrowed eyes.

They don't need to worry. Their activities with the maidens of Angers isn't my aim.

"Oh, what am I to do," I lament, turning to face Charles. "There's nothing to do. Except walk around and look at the countryside from the towers." The Count of Angers smirks. Some of the men chuckle.

They've been doing exactly that for two weeks.

"When last did they get proper exercise, your majesty?" I ask. Charles smiles self-consciously and dips his head.

"When last were they taken out and allowed to run after prey?"

The men cheer. There's fine hunting around here—they've probably been itching to run with the hounds, even if the honor of the kill will go to the nobility and not to them.

I saunter to a table and lean against it, heaving an overly dramatic sigh and crossing my arms.

I hate acting the fool to make people laugh. If only I could have left the real jester alive and not have been forced into this role.

But then I wouldn't have gotten so close to Charles, king in name but not yet ruling the kingdom his father left him.

"I suppose that if your majesty is too busy to take them out, they can always watch the chicken coop. Foxes and ferrets have been getting in somehow." I lean closer to one of the biggest soldiers. "Just think how good the practice would be, chasing down a ferret or cornering a fox. You never know when one might spring up in your midst." I raise my eyebrows.

The man's forehead creases, watching my face. Good.

I lean back, a leg of chicken from his plate in my hand, and take a bite. Before he realizes what I've done, I'm skipping away, waving my bounty like a trophy.

"Oh dear, a fox in our midst," I jeer and take another bite.

The guard rises and turns to me, his face red. He stands a full head and shoulders above me and is probably twice my weight. All my senses come alert. This is when I am most alive, when I am most aware of every muscle and tendon of my being.

He advances, drawing his arm back. I drop and roll, rising to my feet and doing a backflip.

"And the hunter moves forward," I call as he advances once more. I back up, maneuvering into a corner. "Who will win—the fox or the hound?"

I hop one way, plant a foot on the wall, and push. With a skip, I'm around the man and moving into a fluid cartwheel. I land on my feet, take the piece of chicken from my mouth, and chew.

"Hmm. Delicious."

The rest of the men are cheering and applauding, calling to their companion, goading him on.

I use their diverted attention to move to a table and snatch more chicken from another's plate.

"The fox strikes again!" someone calls, applauding.

I smile.

That's what I am, what I've been these past two weeks—a fox. Hiding among the chickens, preparing for my great theft.

The theft of a kingdom.

Before the second man can get over his surprise, I snatch a third piece of chicken from another. Then I move back into the middle of the hall and juggle the three pieces, one of them half-eaten, and smile at my victims.

Two of them will be guarding the chatelet tonight. The other will probably be sleeping innocently in his bed when I become king.

The big one advances, one corner of his mouth raised.

Apparently, he thinks I can't juggle and evade him at the same time.

I duck his punch and leap out of his reach without missing a catch or throw.

"All's well that ends well," I call as the men laugh.

His forehead creases slightly.

I'm close to the king's table and catch the half-eaten piece of chicken in my mouth, toss the other two at their rightful owners, turn and snatch the last piece of chicken from the silver serving dish and present it to the offended man-at-arms with a bow.

The hall erupts with applause. The big man blinks at me, glances at the king, then mumbles something and turns away.

"Well done," someone says behind me, and I turn. The Count of Angers smiles. "You have a skilled jester, Charles. Bold, but skilled."

I smile and dip my head.

If only he knew how bold.

Charles hasn't responded to his host, and I glance at him. He's back in his self-absorbed trance, staring at the spot on the table between golden candlestick and silver platter.

And he's not even rotating the glass this time. Rather, he's running a finger around its lip.

I blink and remove the chicken from my mouth.

He doesn't follow a pattern because he doesn't have one.

Which means I don't have to either. As long as I make it a habit to toy with the glass after meals, shifting between his routines, no one except the most observant will realize that I am not him.

I smile and bow to the young king.

I am ready.

•••●♣●•••

The light of the crescent moon struggles to pierce through the veil of wispy clouds as I slip from the royal lodgings and move to the chatelet. The scent of rosemary hangs in the air, rising from the few well-placed bushes in the small courtyard.

The ancient Romans believed it granted courage and used its aromatic oil before battle. I pause now and crush some of the fresh herb in my hand, hold it to my nose, and inhale.

Then I move to the chatelet and the gate separating the inner ward from the rest of the mighty Chateau d'Angers.

The guards at the chatelet's gate are talking. A nightingale calls, presumably from the gardens beyond the lodgings.

I walk to the chatelet's gate, fighting the urge to become the killer I am.

Soon.

The guards fall silent as I approach, my footsteps crunching over gravel.

"Bit late to be out, Triboulet," one remarks.

"Couldn't sleep," I reply. "You can't hear it out here, but our young king snores. Echoes through the entire building."

The guard chuckles. His big companion mumbles under his breath and turns away.

Well, I've found one of the victims of my earlier antics.

"I thought I'd walk in the gardens a bit. Maybe then I'll appreciate the warmth of my bed despite the discomfort."

The smaller guard nods and steps out my way. I pass through the open gate into the chateau's gardens.

Seventeen towers forty-five feet high surround the small fortress. A handful of guards stroll along the top of the wall. They're relaxed, looking out toward Angers and the River Maine. Where they should be. But tonight, the danger is from within. The fox is among the chickens.

I turn and saunter to the main gates.

•••♣•••

"You're up late," one of the guards says.

"Couldn't sleep," I reply.

He glances at me, no doubt wondering what there is to laugh at in such a short response.

The answer is nothing.

My time of being Triboulet the jester is fast drawing to an end.

For a few minutes, an hour at the most, I'll be the assassin I was trained to be.

And then I'll be king.

"It's a fine night," the guard comments.

I nod, my gaze turned to the other side of the moat. The drawbridge is lowered. All that stands between the half-dozen men I'm waiting for and the chateau is the portcullis.

I'll lift that easily.

An owl call rises from the other side of the moat. My pulse spikes, then returns to normal.

My men are ready.

"It is a fine night," I say, turning to the guard and smiling. One of the blades hidden in my sleeves slides into my palm. "A fine night to die."

He blinks, his forehead creasing.

And I kill him.

He dies quietly, his throat slit and me holding him up while I flick the bloodied blade at his companion.

I set the one down, then leap for the second and catch him before he clatters to the ground and alerts the chateau of trouble with the noise.

And the gates of the mighty Chateau d'Angers are mine.

The portcullis has been kept in good repair and rises silently. I don't bother to look for my companions and turn to the dead guards.

I've removed the vambraces and breastplate from one of them when the first man slips through the raised portcullis.

"Nothing for us?" he whispers.

I slip a knife from one of my many hiding places and point it at him.

"Your turn will come."

He raises his hands. "Was just asking."

I slide the breastplate toward him. "Get changed."

Two more slip into the gate while the first reaches for the breastplate. I step back and turn to the gardens as they move to strip the armor from the dead men.

All quiet.

The changing of the guard had just taken place when I left the chatelet. Even though it feels so long ago, the position of the crescent moon in the sky above tells me that less than an hour has passed.

If all goes well, we'll be done before the next change happens.

"Ready," one of the men behind me whispers. I turn.

Two of my companions are now dressed in armor. One fidgets with the straps of his vambrace. The dead guards lie side by side, and I motion to them.

"Make it look natural," I instruct. "Watch for the signal, then raise the alarm."

"Which window?" one of the armored men asks.

"The king's, you fool."

"Which one's his?" another asks from a shadowed corner.

"Does it matter?"

"How are they supposed to know the signal's from you if they don't know which window?"

I raise my hands and turn away. The king is sleeping on the second level of the lodgings, and I scan the windows for his.

One of the other men shifts, and I mutter a curse.

"Just look for two candles in a window that's not ground level," I snap. My guards—how good that sounds—nod.

"Close the portcullis. Let's go."

The rest of my companions move after me.

A fifth shadow shifts in the corner, and I focus on it.

Nothing.

I turn my head away, watching the corner from my peripheral vision.

No shape unnatural to the cold angle of stone reveals itself to me.

"You coming, your majesty?"

I clench my fingers into tight fists. "I'm not king yet," I reply, moving toward the chateau. My gaze falls on the back of the chapel, and a chill rises up my arms. I force myself to not look at the corner with the shifting shadow.

I don't believe in ghosts or that the souls of the men I've killed return to remind me of my sins.

The real jester's face rises in my mind, and I push the thought away.

Even though he wasn't dead when I left him, it would take a skilled physician to keep him alive after the cut I gave him. A very skilled physician.

"Move west," I instruct my men softly. "Keep in the shadow of the wall. Then around to the chatelet. Quickly."

I step into the pale moonlight, reminding myself that I must play the king's fool again. So I saunter through the gardens, hands clasped behind my back, keeping one eye on the movement of my accomplices along the base of the wall.

The towers are built close, far closer than normal. While this turns the chateau into a fortress that is impregnable from without, tonight it aids my men by creating numerous shadows where the wall and towers intercept. The only reason I see their four shadows is because I'm looking for them.

I mirror their movements in the open space, only moving toward the cluster of buildings as they turn to move along the west wall.

A twig snaps to my left, and I whirl, drawing another of my blades.

Louis the Spider's uncle had planted grapevines along the base of the wall before his nephew knocked on the chateau gates and asked for the key. Now, even in the bright moonlight, the rows of tangled vines cast multiple shadows.

My grip on the blade tightens.

Nothing moves among the vines.

The only people in the chateau are those who should be there or those I've let in. No one else crossed the moat—I would have seen them moving across the drawbridge.

An owl call rises behind me. A warning. I suck my lips into my teeth and conceal my knife in the folds of my clothes.

It won't do to have one of the count's or king's men see the glint of moonlight on the blade.

There's still no movement among the vines, and I turn back to the task at hand. I've lost my men among the shadows of the walls.

The plan is for me to reach the chatelet first and distract or deal with the guards. My accomplices will move around the wall without stopping, reaching the chatelet once the entrance is mine.

I walk forward, searching the shadows for movement, calculating where they should be. Have they reached the turn at the back of the great hall yet? Or are they nearing the back of the chapel, close to the chatelet?

I force my steps to remain slow, a man out enjoying the night air. I could cross the distance to the chatelet in a matter of moments and have both guards dead before they realize that someone is running, but that would appear unnatural to the men on the walls. And so I remain calm, meandering through the moonlit garden toward the chatelet while inwardly cursing my earlier jumpiness.

There's too much at stake, too many years of preparation and training, for me to throw it away because of shadows and sounds.

A murmur of voices increases as I near the chatelet. A shadow shifts to my right, and I glance at it. Four men are crouched at the base of the wall, watching me.

I'm late.

I draw two blades and move to the gate. The guards' backs are turned.

Fools.

I step into the shadow of the entrance and flick my wrists. The blades pass through the men's throats, and they crumple. I catch them both before they fall, holding one with each arm. My men slip into the entrance.

"You're late," one whispers, easing the weight of the big guard off me.

"All's well that ends well." The other guard is lifted from my arms, and I rise.

My companion meets my gaze, the whites of his eyes gleaming faintly. "It's not over yet."

"So hurry up and get dressed," I hiss.

He crouches over the dead guard and undoes a buckle.

A shout rises from the gate, echoing strangely in the night air.

We freeze.

"To the gate! We're under attack!"

Shouts rise from the walls, repeating the call. Footsteps reverberate into the chateau as guards race along the top of the wall, making for the gate.

My companions look to me. One raises an eyebrow. I think.

"Hide these," I whisper, pushing a dead guard to the side. "And yourselves. I'll call you when I'm ready."

Shouts are rising from the lodgings behind us. Three of my men leap for the shadows in the chatelet's entrance. One folds his arms.

"What are you going to do?" he demands.

"Improvise," I reply and run through the gate into the moonlight beyond, reforming my plan as I go.

The handful of King's men in the lodgings will be awake and nervous. Moving silently will certainly earn me a confrontation with one or most of them.

I grit my teeth and yank the door open, making sure it bangs.

A shout from within. Hurried footsteps on the floor overhead.

Wonderful. They'll be watching the stairs now, ready to chop up anyone who ascends.

There should be a candlestick somewhere down here.

Pale light pierces through the open door as I scramble to find a light to take with me. My heart isn't pounding. Rather, it's steadily beating out the moments I'm losing, like a clock's pendulum.

My fingers brush against a candlestick, and I grab it.

Now to light it.

A few coals glow in the grate of the downstairs fireplace. I crouch over it and light the three candles, counting my heartbeats.

One. I grab an unburnt portion of a glowing log and raise it to the first candle.

Two. Three. It flares to life, my fingers smarting from the heat.

Four. I toss the log into the fire.

Five. I loosen the lit candle.

Six. The second candle starts burning.

Seven. The third.

Eight. Nine. I push the candle back into its holder.

Ten. I rise and turn to the stairs.

I make my footsteps and breathing heavy as I ascend. A whisper of sound reaches me from above.

They're at the top of the stairs. Even having given them warning of my coming, I could still kill them.

I clench my jaw.

My act isn't over yet. For a few moments, I was the assassin I have trained to be.

Now, I must be the jester once more.

I can kill them later.

A man shifts at the top of the stairs. I remain limp as he grabs the front of my shirt.

"Oi! Let go!" I yell as he drags me the rest of the way up and presses his sword to my throat.

He blinks and leans closer. "What are you doing coming up the stairs?" he demands, thrusting me back.

I add a stumble for their sake and straighten my clothes, scowling. "Can't a man return to his own bed in peace?" I raise the candlestick clutched in my left hand. "I even grabbed light for the benefit of you fools."

"You're the fool tonight," one of the others says from behind. He clamps a hand on my shoulder and I barely keep myself from ripping him to shreds. "Go back to your room and stay there until we know what's going on." He pushes me away from the stairs and toward the bedchambers. I stumble a little again, successfully keeping myself in my role.

I hurry to my room, open the door, blow out the candles, and listen.

Light flickers through the glass window. The guards must have grabbed torches and are now investigating the grounds.

My men won't be able to evade capture for long.

I set the candlestick down, close my door, and move down the hall silently, a killer on the move once more.

The king's room is only a few doors from mine. I pause and glance back at his guards.

Their attention is still down the stairs.

Should I just open the door and slip in? Knock first and announce myself?

Am I the jester or assassin?

I palm a blade and open the door, staying in the hall.

He just might have someone hidden behind the door.

Charles is standing at the window, nightshirt tucked haphazardly into his pants, feet bare and drawn sword clasped in his hand. He turns, raising his blade. Candles flicker in the corner, illuminating one side of his face.

And two candles burn in the window behind him.

"Triboulet," Charles says, lowering his sword.

I turn my hand with the blade, keeping it hidden from him.

At least I can safely enter now.

"Your Majesty. You're safe." I move forward three steps, trying to ignore the two candles, my signal, burning in his window.

Maybe it's just coincidence. He could have set them there after the call was raised.

The young king flexes his fingers about his sword, and I stop.

He's nervous.

I return my knife to its hiding place and hold out empty hands. He studies me a moment and turns back to the window.

"What's going on?" he asks.

"I'm not sure." I take another step.

This kill must be made silently. The king's guards at the stairs mustn't have any reason to investigate. By the time the "king" raises the alarm, the "jester" must be dead and his face marred beyond recognition.

It probably won't hurt if I also have a wound. Nothing too serious, but sufficient to lend credence to my story.

"I think someone tried to enter the chateau." I'm five paces from him.

"How?" Charles demands, turning to face me once more. "The portcullis was down."

"Yes. It was."

He stares at me.

I slip a blade from its hiding place about my waist.

"Someone opened it, didn't they?" Charles asks softly.

I take a step forward. "They must have." My fingers wrap about the hilt comfortably.

"Was it you?"

The question stops me.

"Why would Your Majesty think such a thing of me?" I add a whine to my voice, playing the part of an injured but loyal servant.

Charles shifts his attention to a point over my left shoulder. I dance right and leap for him, thrusting my blade forward.

Smoke puffs up around me, and sulfur fills the air. I cough, and tears smart my eyes. A patter of light footsteps sound to my left. I throw my knife at it. A cry and a thump echo through the room as he falls.

One of the guards from the stairs shouts.

Curse my reflexes.

A whisper of movement from where my target fell.

"Someone's attacked the king!" I shout, moving toward the sound. The smoke clears.

But my eyes are still watering.

The guards are moving toward the king's chamber now.

I cough and rub my eyes. My vision clears.

The room is empty.

Except for me.

The guards are close.

"Your Majesty? Where are you?" I shout.

The first guard skids round the corner and into the room.

"Light! We need light!"

"Where is the king?" the guard demands. Two more join him.

My eyes are still burning. I swipe at the tears that form.

"Someone attacked him," I say.

The guards move in, and I shift toward the door. One strides to the toppled candlestick and raises it, illuminating the room. A semicircular blackened line is in front of the window. I clench my hands.

Black powder. Fast burning. All it takes is a spark to produce thick smoke.

Perfect for concealing activities.

I blink, looking back at the candlestick.

The guard didn't pick it up from where it had been before.

Somehow, it moved.

He steps forward, face grim and candlestick raised. The light falls on spots of blood on the floor.

They lead toward the door.

"Search the building," the guard orders. "Have two men guard the front door. The king must be found."

I sidle to the door and slip out, before they ask me more questions.

Yes, the king must be found.

But not by them.

I pause in the hallway. The rest of the king's guards are still at the top of the stairs, glancing back every now and then.

A gasp of pain sounds to the right, toward the stairs leading to the topmost level.

So. He's going up.

I might still pull this off.

I move quickly, slipping through the shadows after my quarry, trying to ignore the tingling rising up my neck.

Shadows shifting in the gate. Twigs snapping amongst the vines. My signal in the king's window. Candlesticks moving.

I'm being superstitious. There's no such thing as ghosts.

I pause at the bottom of the stairs. The guards are just getting themselves organized. Two hurry down to ground level.

A floorboard creaks above me.

I ascend, leaving the guards and their slow organization behind.

No one was sleeping in the topmost level, leaving it vacant and dark. Apparently, the young king prefers to die alone.

Suits me.

I step to the side of the stairs and cover my eyes for a moment, helping them adjust quickly to the thick darkness while I listen.

A scuff echoes straight down the hall.

He's moving farther in.

I lower my hands and stride forward, keeping close to the wall and avoiding the creaky floorboards.

There aren't many options up here, with only three rooms on either side of the narrow hall. I pass a closed door. Footsteps approach the stairs from below.

I won't have much time.

A gap opens on my left. I move past and press myself to the wall on the other side.

The doors are normally kept closed. Meaning the king is in this room.

The bottommost step creaks.

I move through the open door.

The shutters are open, allowing some of the weak moonlight to probe into the room. It wraps around my target, casting his face into shadow. He still has his sword but is standing with a stoop now, watching the door.

He shifts as I move inside, face turned toward me as he edges into a deeper shadow. "You won't get away with this." His voice is strained.

I smile and draw a blade, twisting it in a beam of moonlight.

"Go on. Call your guards. It'll be over before they get here."

The king twists as I flick my wrist. He gasps and falls, my knife in his chest. Dust puffs up in the moonlight.

I leap onto him, another blade drawn, and grab a fistful of his hair.

Or try to.

It's shorter than it should be.

I grip his throat and pull him up. He cries out, face contorted in pain. The guards shout on the stairs.

"Dear God . . ." I release him and stumble back. "You're dead. Two weeks ago."

The real jester slumps back, panting. "You should have made sure I was," he whispers. "It's hard to kill a true trickster."

Light precedes the guards. I turn, drawing my arm back to throw my knife.

And meet Charles's gaze.

The king swipes diagonally upward, the tip of a borrowed sword slicing the flesh across my chest. I bite back a cry. My blade falls from my hand. Guards burst past him and grab my arms.

"Fool," Charles says, striding forward.

I suck a breath through my teeth, forcing the burning pain from my thoughts. "You won't be king long," I snarl. "Others will rise, others will come, to finish this."

He stops before me. The guards' grip tightens.

"It is God who raises up kings, and God who removes them," he says before looking to one of the men holding me. "Hang him, and any men in the chateau you don't recognize."

The guards drag me toward the door. Pain rips across my chest, and my vision blurs.

"The king," the real jester gasps from behind me.

"Here," Charles replies, his voice gentle.

My vision clears, and I pull against the soldiers' hands, straining for freedom or another knife. Their grip doesn't loosen.

"Long live the king," the jester says. A long sigh whispers through the room.

I stumble, my knees growing weak. The guards drag me into the hall, and I glance back. Charles is kneeling by the dead man, head bowed.

"*Merci*," he whispers.

MADE WITH LOVE

Beka Gremikova

FINAL MEAL CHOICE, Dunbar. What do you want?"

Vic Dunbar lifted his head. He'd thought long and hard, trying to decide between steak and spaghetti. "Got anyone who can cook a good steak?" Nothing beat Lady Love's cooking, but beggars couldn't be *too* picky.

Kate, his prison guard, narrowed her eyes at him. "Not that *I* know of. What do you think this is, the palace?"

Dunbar sighed. Somehow the prospect of a disgusting last meal irritated him more than his upcoming execution. "Prison budget that tight?"

Kate pressed her lips together. "If they could afford someone who cooks a good steak, they could afford to give me a raise." She leaned against his cell's iron bars. "Hurry up and choose."

"Don't rush me." He wanted the right fortification if he had to face Queen Helen's gallows.

She rolled her eyes. "Fine, diva. I'll go ask the other death rows, then I'll circle back." She sauntered away, hands in her pockets.

Dunbar flexed his fingers. Blast, what he wouldn't give for a good steak: rare, seasoned with salt and pepper and maybe lemon. His mouth watered.

But knowing his luck, some dirty-fingered prison cook would spoil his favorite dish.

When Kate returned, he ordered spaghetti.

••••♣•••

"Spaghetti?" Betsy-Lou stared at Kate in disbelief. Over her three years of employment, she'd never felt so offended by a death row inmate's request. "One of the most renowned criminals of our time, and he orders *spaghetti*?"

"Wonder what his girlfriend would say. The infamous Lady Love." Kate fiddled with her badge. "Wonder how she's dated all those criminals without ever committing crimes herself. Now *that's* talent. Not to mention—"

"*She's never lost a man to the gallows.*" Betsy-Lou quoted the popular phrase, and the other women rolled their eyes.

"Well, until this guy, anyway." Kate sidestepped as Marie, another kitchen worker, bustled past to start the spaghetti.

"Criminals must be her type," Marie joked.

Betsy-Lou sniffed in disgust. "Can't believe Dunbar was stupid enough to get caught."

Marie dumped a package of ground beef into her pan. "Dunbar was such a good boy. *I* think Lady Love ruined him. If she'd spent less time on her makeup and more on him—"

Betsy-Lou scoffed. "Maybe he wasn't as good as you think."

"Not a fan?" Marie asked.

"Spaghetti," Betsy-Lou snapped, "is beneath a man connected to Lady Love."

"Oh, you're a Lady Love fanatic." Marie squinted at her. "Makes sense, considering all your makeup. Except *hers* is always done perfectly."

Betsy-Lou ignored Marie's verbal stab and pondered another dilemma. Since being hired, she'd cooked her way through thousands of worthless meals to reach this one. She'd imagined preparing lobster tails and caviar . . . or the perfect steak: rare, with salt and pepper. *Not* spaghetti.

This would be in the *newspaper*, for heaven's sake. Annoyed, she whirled and dashed to the kitchen fridge. Her fellow workers stared at her as she rummaged and produced a small strip steak. She grimaced. "No tenderloin in here?" That would be a *tad* fancier.

Kate snorted. "First Dunbar, now you. We're not the palace, sweetheart. I didn't even know you could cook steak."

Betsy-Lou slammed the fridge door shut. "The other blighters never asked for steak. Consider it my gift to a famous criminal." She hurried over to the spice cabinet where the kitchen workers kept their own supplies from home. "You cook him that blasted spaghetti, Marie. *I'm* going to cook something worthy of my talents."

•••♣•••

"I'm supposed to tell you it was made with love." Kate's voice was edged with laughter.

"Was it made by a fan or something?" Dunbar slid his knife through the perfectly grilled steak. His eyes widened. "It's *rare*." He grinned.

"That good?" Kate shook her head. "Maybe that means I'll get that raise."

Dunbar lifted a forkful to his mouth. The meat was tender and piping hot. He closed his eyes and sighed deeply. As he chewed, the fiery sensation of pepper ignited his taste buds, then died away to reveal . . . His eyes flew open. He sat up straighter, staring down at the steak resting in au jus. *That flavor!* Slight sourness mixed with the pepper in a combination most people only used on fish.

My favorite. And a preference very few knew.

He glanced toward Kate, but she had already moved on to deliver meals to the other death row inmates.

Pondering, he took another bite and frowned. A different, mystery flavor lurked, masked by the sour fire of the lemon-pepper mix. The more he ate, the more that taste heightened—a lingering frostiness, like someone had dragged an ice cube across his tongue.

He finished the steak and licked his lips. Kate had brought him a bowl of spaghetti, too. Though the steak had satisfied him, who knew if they had feasts in hell? He might as well gorge now.

As he slurped spaghetti noodles, the steak's lingering cold tingle punctuated the acid spark of the tomato sauce coating his tongue.

His heart started speeding faster than a runaway horse. His thoughts stretched like taffy.

Saliva filled his mouth, but he couldn't swallow.

His fork fumbled from his fingers and clattered to the ground.

•••♣•••

With a sigh, Betsy-Lou locked the kitchen doors after her. What a long day. Her personal blend of spices rested safely in her pocket. She'd mixed it with poison the prison kept for executing female inmates—Queen Helen considered hanging women to be in poor taste.

Betsy-Lou smiled. Three long years of waiting, working, had led to this day. Now, her reputation protected, her job done, she could go home and change her makeup, get rid of her disguise. *Maybe find a new beau.*

"Sorry, Dunbar," she murmured. "It was nothing personal."

It was a matter of pride more than anything else. After all, Lady Love had never lost a man to the gallows, and she wasn't about to start now.

THE HUMOR IN MURDER

Anne J. Hill

I RODE MY BIKE through the city on my way to Cherry Café, admiring the lazy autumn morning. Dead mildewy leaves littered my path, their spindly trees looking out of place against the quaint row-house backdrop and—

My tire skidded, and my bike jerked out from under me, shooting me toward concrete stairs. Something smacked me in the back of the head—my backpack.

I had always wondered what it'd be like to fly; I just hadn't pictured it quite like this.

"Whoa!" Arms wrapped around me as I knocked their owner onto his back. He groaned. "You okay?" he asked, wincing.

"Yeah. Are *you* okay?" I rolled off him onto the wet leaves and quickly stood, looking over myself because the stinging I felt proved me a liar. My hand stopped on my knee just below my shorts, and I winced. It was warm and oozing, but I didn't bother looking down.

He stayed on the ground, grinning up at me with sparkling, innocent eyes. Wild hair flipped across his forehead from the shuffle. "Besides almost being murdered by a pretty lady, I think I'm all right."

"You would have been my second victim today," I muttered, deadpan.

He blinked at me, his eyes darting to my knee for a second, then back to my face, and he laughed. "Is a bicycle your weapon of choice?"

I reached out with my non-bloody hand and offered to help him up. "I prefer drownings. You know, tie someone up and dump them into a lake. Watch them sink to the bottom." I grinned, letting out a half-hearted chuckle.

"I'm assuming Lake Dolo is the best for murder." This guy didn't miss a beat.

I nodded. "Obviously. No one around for miles. Perfect place to commit a crime." I winked, letting him know he had nothing to worry about. Standing at only four foot nine inches, I was, in fact, usually harmless.

He patted down his hair. "Also good for drowning kittens. Like in the movies. Toss them in a burlap bag, tie it, and chuck them into the water. Just an average murdering Monday." He threw back his head and laughed.

I laughed with him. "Don't forget the puppies, too."

He paused and mocked serious consideration. "True, but kittens are the classic animal to drown, and if you're going to drown an animal, you might as well make it a classic drowning."

"Fair enough." I nodded. "Gotta know what it's like in the movies and all."

"You headed anywhere in particular?" he asked as he looked me over, obviously not one for discretion. And I'm sure I was a sight to see, with my bloody knee, dirt on my face, and leaves in my hair.

I locked eyes with him and blinked once. "I was getting coffee, but the lake is sounding like a better idea now. Care to join?"

He laughed loudly again. Heads turned to look at us. I was amusing to this man, and I didn't mind. I liked being thought of as funny. Better than awkward and weird—a misfit.

"Perfect," he said. "But first, can I fix up that knee of yours?"

I glanced back down at the scrape. "Oh. It's all right. I'll just wash it off in the lake."

"As you're murdering someone, naturally." He started walking, and I picked up my bike and followed him.

"Naturally."

As we arrived, the lake shone like sparkling glass. Red and brown leaves floated calmly on the water and the smell of decayed nature wafted over me. I breathed in its comforting aroma. Funny how something dead can bring such joy.

"It's so peaceful out here." The man smiled at the water, then at me.

"Perfect place for a murder, isn't it?" I leaned my bike against a nearby tree and adjusted the bag on my back.

"Mmm." His eyes danced back to the water. "Yes, but I'll admit, I like to save kitten-drowning for later. More of a third date sort of activity, don't you think?"

I tried to hide the delight in my face, but I couldn't hold back my grin. What can I say? I'm a killer for cheesy romance. "So, this is a *date* then? I don't even know your name."

"Matthew. And you are?"

I picked up a stone and tossed it into the lake, trying to make it skip, but it just splashed and sank lifelessly to the bottom. "Lora Kemp."

"Pleased to meet you, Lora Kemp." Matthew turned and held his hand out.

I shook it, smiled at him, then walked over to the water and rinsed the blood off my knee.

"So, what's in the backpack? Rope and a body bag?" he teased.

"Obviously." I chuckled. Without looking up, I said, "You're pretty handsome, you know that?"

He laughed again, but there were no strangers to stare at us this time. "Who? Me? Or are you talking to the murder lake?"

I glanced over my shoulder at him and grinned. "I was heading to get coffee before, but then I ran into you, and now I'm here, so what do you think?"

"Maybe we can get coffee after." Hopeful anticipation tinged in his voice.

"What's your last name?"

"Jones."

I nodded formally. "I'd like that, Matthew Jones. But you're paying."

"It'd be my pleasure, Miss Bicycle Murderer."

I held out my hand, and we shook on it as if we had just agreed to be lifelong partners in crime.

My eyes moved to his lips, and heat rose in my core. The idea of this man standing beside me through thick and thin ignited a fire inside. I'd never been one to suppress my cravings, so I leaned forward and kissed him. My hands found his waist as I moved my lips against his, searching for any reciprocation.

Matthew touched my hips and pushed me back, parting us. "What are you doing?" His eyebrows furrowed, his voice a soft sting, and my fire burned brighter.

He'd rejected me.

"Sorry. I thought you'd like that." I slipped my bag off my back.

"I don't usually kiss people I just met." He ran a hand over his red cheeks.

I nodded and flashed him a peace offering grin. "It won't happen again."

"Yeah, so I should probably head out." He brushed his fingers through his hair, taking a step back from me, with a breathy chuckle. I decided it would be his last. No one rejects me and lives to tell the tale.

And soon, only one of us was laughing.

And there was no coffee.

And no second date.

And no drowning kittens.

Just me later that day, alone in Cherry Café, listening to rumors of a local drowning, sipping coffee and grinning as a new man walked in. I'd found my next date.

RUSE OF THE ROGUES

When all else
FAILS,
frame your
PARTNER.

FOOL'S GUIDE TO TRICKERY

Part Four

Anne J. Hill

YOU'VE HEARD FROM the masters, you've learned how to bend humor to your will, and you've even refined the art of the twist ending. But as you know, not everything in this business fits into a neat little box. In fact, not much does! And now that we have reached the end of this Fool's Guide to Trickery, here is a mixed bag of tricks to keep in mind as you plan your next moves.

1. Always be one step ahead (see step number two below).

2. Have a backup plan just in case everything goes to shambles. It likely will. It's a casualty of being a trickster. We can't *always* win.

3. Don't be predictable. Always do the unpredictable. And when that gets predictable, do the predictable.

4. Let the law step in once in a while. It'll save you the trouble of killing the enemy, plus it's fun to watch them suffer a little longer.

5. Keep an eye out for people who seem *out of touch.* They're plotting to kill you. Always. Except authors. They're totally harmless. Usually.

6. Be calm and collected because you have a plan. But don't always tell your partner what it is.

7. Assume everyone else is a trickster too. You can never be too careful, and the worst is getting backstabbed by your own partners. Trust me.

8. When all else fails, frame your partner.

9. Keep an open mind. Maybe you're actually in the wrong . . . . Nah. Who really cares?

10. Don't always assume you're the bad guy, either. Even if you've been told you're a villain your whole life.

11. Lastly and most importantly, do not disregard anyone, no matter how much they don't fit into your plans—because they will. And use the people you think matter regardless of what society says. They all come in handy if you play your cards right. And I know you will because a trickster *always* plays with a loaded deck and an ace up the sleeve.

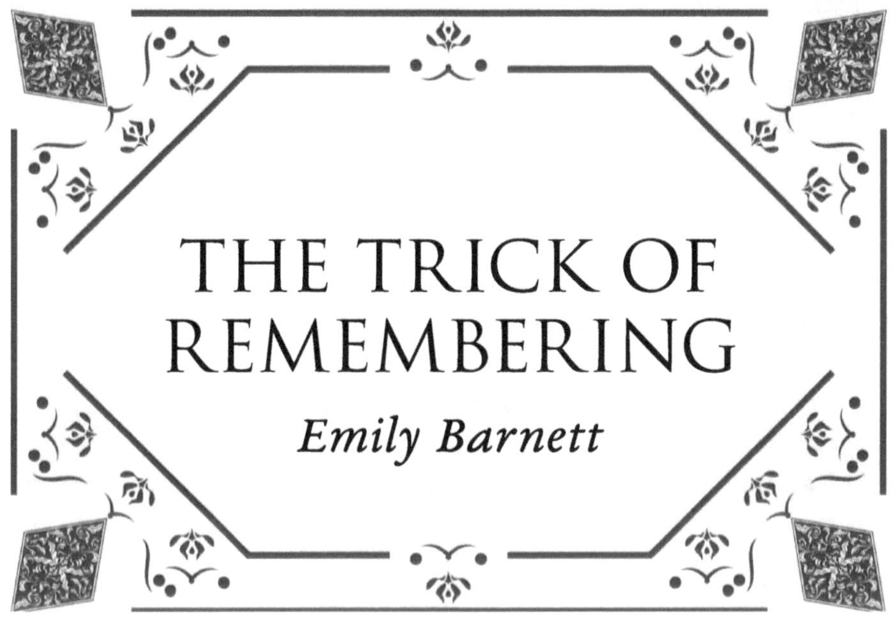

THE TRICK OF REMEMBERING

Emily Barnett

"HERE TO TRY again?"

I smile at the sound of my wife's voice. Usually, Helen's tone is as cold as winter's song, but today there is warmth in it as if spring is awakening. Even her glare doesn't hold the same contempt.

"Of *course* I'm going to try again," I say, straightening my magenta tie. Helen loves magenta. And a man in a suit. "I'll stop when I'm dead, my darling."

I've been trying to win Helen's affections back for five years. And I will. I'm a god in this world, and gods always get what they desire.

Helen huffs, twirling away, her cinnamon-brown hair catching the light of my most recent illusion. The glowing dolphins diving in the blue ocean sky call after her in a sad chatter.

"Quiet," I hiss, swiping my hand and dissolving them into stardust. I easily catch up to Helen, but she can't get far. Her path through the Garden of Remembrance is a forever loop.

Her fingers trail along the head of a Lioness Lily, and it lets out a purr. But she doesn't seem to notice, as she continues in thought—the line between her eyes forming an ever-so-slight wrinkle.

Helen's blue dress sways against her knees, and I gently grab the ribbon that hangs from her waist, pulling her to me. "Do you remember the first time you wore this?"

Helen's green eyes blaze with fury at my touch, but then a brow rises, her vision glazing over in memory. After a moment, her eyelids flutter, and she looks down at the gauzy blue thing that drives me wild. "This dress . . ." she whispers.

My heart speeds. Does she recognize it? Prom, 1980.

But as she stares at the fabric, it begins to fade into a deep brown, like a dying flower in late fall. "No," she says, shoving me hard in the chest. "I don't remember this. I don't remember any of it." She narrows her eyes. "Least of all *you*."

Her words strike like a match, burning me up with grief and rage at this prison keeping away her memories—a prison I should be able to break.

A prison I've trapped her in.

Though sorrow threatens to swallow me, I remind myself that I'm a god of tricks, and I'm good at masking things, even my own emotions.

"It's too bad," I say, with an air of indifference. I flick my fingers, and the blue sky turns to an amber sunset. The clouds, hanging just below the shimmering dome, bleed as red as romance. "You're missing out." I wink.

Helen snorts. "I'm really supposed to believe that my captor is my husband?" She laughs, eyeing the clouds with disdain. "It sounds like we had a *real* charming marriage. Did you illusion up an 'I do' as well?"

Ignoring her, I conjure a dog with silky black fur and ears like dandelion fluff—an exact replica of Benny. Our pup from before the days of magic, before Mayhem hit our world, dousing us all with powers so strange and wonderful that we would never be the same again. The day my wife was entrapped within an illusion, keeping her powers as dormant as seeds in winter.

Benny's bark echoes around the garden, reminding us just how enclosed we are. I pull at my necktie, and it swirls away. I'm in a scratchy red sweater now, the kind she hated at parties. When she eyes the rumpled thing, and no recognition lights up her eyes, I click my tongue at Benny and lead him toward a multi-colored pond in the center of the Garden of Remembrance. Normally, her disgust and anger make me fight harder, but today, I'm tired. Maybe I've used too many illusions.

Maybe it's something else.

Pushing through the horsetails that neigh rudely as we pass, I find a log along the bank and sit heavily. Without looking, I know it has our names carved in its deep bark like a promise etched into steel.

Andrew + Helen.

A crude heart is drawn around it. I carved it when we were sixteen, just old enough to feel the currents of love, yet young enough to not get swept away in them.

Now, I'm drowning, and I can't even conjure myself a boat.

The sunset rolls over on its back to greet the night as stars prick the black velvet above. But I don't call them down tonight. I don't make them dance or form constellations of our past. I don't make them sparkle as brightly as the diamond I gave her when we were twenty-two. They just hang there like normal stars, though our real world is anything but.

If only she could glimpse the world outside these walls. And remember who we were too.

I'm about to push up from the log and make my way out of the garden—out of the gate that, somehow, only I can come in and out of—when I hear the horsetails neighing softly. Turning, I see Helen picking her way down the path I made. My breath catches. She's cloaked in light, and she's wearing her wedding dress. Not a perfect rendition. It's fuzzy around the edges, and with every step, it shifts, its design sliding from one thing to the next. But I can see the truth of it even as it changes.

When she sits beside me and catches my eye, the ice has thawed, as if something has changed. Does she remember?

"You aren't keeping me here, are you?" she asks.

I hesitate. We've been through this before. It's always better to let her believe that I'm the bad guy, that it's me holding her prisoner, not her own weak mind. It always drove her deeper into madness knowing the truth. But tonight, I don't have the heart to tell her I'm the villain. Not again.

"No, I'm not," I say softly.

Her lip quivers, and I stop myself from putting an arm around her. She still smells of uncertainty.

"Why can't I remember my life before?"

"A spell." I sigh. "Our world was attacked by magic, and you were hit with a spell."

She swallows. Though her eyes are still distrusting, I can see a flicker of knowing in them, as if something of our prior life is breaking through. "Will I ever be free from it?" she whispers.

Tentatively, I reach out and touch her hand. She doesn't pull away. "That's what I'm working on."

She slips her fingers through mine, studying my knuckles with curiosity. "Why do you keep coming back?"

"What did I tell you?" Lifting my empty hand, I snap my fingers. "I'll stop trying to win you back when I'm dead." The pond that was a riot of color before now changes to a still, silver mirror. It reflects the glittering stars and a full moon, and . . . a little girl. Helen and I both look up to see the girl across the pond, a faint illusion made stronger by the reflection. She has the same cinnamon hair as Helen's, the same brown eyes as mine.

Helen's breath catches. "Is she . . . *ours?*"

Tears leak down my face, but I don't vanish them. "Yes."

Helen looks at me with a wide-eyed stare. Wonder. Fear. Disbelief. Maybe even remembrance?

"Andy?"

At first, I think it's Helen who has said my name. But then, she frowns, looking through me as if I'm a ghost.

"I'll be back," I yell, but I'm not sure she hears me. My mind is slipping from her prison. It's always disorienting, and it's always too soon. If only I could stay with her forever. Maybe then we wouldn't have to start over again every time.

Maybe then . . .

"Andy?"

I jolt from my trance, the stiff hospital chair under me creaking in surprise. The problem with this type of illusion is that it leaves me completely vulnerable. Anyone can sneak up on me and slit my throat. Or wake me with a single word.

Nurse Jen stands over me, an eyebrow cocked. "Visiting hours are over, Andy. What have I told you about staying so late?"

I grunt, looking at the woman on the bed before us. Her cinnamon hair makes her look so pale in the fluorescent lights.

"I was just napping," I say casually, wondering if I have enough power to illusion Nurse Jen before she catches my lie.

But instead of her expression growing harder, she softens, leaning against the wall full of charts and a magicked X-ray that constantly shows an image of the inside of Helen's brain. To my relief, she doesn't call security. Those guys and their anti-magic tasers are the worst. But I can tell she knows I'm lying.

What else would she think? I'm a dealer of deception—an Illusionist. Though many powers came upon the people of earth five years ago, it's Illusionists no one trusts. They assume the worst of those who conjure lies from thin air.

"The reason I let you in here, though non-healing magic is banned inside these walls, is that Helen's brain activity is off the charts when you *visit* her." She says the word "visit" so forcefully I'm surprised it doesn't slug me in the face. "You may be untrustworthy in our world . . ." She hesitates, looking down at my wife. My wife who's been in a coma for five years. "But in *her* world, you are doing something good."

I smirk, conjuring a spark of light and flicking it between my hands like a baseball. "Come on, Nurse Jen. You act as if I'm a good guy." My expression darkens, and the light fades in my palm. "You know I was the one who did this to her."

She shakes her head. "When Mayhem hit, everyone's new powers were out of control. You're lucky the spell that crashed your car only injured her. She could've died, Andy. Then where would you be?"

"Not in a hospital room, that's for sure."

Nurse Jen nodded. "You aren't the villain, Andy, no matter how hard you try making yourself one. Who cares if you were driving? It was an accident."

"An accident that put her in a coma, stopping any powers she might have manifested. While the rest of the world grows stronger, she—" I look away, clearing my throat and focusing on Helen's serene face. Her closed eyes dance behind her eyelids like ripples in a pond. Is she alone in her garden right now? Does she miss me when I'm gone, or does she simply forget all over again?

The door creaks behind me, and I turn to see a girl of sixteen walk into the room. She looks so much like Helen my heart squeezes painfully. Our daughter slips an arm around my shoulder, kissing the top of my head. "Anything today?"

My throat closes, and I shake my head.

"Actually," Nurse Jen says, tapping the X-ray behind her. "There *has* been a development here." She points to a part of Helen's brain. "In the hippocampus. There's activity."

Hope swells in my chest as I search the magicked screen. A small area of her brain looks to be churning and sparking with light. My eyes prickle with heat, and I blink rapidly, watching the image. "Does this mean . . ."

Nurse Jen smiles. "I think Helen is starting to remember."

I'm at Helen's side in a moment, my emotions sending fireworks and wind through the room. Helen's hair dances in the storm of my illusion, but under those eyelids, in her mind, she is safe. She is *remembering*. The deceptions that have all but exiled me from society have sparked a memory in my wife.

My chest pulls taut and I touch Helen's hand. It's warm, like spring.

Maybe Nurse Jen is right, after all. Maybe I'm not the villain I think I am.

TO LIVE
AND HEAR LIFE
BETWEEN TURNING
PAGES.

OVERTHROWN

Brittany Eden

at the thought of you, I freeze
a fall, a torrent
still

at the memory of you, I speak
a slow drip, a winter sea
silent

at the sight of you
every hint of you
over any throne, your heart claims mine
for all time, all time

but the thought of you,
feels farther, deeper, darker
lost

yet at the memory of you, I weep
waves—no, nothing
will ever keep

your face, your voice
the end of every story
buried, ever-living, below before it ended

and the dreaded then
became now—and still still still
until the hoped-for someday and not then
becomes now, becomes now

for you, I'll be
just in love, just breathing
for you, just willing

and wishing, ever-waking, fighting
for you here, you there
you are everywhere
my love

a story, a book, a hope
my end,
for you—the heart of my love story

to live and hear
life
between turning pages

nothing in me royal
just a fool
overthrown

at the sight of you
every hint of you
over any throne, your heart claiming mine
for all time, all time

if I were stronger, wiser
for this—
I am but yours

if I had only told you
if only, I told you
if only

If I were
to trap the
MUSE
How could I
make it sing?

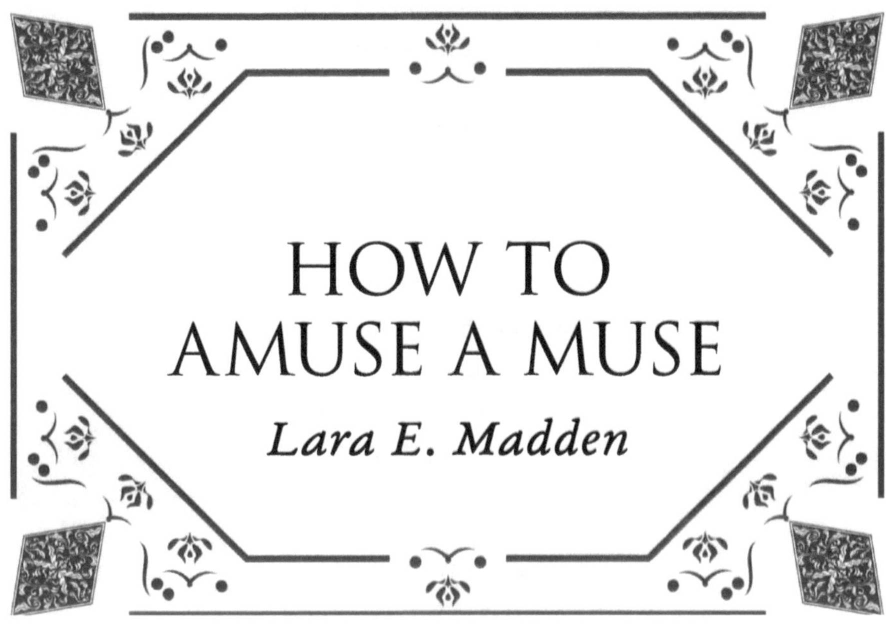

HOW TO AMUSE A MUSE

Lara E. Madden

How could I amuse a muse?
How might I catch its eye?
Would a melody draw it from hiding
Or a picture bring it by?

Will it dance to the tapping of typewriter's keys
Or skip to the scratch of a pen?
If I wait and wonder in silence
Might it creep out from its den?

If I were to trap the muse,
Surely there is no way to force
So fragile and wild a thing

Perhaps if I befriend the muse
It would take me across the sea
If I feed it laughter, grief, and love
It might sing its tale to me

Gently, I enchant the muse
With the honey-wine of Life
And I listen as it drinks its fill
And sings a song of strife

A melody of broken dreams
And tears lost on the wind
I write down all I can before
The Muse escapes again

But ah, I've learned its secret now!
The Muse's favorite vice—
It drinks deeply of the stuff of Life
But won't drink the same stuff twice!

THE RED UMBRELLA

Anne J. Hill

IF ONLY IT hadn't rained that morning, she might have lived.

Slumping on the edge of her broken-down loveseat, Ms. Digger checked and rechecked that her gun was clean, with a full mag, safety off, and a bullet in the chamber. If she were lucky—no, if she did her job well—this would only take two shots.

She screwed the silencer to the end of the barrel with swift, practiced turns, then slipped the firearm into her purse. There were some things even old age couldn't rob her of.

Rain pelted the roof of her ranch-style home as she stepped onto her front porch. She looked up at the sound of a door creaking. Mr. Johnston, the old veteran across the street, was leaving his house. He held a steaming cup of coffee in his right hand and a red umbrella in his left. His slippered feet shuffled across his puddle-laden driveway, and his night robe flapped in the piercing breeze. Reaching the end of the drive, he set his mug on his mailbox, bent down, and scooped up his newspaper. "Morning, Digger!" he called and slipped the paper under his arm.

"Morning, Johnston."

He retrieved his drink and blew on it, and some of it splashed onto his slippers. He scowled down at the mess and asked, "Going to work?"

"Sure am."

Johnston sipped his scorching coffee and spat it onto the gravel, making a pained face. "Have a good day."

Ms. Digger chuckled, shaking her head. "Never did have patience to let your coffee cool, did you?"

"No, ma'am! See you tonight?"

Digger bit her lip in pause, then nodded slowly. "Tonight."

Johnston's eyes lit up, and he shuffled back inside, scolding his coffee for being too hot.

Every morning, he asked to see her that night. She always said yes but never showed up, and he never remembered.

This time, she intended to show. She'd finally let him in. No one wanted to die alone.

But first, she had work to do.

She drove to the nearby city, reminding herself that this would be her last job and then she could finally live. At the age of seventy-five, she would begin her life. Better late than never.

She parked on the street, windshield wipers plowing away the rain. Just in front of her was a couple around her age. Instead of holding hands, they held onto the black umbrella they shared, fingers overlapping. The man leaned over and kissed his lover's cheek. She glanced back and beamed like it was their honeymoon.

Digger's thumbs tapped against her steering wheel. That will be us tonight. She smiled at the thought then got out of the car.

Every building was white or cream except for the one with the green door. She trailed quietly behind the couple, watching the green door get closer as she walked.

She wondered what her targets did to deserve the bullet this time. Murder? Theft? Spying? Could be anything.

The man glanced back at her and offered a smile. She nodded. No one ever suspected an old lady. She had that going for her. Shoot, then fade into the street as a granny looking for her lost cat. Worked every time.

When the man looked away, Digger picked up her pace until she was inches behind them. No one else was on the streets. Most people were still sleeping. Just how she liked it.

The couple stopped in front of the green door. The woman looked back at her this time. "Are you lost, dear?"

"Not me. Lost my cat. Name's Charlie. White fluffy thing. You seen him?"

The lady frowned. "Can't say I have. We'll keep an eye out for you."

"'Preciate it." Ms. Digger gave her a toothy smile. Then she shot the woman through the back and put a round through the old man before he had a chance to react. The silencer-muffled concussions disappeared into the wind like a couple of innocent sneezes.

Two limp, once-happy bodies lay at Ms. Digger's feet. She locked eyes with the lady's forever-unblinking gaze and shook her head, then knocked on the green door and walked away, calling, "Charlie! Here, kitty, kitty!"

The door creaked open behind her, and the sound of dragging bodies grumbled amongst the pattering rain. The blood would wash off the sidewalk soon enough. Easy. Clean. Done.

She never knew what they did with the bodies, but she didn't really care. She knew she'd have a wad of cash in her mailbox when she got home, and frankly, that's all she needed to know.

Digger smiled up at the rain, feeling angels' tears plummet down on her face. She was a free woman. She'd pulled her last trigger and would be rewarded with true love.

If only it hadn't rained that morning, she might have lived.

She glanced back towards the green door and froze. A man stood under a red umbrella, mouth gaping.

"Johnston?" Digger could have sworn the street had been empty.

"Saw you leave the house without an umbrella, so I came to walk you to work so you wouldn't get wet." His face was ghostly white like he'd seen, well, everything.

She glanced to his right. He must have turned down the alley behind her just as she'd pulled the trigger. If only it hadn't been raining. If only Johnston hadn't been so sweet to bring her an umbrella.

If only...

If only Digger hadn't inclined her firearm toward Johnston out of habit. If only Johnston didn't carry his old World War 2 pistol and a strong sense of self-preservation. Then she might have walked down the street under his umbrella to a happily ever after. Instead, she now lay in a pool of her own blood with a hole between her eyes.

Nobody likes to die alone.

Truly,
I am not
CRUEL
at heart.

SHADES AND FEATHERS

Mariella Taylor

The more you press the more
I am provoked
to deny what you desire.

Truly, I am not cruel at heart,
but I hate all the
begging and nagging and lies.

Manipulation unfolds
such a well-known face,
but at least it is not masked.

The only thing I hate more
than seeing your lies
is hiding myself from you.

Harsh but necessary so
I hide my gray shades
behind your peacock feathers.

Keeping hidden is why
when you press I bow
It's a beautiful blend

—my shades and your feathers.

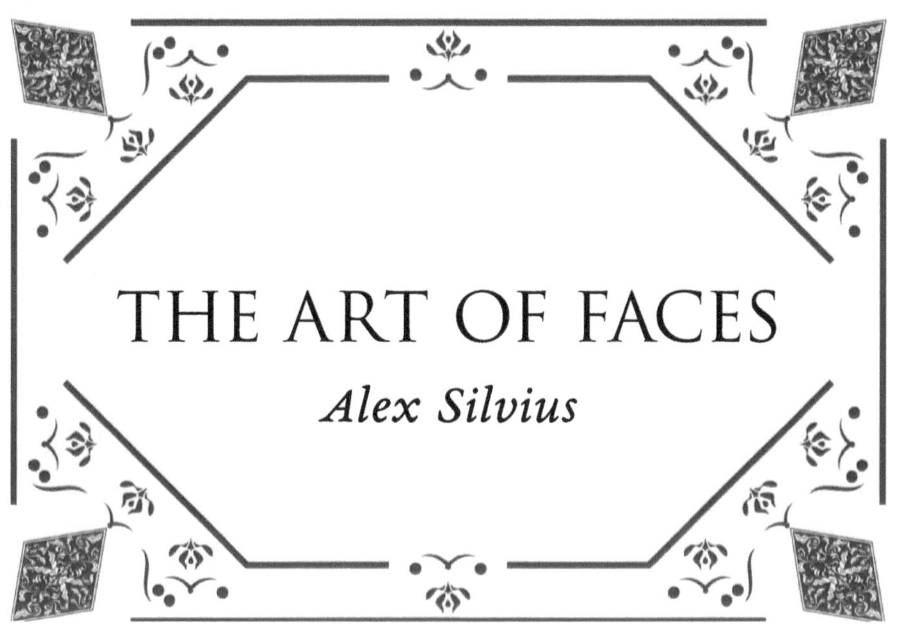

THE ART OF FACES

Alex Silvius

Tell me, do you like my second face?
You've probably never noticed it,
So smooth, so human,
Feminine with grace.

I only put it on when you're around,
For you like me this way,
Untouchable, a goddess
Living on the ground.

Let me know when you're through,
Your love for me dwindling,
For I'll pull out a third face,
And use it to keep loving you.

Now that she's

DEAD

Echo's power

has only

STRENGTHENED.

PRISON OF STARS

Beka Gremikova

EARTH TO ECHO."

Electricity courses through Echo as Darbo's deep voice prods her consciousness. She stirs, blinking out at the spaceship's main chamber. Her jail cell.

Darbo stands by the main control panel, pressing the button that shoots shock waves across Echo's incorporeal form. Nearby, his daughter Lilah crunches on star-puffs while skimming travel magazines. Her younger brother, Adrian, stares out the viewscreen, his nose smudging the glass as he watches stars slide by.

Echo pokes her head from the spaceship's wall. Ever since Darbo murdered her aboard this ship, she's been completely tethered to it—with Darbo as her master. "Your *request*?" She barely keeps the acidity from her voice.

"We've entered a new galaxy. Are there any black holes in the area?" Darbo's voice is tense, and his gaze slides to Lilah and Adrian.

Still views me as his personal glorified computer program, I see. But she's got nothing else to do, and at least checking will distract her from the anger that's starting to crackle inside. "Let me check." She closes her eyes, waiting for the tug on her mind that will alert her to the presence of danger. Black holes used to be a rare problem—but now that all the bored rich kids started blowing up stars for fun, they're all over the place.

And Echo's parents couldn't keep silent that *their* daughter had been born with the special power to sense them. Now that she's dead, Echo's power has only strengthened—enough to feel them light-years away, with ample warning. This, she knows, is the entire reason Darbo killed her. To have a black-hole-sensing ghost at his beck and call. Bound to this ship—and him—as long as he commands the vessel.

"You sure we'll be safe, Dad?" Lilah glances up from her magazine, biting her bottom lip.

"Of course." Darbo kisses the top of her head. "That's what we've got Echo for. I promised you kids we'd get away from it all after your mother died, and I'm sticking to my word."

The presence of a black hole just ahead tickles Echo's mind. A mass of swirling darkness that threatens to suck in the ship, stripping every living creature to the bone, leaving only souls behind.

And, light years beyond that one, another.

Shivers curl through her. "Da—" Then the thought strikes. *Don't tell him.*

She swallows. As a ghost, she'll survive if the spaceship gets sucked into a black hole. With the ship destroyed and Darbo dead . . . she'd be free.

"What is it?" Darbo cuts into her swirling thoughts.

"There's no . . ." The words slip out so easily. "No black holes in the area."

Darbo nods, waving her away. She sinks back into the spaceship walls, alone with her musings. The walls hum, but her thoughts are louder. *Is it murder if you're just killing the person who killed you first?*

They speed into an asteroid belt, and Adrian whoops, pumping his fist. "Faster, Dad!"

He bounces around the chamber, pretending to be a pilot.

Lilah clings to her seat. "Slow down, Dad! We could lose the ship for going this fast!" She stares out the viewscreen, as if trying to glimpse the space patrols said to hover near asteroid belts, just waiting to nab speeding ships.

"Only if the patrol catches us." Darbo grips the controller, his lips pressed tightly together. "And I don't like being in asteroid belts any longer than we need to be."

The presence of the first gravity well clogs Echo's mind with its whirling mass.

Is freedom worth her soul? Can she enter the Final Universe with deaths on her conscience?

She's so close to being free of this ship, of these people.

But the cost . . .

She shuts herself off from her mind, connects herself to the blinking lights of the spaceship. *I'm not real. Not culpable. I'm nothing but metal and lights and—*

The high-pitched sirens of the ship's proximity alert squeal through the control room, yanking Echo back to full consciousness. Multiple dots flash on the screen.

Darbo hisses through his teeth and jabs at buttons, his face white.

"Space patrol!" Adrian crows.

Lilah scowls at him. "This is *bad*!"

Echo's heart thunders. If she leads this family into death, the space patrol will follow. *I can't do this. I could kill Darbo. But not so many innocent people.*

She bursts from the walls in a flickering mass of blue and yellow light. "Swing right!" she yells.

Darbo stares at her from the control panel, his jaw dropped. "What?"

"A black hole! Less than a light-year—"

Darbo yanks on a handle, slowing their momentum and preparing for the turn. Glowering at Echo, he gently swings the spaceship around in a half-circle. "Coordinates," he snaps.

She leads him around both black holes, hoping the patrol officers will follow their path.

The ship chugs forward, the threat of being sucked into a vortex too great to risk driving too quickly.

Another idea floats through Echo's mind, and she smiles to herself.

When the ship clears the black holes, she says nothing.

Darbo continues to proceed cautiously, unaware they're out of potential danger.

Their ship comes to a shuddering halt. Metal crunches across its hull. Echo pokes her head outside. A robot hand clamps their spaceship, attached to a patrol vessel.

She barely restrains a gleeful cackle.

Boots tromp through the ship as the officers board, flashing their badges.

Lilah hides behind her magazines, and Adrian shrinks against the window, frozen.

Darbo opens his mouth, but the leading officer cuts him off."You might've slowed down, but you still broke Galaxy Regulation 13-50-832: Speeding Over 1200 Star-blinks in an Asteroid Belt. We'll be confiscating the ship."

"I—but—" Darbo sputters. His eyes flicker wildly. The patrol surrounds him, ushering him and his children toward the exit hatch.

The leading officer lingers, frowning and shaking his head. "And such erratic driving," he mutters.

"It was a black hole belt, that's why." Echo pops up behind him.

"Black holes? How would you know—" As the man turns, his dark eyes widen. He removes his navy-blue uniform cap and presses it against his chest. "You—!"

"Dead? Yes." It feels good to finally have someone learn the truth. She points after Darbo. "I can sense black holes, and this man murdered me to better use my abilities. I've been tied to this ship for *months*." Anger courses through her, and the ship's lights blink erratically.

The officer sinks into the control chair, hands clasped against his knees. "Oh, mercies. I'm so sorry."

Echo hovers in front of him. "Please," she whispers, "I just want this thing scrapped so I can go free."

"Of course, of course." The man nods, fiddling with one of the levers. "We'll scrap it, sell it for parts, and give your family the money from the sale," he adds. He bows his head. "I know that can't bring you back . . ."

Echo's anger wanes, and the flickering lights blink out. "I still appreciate it."

The officer's fiddling intensifies, and his shoulders quiver. "I know some sort of alert system is needed, but to *kill* for one?" He glares at the screen in front of them. "If I have anything to say about it, that disgusting star-puff is going away for life." Then he sighs. "I'm just sorry we weren't in time to save you."

Echo smiles softly. Perhaps they can't save her body. But now she can return to her family and say goodbye. She can search out the Final Universe without regrets marring her soul. She can finally leave this prison of stars.

"You were, actually," she says.

APRIL 1, 1933

Richard S.

Today it's considered a joke,
To be bandied about by any old bloke.
But being born on this date
Is not something to hate,
Not something on which you should croak.

That fateful day, many years ago
When most things moved rather slow—
My parents were in disbelief,
Causing some undealt with grief.
They said, "This kid better grow!"

I've enjoyed this for 89 years.
It hasn't really brought me to tears,
In fact, it frequently brings levity.
And in the interest of brevity,
I'll stop, as outside darkness nears.

I WOULD
KILL FOR
JUSTICE

THE GOLDEN COW MAKES THE RULES

Elaine Wells

You did the right thing for the wrong reason;
I did the wrong thing for the right reason.
I was never as selfish as you,
you were just nicer about it,
I would kill for justice,
you would save me to make yourself happy,
because wasn't it always just charity to you?
Pocket change to the pauper,
you did it for a good word,
you did it to follow the rules,
you make all the rules that you follow,
and all of the ones that you don't,
these people are just cogs in a machine to you,
and you butter them up to keep it turning,
to keep the clock ticking,
to keep them happy,
because if it weren't for greed,

you'd never feed the hungry urchin on the street.
But me,
a thief in the night,
the piece that wouldn't fit,
the one that refused your beguiling smile,
I knew the game and wouldn't play by your rules,
I hop the train without paying for the ticket,
I steal the bread and cock the gun,
I pick the pockets of people like you,
men in gold-trimmed suits and top hats,
because you let them eat cake,
you sit on your throne of philanthropy and good intent,
but one day I will have your head,
and I will bury you in an unmarked grave,
throw pocket change onto the dirt,
because I am the revolution,
and you are an aristocratic stirk.

A STONE'S THROW

Anne J. Hill

WALDREN PACED BY the cell bars, his fingers yanking through his shaggy hair. "There's gotta be a way out of this mess!" His boots tracked muddy water across the rock floor.

Boyer, his companion of four months, tossed a stone against the wall and caught it, just like he'd done a dozen times before. Apparently, the only thing that mattered in his world was hitting the wall just right with his stone.

"I'm talking to you, Boyer," Waldren snapped at him.

"I noticed." The stone landed in a puddle, and Boyer quickly fished it out. "You're going to go bald if you keep pulling your hair like that."

He might go bald, but he was taller and more toned than his companion would ever be. He stopped his pacing and glared at Boyer. "At least I'm trying to think of a way to get us out of here." The strong smell of urine only intensified his desire to flee.

Thud-um. Boyer's stone hit the wall again. "That's funny, seeing as it's your fault we're here in the first place."

"Should have just sliced the guards' heads off. Now we're going to hang for murdering Friddan." He tapped his foot on the floor, outdoing the beat of Boyer's stone.

"Ironic." Boyer dipped his temple against the wall. "Guess we're pretty fortunate they didn't lop our heads off right on the spot."

Gripping the cell bars, Waldren pressed his face through, his skull blocking him from going any farther. "Hello? I need to take a leak!"

Boyer chuckled from his corner.

He glanced back at him. "What—"

"Piss in your cell, half-blood!" a guard yelled from where he sat.

"That's what," Boyer said with a smirk. "You've not spent much time locked up, have you?"

Waldren glanced down at what he had thought was water and shuddered. "No, because I don't *get* caught."

"Mmm. Clearly." Boyer's stone hit a ridge with a maddening clatter and shot to his left.

Waldren booted the rock against Boyer's leg. "This is why I never go after higher ranks."

Boyer snatched the stone, his face pinching.

"Gets you thrown in their personal little prisons," Waldren continued. "Who has this sort of money to spend on a special room for crooks?"

Boyer glanced at him before looking back at his wet rock. "Where've you been living? This is rather pathetic, really. Only one guard on watch and *one* cell."

"Apparently—" Waldren stuck his face between the bars again, "—this guard can't be bothered to clean up piss!"

The guard stood. "Shut your talk-hole, elf! Murderers don't deserve a clean cell!"

"I'm not an elf," Waldren screamed, and the guard took a step closer.

"Wally, sit down and leave the nice guard alone. He's just trying to feed his family, like anyone else," Boyer scolded without looking over.

"When I die, I'm coming back to haunt him and make sure he knows the difference between me and an elf." Waldren pushed away from the bars, and leaned his back against the wall opposite Boyer, refusing to sit. The coldness of the rough wall seeped through his clothes.

Boyer yawned, the scruff on his jaw bristling. "You have elvish blood."

Clank, clank, clank. The hairs on Waldren's arms stood on end at his fellow assassin's obsessive stone-throwing.

"And human blood. He was more accurate when he said half-blood." Waldren splayed his fingers behind his head.

Boyer shrugged. "Full, half, either one will get you killed."

Waldren narrowed his eyes at him. "That's already underway. You got any genius plans, or you going to keep slamming that stone against the wall?"

Boyer smiled, rubbing the stone under his thumb before tossing it again. "Do you promise me you'll stop going out of your way to steal things in the midst of our assassinations?"

Waldren rapped his fingers against the wall. "I'm an opportunist, Boyer. I take what I can when I can, and I never shoot higher than I can aim."

Boyer rolled his eyes.

"Well, I try not to," Waldren went on. "Friddan's personal treasury was just down the hall like you said. If you had focused on your job and gotten out after you slit that noble's throat, I could have stolen the gold, and we'd be paid twice over. *You're* the one who felt the need to come warn me of the dangers. I *knew* the dangers."

"Oh, I wasn't trying to warn you." Boyer's smile twitched as his stone made another *clink* against the wall. He moved his finger to his lips, then leaned over and scraped a key out from under a crevice in the wall.

Waldren's eyes widened, and his mouth gaped as realization dawned on him. "Yeah, I was about to steal the treasures, but you made too much noise coming after me." He kept up his rambling so nothing sounded suspicious to the guard. He wasn't sure what Boyer was doing, but he'd play along.

"How would you have stolen the gold if I hadn't followed you?" Boyer asked, moving to stand.

"I'd have picked the lock . . . ." Waldren stood.

Boyer peered out of the cell.

"And snuck into the room . . . ."

Boyer shushed him, slipped the key into the keyhole, and twisted.

Waldren noticed the guard was away from his post. He lowered his voice. "Paid the guard?"

Boyer nodded, adding, "Changing of the guard," and slowly eased the door open. Waldren slipped out first, with Boyer following close behind.

"With what?" Waldren whispered.

"Friddan's gold."

Waldren is too easy to impress. Boyer stifled a chuckle when Waldren's eyes widened in surprise.

They turned the corner and slinked up the dark stairwell that led out of the dungeon. Boyer could hear Kilm, the guard who'd been watching them moments before, chatting up his replacement just as planned.

As quiet as feathers, Boyer and Waldren walked up behind the unexpecting guard facing Kilm. Boyer winked at Kilm and slipped down the adjacent hall. Waldren paused behind him briefly but was soon beside him again.

They had exactly one minute to get out of Friddan's castle if the guard could keep his end of the deal.

Thank goodness for disloyal guards like Kilm.

The sound of shuffling boots echoed from up ahead, and Boyer grabbed Waldren's arm, yanking him down a hall. They disappeared into the shadows and waited with silent breaths as two guards clipped by. Boyer gritted his teeth. *Blast that Waldren for messing up my timing with his chatter.*

Dawn was near, and soon the halls would fill with servants and nobles. This was the prime time for an escape when the guards were switching and less focused.

Boyer waited a few seconds after the guards had moved past before jutting back out into the hallway, Waldren at his heels. Reflections danced with the slowly rising sun through the windows that lined the hall. He needed to find just one thing—a secret passageway behind a tapestry that Kilm had told him about. Just a little further and—

Alarm bells shattered the morning quiet and shouts filled the hall. Boyer cursed. No time to find the passage now.

Waldren lifted his foot and kicked through a window, sending shards of glass clattering to the floor. He stuck his head out of the opening, glanced over his shoulder and grinned at Boyer. "Let's go."

Boyer could not resist giving him a shove as he slipped out the broken window.

Alone now, Boyer glanced down the hall and saw light shimmering on the walls as the guards drew nearer. He leaned out the window just in time to witness Waldren land in a pile of hay and roll off. Boyer climbed onto the ledge, dislodging pieces of glass. He smiled to himself and jumped. Wind pressed against his body as he fell. He never felt more alive than when he was falling through air.

The drop was short, as they were only just above the dungeon, but he appreciated it nonetheless. He landed in the hay with a grunt and spat out the straws in his mouth.

"Stop them!" An arrow whizzed by his head as he scrambled onto the ground.

"Boyer!" Waldren waved him over from the stables where he was untying their horses.

Boyer darted the short distance and scaled his mount, dodging another arrow. He clicked his tongue and dug in his heels, spurring the animal forward.

"The gate! Close the gate!" a guard yelled.

"Oh no, you don't," Boyer hissed and pressed his horse on faster as the portcullis slowly cranked down. Before it could shut, the two assassins slipped underneath and out to freedom.

The same guard cursed loudly. "Open the gate! Open the gate!"

Boyer chuckled. *So long, fools.* He and Waldren rode into the forest and split off from each other, disorienting their pursuers and slipping into the morning light.

Several hours later, they joined at their agreed upon narrow path, all traces of the noble's guards gone.

Boyer wouldn't admit it, but he was relieved to see Waldren had made it safely.

"So . . . how'd you do it?" Waldren asked.

Boyer smirked, riding his horse at a walk beside him. "I know the guard. We've had . . . run-ins there before. When they caught us, Kilm was the one who led me to the cell, and we hatched the plan in just a few moments. He said the guard would change in an hour, so I tracked the time, using the stone taps to help, but you kept interrupting me. And of course, he wanted payment for his pains."

"Yeah, with the noble's gold. How did you—"

"When you were off picking locks to a room that definitely didn't lead to the gold, I snatched it from Friddan's chest under his bed. Broke the lock."

"Then why'd you tell me—"

"The gold was in that room? Because I was hoping you'd get hanged, and I could be free of you." He leaned back in his saddle with a careless yawn.

Waldren scowled. "That's a bit harsh for a new partner."

Boyer laughed, enjoying the peeved look on his face. "I jest. There were guards coming, and I needed a distraction. You worked perfectly. And Kilm is always making his rounds at that time, so I knew I could strike a deal with him."

Waldren nodded slowly, then his eyes lit up. "I know something you don't." He puffed out his chest and opened his mouth—

"You stole the gold off Kilm on our way out." Boyer fished the pouch out of his pocket and dangled it out of his reach.

Waldren clamped his mouth shut, checking his belt. "How'd you . . . ?" His eyes followed the weighty sack as it swayed. He shook his head and cleared his throat, his shoulders drooping. "Explain."

"I was betting you'd snatch it. You paused when we passed Kilm, and the guards were after us too soon. He must have noticed the gold was gone and sent the alarm."

Waldren blinked. "Well . . . I got our horses."

"Mhm, Kilm made sure they were tied up by the stable for us. But yes, you . . . *helped*."

Waldren shook his head, pinching the bridge of his nose. "But how did you get it from me? I'm the trained thief, not you."

Breathing in the fresh air of victory, Boyer tucked the gold at his side. "When you jumped out of the window, I yanked it off you. Didn't feel it with your momentum."

Waldren studied him, his forehead wrinkling. "Working with you is not going to be fun."

"Maybe not, but it will be memorable."

Boyer and Waldren will return in Anne J. Hill's debut series.

ACKNOWLEDGMENTS

We'd first like to thank all the authors who poured their hearts and souls into each of their stories and poems. This is truly a talented group of writers we got to work with. Thank you to the authors who jumped in to help with edits. So many pitched in and it means the world to us. A special thanks to Crystal Grant, Maseeha Seedat, Hannah Carter, and Anna Agustine, who helped edit most, if not all, of the pieces. Thank you to Brittany Eden for long discussions over Anne J. Hill's *The Man of Twist and Turns* short story, and to Andrew Winch for his edits on select pieces. Thank you to Elaine Wells for helping to choose the poetry.

Thank you to everyone who helped promote this book and cheered us on. Who encouraged us to not give up even after little sleep and too much coffee.

-Anne J. Hill and Lara E. Madden

ABOUT THE AUTHORS

ANNE J. HILL

Anne J. Hill is an author who enjoys writing fantasy for all ages. Her love of words has also led to her career as a freelance writer and editor. She spends her days dreaming up fantastical realms, talking out loud to the characters in her head, and rearranging her personal library, which has been affectionately dubbed the "Book Dungeon."

Instagram @anne.j.hill.editing
Twitter @AnneJHillAuthor
www.annejhill.com

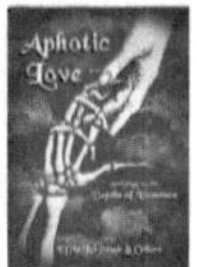

LARA E. MADDEN

She might be crazy—the jury's still out—but Lara E. Madden would consider herself to be widely fascinated, with an affinity for wonder. She is madly in love with Jesus, with storytelling, and with the tribe of colorful characters that is her family and friends. When her feet are on the ground, she lives in Lancaster, PA with her housemate, Anne J. Hill, without whom she would likely never finish any project she starts. She is a novelist at heart but is currently focused on creating short fiction as she hones her writing craft.

Instagram @lara.e.madden
Facebook @Lara Madden
LaraTheWanderer.blogspot.com

Elaine Wells

Elaine Wells is a 17-year-old crazy cat lady, and an aspiring author with a poet's heart. Her poetry portrays her truth-seeking attitude. Some of her favorite poets include Edgar Allen Poe and Emily Dickinson, while drawing inspiration from Olivia Gatwood. She has a passion for writing about mental health, and she also loves photography, good books, deep conversations, and soft blankets.

Instagram @elaine.wells.poetry

Beka Gremikova

Beka Gremikova writes folkloric fantasy from her little nook in the Ottawa Valley, Ontario, Canada. Her flash fiction can be found on Havok Publishing's website and in several of their anthologies. When she's not traveling, playing video games, or sketching, she's often curled up with a mystery novel. Currently, she's plotting a plethora of fairy tale retellings and planning to release her dark fantasy thriller short, "Perchance to Dream," in late 2022. *Photo credit Sarah-Ann Wijngaarden.*

Instagram @beka.gremikova
Twitter @DreamofWriting
Facebook @bekagremikova
www.bekagremikova.com

Maseeha Seedat

Maseeha Seedat is a 17-year-old author, born and raised in sunny South Africa before moving to the Middle East in 2011. She made her publishing debut in *What Darkness Fears*, and since then has made her mark on the writing world. When she's not writing, Maseeha can be found chasing after her toddler cousin, hitting the padel courts, or clawing her way toward a degree in physiotherapy.

Instagram @sincerelymaseeha
Twitter @maseeha_writer
sincerelymaseeha.weebly.com

Crystal Grant

Crystal Grant grew up LOVING books and stories and sometimes spent more time in her imaginary worlds than the real one. She spent fifteen years teaching first grade and shared her love of books with her students. Recently, she's had three stories published through Havok Publishing and a poem in the *What Darkness Fears* anthology, and does a little freelance editing on the side. Currently, she has an epic fantasy out on submission. She spends her spare time writing, watching old movies and TV shows, or reading books that sweep her away to another time and place.

Instagram @crystalgrantfaithandfiction
Facebook @crystalgrantauthor
www.crystalgrantfaithandfiction.com

L.A. Thornhill

L.A. Thornhill is an epic fantasy and steampunk writer who deeply loves her Savior, and has a severe addiction to caffeine. She currently has one novella "The Lost Descendants" in her fantasy series *The King and Prophet Chronicles* which is available in ebook, print, and also in audiobook in the near future.

Facebook @l.a.thornhillauthor
Instagram @l.a.thornhill

Mariella Taylor

Mariella Taylor was raised on fairy lit paths somewhere between the backstreet alleys of Jackson, Mississippi, and the jazz infested avenues of New Orleans. She graduated with her terminal degree in Writing and Editing from University of Nebraska (Omaha) in 2018, and now she delegates her writing efforts to mentoring young authors, providing editing services to Indie writers, and grumbling at her uncooperative characters. Her work appears in *For the Love of a Word, Whispers From Before: Tales of Myth and Legend, Aphotic Love,* and T*he Depths We'll Go To*, as well as other publications.

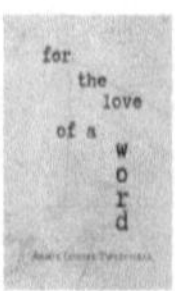

Instagram @thefoldedworld
Pinterest @thefoldedworld
https://thefoldedworld.wordpress.com

Emily Barnett

Emily Barnett resides in Colorado with her husband and two sons writing young adult fantasy full of feels. She has had short stories published in *Spark Flash Fiction*, *Havok*, and *What Darkness Fears*.

Instagram @embarnettauthor
Facebook @emilybarnettauthor
Twitter @embarnettauthor
www.emilybarnettauthor.com

Richard S.

Richard S. is Anne J. Hill's granddad. He was an English teacher and a tutor for many years. He loves words and discussing their meaning. He's been writing poetry for a long time and has blessed a lot of people through his words.

AJ Skelly

AJ Skelly is an author, blogger, and lover of all things fantasy, medieval, and fairy-tale-romance. And werewolves. An avid reader and a former high school English teacher, she lives with her husband, children, and many imaginary friends who often find their way into her stories. They all drink copious amounts of tea together and stay up reading far later than they should.

Instagram @a.j.skelly
www.ajskelly.com

Effie Joe Stock

Effie Joe Stock is the author of *The Shadows of Light* series and the creator of the world Rasa. You can usually find her working outside on her small homestead farm, playing music, studying psychology, theology, or philosophy, running her small businesses, or riding her dirt bike. She looks forward to continuing her publishing dream with the six books and multiple companion novels she has written for her epic fantasy series, along with a few other works in progress.

Instagram @effie.joe.stock.author
YouTube @Effie Joe Stock
www.effiejoestock.com

Hannah Carter

Hannah Carter is just a girl who loves to dream and write and still wakes up every day hoping to figure out she's secretly a mermaid. Her short stories and award-winning flash fiction pieces have been published in anthologies such as: *Whispers From Before, Prismatic, The Depth's We'll Go To, Aphotic Love,* and *The Willow Tree Swing*. She also won a competition with her short story, "Lara." She currently has two published novellas, *Amir and the Moon* and *Seashells*. In addition to fiction, she also has had over a dozen devotionals published in various magazines.

Instagram @introvertedmermaid3
introvertedmermaid3.mailerpage.com

David Lasley

David Lasley is an aspiring poet who resides in Illinois with his wife and kids. He writes to process through everyday experiences of life and faith. He enjoys reading, watching sports, eating tacos and floating muddy Illinois creeks in his kayak. His poetry can currently be found in *The Depths We'll Go To* anthology. He will also have works in two upcoming anthologies: *The Heights We'll Fly To* and *Exquisite Poison*.

Instagram @dlasleyramblings

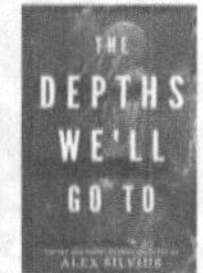

Nobel Shut Chan

My name is Nobel Chan and I'm a student at Boston University, majoring in English and minoring in Deaf Studies. Hailing from Hong Kong, I love reading, writing, and musical theatre. My poetry has been published in various school and nation-wide magazines. In the future, I hope to continue honing my craft and writing more poetry and short stories.

Alex Silvius

Alex Silvius is a Canadian poet. He started publishing last year with his debut collection The Irrelevance of Knives. Near the end of the year, he ran an anthology called The Depths We'll Go To. His goal in publishing is to not only publish his own writing, but to help other writers get themselves out there.

Instagram @alexsilviuswriter

Claire Tucker

Claire Tucker is a copyeditor, proofreader, science tutor, and violin teacher who lives in South Africa but frequently visits other worlds through books. She adores the world of fiction and loves to explore Christian themes through writing, particularly fantasy. Claire also enjoys being in nature, especially if it involves hiking in the beautiful Drakensberg.

Instagram @clairetucker_writer / @clairetucker_editor
LinkedIn @claire-tucker-editor
www.editwithclaire.com

Nathaniel Luscombe

Nathaniel Luscombe is a 19 year old author from Ontario, Canada. He spends his days working and his nights expanding his digital footprint and preparing stories for publication. He has always been an avid reader and writer. He was first published in 2020 in the *There is Us* anthology. In 2021 he ran and published his first anthology, *Among Other Worlds*, and was involved in some other exciting projects, such as *The Animals of Pink and Yellow* by Alex Silvius. The things that inspire his writing the most are his faith, his friends and family, and the need to create something bigger than himself (which is hard, considering he's 6'7").

Instagram @ hecticreadinglife

Julia Skinner

Julia Skinner is a modern day hobbit with a love for good stories and chocolate ice cream. Abiding in South Texas with her parents, and six siblings, she spends her days juggling college, writing, family adventures, and random entrepreneurial dreams. She is a sinner saved by Jesus, and she wouldn't be the person she is today without her Savior, Jesus Christ. Even though she has yet to publish one of her many fantasy novels, her flash fiction has been published in a number of anthologies, including: *Prismatic, Aphotic Love, The Willow Tree Swing*, and *Fool's Honor*.

Instagram @litaflameblog

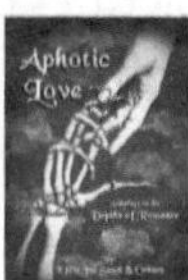

Natalie Noel Truitt

Natalie Noel Truitt is an aspiring Christian author who is pursuing a degree in psychology. She is often on her front porch drinking a chai latte, reading a good book, and hanging out with one of her cats.

Instagram @life_frommydesk

Brittany's fascination with Wonderland may have given her the courage to use a sparkly Cinderella book bag while completing her First Class Honours degree in Greek & Roman Civilization and Political Science at the National University of Ireland. She's travelled to over twenty-five countries and has walked the Great Wall of China in Beijing, the Acropolis in Athens, Table Mountain in Cape Town, and Ipanema in Rio. She also once lived in a Circus. You'll find her writing starcrossed romance with timeless endings or on Instagram oversharing pictures of her home in Vancouver, Canada.

Instagram @brittanyedenauthor
brittanyeden.com

Anna Augustine

Anna Augustine lives with her family of eight in a small, midwestern town with two dogs and a whole lot of crazy. Anna is the author of romantic fantasy *When You Found Me*, is in a number of anthologies, and has been published on Havok. When she's not writing, Anna is either working as a teacher's aide in her local elementary school, taking photos for her bookstagram, or trying to put a dent in her never ending tbr.

Instagram @anna_augustine_author
www.anna-augustine-author.com

Laurie Lucking

Laurie Lucking loves books, music, and spending time with her family in beautiful Minnesota. When she finds a spare moment from herding her four rambunctious kids, she writes young adult romantic fantasy. Laurie's debut novel, *Common*, won the Excellence in Editing Award, and her short stories have been published in a variety of anthologies. She is a co-founder of the Facebook group Faith and Fairy Tales and contributes to Lands Uncharted, a blog dedicated to clean fantasy and science fiction.

Instagram @laurielucking
Facebook @AuthorLaurieLucking
www.laurielucking.com

Kaitlyn Emery

Kaitlyn Emery was obsessed with dragons and fantasy at a young age. When she grew up, she learned reality was darker than anything she read in a book. Through writing, she learned to cope with the world around her and find a voice in fiction. Kaitlyn has written short stories for various magazines, Flash Fiction for Havok Publishing, and been published in several anthologies including *Rebirth, Sensational, Prismatic, When Your Beauty is the Beast, Moonlight and Claws, Tales From The Tower, The Depths We'll Go To*, and *Aphotic Love*.

Instagram @kaitlyn_scribbling
Kaitlyn-Emery.com

Tasha Kazanjian

Tasha Kazanjian is currently pursuing her masters in clinical counseling and writes fantasy to escape APA citations. She loves losing herself in books, especially very old ones that smell strongly of ink and dust, and has been known to disappear into used book shops for hours at a time. Tasha's writing process usually involves stacks of historical nonfiction, a hundred index cards stuck up on her wall, and copious amounts of coffee, tea, and colored pens. She is currently revising a dark fantasy novel involving ice age dragons.

Savannah Jezowski

Savannah Jezowski lives in a drafty farmhouse in Michigan with her Knight and two wee warrior princesses. She specializes in epic fantasy worlds with emotional themes and characters that defy the norm. Her works include *When Ravens Fall, Curse and Consequence* and more. She also writes sweet romantic fantasy under the penname Everly Haywood.

Instagram @savannahjezowskiauthor
Facebook @savannahjezowskiauthor
www.dragonpenpress.com

www.annejhill.com/twenty-hills-publishing
Instagram @twenty_hills